The Conspiracy of One

A STORY OF WITCHKIND

DON JONES

DONJONES.COM

Copyright © 2024 by Don Jones

All rights reserved.

No part of this book may be reproduced in any form or by any electronic or mechanical means, including information storage and retrieval systems, without written permission from the author, except for the use of brief quotations in a book review.

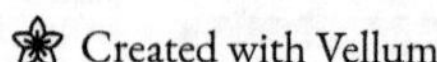 Created with Vellum

For the 'doodles,
Cory & Dylan

Also by Don Jones

stories of witchkind®

<u>Age of the Adherents</u>:

Daniel Scratch • Master of the Tower • The Fifth Axis

<u>The Order</u>:

The Order of Some • The Conspiracy of One • The Truth of All

Clara Thorn

Clara Thorn, the witch that was found

Clara Thorn, the witch that fought

Clara Thorn, the witch that won

Endless Sky®

Truthsayer • New Worlds

Tales from the Broken Claw

Pubs & Pegasi

The Never: A Tale of Peter and the Fae

Find more at DonJones.com, including a free fantasy trilogy, a free superhero duology, two collections of short stories, and even more short stories and flash fiction. You can even listen to free music inspired by the books!

Contents

the world
Brysst
Lastpointe
Greensea
Rushford
Soloton
Northsea
Farreach
Evermore
Doocastella's
Westhead
Fyngershire
Lakewood
Withring
Turynsitts
Cuppton
Little Bay
Hook
Disemstoke's
Baythorpe
Carvendam
Meadowside
Nuvorlons
Nek
Haydsmouth
Peasc
Thornwraith's
Wisdng
Soysea
Farreach
Chilton
Taliesin
Landshire
Spurham
The Tower
of Endings

CHAPTER 1

Apprentice Review

"So I gather your first mission didn't go so well?" Finley Coughlin offered an gentle smile to Rey Rinwander, his newest apprentice, as they strolled along the packed-earth road that led to Sowsea. "I remember my first time out. It was definitely stressful. Mind telling me what happened?"

Rey sighed. "It was in Reedsedge. You know it?"

Finley considered. "Tiny little village along the southern coast, right?"

"Calling it a village is overselling it, but yeah."

"What was the mission?"

"Printing press." Rey looked up at Finley with a bit of suspicion. "They plant those, don't they?"

"The Order? Possibly," Finley allowed. "First missions aren't supposed to be all that complicated. But... well, there are some measures in place specifically for printing presses." He'd invented those measures, relying on printers' almost inevitable tendency to use the human religion books as their first printing project. New runes carved into the foundations of every church on the continent ensured the projects didn't get far. "So yeah, it might have been a setup."

"Well, it didn't go well."

I gathered, since they sent you on a second one with me. "Who were you with?"

"Ujjwal."

"Ah." An older member of the Order with the curmudgeonly demeanor of most older witchkind with an Earth affinity.

"So you know him."

"Let's just say I'm surprised they sent him out with an apprentice. But you're Earth affinity as well, right?"

"Yeah, but nothing was good enough for him. I can't work if I can't concentrate, and if he wasn't staring through the back of my head, he was making that sound he makes. To let you know you're never going to be good enough."

Having been on the receiving end of Ujjwal's *harrumphs,* Finley could only grin. "But what about the mission itself?"

Rey sighed even more deeply. "I blew it. Ujjwal gave me the rune construct to use, but I couldn't get it empowered. It… kind of backfired."

"How badly?"

"The entire cottage was swallowed by the earth."

"Oh, my."

"Yeah. So Ujjwal had to conjure up a quake and damage a few more, so it looked natural. Then he had to call four others to keep the quakes going for a few days, and put out the story that it was a sinkhole."

"Anyone hurt?"

"No."

"Well, there's that. And they're giving you a second chance, with me."

"And you're Earth affinity, too?"

"I am. Earth and Flame, actually."

"That's an odd combination."

"My whole family's an odd combination," Finley chuckled. "In a good way." He scanned the road ahead. "We should be in sight of the village pretty soon. Want to go over the plan?"

Rey sighed again, and Finley wondered if the constant, dramatic exhalations had been part of what set Ujjwal off. "We touch base with the local reseller."

"Right." The Order's cover story for having agents traveling all over the continent was its kitchenwares business—an extremely real, and quite lucrative, business. Standard procedure in most cases was to stop in and check on the merchants— almost always human shopkeepers—who purchased and resold their products. "Then what?"

"I didn't understand the brief," Rey admitted. "It sounds like something to do with dirt and bricks."

And with an Earth affinity, that didn't interest you more? Finley thought sharply. *Where'd they recruit this kid?* "Well, I can assure you it's not a plant. It says someone's found a process to create a stronger brick. Like, *massively* stronger. And it's apparently quite an involved process, which is good for us."

"Why are bricks bad?"

Seriously? "What would your trainer say?"

Another sigh preceded a desultory recitation. "We can't have humans building better structures, because one, it'll reduce their reliance on magic should they ever find out about witchkind, and two, it'll just encourage them to spread out more. Their population is already large and limiting structures helps rein them in."

That's the theory, Finley thought a bit sourly. *Although there's no evidence it's true.* But better to stick with the official narrative for now. "Correct. And why is it good for us that it's a complex process?"

Rey had to think about that one. "Easier to mess up?"

"Basically," Finley confirmed. "The more steps that are involved, the more opportunity we can usually find to break part of it in a way that'll look natural. And after we do that?"

Rey took longer this time. "Mind-wipe the inventor?"

"*Memory* wipe," Finley corrected, "but yes. Have you practiced that one?"

"No. It's Sky magic and I'm no good at it."

"So what would you do if I wasn't here?"

"Call someone else?"

"Correct. And it *is* tricky magic, so it's definitely better to not even try it if you're not pretty skilled at it."

"Are you?"

"I can get by." *Understatement of the era.* Finley might not have a direct affinity for Sky magic, but his talent as a runewright—and more importantly as a far rarer Rune Smith —gave him an uncanny knack for whatever magic he put his mind to. *Although my talent still isn't talking to me after Harbsmouth.* He worried, some days, that the encounter with the human weapon maker in that little fishing village had damaged his talent, somehow. Other days, he could almost swear he heard it muttering in the back of his brain, only to vanish when he considered it too closely.

He shook his head. *Mind on the game.* "There's the edge of the village, ahead," he pointed out. "Ready to prove you can do this?"

Another sigh. "I guess."

Don't act all enthusiastic about it, Finley thought sarcastically, wondering for the first time if maybe Ujjwal'd had the right of it with this one.

***

The village had turned out to be surprisingly small and barely worth the title—little more than a dozen buildings clustered together, with various barns and shacks scattered around the perimeter. Their "reseller" ran the community's tiny dry good store, and had dourly proclaimed himself well-stocked with pots and pans. They'd taken a light lunch at a similarly minuscule inn before walking as discretely as possible toward their target.

"Did you notice," Finley said softly as they strolled to the edge of the clustered buildings, "that there's no church?"

Rey shook her head and Finley rolled his eyes. Even as an apprentice, she should know how much the Order made use of the humans' churches. Magically modifying their religious texts in subtle ways, adding magic runes to the structures themselves, and other tricks helped suppress dangerous human innovation. Other runes helped connect Order agents with each other, while still others provided primitive monitoring of every human community. "Without a church..." he murmured. *Without a church, they could be doing anything here.* "I wonder how we found this one."

"The brief said the new bricks were being shipped to a larger town," Rey said.

Finley flushed slightly. *How did I miss that?*

They continued past the edge of the "village," where the landscape flattened into hardscrabble dirt, tall grass, and the thick, low shrubs that led to the adjacent farmlands. The sun was growing low, and as they walked Finley cast a light glamour about them, encouraging human eyes to look elsewhere.

"Why are we skulking?" Rey asked. "That glamour makes my eyes itch."

No sense of discretion, Finley thought, gritting his teeth. "Are you saying you and Ujjwal just strolled up to that cottage?"

Rey shrugged. "Basically."

"It's so surprising it didn't go well." Finley kept his own

voice barely above a whisper as they surveyed the workshop. Situated on the very edge of the small village, it looked as if it had once been used to keep livestock. A small, ramshackle building was surrounded by a large yard, enclosed by an even more ramshackle split-log fence. Where pigs and chickens had once roamed, there were now large piles of... sand? "What do you think it all is?"

"Who can tell?" Rey sounded completely disinterested.

Finley suppressed the urge to shout. "Someone with Earth affinity, perhaps?"

"So then why can't you—oh, right."

"Right."

"Sure, just a second." Rey closed her eyes and concentrated, while Finley rolled his own again in exasperation. He listened—not with his ears, but with his on-again, off-again Rune Smith talent—to see if he could sense what she was doing. But this afternoon was his talent's day off again, and he could detect nothing.

"That pile is just rocks. Small ones. Probably leavings from the granite quarry not too far away." Finley had known that much at a glance, but at least Rey was trying, now. "Second one is sand. From the shore line. Nothing special." Her eyes squeezed shut even harder, and Finley wondered for a moment who'd taught this girl to use magic. "The white stuff isn't sand, it's ground limestone. Weird." She opened her eyes. "That other pile is firewood."

"Fire—" Finley stopped himself with a quiet sigh, forcing his jaw to unclench. "Then he frowned. "What are they heating?"

"Maybe something in the shack?"

"Possibly." In his mind, Finley pictured a rune of seeing, called *matau pro sienas* in the True Language of magic. Feeding it a touch of Sky magic, he let his eyes drift slightly out of focus as the walls of the shed seemed to grow translucent. "Odd," he said softly.

"What?"

"It's like a tube made of rock," he mused. "Roughly made, at that. As long as the shack itself. Actually," he added, letting his eyes snap back into focus. "It extends out the far side. They've been lighting a fire underneath it, although it's cold now." He shook his head. "I've no idea what—ah, here we go."

On the far side of the shack, a human man was stepping through a gap in the fence, whistling happily. Finley stood at once and waved, urging Rey to step through a similar gap on their side.

"Hello!" the man called. "Hello, hello! What can I help you with?"

"My apprentice and I were noticing your supplies. My employer works with a number of specialized earths—clays, glazes, that sort of thing. I was just wondering if you might have any interest?"

"Clays—oh, spirits no!" the man laughed. "No, you must think we're manufacturing stoneware or something!" He chuckled, shaking his head. "No, we're up to something else entirely!"

"Oh?" Finley asked curiously, elbowing Rey. This was *her* apprentice mission, after all.

"We're making a new type of construction material," the human continued. "Officially, it's called *portlandcementis*, but trust me, we're working on something less of a tongue-twister."

Finley's eyes widened—the word sounded very much like one from the True Language.

"Port—" Rey attempted. She gave up with a quick shake of her head. "What's it do?"

"Well, the process is a bit secret, but the end product is a gray powder. Mix it with pure water and within a couple of marks it begins to solidify. Give it two or three days and it's hard as any rock. It will even cure underwater! Far stronger than wood, all but impervious to seawater! It's going to revolutionize building!"

Finley's eyes had widened even more. "That... sounds amazing." *More than amazing,* he thought quickly. *That sounds like magic.* "You've been able to do this consistently?"

The man nodded proudly. "Once we got the specifics of the process figured out. In fact, we're just about to close up this shop. We've built a much larger one further down the coast. Should be able to produce a ton of the stuff every few days." He grinned and gave them a wink. "The stuff's incredibly durable, too. Great with heat. I imagine your employer could use it to build kilns. Mix it with small rocks and it'll support an entire house."

Finley blinked a few times, and then forced himself to smile and nod. "Could be! I'll certainly pass that along—what was your name?"

"Tomas Clincker," the man said, extending his hand for Finley to shake. "Going to revolutionize the world!"

No, you're not, Finley thought to himself.

***

The twin moons hung low and pregnant in the night sky, bathing the countryside in an ethereal silver glow. Crickets and night birds sang their nocturnal chorus as Finley and Rey crept silently through the tall grass toward the abandoned shack.

A light breeze whispered through the leaves of the nearby trees, carrying with it the rich scents of earth and growing things. Finley breathed deeply, feeling his Earth affinity resonate with the living land around them. He glanced over at Rey, noting how the moonlight glinted off her dark hair and made her green eyes gleam like a cat's. She moved with a fluid grace, barely disturbing a blade of grass. Maybe there was hope for this apprentice after all.

As they drew closer, the ramshackle structure resolved out of the shadows. It slouched tiredly against the landscape, looking even more dilapidated in the moonlight. The rough hewn logs were weathered to a silvery gray and the thatched roof sagged in the middle. No light shone from the single shuttered window.

Finley held up a hand, signaling Rey to stop. He closed his eyes and waited.

There were no lights in the shack itself, and even after several moments no movement. He signaled Rey again, and they crept forward, easing through the same gap in the fence Tomas had used earlier. They crossed the yard, weaving between the piles of rock, dirt, and wood, and slipped into the shack.

"*Minkštiausia šviesa,*" Rey whispered, and the interior of the shack took on a faint glow.

Finley nodded approvingly. Earth affinity was terrible for delicate illumination, and he knew Rey must have concentrated intently to empower the rune she'd held in her mind.

In the dim magical light, the strange stone contraption dominated the interior of the shack. It was a long, narrow tube, roughly the length and height of a tall man lying down, carved out of a single massive piece of granite. The surface was rough hewn, with chisel marks still visible, as if the maker had been more concerned with function than aesthetics.

One end of the tube was raised up on a sturdy platform of clay bricks, elevating it about three feet off the packed dirt floor. Directly beneath this end was a fire ring, also crafted from clay bricks. The bricks were blackened and cracked from repeated heating and cooling cycles. A few chunks of charred wood and a fine layer of ash dusted the inside of the ring, evidencing its recent use.

From the raised end, the stone tube sloped gradually downward, extending through the wall of the shack. The far end disappeared into the night outside, aiming toward a pit dug into the earth where the processed material would be collected. Along the bottom of the tube, a series of small holes had been bored into the rock at regular intervals, allowing heat and gases to flow through the interior.

Rey walked slowly around the apparatus, running her hand over its rough surface. Finley sniffed, and wrinkled his nose. "It smells like burned rock."

"What do we do with it?"

Finley gave her a sharp look. "This is your mission. What would you suggest?"

"We could break it."

He nodded. "We could. And that would doubtless slow them down. But he mentioned they're already building a larger one."

"Right." Rey chewed her lip as she thought. "We could change how it works."

Finley nodded encouragingly. "Go on."

Rey stared at the rock tube, and Finley knew she was using magic to study how it had been used. "They're heating the limestone. And pushing it down the tube to cool." She tilted her head. "Limestone and clay. Hmm."

Finley waited patiently while Rey continued to study the tube. He resisted the urge to use his own magic to do the same.

"There's something else."

"Oh?"

"It's a sulfate."

Finley raised an eyebrow. *"Gipsas?"*

She nodded. "I think so."

"How odd. I didn't think the humans had any use for it." The soft white powder had specific uses for several highly specialized Earth magic workings, but he'd never heard of humans bothering with the stuff.

"It's easy to decompose," Rey said thoughtfully. "It's a simple rune."

Finley knew it well. "And so…" he prompted.

"Carve it on the bottom of the tube," Rey said. "Really small. If that's really important, it should ruin the result."

"And then?"

She considered. "We'd need to have people go do it to the other one. Maybe if their process stops working, they'll give up. These can't be easy to make."

"Nor cheap," Finley agreed. "All right, then. Go ahead."

"What, now?" Rey looked surprised.

"Did you have some other plans this evening?"

Rey stared at him for a moment, shrugged, and turned back to the tube. She knelt and reached up to the blackened underside, where whatever she carved would be quickly covered by more soot once the humans relit their fire. She reached up to the stone, and Finley dimly sensed power gathering at her extended fingertip.

Odd technique, he thought. Most of witchkind would carve first and empower second, rather than doing both at once. He wondered if someone had taught her differently, or if she was just being lazy. *Lazy and dangerous.* Small mistakes would be amplified this way.

She began tracing her finger through the soot, leaving a shallow furrow in the rock itself, her brow furrowed in concentration.

"Focus, Rey," Finley instructed softly. A *twang* in his mind suggested she wasn't holding her magic in check. *Good timing,* he told his erratic talent. "Your alignment is all over the place. Gather it. Control is key."

"I'm trying," Rey snapped back, the air around her suddenly crackling with uncontrolled energy. A bead of sweat rolled down her forehead. Within seconds, her frustration became palpable, an aura of desperation emanating from her as she struggled to align her magic with the task at hand.

"Trying isn't enough." Finley warned, sensing the chaotic dance of power swirling around Rey. "Magic is about balance, especially for those of us with Earth affinity. You must learn to wield with precision, not brute force." Already, the tracery in the stone was widening and deepening as she fed too much power. "Maybe you should—"

Rey exhaled sharply, and then, with a sudden burst of determination, her finger darted along the granite, her fingertip whitening as she pressed down hard. The half-finished rune she'd carved glowed briefly before fizzling out like a dying star. She cursed under her breath.

"Language," Finley chided.

"Sorry," Rey mumbled, her shoulders slumping. "It's just... hard."

"Hard is what we do. But you've obviously got potential. That's why they paired you with me, instead of accepting Ujjwal's judgement of you."

"Potential to do what? I can barely manage basic spells." Rey's voice wavered, and Finley could see the doubt clouding her green eyes.

"For one, stick with carving first and empowering later. Who taught you that, anyway?"

"Uncle," she mumbled.

"Well, he's wrong." Her eyes fell. "But you do have potential. Potential to make decisions that matter," Finley added, his thoughts returning to the mission—an 'easy' task, they'd called it. A chance to prove Rey's worth to the Order. "Let's try again. This time, clear your mind. Picture the rune. Feel its shape, its edges, and let your magic flow through it. Carve first, without empowering it. Just that much." Finley watched as Rey closed her eyes, taking a deep breath.

She waved her hand over the charred rock, erasing her previous carving. Finley grinned. *Only Earth affinity gets a redo with rock.* As she extended her finger and began the carving anew, Finley couldn't help but admire her resolve. She was raw, unpolished—but there was a spark there, something that reminded him of his own early days in the Order.

The rune took shape, more slowly this time, and without magic flowing into it. Finley nodded. "Good. Now empower it. Steadily. Slowly."

"Like this?" Rey's voice held a hint of hope as the rune began to glow softly.

"Exactly like that," Finley confirmed, allowing himself a small smile. "You see? You're capable."

"But what if I fail?" Rey's concern was evident, even as, with growing confidence, she maintained the trickle of power flowing into the rune. The glow faded as the magic took hold in the loops and lines of her carving.

"Then we reassess. But failure is not the end, Rey. It's merely a step on the path to mastery." Finley's voice was firm, bolstering.

"Is that what happened to you?" Rey asked, her curiosity piqued as she finally lowered her hands, the rune dissipating into the ether. "Did you fail before you succeeded?"

"More times than I care to count," Finley admitted with a wry chuckle. "But each failure taught me something new."

Rey seemed to consider this, her expression softening. "So, what's the verdict, then? Am I ready or not?"

Finley contemplated the question, weighing the potential he saw against the stakes of their mission. It was his call to make —a go/no-go decision that could alter Rey's path forever.

He met her gaze squarely. "You're ready to take the next step. Just remember, it's about more than the spells. It's about making choices that uphold the balance. Can you do that, Rey?"

"I can," she said, her voice steady now, filled with newfound determination.

"Then let's get out of here." Finley extended his hand, offering to help her to her feet.

"Let's," Rey agreed, taking his hand firmly in hers. Then she frowned. "Do we have to go do the other one? The one he said they're building?"

Finley chuckled. "You know someone else who's going to?"

***

Finley and Rey had traveled for two days, following the vague directions Tomas had provided, until they reached the larger coastal village. It was a bustling hub compared to the tiny hamlet they had left behind, with sturdy wooden buildings, cobblestone streets, and a busy marketplace filled with merchants hawking their wares. The salty tang of the sea hung heavy in the air, mingling with the earthy scents of livestock and freshly baked bread.

As the sun dipped below the horizon, painting the sky in vibrant hues of orange and pink, Finley and Rey made their way to the outskirts of the village. There, nestled against a rocky hillside, stood an enormous barn. Its weathered wooden walls rose two stories high, dwarfing the other structures nearby. A heavy brass padlock secured the oversized doors, but it proved no match for Finley's deft manipulation of a simple unlocking rune.

They slipped inside, closing the doors behind them with a soft thud. Pale moonlight filtered in through gaps in the walls, casting long shadows across the dirt floor. At Finley's nod, Rey conjured a small orb of soft white light, no larger than a pearl.

The orb of light floated upward, illuminating the cavernous interior of the barn. Finley and Rey gasped in unison as the true scale of the operation was revealed. The barn was filled with an enormous, crudely constructed cement kiln, a rough stone tube whose end rose nearly to the rafters, an enormous cousin of the one they'd seen before. The kiln stretched the entire length of the barn, a behemoth of granite that radiated a palpable heat, even in its dormant state.

Surrounding the kiln were towering piles of aggregate—mounds of sand and gravel that glittered in the magical light. The sand was a pale, moonlit silver, its fine grains shifting and whispering with every errant breeze. In contrast, the gravel was a riot of earthy hues—rich browns, rusty reds, and deep, inky blacks—the stones worn smooth by the relentless pounding of the sea.

Stacked neatly along one wall were rows upon rows of sturdy gray bricks, each one bearing the word "Betono" stamped deeply into its surface. The bricks were uniform in size and shape, their edges crisp and their faces smooth, a testament to the efficiency of whatever process the humans had developed.

"Let's get this over with," Finley muttered, his eyes rising to the underside of the kiln, high above them both.

Rey nodded, her brow furrowing in concentration as she reached out with her magic, attempting to trace the delicate lines of the rune into the soot-stained underside of the massive kiln. The rough granite surface seemed to resist her efforts, the stone unyielding beneath her ethereal touch.

Finley watched closely, his own magic at the ready, as Rey struggled to maintain control. Her hand trembled slightly as she carved, pouring her power into the nascent rune even as she shaped it.

Finley's eyes widened. "Rey—"

The air around them began to hum with barely restrained energy, the hairs on Finley's arms standing on end.

"Careful," he cautioned, struggling to keep his voice low and steady. "Remember, precision over power. Just carve it first."

Rey gritted her teeth, sweat beading on her forehead as she redoubled her efforts. The rune began to take shape, its lines glowing with a faint, pulsing light. But even as it formed, Finley could sense the imbalance in Rey's magic, the way her Earth affinity strained against the confines of the spell.

And then, with a sudden, sickening lurch, Rey's control slipped. Without warning, the incomplete rune flared to life, a blinding white light erupting from its core. The massive kiln shuddered and groaned, the stone writhing as if in pain. Spiderweb cracks raced along its surface, spreading outward from the glowing rune like bolts of lightning.

Rey cried out, her voice lost in the cacophony of splitting rock and surging magic. The backlash of power slammed into her like a physical blow, hurling her backwards. She crashed into a towering stack of bricks, sending them tumbling to the ground in a deafening avalanche of stone and dust.

Finley threw up a hasty shield, a shimmering barrier of Earth magic that deflected the worst of the debris. But even his quick reflexes couldn't fully protect him from the wild, untamed energy that ricocheted through the barn. It struck him like a fist, driving the air from his lungs and sending him staggering.

The orb of light Rey had conjured flickered and died, plunging the barn into darkness. In the sudden gloom, the rune's glow was a brief beacon, pulsing with an angry, malevolent light that slowly faded.

Finley fought to catch his breath as he pushed himself to his feet, ignoring the sharp pain lancing through his ribs. His eyes darted around the darkened barn, searching for Rey amidst the rubble and settling dust.

"Rey!" he called out softly, his voice raw and strained. "Rey, where are you?"

A muffled groan answered him from the far side of the barn. Finley stumbled forward, his feet crunching on shattered bricks as he made his way towards the sound. As his eyes adjusted to the gloom, he spotted Rey's crumpled form, half-buried beneath a pile of debris.

"I'm here," she croaked, pushing feebly at the stones that pinned her. "I'm sorry, Finley. I tried, but—"

"Hush now," Finley soothed, kneeling beside her. With a flick of his wrist, he summoned a gentle gust of wind, carefully shifting the rubble away from Rey's battered body. "We need to get you out of here. There's no way nobody heard that."

Rey nodded weakly, her face pale and streaked with dust. Finley helped her to her feet, slinging her arm over his shoulder as he supported her weight. Together, they limped towards the barn doors, each step an agonizing effort.

Outside, the night had come alive with shouts and the flickering glow of torches. Villagers were emerging from their homes, roused by the thunderous noise that had shattered the evening calm. Finley could hear the pounding of footsteps drawing nearer, the clamor of voices raised in alarm and confusion.

"We need to move," he urged, half-dragging Rey along as they skirted the edge of the barn. "Can you cast a cloak?" This was still her mission, after all.

Rey shook her head, her breath coming in ragged gasps. "I'm sorry, I don't think I can..."

Finley nodded grimly, understanding all too well the toll the failed spell had taken on her. Summoning his own magic, he sketched a hasty rune in his mind, blurring their forms and allowing them to blend into the deepening shadows. It was a weak glamour, one that wouldn't hold up under close scrutiny, but it would have to suffice.

This was, at least, a large enough village to have a population of witchkind. They'd find shelter, hopefully a healing specialist, and see what the humans made of their shattered kiln.

And then they'd share a difficult journey home.

CHAPTER 2

The Weary Soldier

As the sun began its descent, the sprawling fields of the Order's headquarters known as "the Farm" were cast in shadows that stretched long and thin across the landscape. The air was infused with a heady scent of earth and growth, a tangible reminder of the powerful magic that permeated every inch of this hidden retreat. It was as if the very soil itself had absorbed the mystical energy, giving life to the plants and creatures that called this place home. Even the delicate breeze carried a faint whisper of enchantment, stirring the senses and beckoning one deeper into the heart of the Farm.

Finley sat at a worn desk in one of the main building's many side rooms, a stack of parchment dispatches spread out before him like fallen leaves, a fireplace flickering calmly to one side. His green eyes moved swiftly over the inked reports, each one a whisper from the field, a tale of concerns and unseen influences.

Many were simply new versions of old problems. While Finley believed they'd solved the printing press problem for good, humans were forever trying new ways of joining wood for fishing boat hulls, new ways of building lamps that wouldn't blow out in a wind, and new ways of forging metals—including their precious iron.

He frowned at a dispatch which described exactly that: a new means of more efficiently producing rails for their hated Iron Roadway. The Order had been plagued by it since its founding, back in the days of the Last Adherent. Witchkind had sorely underestimated the effect of magic-blocking iron rails spanning the continent, of iron horses and carriages plying those roads laden with goods. Witchkind had been forced to evacuate entire sections of cities where the iron depots had been built, fleeing ahead of their own magic collapsing. Iron remained one of the biggest—

"Finley," boomed a voice, powerful despite the creeping touch of age.

He looked up to see Ram filling the doorway. Formally, Ramirokovit Siuta, although few of the Order likely remembered his full name, let alone used it. The Head of the Order stood with shoulders back, his pale, yellowed hair almost glowing in the dimming light of the room. His intense orange-brown eyes fixed Finley with a gaze that commanded attention.

"Hey Ram," Finley smiled, standing. He placed his hands respectfully behind his back, noting how the evening light played upon the rugged lines of Ram's face.

"No, sit," Ram ordered curtly, making his way to the opposite side of the wooden desk. "I need to discuss Rey with you."

Had to happen eventually, Finley thought. He'd been expecting this conversation for days, and was beginning to wonder if the Head even knew Rey was preparing to go home. "Of course." He resumed his seat, a mild tension building within him. He folded his hands atop the dispatches, his mind already formulating thoughts on the young girl of witchkind whose control over her magic had become the subject of many whispered conversations.

"Give me your honest evaluation," Ram said as he leaned forward, hands resting heavily on the desk. "No platitudes. Her audition... was it truly as dire as they say?"

"Her control is lacking," Finley admitted, recalling the chaotic energy that had radiated from Rey in the barn. "But she has potential—her strength is undeniable, if raw."

"Strength means nothing without direction." Ram's eyes narrowed slightly. "Can she be trained? Or is she a danger to herself and to the Order?"

Finley considered the question, weighing his words carefully. "Training could harness her power, but it will require patience and a skilled mentor. Unfortunately..."

"Go on."

Finley sighed. "She doesn't seem even vaguely interested. Even her own magic seems largely disinteresting to her. She sparked up a bit at one point, but..." He spread his hands.

"Undirected," Ram echoed, a frown creasing his forehead. "And disinterested. That is a combination we cannot afford. Not now, not with the humans' advancements. Their 'Benoto' blocks are crude, yet they show an alarming ingenuity."

"They do," Finley agreed, thinking of the human attempts contained within the reports in front of him. "Their progress is worrying on several fronts. But as long as the Veil holds, their reliance on our magic remains our advantage."

"Advantage?" Ram gave a short, humorless chuckle. "You speak as though we play a game, Finley. This is about survival—the survival of our kind above all else. Humans are ignorant, yes, but ignorance paired with ambition is a dangerous combination. And they outnumber us by the hundreds."

"Understood," Finley acquiesced. He respected Ram's wisdom, even if his own views were sometimes less stringent.

"Your talent for runes, it could be the key to reinforcing our position," Ram stated, his gaze piercing. "What are your thoughts on this? Is there a rune, some construct, that could tighten our hold?"

"You mean like I've done before?"

"Exactly that," Ram smiled. "Something we can carve in their villages, on their churches, that will suppress this... *innovation*. Keep them docile, happy with what they have."

"Runes are a focus for shaping magic," Finley replied slowly, his fingers absently tracing the edge of a parchment. "They're not inherently magical. It's possible that there could be a more efficient approach, a new method that we haven't yet discovered. We had some success with persistent runes. But this village Rey and I were in—even calling it a 'village' is generous—didn't have a church. We've focused much of our efforts on using the humans' religion."

"But," Ram pressed, "what about something more *global?*"

Finley frowned. "You're talking about something to literally keep them... docile." His stomach churned with disgust.

"Yes."

"It wouldn't work. Runes exist for that, of course. I could probably increase their area of effect. We could put them on every building on the continent. But how would we cover the fields? If we dulled their minds and dimmed their aspirations, would they still go out on boats and fish every morning? Would they still plow their fields? We *need* them, as much as they need us and our magic."

"Hmm," Ram murmured, pushing himself upright. "Perhaps. But we must always be ten steps ahead, Finley. Remember that." He turned to go.

"Sir?" Finley's fingers ceased their absent tracing as he considered his next words with care. The quiet of the room seemed to press upon him, urging him to speak. "About Rey," he began tentatively. "We were speaking of Rey. Her control over magic is... erratic at best."

"Erratic?" Ram's voice was cutting. He turned on his heel, his eyes flashing. "I've seen the reports. Her magic isn't just erratic—it's dangerous."

"Indeed." Finley nodded, collecting his thoughts. "Her habit of empowering runes as she goes... I cautioned her against it, and she had far greater success. But the second time, she forgot. It's habitual. She claims an Uncle—"

"Hah!" Ram barked, shaking his head.

"Sir?"

"Did you know that the girl is my great-grandniece?"

Finley blinked. "I, ah... did not."

"Her audition was no more than a favor," Ram confided, his voice taking on a harder edge. "A nod to the family. Too many of whom know of our existence, to be frank. But now..." He paused, and for a moment, vulnerability flickered across his weathered face before it was quickly masked. "Now I have a reason to erase the Order from all of their memories."

"Is there truly no other way?" Finley asked, although he knew the answer even before Ram responded.

"None. She's spoiled—always has been—and clearly lacks the discipline required of our Order." Ram's gaze drifted toward the window, where the stars seemed to mock them with their serene glow. "It's a pity. I had hoped she might rise above her upbringing." Then he shook his head. "Did you know all of the Great Schools refused her?"

"Truly?"

The older man nodded slowly. "Truly. She was tutored privately. An indulgence. Her mother is... little better, frankly."

Finley felt the weight of Ram's disappointment, mirrored by his own disillusionment. The potential of a new member always brought a spark of hope, yet here they were again, confronting the stark reality that not all who wielded magic were fit to stand among them.

"Then it shall be done," Finley said quietly, knowing full well the gravity of what they were agreeing to. "We must protect the Order above all else."

"Indeed." Ram gave a curt nod, the finality in his voice echoing off the stone walls. With one last piercing look, he turned and strode out of the room, leaving Finley alone once more.

Alone with his thoughts and the disquieting notion that perhaps they were too quick to judge. And yet, the necessity of their actions was undeniable. For the survival of witchkind, they would do what must be done. That was the Order's mission, its mantra.

Still... Finley thought sadly. *Do better building blocks truly threaten us?*

He shuffled through the dispatches, his fingers again grazing over the parchment as if by touch alone he might discern the urgency of their contents. Amongst them lay a report that caught his attention, its seal broken hastily as if the messenger couldn't deliver it fast enough.

"Benoto blocks," Finley murmured, eyes scanning the text. "So it wasn't just the one village."

"Finley?"

He looked up at the new voice. "Jasen! I didn't know you were here!"

Jasen grinned, running a hand through his thick, black, ever-unruly hair. "Just yesterday. Did I hear you say 'benoto?'"

Finley tapped the dispatch. "Just going through the field reports."

"That one was mine. They've come up with some process—"

"Heating limestone and some other minerals? Cooling the

result, mixing it with water, forming incredibly strong blocks? Like gray bricks?"

Jasen's eyes widened. "I thought I'd caught the first one."

Finley grimaced. "Afraid not. I took a new apprentice out—no, don't ask," he added as Jasen opened his mouth, "and we compromised a small kiln and destroyed a larger one. But it's apparently already spread." He looked down at the dispatch. "Where is Rinceriver?"

"Minuscule little collection of hovels on the western coast, just a bit south of the Great Northern Wood."

A trickle of chill slid through Finley's heart. "No church?"

Jasen frowned. "No, not big enough. Why?"

"I don't believe in coincidences. Small kiln, then? Experimental?"

"Yeah."

"What did you do?"

"Compromised it, as you said."

"Yes, but specifically."

"Oh. I was with Kayte Goldrun. She's amazing with Flame magic. No matter what they do, they'll never get the heat right again. The stone tube will dissipate it far too quickly now, until suddenly... it doesn't. It should shatter."

Finley nodded. "Good enough, I suppose. We modified ours to split the gypsum they use. I doubt they'll ever find a working recipe again."

"So then we're good." Jasen's voice was hopeful.

"Doubtful. I was far to the south. If you've found this... there will be more. Tiny communities, no church."

"I don't get the church connection."

Finley sighed and looked out the window. The grassy fields of the Farm always seemed to promise relaxation and respite, but they always seemed to wave mockingly as the crisis of the day took over. "I think the humans know we're watching them. Manipulating them."

"We believed we'd dealt with that." Jasen turned to the door, and Finley looked past him to see Ram stalking back into the room. *Was he standing out there listening?* "No?"

"We dealt with that a few *inventions*," Finley said. "The carronade. Their printing press. But no, we didn't deal with the... watches. There's at least a small group that's aware of us, and resentful."

Jasen's brow furrowed. "And they're... what? Moving their experiments to smaller settlements?"

"Indeed." Ram's voice was hard. "Their latest tactic, it seems. Away from what monitoring we can conduct."

Finley looked up, meeting Ram's intense gaze. "They've progressed further than anticipated."

"An advancement, yes," Ram conceded, his lips thinning. "But they'll try again. These benoto blocks could be a considerable threat if developed further."

"Are they truly so dangerous?" Finley questioned, skepticism inching into his tone. "Or merely an inconvenience? They're just brick. They've had—"

Ram's expression hardened. "You underestimate the peril, Finley. Humans are persistent. Like pests, they burrow and gnaw through barriers with relentless ambition." He thought for a moment before continuing. "Remember, our dominion over magic is what separates us from them," Ram recited, his voice falling into a lecturing tone. It was an argument Finley had heard him make often in the past few years. "It is the fulcrum upon which the balance of power rests. Should humans discover us—our true nature—and we did not have the threat of withholding magic to hold over them..."

He trailed off, leaving an ominous silence. Ram fixed Finley with a piercing look, as if to brand the significance of his words upon him.

"Then we become obsolete," Jasen finished the thought aloud, the gravity of the statement settling heavily in the room. "If they can build stronger buildings without magic—"

"Buildings. Bridges. Roads. *Walls.*" He nodded to Finley's desk. "Jasen, is that your dispatch?" The other man nodded. "I've read it. You said they've subjected those bricks to pressures that would crush an ordinary brick of baked clay, no? Stronger than rocks, even, and shaped perfectly for stacking?"

"Yes."

"And they have emerged in *two* small villages, each well separated?"

"Yes," Finley confirmed. "Although if they're stamping the same name into them, it's likely that it's just one—"

"Don't you see what they're doing?" Ram snapped. "Do you have a rune, runewright, that can affect them across those two villages?"

Finley shook his head.

"They're spreading out. Making it harder for us to monitor them. Making it harder for us to *counter* them."

"They're actively working against us," Jasen whispered.

"Exactly," Ram said sharply. "And if they succeed, they can tell everyone about us. It would be genocide. We have magic, but they have iron. And numbers. Only their unwitting reliance on magic, gathered and wielded by witchkind alone, is our lever over them. Should we lose that advantage..." He let the implication hang in the air like a specter.

Finley's eyes flicked to Jasen, who'd paled.

"Without that leverage," Ram continued, his voice cold and curt, "humans would see us as equals—or worse, as threats. And we know it will be threats—we've tried for centuries to shape their religion away from a hatred of witches. We must never allow them the luxury of autonomy."

"*Nekęsk ragana gyventi,*" Jasen whispered. *Suffer not a witch to live.* One of the oldest phrases witchkind and humans still shared, a phrase that meant as much in the True Language as it did in the humans' religious texts. "It would be chaos."

"Chaos," Ram echoed, nodding slowly. "And chaos is a luxury we cannot afford. Not now, not ever."

"What can we do?" Jasen asked.

"Send warnings. Practice care with magic. Stay hidden. Let the Veil work. Report signs of human advancement, of suspicious activity." Ram's jaw set. "More patrols. We have the kitchenware business as cover. We clearly need to be visiting more of these small, churchless towns."

The Head of the Order turned away, his silhouette framed against the flickering flames in the fireplace. In his stance was the unyielding resolve that had guided witchkind for close to a century. Finley watched him, knowing that beneath the surface of their conversation lurked an unspoken truth.

Stay hidden. Practice care with magic. Finley was careful to keep his expression neutral, but he heard the underlying directive. *We don't just hold the humans in check. It's all of witchkind as well.*

"Jasen, come with me. We'll review the patrol assignments."

"Yes, sir."

They left, and Finley listened as their footsteps receded. Alone now, Finley sank into the high-backed chair, its wooden frame creaking slightly under his weight. His gaze drifted toward the window where the sun dipped low, casting long shadows across the room.

It was true, what Ram had said about humans. Their lives were brief and fraught with struggle, absent the grace of magic that flowed so naturally through witchkind. They toiled upon the earth, ignorant of the arcane currents that danced just beyond their perception—a dance that could uplift or obliterate, depending on who led it.

Finley's thoughts, unbidden, shifted to Rey—specifically, to the rune she had been carving when he last saw her. The lines had been rough, yet imbued with a promise of power that she couldn't quite harness. It was a fairly simple Earth sigil, meant to separate the fundamental components of minerals. Yet it had seemed... overwrought.

It wasn't just her, he thought idly as his hands shuffled the dispatches into a neat stack. *With a more direct rune, she'd have been fine. Even empowering it as she carved.* The problem with runes were that they were each a creation, a complete work. Partly finished, they were unstable, their alignments unable to process magic. Finished, of course, they let witchkind's minds shape magic. That's what they were for. *They represent outcomes. Intent.*

His fingers twitched as if they yearned to correct her work, to smooth the jagged edges of her intent into something purer, more potent. Such was the burden of his talents: the uncommon runewright, coupled with the secretive whisper of the Rune Smith within him, always urging him toward creation, toward perfection.

"Hmm," he murmured, the sound hanging in the air like a question. The potential in Rey's magic had been raw, untamed —dangerous, even—but wasn't the problem more in how it was being applied? *Isn't that the problem with all of us? The magic is* there, *we just shape it. Why can't it be shaped as we go?* There was something there, something itching behind his eyes, refusing to let this go.

He closed his eyes, envisioning the rune again, feeling the thrum of the Earth magic inside him. His mind reached out, his talent prodding at the edges of the memory, seeking the core of what Rey had tried to invoke. There was something there, a spark waiting to be stoked by a steady hand.

"Control," he whispered, the word a mantra. "Control and understanding."

The Farm settled around him in silence, the quiet hum of gathered magic vibrating through the walls. In this moment of solitude, Finley Coughlan, pragmatic yet hopeful, stood at the precipice of discovery, wondering not for the first time if there might be a path forward—one that could bridge the chasm between human and witchkind, chaos and control.

"Finley, do you have a moment?"

Finley's eyes flew open before he even realized they'd fallen shut. "Dmitry?"

Dmitry Aganin was a slightly built man with the jet-black skin of the southwest and a shock of unruly, coarse white hair. He was Ram's personal assistant, and had been for decades. He gave Finley a hesitant smile. "I was waiting until Ram left."

"He's... intense, today."

Dmitry nodded sadly. "The pressure has been weighing on him. The responsibility. We've never been *actively* opposed, you know."

"This cabal of humans has been doing this since I joined."

"Probably before," Dmitry acknowledged. He stepped into the room and leaned against the wall next to the doorway. "Ram's starting to worry we might not be enough."

Finley frowned.

"We've never been large, and right now we have more field operatives than we've ever had. More people running the kitchenware business. More eyes, all across the continent. Yet... they're still finding ways to elude us."

"And we're allowing them fewer and fewer inventions," Finley pointed out.

"Ram's starting to regret every one we've let slide."

"It's not sustainable."

Dmitry looked away for a moment and sighed. "I know. Something has to give."

"What will it be?"

"It may be *us*. I've... there's some pressure for Ram to end the secrecy around the Order."

Finley's frown deepened. "To what end?"

"To enlist all of witchkind."

"Wouldn't that be... dangerous? We've always stayed small, always stayed secret, precisely to—"

"To specialize, and to protect everyone else. I know." Dmitry gave Finley a wan smile. "I helped develop the current policy, you know. And the recruiting process."

"Oh." Dmitry had been in the Order for a *very* long time, then. "But to end the secrecy... it would be declaring all-out war against the humans."

Dmitry's eyes narrowed and he nodded slowly. "It would."

Finley's chest tightened slightly. "Dmitry, they outnumber us hundreds to one."

"But we have magic."

"We *need* them. The farms, the fishing fleets, we can't—"

"We wouldn't destroy them. Not like they'd do to us, if they knew." Dmitry's voice had gone hard. "We'd simply need to... keep them under control."

Finley suddenly felt sick. "It... we can't let it come to that."

Dmitry's expression relaxed and he stood upright. "No. No, we can't. And we won't." He smiled, but there was no joy in it. "We'll hold the line." And with another curt nod, he turned and stepped out.

Finley watched him go, whatever energy he had remaining seeming to drain out of his body.

· · ·

***

Finley abandoned his dispatches and the small office, commandeered a mug of hot, spicy *kava* from the kitchen, and returned to his room. The conversations with Ram and Dmitry had left him feeling tense, and a sullen weariness pulled at the edges of his mind.

He could *feel* something—his talent, he hoped—rolling something around in his brain. Something even it wasn't certain of, something Rey had sparked. *I've known that rune for years,* he thought, picturing it in his mind. He'd learned it from his parents, even before he'd gone to school. They used a version of it to strengthen the mortar in the sea wall of their village.

"Runes," he said to himself, the word falling flat in the silence of the room. "They're not the magic itself; they merely give it shape." He contemplated the history of runic orders, each evolving from its predecessor—Old Runic's angular markings giving way to Middle Runic's flowing scripts, and now New Runic's sharp geometries, brimming with potential.

"We've used many different shapes to achieve the same outcomes. The shapes don't matter." Old Runic had required great power and fairly little precision, and power had been abundant back then. After the Forging of the Axes and the rise of the Adherents, magic had grown thin in the world, far too insufficient to power the runes. Middle Runic had been the answer: simpler, thick strokes that could be filled with what little magic witchkind had available. But they'd been *too* simple once the Last Adherent fell and magic splintered, flowing back into the world like a flood. New Runic harkened back to Old, but explicitly recognized the elemental alignments of Earth, Sea,

Flame, and Sky that had been more lore than fact in the oldest days.

He recalled the harvest spell that his professors had used to illustrate the differences, and summoned the Old Runic version in his mind.

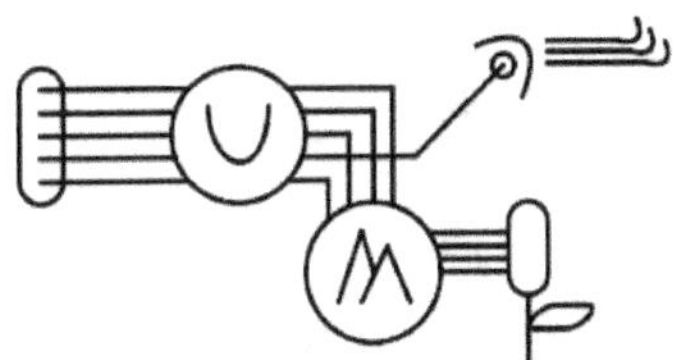

Straight lines and sharp angles carried magic from rune to rune. *They even called them Intents,* he remembered, ways of shaping the mind's desire in a way to which magic would respond. Some professors theorized that even these constructs were greatly simplified from witchkind's originals, from structures vastly more intricate.

Middle Runic's calligraphy-like strokes captured the same intent, but with a blunter, less nuanced approach.

They were better suited for carving into things, he thought wryly as his talent sketched how magic would flow through the heavy loops and whirls.

And New Runic, the language he'd known his entire life.

So similar to Old Runic, in many ways. Intent was depicted in much the same way, although the flow of magic was much the same. *They tell a story, of sorts.* This is the sun, this is the Earth magic we'll use. This is the outcome, directing strength and nutrients into the crop. Magic neatly categorized, neatly structured.

He pondered the purpose behind the intricate designs, how each curve and line must be understood by the caster to properly channel the magic. The runes were like a complex language spoken between the mage and the forces at play—a language that required fluency for mastery.

"Yet, what if..." Finley's voice trailed off, his mind racing ahead. He walked over to the expansive window that looked out over the Farm's lush grounds, the greenery a stark contrast to the dark thoughts clouding his mind.

"Magic is formless, bound only by our understanding of it," he continued, speaking as much to the wind as to himself. "What if the runes themselves are a limitation? A crutch we've grown too dependent upon?"

The idea was heretical, almost blasphemous within the Order's hallowed halls. Runes were the bedrock of their practice, the foundation upon which all witchkind's magical prowess was built. Yet, the Rune Smith within him—the rare gift that allowed him to craft new magic from the ether—whispered of possibilities unexplored, of boundaries yet to be pushed.

"Perhaps there is a way to transcend the runes," Finley mused, his heart quickening at the thought. "To tap directly into the essence of magic itself, without the intermediary of these prescribed symbols."

But still, magic had to be *shaped*. The caster's mind must be in a precise configuration, focused on its intent. That's what the runes did: they provided structure, along with cantrips recited in the True Language. Without placing your mind into the proper set, the magic couldn't flow.

Is that really true? something whispered in his own mind.

His gaze drifted back to the materials scattered across the

table: scrolls, quills, and various implements for carving. They seemed suddenly antiquarian, relics of a bygone era that begged to be surpassed.

"Efficiency...directness...purity," he uttered, as if casting a spell with his words alone. Each term resonated with the power of untapped potential. Finley's green eyes gleamed with the reflection of the late afternoon sun filtering through the window, igniting a fire within him.

"Could it be?" he whispered to the empty room, the question hanging in the air, charged with the promise of revolutionizing magic as they knew it. "Is there a more efficient way?" A more efficient form of magic would be more *powerful.* Less waste meant more outcome, and already his talent was pointing out areas where New Runic wasted magic in its precise, geometric structures. *Circles contain, lines transmit,* he considered. *But is magic truly so banal?*

If he could devise a broader, more powerful way of discouraging humans from their inventions, then Ram would quickly turn to other priorities. Speeches about *docility* would give way to the practical matters of the day. Would it be possible, practical, for magic to stretch across the continent? Something akin to the Veil, but designed to gently steer humans to more pastoral tasks than inventing weapons and new building methods?

In that moment, Finley stood on the cusp of something monumental. If he could just unravel the mysteries that beckoned, he might forge a new path for all witchkind—one where the shackles of tradition would fall away, leaving pure, unbridled magic in their stead.

His eyelids felt suddenly heavy, and he turned to his bed.

CHAPTER 3

Everburn

Finley's eyes flew open at a pounding on the sturdy wooden door of his room. He flew out of bed, pulling the door open. Before him was Marlowe, one of the oldest members of the Order aside from Ram himself. "What is it?" His eyes were still swimming with sleep, and half-formed runes skittered through his mind, a side effect of his talent reawakening.

"Finley," Marlowe began, his voice carrying the weight of urgency, "Dmitry sent me. We have a situation that requires your unique talents."

"What kind of situation?"

"A report has come in. A human—reckless as usual—has concocted something... dangerous. They call it Everburn. Our agent describes it as a fuel of some kind, says it burns extremely hot." Marlowe's fingers drummed on the wooden door frame, betraying his concern. "It burns without ceasing, water or no. It could decimate entire cities if left unchecked. The man is distilling it into glass containers, which can be..." he swallowed heavily before continuing. "Launched. Or thrown."

Finley felt a surge of adrenaline. This was no mundane task; it was a mission that could tip the scales. "You believe I can stop it?"

"Your runewright abilities are second to none, and your secret talent..." Marlowe let the sentence hang, a coded nod to Finley's rare Rune Smith gift. The oldest members of the Order knew of it, although they were careful to contain that knowledge. Having a Rune Smith in the Order was a rare advantage, one that witchkind's great council, the Taryba, might deny them if discovered. "We require a *permanent* solution, if one can be devised. Ram is concerned—"

Finley nodded quickly. "It's likely this has already been spread to other villages, like the bricks were."

"Exactly."

"Understood." Finley's mind raced. He would need to invent new magic, something that could counteract the Everburn without causing further destruction.

"Finley," Marlowe added urgently, "some of the larger human towns have been... agitating. You know how they are."

Finley's heart beat more quickly. "Have there been attacks?"

"Not as such, but... yes. Not attacks exactly. More along the lines of bandits. But curiously only against caravans originating from specific towns."

Finley sighed heavily. "So they're boiling again."

"Simmering heavily, at the least, yes," Marlowe agreed. "Which is why it's imperative—"

"—that they not have efficient new weapons, yes," Finley nodded. One of the best outcomes of the Order's work had been depriving humans of any kind of effective weapons for centuries. They'd left humans with little more than rocks and sticks to work with until they'd figured out how to forge spears and swords, and the result had been centuries of relative peace between the notoriously combative population.

"Ram asks that you remember that time is not our ally. You must act with both precision and discretion." Marlowe leaned forward, his gaze locking onto Finley's. "The balance between humans and witchkind must be maintained."

"And between humans," Finley agreed. "I'll begin at once."

Finley nodded and turned away, his thoughts already weaving through the complexities of his Alignments. This mission would need to use Control to manage the delicate balance of the spell, Reach to ensure it covered the necessary area, and Destroy to dismantle the Everburn's effectiveness. *A tricky combination.* Destroy often contradicted control, although it was compatible enough with Reach. *Perhaps there's a way to modify the Everburn, limit is own reach. Turn something destructive into something useful.*

As he closed the door to his room and began tossing clothing into a traveling bag, Finley concentrated on the task ahead. Stopping the Everburn wouldn't just be about harnessing his affinity for Flame; it would be about—once again—bending the principles of magic to his will. He had no doubt that more than one agent of the Order had already considered this problem—Ram himself was exceptionally clever with runes. But they'd obviously come up empty, and when that happened these days, Finley was inevitably the one they turned to. It wasn't just his Rune Smith talent, or even his lesser runewright ability. *It's my dual affinities and the dual-gender affinity.* Gifts from his sister, who'd died before they'd come into their magic, leaving him with a combination of abilities.

"Expandable, durable, detailed, adaptable..." Finley murmured, listing the qualities he'd need as he strode through the quiet streets. Each word sparked an idea, a potential rune that could form the linchpin of his plan. The thought of creating new magic always thrilled him—a whisper of excitement that danced through his veins. But tonight, it was tempered by the knowledge that lives hung in the balance. He couldn't afford to get this wrong.

***

Finley's boots scuffed against the hard-packed dirt, his shadow stretching long and thin beneath the crescent moon. He knew every second mattered; the Order's efforts to suppress human weapons had been a delicate dance of magic and secrecy. Everburn threatened that balance. The substance had been detected in—once again—a tiny settlement that lacked a church, a true general store, or any of the other amenities of civilization. Rockpoint, as it was called, lay a half-day's walk from Cuppton, along the continent's west coast, bracketed by sea and forest. According to the dispatch he'd been given, fewer than three dozen buildings formed the tiny village, along with a rickety pier and a surprisingly robust seawall.

And no church.

And none of witchkind living there.

This isn't coincidence, all these tiny settlements cropping up without any of us living there, and without the trappings of a normal human village.

He'd used travel magic to speed his way to Cuppton, and then set out at a brisk pace, just as the sun was beginning to peek over the horizon. Now he strode along the caravan path, his boots crunching softly on the dew-laden grass. The sky was a deep indigo, the stars beginning to fade as the horizon lightened to a pale lavender. The two moons hung low, their silver light casting long shadows across the rolling hills.

The air was crisp and cool, carrying the earthy scent of the soil and the sweet perfume of night-blooming flowers. Finley breathed deeply, letting the fresh air fill his lungs and clear his mind. As he walked, he let his senses expand, feeling the thrum of magic that pulsed through the land. It was a subtle thing, a whisper on the wind, but to Finley it was as tangible as the ground beneath his feet.

The path wound its way through the hills, following the natural contours of the land. It was well-worn from the passage of countless caravans, the grass trampled down to bare earth in places. Finley could almost hear the creaking of wagon wheels and the soft nicker of horses, though the path was empty now, save for himself.

He crested a particularly steep hill, and there was Rockpoint.

The dispatch had been quite accurate: the low, two-story wood-and-stone buildings hunkered just back from the pier, arranged around a cross-shaped road that led straight through from north to south, and from the pier to the thick forest from west to east. None sported the characteristic steeple of the humans' churches. While all of the buildings looked sturdy...

Finley frowned as he set off down the hill toward the town, his discerning eye picking out details the dispatch had omitted.

They're sturdy, but they're new. Very new. Rough-hewn lumber hadn't yet been worn by wind and rain. Thatched roofs still glowed a honey-gold in the growing light, not yet faded to gray and black. And even the rickety pier was new—and as he approached, Finley detected workers clambering over the structure, wrapping lengths of heavy rope around the wood joints to strengthen them. *They're still working on it.*

He scanned the village one last time, looking for one that seemed a bit set back, or a bit more heavily built. A structure designed to accommodate someone working on deadly mass-effect weapons.

That'll be it, he thought as his eye lit on the most likely candidate. The only building in town with two-story stone walls, tightly mortared, rather than wood set atop a waist-high stone foundation. Its roof was black slate rather than thatch, and its neighbors were at least a narrow alley away, rather than directly against it.

In a town this size, it would be difficult for a stranger to pass unnoticed. As Finley walked into the village's center, his eyes scanned for an excuse. *Ah, there.* An inn was always a good starting point. This one sat along the north-south road, just one building from where the roads intersected. *Although not much of an inn,* he thought with disappointment as he stepped inside.

The inn's interior was as rough and new as the rest of the village. The common room held a scattering of mismatched tables and chairs, the wood still pale and unvarnished. A long bar ran along one wall, its surface still rough from the mill. A few early rising patrons—*locals, if I'm any judge,* Finley thought—sat hunched over their meals, their conversation a low murmur that ceased as Finley entered.

The innkeeper, a burly man with a thick beard and suspicious eyes, looked up from wiping down the bar. "What'll it be?" he grunted.

Finley approached the bar, offering a friendly smile. "A room for the night, if you have one available. And perhaps a meal and a mug of ale."

The innkeeper's eyes narrowed, his gaze flicking over Finley's travel-worn clothing and the pack slung over his shoulder. "We don't get many visitors here," he said slowly. "What brings you to Rockpoint?"

"Just passing through," Finley replied easily. "I'm a trader, headed down the coast. Thought I'd stop for the night, rest my feet a bit before moving on. And if you've a dry good store or any such, I might try and ply my wares. Some of the best kitchenwares in the world!"

The innkeeper grunted. "No dry goods. Goods come in on wagon from Cuppton, fish goes back. Room's two for the night. Meal's one extra each." He paused, and then in a friendlier tone, added, "Not much to do or see here. Tomorrow's wagon will continue on south."

Finley nodded amiably. "I'm ultimately headed for Farreach in the South. Might see if they've room."

Although a few of the other patrons were still eyeing Finley suspiciously, most returned to their meals and muttered conversations. Finley slid payment—one room, four meals—across the bar and settled into a stool as the innkeeper stepped into the back to retrieve his food.

The meal was a simple yet satisfying one. A small, crispy rasher of bacon sat atop a thick slice of bread, its edges glistening with the drippings that had been smeared generously. A perfectly fried egg rested on top, its yolk still runny and inviting. Finley wasted no time in eagerly digging into the dish, savoring each bite with gusto as the flavors melded together in his mouth.

He pretended to be so completely absorbed by his meal that he didn't notice what was happening around him.

He wasn't by any means an expert on humans, but these ones acted... strange. He quickly cast *akys pakaušyje* and then squinted as his eyes were filled with an oddly distorted image of the entire room, as if he'd grown eyes on the back and sides of his head.

Finley kept his eyes down, focused on his meal, but his magically enhanced senses took in every detail of the room. The inn's patrons were a rough-looking lot, with weathered faces and calloused hands that spoke of hard labor. They huddled together in small groups, their voices low and urgent as they conversed.

One man, his face half-hidden beneath a wide-brimmed

hat, kept casting furtive glances in Finley's direction. Another, a burly fellow with a scar running down his cheek, leaned in close to his companion, muttering something that made the other man's eyes widen in alarm. A third patron, a wiry man with sharp features, slipped out of his chair and made his way to the door, his movements quick and furtive like a startled hare.

There was a palpable sense of unease in the room, a tension that hung thick in the air like smoke. These men had the look of those who were hunted or had been, their eyes darting to the shadows as if expecting danger to leap out at any moment. They carried themselves with a wary alertness, their muscles coiled and ready to spring into action at the slightest provocation.

"What takes you to Farreach?" the innkeeper asked in his gruff, gravelly voice.

Conversation in the room stopped, and Finley could see everyone looking at him out of the corners of their eyes.

A strategy fitted itself into his mind. It was sure, certain, and calm.

Yet it hadn't come from his own mind.

Still, he wasn't one to look askance at a gift, so he went with it.

"If I'm being honest," he said quietly, watching everyone else in the room lean very slightly toward him, "I've had a bit of trouble." He shrugged. "If I'm being more honest, those six pieces I gave you are close to all I have left."

"You said you sold kitchenwares," the innkeeper growled.

Right, I did do that, didn't I? "Sold. Past tense. Lost that job a fortnight ago."

"Stealing?" the innkeeper asked gently.

Finley shrugged. "That's what the owner claimed. I didn't, but he put it out, and every door was closed to me."

The innkeeper's eyes tracked slowly to the left, then to the far right, and then back to Finley. "What kind of work do you know?"

"Not fishing," Finley said quickly. *For all that my parents are fisherwitches. I can barely be on a boat before I'm getting sick, and it's gotten worse as I get older.* "But good with my hands. Woodwork. Stone. I can make bricks, if you've a kiln." He took another bite of food, chewed, and looked into the innkeeper's eyes. "I know how to keep my mouth shut."

"Now why," said the man sitting next to him at the bar, "would that be important?"

The man who had spoken was of average height, but his broad shoulders and thick, muscular arms suggested a life of hard labor. His skin was tanned and weathered, the creases around his eyes and mouth etched deep by years of squinting into the sun and salt-spray. His hair, once a rich chestnut brown, was now liberally shot through with gray, and a short, neatly trimmed beard covered his jaw.

He wore a well-made linen shirt, the fabric a crisp white that stood out in stark contrast to the rough, homespun garments of the other patrons. Over this, he had donned a leather vest, the hide supple and well-oiled, adorned with intricate tooling along the edges. His trousers, tucked into sturdy leather boots, were of a finer weave than those around him, the deep blue fabric unmarred by patches or darning.

There was an air of authority about the man, a quiet confidence that spoke of a life spent giving orders and having them obeyed without question. Yet there was also a roughness to him, a sense that he was no stranger to getting his hands dirty when the need arose.

"Just saying a lot of men talk too much," Finley said, nodding politely at the man. "Can get on your nerves, after a long day of hard work. I'm no gossip."

The man looked at Finley for a long moment, and then

nodded slightly. "Might be we could use a man like you, then. Can you lift a brace?"

About half my own weight, Finley thought quickly, remembering the heavy crates the fisherfolk used in his parents' town. He nodded slowly. "I believe I can."

The innkeeper had backed away, busying himself polishing a tankard, but he kept an eye on the two. Everyone else had turned back to their own business, and Finley let his magic dissipate, blinking hard as his vision snapped back to normal.

"Ever work with fire?" the man asked. "Forge, maybe? See, we need men who can lift, who can be quiet, and who know how to be careful. Respectful, you might say."

Everburn, Finley thought, excitement rising in his chest. *But there's no way they're asking a complete stranger to see their new invention. Either this is some kind of test, or they've been going through menial assistants really fast. Maybe both.* "I know how to be careful. Follow instructions. Real good at following instructions." It was too late to make a play as a thick-skulled laborer, but he could certainly try for *desperate* and *obedient.*

That earned him another long, searching look, which was followed by a gap-toothed grin. "Name's Harm," the man said. "Finish your meal and I'll show you the job."

***

Harm led Finley directly to the all-stone, slate-roofed building Finley had noticed earlier. Harm pushed open the heavy wooden door, its new leather hinges creaking. Finley followed him inside, his eyes taking a moment to adjust to the dim interior after the brightness of the morning sun.

The first thing that struck Finley was the smell—a pungent, chemical odor that stung his nostrils and made his eyes water. It was a sharp, acrid scent, like burning oil mixed with something else, something harsher and more caustic. The air was thick with it, hanging heavy and oppressive in the stale, unmoving air of the building.

As his vision cleared, Finley took in the details of the room. The walls were of rough-hewn stone, the blocks fitted tightly together with only the thinnest lines of mortar visible between them. The ceiling was low, supported by heavy wooden beams that looked as though they had been hewn from ancient trees, their surfaces rough and unfinished. *They took great care with this building,* he thought.

Along one wall stood a row of large, cylindrical glass canisters, each one taller than a man and nearly as wide. They were scuffed and chipped, but whole. Piles of some white substance —it reminded him of limestone powder, but there was something different about it—sat on the opposite side of the room. In one corner, a testing area of sorts had been erected. It was little more than three double-thick stone walls, capped with—

Finley's breath caught as he felt the unmistakable pull of iron on his magic. He quickly cast the rune that locked his magic inside him.

Iron rails, looking for all the world like those used on the iron roadway, were laid across the testing area, providing a sturdy roof. The interior of the three walls were chipped and blackened, testament to the power of this new weapon.

The room was cluttered with an array of smaller glass

containers and wooden barrels, each one carefully placed in a specific location. Finley's gaze traced across the space, taking in the organized chaos before him. The delicate bottles glimmered in the light, their contents unknown but undoubtedly precious. The barrels appeared old and well-worn, hinting at years of use and refinement. Despite their seemingly random distribution, there was a clear method to their placement.

"You're to stand guard, and carry as needed," Harm said. He pointed to a reed-thin young man who was struggling to pry the top from a small barrel. "Aldarae!" The man turned with a start, his eyes blinking owlishly in the dim light. "Got you another helper." Then, to Finley, "Man's a genius, but distracted. Just help him however he asks."

"You said 'stand guard?'"

Harm waved it away. "Everyone knows not to come in here uninvited. Just make sure of it."

"What's all this for?"

Harm's eyes narrowed. "Forgot to mention that we don't like questions, either."

Finley smiled affably. "Then just one more. What's the pay?"

Harm's expression relaxed. "Ten a day."

"I'll take it."

"Then I'll leave you at it. Work day ends when he says so, but take yourself a break for nuncheon."

"Understood."

***

"Do you know what we do here?" Aldarae asked.

"I don't really ask questions," Finley replied carefully.

Aldarae turned to fully face Finley, his movements quick and birdlike. He was a thin man, with pale skin that looked like it had rarely seen the sun. His hair was a shock of unkempt brown curls, sticking out at odd angles as if he had been running his hands through it in thought.

But it was his eyes that truly caught Finley's attention. They were large and round, a striking pale blue, and seemed to take up half his face. They darted about the room, never resting on one spot for long, as if his mind was constantly racing ahead, wrestling with a thousand ideas at once.

There was an intensity to Aldarae's gaze, a sharp intelligence that burned bright and hot. It was the look of a man consumed by his work, driven by a relentless need to discover, to invent, to push the boundaries of what was possible.

He wore a simple tunic and trousers, both liberally splattered with stains and scorch marks. His sleeves were rolled up to the elbow, revealing forearms crisscrossed with thin, pale scars - a testament to the hazards of his craft.

He snorted. "Don't mind Harm. It's important that you know a bit about this, so you know to be careful. Respectful."

"He used those exact words."

Another snort. "Well he should. What we make here is a kind of chemical—do you know what a chemical is?" Finley shrugged. "It burns. Once set alight, it is almost impossible to extinguish it. It will burn underwater, even. Even if smothered in sand, it will remain hot for hours—dozens of hours—and re-ignite at the slightest touch of air. That means it is *dangerous,* do you understand?"

Finley nodded vigorously.

"Good. Most of the components are not dangerous by themselves, but if combined, they can be dangerous. The white powder there," and he waved to the neat piles Finley had seen, "is called *kalcio oksidas.* Have you heard of it?"

Finley shook his head, although he was once again struck at a human's use of the True Language.

"Don't touch it with bare hands. Always wear gloves, long sleeves, and ideally move it only with a long-handled shovel. It prefers to be in glass or wood containers, not metal."

"Okay." Finley paused. "Can I ask a question?"

Aldarae's response was enthusiastic. "Of course! Questions beg answers, and finding answers is how we learn!" He smiled encouragingly.

"What's it for?"

"Ah, well, nothing nice, I'm afraid," the slim man said, shaking his head sorrowfully. "It is mainly used as a weapon. We will be packaging it into glass jars. When thrown, they shatter, and quickly ignite. As I've said, once ignited they tend to keep burning."

"So... we're attacking someone?"

"God in his heaven, no," Aldarae said, his eyes widening further. "Not us. Well, certainly not me. No, the intent, which I have been given to understand... that is, it is mainly as a defense."

Finley's brow furrowed. "I don't understand."

"I'm told the point is that only an insane person would attack a party that was liberally equipped with Everburn. Which is what I've named it. Everburn. Because it burns for quite a long time, do you see?"

Finley nodded.

"And so, if one opponent was well-supplied with Everburn, nobody would dare attack them, for fear of retribution."

"I see." *They're mad.*

"So these won't actually hurt anyone."

"Of course."

Aldarae paused for a moment, his eyes settling on Finley's

for several moments. "Can you help me open a barrel of sulphur? I'll warn you, the stuff reeks."

***

Finley spent the day assisting Aldarae in his work, moving barrels and containers of various substances around the cramped workshop. The physical labor was taxing under normal circumstances, but with the added complication of the heavy, acrid air, it quickly became exhausting. Sweat poured down Finley's face as he hefted the weighty materials, his lungs burning with each breath of the noxious fumes.

As he worked, Finley surreptitiously called upon his Earth magic, letting his senses probe the composition of the materials he handled. The *kalcio oksidas* felt curiously inert to his magical senses, almost as if it existed outside the realm of Earth entirely. It was an unsettling sensation, like a void where substance should be.

The sulphur, on the other hand, fairly buzzed with potential energy, its essence almost eager to combine and transform. Finley could sense the latent power within it, a kind of chemical hunger waiting to be unleashed. He made a mental note to be especially cautious when handling it.

Throughout the day, Finley's Rune Smith talent whispered in the back of his mind, offering tantalizing glimpses of potential solutions. He could sense the intricate interplay of the chemicals, the delicate balance that allowed them to combine into such a volatile substance. With each new insight, a corresponding rune would flicker through his thoughts—a twist here, a flourish there, each one a key to potentially neutralizing Everburn.

But he couldn't risk experimenting here, not with Aldarae watching his every move. He needed time and space to fully explore the possibilities his talent presented. And so he bided his time, committing each fleeting rune to memory, building a mental library of potential countermeasures.

And... *I'm reticent,* he admitted. *All my talent wants to do is invent new things, invent new runes. Invent new* magic. *When will that get away from me?* The whispering had grown more interested and more insistent throughout the day, and for the first time, Finley wondered if his talent was *his* talent, or if he was just a body for his talent to live in.

As the sun began to dip towards the horizon, Aldarae finally called a halt to their labors. "That's enough for today," he said, his voice hoarse from the fumes. "You've done well. I think you'll fit in nicely here."

Finley nodded his thanks, his mind already racing ahead to the solitude of his rented room at the inn. There, he could finally give his Rune Smith some room to wander, and see what it came up with.

One thing was for sure: he didn't know a single existing rune construct that would change Everburn. Every element was too basic, too focused on what it did. Oil *would burn,* no matter what you did.

But a tickle at the back of his brain was saying, *nothing is impossible.*

***

Finley hurried back to the inn, his mind awhirl with the day's discoveries. The common room was bustling with the evening crowd, the air thick with the scent of roasted meat and the clamor of raised voices. He made his way to the bar, signaling the innkeeper for a meal.

"Job working out?"

Finley shrugged, but said nothing.

The innkeeper nodded approvingly. "You'll be looking for something more permanent, then? Someplace to stay?"

Another shrug.

"Go see Kemal around noon tomorrow. He's got a room to let. Last place along the north-south road, east side."

Finley nodded silently, and the innkeeper stepped away. A few minutes later, a plate was slid in front of him - a slab of dark bread, a wedge of sharp cheese, and a bowl of hearty stew, steam curling invitingly from its surface. Finley ate quickly, barely tasting the food, his thoughts consumed by the challenge that lay ahead.

The Rune Smith talent whispered insistently in his mind, a constant stream of possibilities and permutations. It was eager, almost impatient, straining against Finley's restraint like a hound pulling at its leash. He could feel it pulsing through his veins, a living thing with a will of its own. *Something new*, it muttered eagerly. *Why does oil burn? Why does the* kalcio oksidas *encourage it? How do you shape an intent that you don't understand?*

That last piece is what bothered him the most.

Finley finished his meal in record time, pushing away from the table with a nod of thanks to the innkeeper. He made his way up the narrow stairs to his room, the worn floorboards creaking under his feet.

Let's see if I can rest a bit before nightfall, he thought tiredly.

***

. . .

"Odd time for a stroll," a voice sliced through the silence, tethering Finley's swift steps.

Finley had taken a fitful nap of just a couple of hours as the sun set and the air cooled. His mind had churned restlessly, his Rune Smith talent weaving intricate patterns behind his eyelids, teasing him with glimpses of a solution just out of reach. When he could bear it no longer, he'd thrown off the thin blanket and risen from the narrow bed, his body protesting the sudden movement.

He'd dressed quickly in the dim light, pulling on his sturdy trousers and tunic, fingers fumbling with the laces. He'd reached for his boots, the leather soft and supple from years of wear, and tugged them on, the soles whispering against the rough floorboards.

And then he had paused for a moment, his hand resting on the cool metal of the door handle. He'd closed his eyes, reaching for the well of magic that pulsed within him, and carefully started to weave a glamour. It was a subtle thing, a gentle nudge to the mind rather than an outright illusion. It would make him less noticeable, encouraging the eye to slide past him without registering his presence.

And despite that, someone had seen him.

He turned, spotting the figure leaning against a building's rough brickwork. She was inconspicuous, almost too much so, with keen eyes that didn't miss a beat. "And you're out here because...?" Finley quirked an eyebrow, his voice steady despite the prickle of suspicion crawling up his spine.

"Curiosity," she said, pushing away from the wall. "You're Finley, aren't you? The Order's golden boy."

Finley's heart nearly stopped.

His mind began weaving a dozen runes: this one for shielding, this one to launch an attack, another to carry him far from this town, a fourth to imprison this stranger. It wasn't until he dropped the magic that had been holding his power inside him that he remembered casting it in the first place.

"Golden is a bit much. I prefer just 'boy,'" Finley retorted, clasping his hands behind his back to conceal the sudden shaking in his hands. *This is a trap. It always was.* "What does your curiosity want with me?"

He could feel his magic licking out of him, drawn to the woman. *She's wearing iron,* he realized. He reinstated the protective magic, torn between protecting himself and giving himself options.

"Everburn," she stated flatly, locking her gaze with his. "You're here to extinguish it."

"Maybe I'm just fond of fires," he shot back, though his mind raced. She knew more than she should—more than any human ought to know about witchkind.

"Or maybe you're trying to maintain a status quo that's suffocating us," she countered, crossing her arms. "Humans deserve to forge their own path, free from your chains."

"Chains? Those 'chains' keep your world from collapsing under the weight of its own chaos." Finley's tone was a mix of frustration and an unyielding sense of duty. "You don't understand the forces you're meddling with."

"Enlighten me, then," she challenged, taking a step closer.

He suppressed an urge to step back. *She's with the cabal. The ones who know about us. The ones who trapped me.* He forced his mind to focus, forced it to put off the flashback he felt coming. "War. Destruction. Suffering. All held at bay by what you call 'chains.' Without us, your path would lead straight into darkness," Finley explained, his green eyes reflecting his earnest belief. "Everburn is the best example. Why do you need so badly to destroy each other?"

"Your kind always thinks they know best," she huffed, but there was a flicker of doubt in her eyes now.

"Because we've seen the worst," Finley replied softly. "You hunted us, and you warred against each other. Our oldest stories, that's all they're about. This isn't just about better bricks or printing books faster. And we don't hold you back. We just..." He struggled to finish the sentence. "You go too fast. You reach for things you don't need. We're just..."

"Slowing us down?" she asked, a smirk in her voice.

He shrugged. "Maybe. A bit."

"Even if it means denying us our potential?" There was a tremor in her voice now, a crack in her resolve.

"Especially then," Finley affirmed, turning away from her. In a single mental motion, he dropped his protective magic and engaged a more powerful glamour, his eyes itching as the magic took hold, cloaking him from sight. "Goodnight," he murmured, disappearing into the shadows.

He cast one additional rune.

Nesek paskui mane was anti-tracking magic, one not known to most of witchkind but an old friend to the agents of the Order. Finley reached into a pocket for one of the segmented wooden coins the Order used, planning to snap off pieces in a brief message, before he remembered that this little settlement didn't have a church. No church, no donation box. No box, no way of getting the coin back to the Order.

I'm truly alone, he thought.

We always are, his talent whispered.

***

The factory was dark and quiet at this time of night. A quick rune of sleeping dispatched the single already sleepy guard standing next to the door, and a moment later Finley was inside.

The interior of the factory loomed dark, its stone walls black and forbidding in the moonlight. The building seemed to absorb the faint illumination, hunching in on itself like a great beast. The high, narrow windows were like eyes, staring down at him accusingly.

The heavy wooden door creaked shut behind him with a dull thud that echoed through the cavernous space. The air was thick and still, heavy with the acrid tang of chemicals. It coated his tongue and stung his eyes, making them water.

In the dim light filtering through the slit windows high above, the contents of the factory took on a sinister aspect. The towering glass canisters glinted dully, their curves distorting the faint moonbeams into twisted shapes. They stood in silent rows like an army of ghosts, sentinel and waiting. Who knew what volatile substances they contained, just waiting for the right spark to erupt into deadly conflagration?

The piles of white *kalcio oksidas* powder formed eerie mounds, their surfaces smooth and unnaturally pristine. In the shadows, they looked like snowdrifts or piles of bone meal.

He had no idea what he was going to do.

He'd initially thought to render some of the materials inert, an achievable enough goal for someone with Earth affinity as strong as his. But the woman in the street... there was no possible way that the cabal didn't have another factory just like this one, elsewhere. Probably more than one.

The petroleum oil is pretty bad stuff, his talent whispered, more lucid than he'd ever experienced. *We could probably just end it. It doesn't even belong here.*

What? Finley asked silently.

His only reply was a muffled sense of irritation, a shaking of the head and a grumbling return to slumber.

But of all the ingredients, the oil was the most intriguing. He'd read about the stuff, but never encountered it. Might as well introduce himself.

A new rune flared in his mind as he stepped toward a wooden barrel of the black, sticky substance. Thinner than pitch but smelling exactly the same, capable of burning hotter than tallow.

Papasakok man apie save.

A phrase in the True Language, one that, according to the stories, predated witchkind itself.

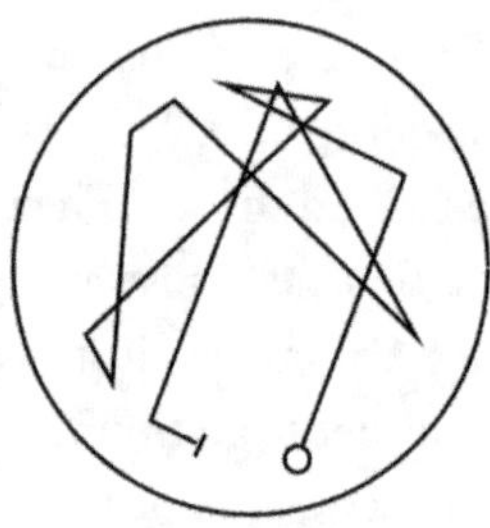

What in the name of the elements? Finley asked himself, startled at the image that appeared in his mind. This wasn't the rune he'd pictured. This was something... new. Different.

Unwelcome, at this particular moment.

But it worked.

Trees, even small animals. Born, growing to reach high into the sky, and then dying. Falling, lying on the soft ground. The rains come, and wood rots. What was once structured, is no more. Is instead a collapsing mass, rejoining the earth from which it came. Years go by, new growth above reaches high, dies, falls, and disintegrates. Over and over in the endless cycle, the infinite circle.

Pressure now, as more and more from above pushes down and down. More and more pressure, until nothing solid can remain, and all that is left is a liquid. The components of life, distilled into a slick elixir.

Finley gasped.

His mind still whirling, a new rune took shape in his mind.

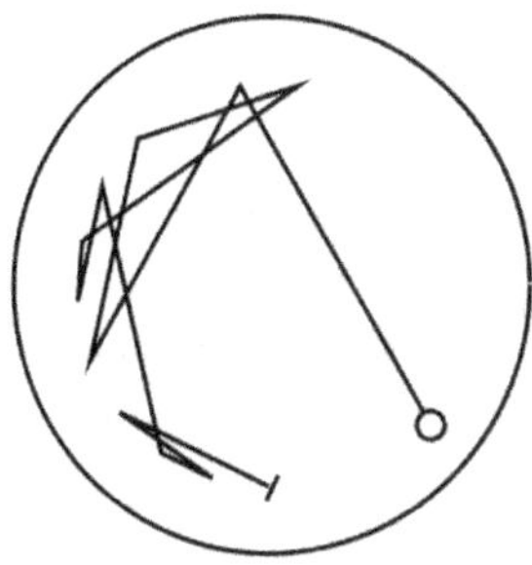

He gasped again at the grandeur of it, the compelling asymmetry, the *purpose.*

Inelegant, his talent muttered unhappily, before turning over and returning to its sleep.

It isn't... there's no shape to it. Except that there was. A shape that had less to do with intent, and less to do with outcome, and more to do with *action.* With what the magic must *do,* here in this moment.

Finley's mind spun and he fell to his knees.

Earth magic drained from Finley as the new rune empowered, energy driving deep into the earth, small tendrils spinning lazily around him as if examining the containers there.

This is change, he thought to himself in awe as he sensed his magic spiraling away. He quickly activated a rune for Gathering, drawing more magic into himself despite the hulking, glowering presence of iron nearby.

Finley's magic surged, thick tendrils of earth magic rushing down into the depths of the earth. He could feel the magic reaching, probing, seeking the hidden reservoirs of oil far below. They lay in layers, each representing an epoch from the past, each one pressed down by the present and future, crushed until nothing but this thick liquid remains. It was as if his consciousness expanded, merging with the very soil and stone, sensing the vast interconnected web of the earth itself.

The magic found what it sought, and Finley inhaled sharply as he felt the raw power of his spell take hold. It started as a tremor, deep in the earth's bones. A slow, inexorable shift, like the grinding of continents. The oil began to change, its structure unraveling and reforming under the guidance of Finley's magic.

He could see it in his mind's eye—countless tiny chains of matter breaking apart, the building blocks of the oil rearranging themselves into new configurations. The long, sinuous elements coiled and twisted, latching onto particles of rock and soil, imbuing them with their essence.

In the hidden chambers of the earth, the liquid oil thickened, grew dense, and became heavy. Its glossy black sheen dulled to a matte, earthen hue as it absorbed the minerals around it.

What was left was simple clay.

Finley passed out.

CHAPTER 4

The Mentor

It was afternoon at the Farm, and Finley had decided to abandon his usual office for a small table on the main building's wide front patio, under the shade of a broad overhang. *There are always more dispatches,* he thought tiredly as he perused a stack of them, *but there's no reason to huddle inside when it's so nice out.*

"Finley."

He looked up. "Ah, Ram. They said you wouldn't be back until tomorrow."

The older man shrugged and pulled an empty chair over to Finley's table. "My business in Evermore ended early, and I'd prefer to be here. It's more peaceful." He settled into the chair with a sigh. "I'm told your mission was a success."

Finley hesitated. He'd glossed over most of the details in his own dispatch, which he was sure Ram had already seen. "The basic mission, yes. It obviously raised even more concerns."

"Let's start with the basic mission."

"They were making some kind of long-burning substance. I

was able to neutralize all of it, and their current stock of supplies."

"But they'll be able to start over."

Finley nodded, and pushed his dispatches back into a neat pile. "We should assume so. We should probably assume they already have. It would be reasonable to assume they're doing this in multiple locations already, and that my work will have no practical impact on their efforts."

His mind drifted back to the little village. His blackout had fortunately lasted only a few minutes. He'd come to in the same dark building, slowly and carefully made his way out, and snuck to the edge of town. He'd taken great pains to ensure he was unobserved before using travel magic to whisk himself away. He'd avoided any towns or villages on his return to the Farm, fearful of being seen by agents of the human cabal.

"Which leads us to the bigger issue," Ram was saying.

"Yes," Finley nodded, dragging his thoughts back to the present.

"Walk me through it."

"There was a human woman. She recognized me. Called me 'the golden boy of the Order,' or something like that. Which means they know of me, and they know of us. She spoke specifically of us holding them back—although she hesitated a bit when it came to weaponry."

"So you exchanged words."

"I did." Finley hesitated a moment before continuing. "It seemed pointless not to. And now I know that they're not universally aligned on their principles. She *did* genuinely hesitate about the weapons. We've always tried to keep them from killing each other, after all."

"Go on."

"She didn't say much more of use. But the fact that this happened in a tiny settlement—one new-built in the last year or so, I would say, based on the condition of the buildings—without a church and without any of the things we normally use to cover ourselves... that's pretty telling. And that's on top of the two with the new bricks they've developed. They're clearly aware of us, and they're clearly taking steps to mitigate our interference."

Ram frowned. "Interference?"

"I mean, it is. It's to our benefit, but obviously they don't see it that way."

Ram nodded once, and the fingers of one hand began drumming out a slow beat on the tabletop. "You said you nullified their materials. Could this rune be replicated?"

I'm not even sure it was a rune as we understand them, Finley thought. Aloud, he merely said, "Of course."

"Then—"

"But *where?*"

Ram's brow furrowed. "What do you mean?"

"The area effect of that magic was maybe a hundred steps. You know Earth magic doesn't lend itself to wide-area effects. So where would we put the rune? This isn't one we can just carve into the walls of their churches—that's Sky magic, and only a limited set of things work that way even then. Do we start carving it into every building in the world? Someone's bound to notice, especially since this cabal is looking for us. And what about the buildings we don't even know about? The people in that... village, if you like... were suspicious. The population is so small that any stranger will stand out instantly, and be watched. I very much got the impression that the men working there were... if not criminals, then at least down on their luck. They've probably been *told* to watch for strangers."

"Odd," Ram mused, "that one woman knew you, yet the others did not."

Finley sighed heavily. "I'm not at all certain they didn't *all* know who I was. Or at least *what* I was."

"What do you mean?"

"Look, the first thing they offered me was a job working in the exact building they'd have known I was looking for."

"So a trap."

"One that they didn't spring, which begs the question why they didn't."

"Trapping you didn't work the last time," Ram pointed out.

"It damn well nearly did," Finley countered.

"So they *knew* you'd find a way to neutralize them."

"Yes, and what if *that's* what they wanted? To see what I would do? After all, if they've set up similar operations else-where—and there's no reason to think they haven't—they had little to risk and much to learn."

"Because the other operations will be unaffected," Ram agreed.

Well. Yes, although no, because I haven't told you that I somehow managed to use Earth magic to neutralize petroleum oil across the entire continent. And now our enemies will know that, too, and that has me worried that I went too far.

It had, in fact, kept Finley up every night since his return. *I did nothing to eliminate* knowledge *of oil, and in that time-frame I'm not sure I could have done anything along those lines anyway. So now there's a world full of people who know about oil, living in a world that doesn't actually contain any. Stupid.*

But it had been his Rune Smith talent, carried away with itself, eager to invent something new.

What if a change is neither a beginning nor an end? it whis-pered sleepily in the back of his mind.

"The point is that every member of the Order is in danger. The humans know us, they know about us, they know our faces, and they know our mission. Anything that this cabal is overseeing is going to be well-guarded, and I fear that they've grown better at deceit and trickery than we have." Finley's eyes were drawn to Ram's gently tapping fingers, thumping the table almost hypnotically.

"Then we must change our ways." *Thumpa-thump.*

"How so?"

"We have always been reactive." *Thumpy-thumpy-thump.*

"Yes, but—"

"Waiting for humans to innovate, then stopping them." *Thump-thump.* "Covering their tracks." *Thumpa-thumpa.*

"When we—"

"And so now they have caught us at our game." *Thump.* His fingers stopped moving and he stared at Finley. "And they move to counter us."

"You've said this isn't a game," Finley said quietly.

"I have. And it is not. It is survival. We were threatened, and we countered the threat. And now our enemy has countered *us*, and so we must counter *back*."

"Meaning...?"

"I am taking you off of active assignments," Ram announced.

Finley blinked several times. "Okay."

"We must find a new way. And so I am assigning you an apprentice."

"I thought the mission with Rey—"

Ram waved that away. "No. I had doubts about her from the outset. We should have put you to something simpler, something contrived. It was stupid to risk you with such a person. No, I have someone else in mind. Someone newly come to us, with a background different from our usual recruits."

Finley was intrigued despite himself. "Different how?"

"Where do our recruits traditionally come from?"

"Duocastella's and Disemstoke's. Well, with the odd exception, like—"

"Yes, yes, I made that exception for Rey just to get it over with," Ram said testily. "I have no other young relatives, so it will not happen again. And yes, from those two schools. But," he added, a sly grin spreading over his features, "are there not *three* Great Schools of witchkind?"

Finley sat back. "Thornwaithe's has never—"

But Ram was already nodding. "They have not, but we have found ourselves a unique opportunity, it seems. And a timely one, as we seek to adapt our tactics to the world in which we find ourselves."

"You're saying we have an apprentice from *Thornwaithe's?*"

"I am saying," Ram said, his smile growing wider, "that *you* do."

***

Finley made his way to Challa's office. The spry old woman had taken over from Cat, who had overseen much of Finley's apprenticeship.

She looked up as he entered and smiled. "Finley! I take it you've heard the good news?"

"That I'm to be a babysitter?" he joked. "Indeed, Ram just filled me in."

"Your 'baby' should be here momentarily—ah, right on time, Kelden!"

Finley turned as Kelden Stirrim stepped into the warmly lit room. They were taller than Finley had expected, their presence commanding even in silence. Short-cropped white hair framed a face that seemed carved from stone, with violet eyes that held a gravity Finley seldom saw in someone so young.

"Kelden, this is Finley Coughlan," Challa said, her sunny voice bridging the gap between them like a handshake. "Finley will be your guide and mentor during your time here."

"An honor," Kelden said, their voice methodical and concise. "I've heard much about your work with runes."

Finley nodded, feeling the elephant in the room swell. "And I, about your achievements at Thornwaithe's. Rare for one of their kind to join us."

"Unheard-of," Kelden agreed, "but alignments and affinities know no school loyalty. It's the application that matters."

"Indeed." Finley gestured towards the door. "Shall we? The farm's different in the afternoon. Easier to feel the magic in the soil."

"I'm more Sky-aligned than Earth, but certainly."

"I should point out," Challa said quickly as they turned to go, "that Kelvin's technically already cleared his initial assessments. We'd normally put them right on field work, but Ram had something a bit different in mind. I assume he's shared that?"

Finley nodded hesitantly, then more firmly. "I'm sure we'll be fine. Thank you, Challa. Always so good to see you."

"Don't be a stranger!"

Finley and Kelden stepped outside into the warm afternoon air, where distant rows of crops whispered secrets to the wind. "How long have you been here, then?" Finley asked.

"Here, just an evening. My evaluation was held elsewhere, and my escorted mission was in Harbsmouth."

Finley shuddered involuntarily at the name. "I know the place... well."

Kelden merely nodded politely, and Finley turned to change the topic, gesturing to the fields that lay beyond the

Farm's central clearing. "Here we cultivate more than just food," Finley explained. "Many of these plants have uses in more advanced magic, or take to magic particularly well. There are whisperwillows—they carry messages on the breeze. And there, the glowleaf. It absorbs moonlight, useful for night spells."

Kelden listened intently, their eyes scanning the landscape with a scholar's curiosity. "We didn't do much herb lore at Thornwaithe's obviously. But the interplay of Earth and Sky must be strong here. I can almost hear it hum."

"Exactly," Finley replied, impressed. *I wonder if that's a natural sensitivity, or something Thornwaithe's cultivated?* "We use the natural alignments to enhance growth and protect against pests. No fences needed when you have a hedge of firethorn—the secretions from the tips of its leaves keep the unwanted at bay."

"Resourceful," Kelden noted, stopping before a particularly robust plant. "And this?"

"Ah, that's heartroot. Heals the flesh, mends the spirit. Hard to grow but worth the effort. All but useless to anyone who hasn't specialized in healing, by the way. But worth the effort."

"Much like our talents," Kelden mused, a hint of a smile touching their lips.

"Indeed," Finley echoed, the word becoming their refrain. They continued the tour, steps falling into a comfortable rhythm, until afternoon cooled into evening.

"Thank you, Finley," Kelden said as they circled back to the farmhouse. "This place... it's unlike any other I've seen. I suspect there's much I can learn here." They raised an eyebrow. "Assuming we will be staying here?"

"We'll learn from each other, I reckon," Finley admitted, finding hope in the idea. "And... honestly, I doubt it. I don't know if Ram or anyone has filled you in on our current... priorities?" Kelden shook their head and Finley sighed. "Let's head back to the main building, they'll have dinner on soon. But... I suspect we'll be on the road a good bit. The humans... well. I don't know how much of this is common knowledge, but if we're going to be working together, you need to know."

As they walked, Finley filled Kelden in on the events of the past few weeks. The apprentice's eyes grew wider and wider as they went.

"If I may summarize," Kelden said politely when Finley had finished, "the humans know about us, can identify at least some of us on sight, and are actively mitigating our efforts. We can expect many new inventions from off-the-map settlements with no connection to the Order's usual tactics, such as the churches or general stores."

"That's pretty much it."

"And do you have a plan to deal with this... change?"

Change is good, came a whisper in Finley's mind. His talent, rolling over in its sleep.

"I have... look, really honestly, one of my strengths had been kind of figuring it out as I go."

"Ah." Kelden smiled. "Mine too."

Finley grinned. "Then let's begin by figuring out dinner."
***

The small dining hall was especially crowded, and so Finley and Kelden kept their conversation to small talk as they ate. When they finished, Kelden explained he was to check in with the Order's quartermaster to draw some supplies and clothing.

"Go take care of that," Finley agreed. "I think I'm going to go through some more dispatches, maybe get a feel for the big picture we're looking at. If I'm not on the covered porch of the main building, I'll be in one of the little offices. Come find me, and we'll pick up where we left off."

Kelden nodded politely and strolled off toward the large barn the Order used as a warehouse.

Finley settled back into the table where Ram had met him earlier. The evening, while cool, was still pleasant. The usual hordes of biting bugs, so common to this part of the continent, were held at bay by the plantings of thistlespark the Order's gardeners had cultivated. Even at a dozen paces away, Finley could feel the trickle of Earth magic feeding the plants, and could almost taste their gentle, yet persistent, discouragement of the insects.

"Tų dokumentų man reikia," he said softly, picturing the accompanying rune in his mind. A pile of dispatches appeared before him. Again, he found himself distracted by the process of it. Words and runes to guide the mind, the mind to shape the magic, the magic to effect change in the world. But why did the words have to be in the True Language? Haltingly, he translated the ancient phrase into the modern tongue: *Bring me the documents I need.* Astoundingly vague! And the rune was no better. But his mind had known what he wanted, and the magic had responded.

As a test, he pictured another stack of documents, but none appeared. So the words and rune acted more like... *a trigger,* he thought suddenly. *Otherwise, every little thing that flitted to my mind would set off the magic, no?*

But could the words be from a different language? He chuckled. *And what language would that be? Horse? Dragon?* The world *had* only one language, and it had, over centuries, evolved from the True Language. Even humans had never evolved their own distinct language, maturing alongside witchkind as they had.

But what about the rune? Everyone knew there were different ones to choose from. Old Runic, although it was a bit overwrought. Middle Runic. *Imprecise.* New Runic... *Which is fine, but it's so... structured.* Wasn't Middle Runic proof that you didn't need something so complex to guide the mind?

Another flick of magic summoned a quill to his hand, and he turned over one of the dispatches and began sketching. He let his hand work on its own, free of supervision from his conscious mind, and wasn't wholly surprised when a version of the oil-negating rune began to take shape. *Not really a rune,* he mused as he began paying attention, filling in the smaller details his memory provided. *Construct is a better word. Diagram, maybe.* A map to an outcome, a complex set of instructions that had turned one Earthen substance into another.

"What's this?"

Finley jumped and looked up to see Kelden looking over his shoulder. "Sorry, you startled me," he chuckled. "Not a very good role model for field work, am I?"

Kelden grinned. "You just seemed a bit engrossed." They looked closer. "Is that... it's not a rune construct?"

Finley turned back to his drawing. "It's not... traditional."

Kelden sank into an empty chair, their eyes still on the sketch. "It certainly isn't. But it does... it feels like magic, doesn't it?"

Finley looked up. "What do you mean?"

Kelden met his eyes. "It just does." Then they tilted their head. "What do you know about Thornwaithe's alum?"

Finley laughed. "You could fill a thimble with what people know, and an ocean with what they don't. It's a very mysterious school."

Kelden smiled, but their eyes remained serious. "It isn't exactly a secret but it's... very personal. We don't speak of it often. Still, as you say, if we're to be working together, then you should know."

They took a deep breath. "You get to Thornwaithe's because you're a... problem. Elsewhere. I spent two years at

Duocastella's. I never fit in. My magic was... strange. Not unstable, but it didn't respond like everyone expected. I used the same runes, the same words, but it was always a struggle." They sighed. "I got into fights. I don't even know why. People just felt... strange around me.

"My little sister, Tabeka, she... died. When we were really young. She'd always been weak, and it was a really bad winter. She got sick, and the healers couldn't do anything for her. She went fast." They looked away. "I got her power. Her affinity. It sets people off sometimes, it's—"

"It happened to me too," Finley said softly. Kelvin's eyes snapped back to his. "School was definitely tough. but I got lucky, I had good friends."

Kelden nodded slowly. "I appreciate that. Thank you. I think... I just didn't have friends."

"I'm sure you—"

"No, that's the point, though. Sorry. But that's the point. A few dozen kids a year, that's what happens. Their magic is strange. People feel strange around them. They don't make friends." They chuckled. "You know, one of my professors—and she was the nicest one I had—told me, 'It's like you know something about magic that nobody else does, and you're not telling them. It feels weird.'"

Finley spoke slowly. "But that's actually it, isn't it?"

"It is," Kelden confirmed. "Although you don't find that out until you're at Thornwaithe's. Do you know the school has no sports? No contests? Absolutely no organized competition whatsoever?"

"I... did not."

"Even between years. It sounds impossible at first, doesn't it? Kids are so competitive. But once you've been there for a few days... you don't even want to. Everyone helps you out. And nobody feels weird."

"There are legends..." Finley prompted.

"All true. Every word, most of them. Not even exaggerations." Finley raised his eyebrows. "No, I'm serious. If there's ever a big enough threat to witchkind, to magic itself... Thornwaithe's is called. Every alum. You know how much power true teleportation takes? What they used to call translocation magic, before the Age of the Adherents?"

"Impossible amounts," Finley agreed.

"Not if we're summoned. We... it's never happened to me, but the faculty and staff are all alum too, and they try to prepare us. It's like you're taken over. You're still in your body, but something else is with you, and it's telling you what to do. *Magic* itself. And it'll lash out at whatever's attacking it. Usually with brute force."

"Entire armies smashed to the ground."

"Well, mobs. But yes, that's actually happened. You can still find some of the depressions, if you know where to look."

"That's incredible."

"But that closeness to magic... it's with us all the time. It's why, when you leave Thornwaithe's, you tend to go into more solitary jobs. People still find us weird. Strange to be around. Even our families. Did you know that no family, ever, has sent two consecutive generations to Thornwaithe's?"

"Again, I did not."

"It's true. Whatever it is skips a generation at least. Usually a dozen or more."

"So... what brought you to the Order? Ram said we'd never had a Thornwaithe's alum."

Kelden shrugged. "They recruited me."

"Yes, but why *you?* Why now?"

"Oh, I think it's because I'm immune to iron."

. . .

***

Finley stood with Kelden at the edge of a clearing, the ground soft and yielding underfoot. The sun was still low in the morning sky, and they'd both slept well. "You sure you're okay with a little practice?" Finley asked.

"Of course. And it's beautiful out, so why not?"

"Perfect. But the thing is, I'm not sure if this is going to make any sense to you or not, but I'd like to try. At least show you what the rest of us have to do. The first step in protecting against iron is to sense its presence," he said, his voice steady as he retrieved a small, dull iron nail from his pocket.

"Right," Kelden replied, their eyes narrowing in focus. "Feel it draw the magic in, like a sinkhole for power. Except mine doesn't get drawn in."

"Exactly. Well, except for that last bit. But can you at least sense it?" Finley held the nail out before him, letting his inner reserve of magic rise to the surface. The air around them hummed with potential as he channeled Earth's resilience and Flame's defiance into a shield around the iron spike. "Now you try."

Kelden extended their hand. "I can try and *send* it to the spike."

Finley's wide-open senses, and a curious second set of mental eyes that he attributed to his talent, watched carefully. Magic *was* flowing. "And you don't feel that a bit?"

"I mean, I can feel my magic leaving. I'm telling it to."

"But if you just stop?"

They did so, and Finley sensed the *snap* as Kelden's magic snapped back, exactly as magic would do with any of witchkind who'd simply stopped using it.

"That's incredible. And you've always been able to do that?"

"I never *started* doing it. It wasn't until we were doing drills at school that anyone realized I *was* doing it."

"You drilled with iron?"

Kelden nodded. "Pretty standard. If you can amass enough magic, you can get by. Iron can only absorb so much."

"We have a technique for blocking it."

Kelden laughed. "I was told. And you developed it. But it bottles you up, right? You can't *use* your magic, it just helps you hold it in?"

"True. Yours is better."

"I wish I could tell you how it's done."

"Hold that thought. You might do just that, before it's all over."

"Deal."

"Okay, while we're here, let's practice rapid Gathering," Finley transitioned, feeling the weight of responsibility settle on his shoulders. He demonstrated, drawing energy quickly from the surroundings—pulling from the earth beneath their feet and the air around them. He exhaled slowly as his body filled with magic. "This comes up more than you'd believe in the field."

"And not something we practiced at school," Kelden said. "The assumption is that if we're ever summoned, we'll have basically all the magic we can handle."

"Try to get it aligned to breathing. That's how most people Gather anyway, right? Throughout the day, with each breath, even at night."

"Sure."

"So just make it deeper." Again, Finley inhaled deeply, focusing on pulling in magic along with air. Already full, he couldn't pull in much more, so he exhaled more quickly. "Your turn," he prompted, watching Kelden mimic the motion.

Kelden's face relaxed as they inhaled, and a telltale breeze of Sky magic played through their short-cropped hair. They exhaled, and Finley could dimly sense the magic gathering in their chest.

"Nice work," Finley praised, genuinely impressed. "You wouldn't know you'd never done that before."

"It's just like breathing, as you say."

"Now, for travel magic. We don't need to do everything, but I do need to know which ones you're comfortable with."

Kelden grimaced. "Honestly my weakest subject at school. I can do *Nuvesti mane ten* and *Dešimties lygos žingsnis.* I can manage *Grupinė procesija,* but not with more than four or five others. Almost anything else will fizzle."

Finley considered. "What about *Išeik iš miesto?*"

"Not with any confidence."

"That's one you should practice, I think. We use it a lot."

Kelden looked confused. "It's short-distance, though."

"The idea is to get away from where you are right then, stop, and reassess. Less about escaping, more about giving yourself room to think."

"Hmm. I'll work on it."

Finley hesitated. "While we're out here... actually, wait." He summoned a rune to mind. *"Tylos kūgis,"* he intoned softly.

The clearing, which moments before had been alive with the chatter of birds and the rustle of small creatures in the underbrush, fell into an eerie hush as Finley's magic took hold. It was as if a heavy blanket had been draped over the glade, muffling the usual symphony of the forest. The breeze still stirred the leaves overhead, but the sound of their whispering was distant, as if heard from the bottom of a deep well.

Even the colors seemed more muted, the vibrant greens and

browns of the foliage fading to more somber shades within the spell's influence. Shafts of sunlight still lanced down through gaps in the dense canopy, but they had a filtered quality, as if passing through gauze on their way to dapple the forest floor.

Finley could feel the weight of the magic settling around them, a palpable pressure that seemed to press against his ears. It wasn't uncomfortable, but it was impossible to ignore—a constant reminder of the power he had brought to bear. The air within the clearing felt thicker somehow, laden with the potential of their words, which would now fall only upon each other's ears.

"I've never experienced this," Kelden murmured. Their words felt thicker, softer, almost deadened.

"This isn't common knowledge," Finley said, "and both I and the Order have reason to keep it that way. But, as we've said, we'll be working together. Do you know what a runewright is?"

"One of you," Kelden grinned. "But yes. You can recombine existing rune elements to make entirely new constructs."

"And what about a Rune Smith?"

Kelden's grin faded. "There arc legends."

"We're pretty rare." Kelden's eyes widened, and Finley smiled back. "And yes, I am one." His own smile faded. "It means I can create entirely new... well, at least runes. New constructs, entirely from scratch. I'm starting to think it means more. New magic."

"Your sketch, from last night...?"

Finley nodded confirmation. "That was a construct I... imagined. On the spot. It's difficult to—actually, for you, it probably isn't. You've said magic kind of talks to you, right?"

"Not *talk* exactly, but... there's an awareness."

Finley's expression changed as he spoke, his focus shifting to some distant memory. "My Rune Smith talent... I think of it as a separate being. It speaks to me. In actual words sometimes. And that night, it had a lot to say." He recounted the events of the mission to Kelden, his voice filled with a mix of awe and disbelief. "And that rune—construct, diagram, whatever it is— was what did it all."

Kelden's doubt was evident in his tone. "It turned all the oil in the world into clay?"

"Yes, unbelievable as it may sound. But I assure you, it did. At least, from what I can gather. There used to be a rune for locating oil deposits—they tend to gather just below the surface —but since that night, I haven't been able to make it work. The magic seems to have disappeared from the rune, as if it no longer serves its purpose. I know what it looks like, but it just won't take power anymore." Finley shook his head, still trying to make sense of it all.

"That is... if I may say so, frightening."

"You're telling me."

"I begin to imagine why you might not want a great many people to know this about you."

"Yeah even..." Finley paused, thinking back to the recent conversations he'd had with Ram. "Kelden, can I be really honest with you?"

Kelden's expression grew somber. "Of course."

Finley took a deep breath, held it for a moment, and then exhaled heavily. "Ram—the Head of the Order, I don't know if you've—"

"Briefly."

"Okay. So... he's been at this a long time. And what the Order does is necessary. That Everburn wouldn't have affected witchkind, but the humans would have used it to wage battles against each other. Wars, maybe. We haven't had a significant battle between towns in *centuries,* because the Order stops humans from creating any kind of weapon that would be useful in battles. They're left to bash at each other with swords."

"Agreed."

"And the argument for stopping other inventions... I get it. If humans ever discover us, if the Veil ever falls, we can say, 'look, your whole society will collapse without magic, so let's just work together.'"

"It's a theory."

Finley cocked his head to one side. "You disagree?"

Kelden shrugged. "The Veil *did* fall, one time. Or nearly did."

"You're talking about the Last Adherent."

"Yes. A Thornwaithe's alum was there. Involved. Many were, actually—magic was threatened. We have *detailed* archives at the school."

"I... would love to read those sometime."

"They won't let you."

"Okay. But you still don't think it'll work?"

Kelden sighed and looked away. "Everything in them says that the humans called for Hunts. That they tried to burn people. They relied upon magic as much then as now, and there was never any *time* to make that conversation. Even the Adherent of the Sixth Axis couldn't stop them. He barely slowed them down. I think, if it happens, that humans will come for us regardless."

"Yeah, but back then they never went to the lengths of withdrawing magic. They didn't have house collapsing, boats sinking, that kind of thing."

"True, but could we do so much so quickly? We eat fish, too. We live in the same buildings, in our hidden spaces."

Finley hesitated, then nodded. "True. But you're almost making my point for me."

Kelden turned back to him with a confused expression. "I am?"

"Ram's going... further. He's asked me to create a rune that will... I don't know, exactly. Make humans calmer. More domesticated."

"Like what, livestock?"

Finley nodded sadly. "He doesn't know what I did to the oil."

Kelden's eyes widened. "Ah. And if he does, he will know you can do large-area magic."

"Yeah."

"Possibly the entire world."

"Yeah."

"Yet you continue, because the Order's ordinary work is still worthwhile."

"I believe so, yes."

Kelden smiled. "Then, for the time we are together, I will have your back, and keep your secret." Their smile widened. "You will find that Thornwaith's alum are *very* good at keeping secrets."

"Well, there's one more for you." Kelden raised an eyebrow. "There's a group of humans, probably small, who know we exist."

Both of Kelden's eyebrows climbed to their hairline as they paled. "You're joking."

"I wouldn't joke about that."

"How? Who?"

"I call them 'the cabal.' I met one of them, once. Shortly after my own apprenticeship. They've been... quiet, since then. But we know they work against us."

Kelden's alarm grew. "Work against us how?"

"Preserving knowledge we'd suppress. They've set traps for

witchkind, although not recently. Not that we can tell. I suspect they watch us."

"Ram knows?"

"He does."

"And... we do nothing?"

Finley shrugged. "They stay hidden. They're small enough —they know we could eliminate them, if we could find them. I think they test us. See what we'll notice, see what they can keep hidden from us. See what we'll respond to. See what we'll take action against, what we'll leave alone."

"Finley, if they threaten magic itself..."

"I know. It's frustrating. Intellectually, I can understand their motives. We hold them back. But if *more* of them knew of us, if the Hunts began, if Evermore was exposed..."

"This is bad."

"It is."

"So what do we do?"

Finley sighed and looked away. "We keep an eye out. We deal with their agents as we can. We remain alert. We try to learn more about them, if we can. We can't move openly any more than they can. Less so, even."

Kelden nodded slowly, their eyes still wide with alarm. "This adds some... urgency to our work."

Finley responded with a dark, humorless laugh. "You think?"

CHAPTER 5

Blue Bread Mold

The sapphire expanse of Lake Serein lapped gently at the hull of their modest vessel, a speck upon its vast, mirror-like surface. Kelden set their gaze upon the distant shore where the quaint village of Little Bay nestled. Beside them, Finley stood with his hands clasped behind his back, his dark eyes reflecting the water's serenity.

"We couldn't go by land?" Kelden grumbled. "I've never been a fan of boats."

"Other than the Fisherwitches," Finley smiled, "few are. I myself have been seasick the entire day."

It took Kelden only a moment. "This is meant as a disguise, then."

Finley nodded. "In truth, the voyage by land from Harbsmouth isn't that bad. You have to be in a hurry, or fairly poor, or both, to go by boat."

"The smell alone…"

The pungent aroma of the day's catch permeated the air, an inescapable reminder of their maritime disguise. Baskets of silvery fish, scales glistening in the midday sun, were stacked haphazardly across the deck. The sharp tang of brine mingled with the earthy scent of wet wood, creating a unique bouquet that seemed to cling to every surface.

Beneath their feet, the weathered planks creaked and groaned with each gentle swell, a symphony of the sea accompanied by the rhythmic slap of waves against the hull. Overhead, seagulls wheeled and cried, their raucous calls carrying across the tranquil waters of Lake Serein.

Kelden wrinkled their nose, unaccustomed to the assault on their senses. "How do the Fisherwitches stand it?" they asked.

Finley chuckled, his eyes crinkling at the corners. "Years of practice, I suppose. And a genuine love for their craft. To them, this," he gestured to the aromatic chaos surrounding them, "is home. I grew up in a fishing village, you know."

"So you're used to it."

"You would think. The motion still upsets me."

Kelden lowered their voice. "A rune?"

Finley nodded. "I can show it to you sometime. It's called *jokio vémimo.* It was quite the scandal in my family when my mother had to show it to me, but she's never been comfortable on the water, either."

"Making a fishing village an odd choice."

"Oh, there's always plenty of land work. Sorting fish, packing fish, shipping fish. Repairing the docks—my parents were specialists in sea walls, actually. Not much call for the meeting of Earth and Sea anywhere else."

As they spoke, the bustling activity of the fishing vessel continued around them, a microcosm of life and labor upon the peaceful lake. Weathered fishermen, their skin tanned and hands calloused from years of toil, moved about the deck with practiced efficiency. They carried baskets and crates laden with silvery fish, their muscles straining against the weight. The air was filled with the grunts and shouts of the ship's crew as they worked in unison, a well-oiled machine born of necessity and camaraderie.

Nearby, a grizzled sailor with a salt-and-pepper beard expertly mended a torn net, his nimble fingers weaving the frayed strands back together with the skill of a master craftsman. He hummed a sea shanty under his breath, the melody lost amidst the cacophony of the boat's daily operations.

A young deckhand, no more than sixteen, scurried past Finley and Kelden, his arms laden with coils of rope. His face was flushed with exertion, but his eyes sparkled with the excitement of youth, eager to prove himself among the seasoned crew.

"According to the missive, it's here in Little Bay," Finley said, breaking the silence that had settled between them like a soft shroud. "A healer whose prowess borders on the miraculous." His voice was thick with sarcasm.

"Or so they claim," Kelden smirked, their voice a study in measured skepticism. "Many have claimed miracles before, only for us to find clever tricks or fortunate coincidences. Rarely true innovation, from what I've read."

Finley hummed thoughtfully, watching as the shore drew closer. A pragmatic edge sharpened his demeanor; his mind revolving around the gravitational pull of logic and possibility. His Rune Smith talent whispered at the fringes of his consciousness, the promise of an undiscovered *something* like a melody only he could hear. "Probably," he mused aloud, "but if there's truth to it, we must understand how."

"And stop it?"

"That depends."

"Oh?"

"Mmm. Some years ago, before I was with the Order, there was a similar investigation. Some healer had, it was said, gained the ability to reduce aching heads. Initially, I gather it was the town drunks who took him up on his miracle cure, but before long everyone was swearing by it."

"Surely you're not referring to willow bark," Kelden chuckled.

"Oh, don't laugh. That's exactly it."

The apprentices's eyes widened. "Truly?"

"No magic to it at all. Just a fortunate coincidence. The tale is, the healer had been making teas out of all manner of things. Most made people sick as could be, but that one was a miracle cure. We could be sailing into another such circumstance."

Kelden nodded slowly. "Makes sense. And what would the alternative be?"

"You mean something that we'd have to stop?" Finley asked quietly. "I'm not sure. We typically stay out of healer affairs. They have little downside. I think, at present, there's more a... heightened sense of alertness. But there have been a couple of instances, I suppose."

"Oh?"

"Mmm. I'm thinking of one... this would have been a century ago. Actually, two, if I'm remembering correctly. You know how... humans"—and he pronounced this word more quietly, glancing quickly at the fishermen and sailors around them—"sometimes suffer an injury so bad, a limb must be removed entirely?"

Kelden grimaced and nodded.

"Normally, they dose the patient with ample alcoholic beverage before doing so. *Likeris* is popular, as it's cheap. *Viskis*, for those who can afford it. *Degtinė* is popular in the east."

"You know an awful lot about this."

"I read a lot. And have had some unpleasant missions. Anyway, this human healer, a chirurgeon, discovered a means of making someone pass out so completely they wouldn't feel a thing until they woke up."

"Is this *Eteris?*"

"In the True Language, yes, although at the time the... *they* called it letheon. In any event, the Order judged it to be too dangerous."

"I'd think the patients would have suggested differently," Kelden said wryly.

"No doubt. But the Order substituted opijus instead."

"Not exactly safe stuff."

"No, but incapable of being delivered as a gas. That was the concern, you see. Weaponizing it. That's very much the point—the fear that what started as a very beneficial tool to help those in need would be repurposed to gas an entire neighborhood. And you know how witchkind react to *Eteris.*"

"No. Badly?"

Finley snorted. "To say the least. You start hallucinating runes, and they just... activate. Pretty obvious stuff, not easy to hide. Enough to thin the Veil."

"I had no idea."

"Read some of the legends about the oldest Hunts. It was one way the humans who were railing against witchkind would drum up fear of us."

"Well," Kelden said softly, "let's hope that's not what we're walking into." They paused and lowered their voice further. "Is it actually *possible* they've found some magical substance?"

Finley hesitated, then nodded. "Nothing naturally occurring, obviously. No such thing. But there are Earth magics that... linger. Our own healers gather moss from the edges of fields that have been empowered for health."

"So they could have found something like that."

Finley's jaw tightened. "And that, we would have to do something about."

"Like?"

"Let's hope it doesn't come to that."

"So just keep an open mind."

"Indeed," Finley responded more loudly, standing up straighter, his violet eyes scanning the approaching docks. "But let's not get ahead of ourselves. First, we must find this healer."

"Any concern," Kelden asked in a whisper, "about a trap?"

Finley shook his head slowly. "No. I mean, always, yes, but this isn't the pattern we've seen. Little Bay is a good-sized village, with multiple general stores and at least two churches. A *normal* village. We may be seen, but this doesn't feel like how I'd expect a trap to go."

The two men remained silent for the short duration of the voyage, watching over the boat's rails as Little Bay's harbor slid closer and closer.

The boat touched land with a gentle thud, and they disembarked onto the wooden planks of the dock. They advanced towards the heart of Little Bay, the small village alive with the sounds of daily hustle. The fragrance of fresh fish and baked bread wafted through the air, mingling with the gentle scent of lake water.

"Shall we split up, or would you prefer to stick together?" Kelden asked.

"Stick together," Finley decided. "Two sets of ears are better than one. And if this 'magical' substance is real, I want to be there when we find it."

"Very well," Kelden conceded, their solid build moving with effortless grace as they made their way through the throng of villagers. He turned to the first villager who walked close by them, a slightly built woman carrying a basket of linens. "Excuse me. We've heard tell of a..."

"My pardon," Finley said smoothly, cutting off his apprentice. "I believe I know the way."

The woman shrugged and continued on her way.

"What was that for?" Kelden asked.

"A bit of discretion. This *could* be a trap. We want to be seen as normal travelers. Neither of us has any obvious injury; why would we be seeking some miracle healer?"

Kelden's eyes lowered. "Sorry."

"No harm done. Come, I'll show you how I usually do this."

They walked casually away from the docks and into the heart of the town. "It's rare for healers to be located so close to the docks," Finley murmured as they walked. "The spaces are too valuable. What isn't taken by storehouses and fishmongers will be for taverns and inns and the like. Same with the edges of the village where the trade road intersects. Where that road winds through you'll find more inns, more taverns, and the more prosperous merchants. Moneylenders, as well."

"So where do we head?"

"Usually off that main road, usually a bit away from the docks. Not too rich, not too poor. Often close to a church. There'll be a sign, shaped like a serpent coiled around a staff. All healers post one. And in the meantime," he added, giving Kelden a significant look, "keep an eye out. See if anyone appears to be paying more than a little attention to us."

Kelden's eyes widened slightly, and they nodded.

The village wasn't large, and it spread itself out along the lakeside, hugging the trade road. It wasn't long before the two men rounded a corner and spotted the tall steeple of a church.

"There," Kelden said, nodding to it.

"Let's stop for a bite," Finley said abruptly, turning sharply into a small tavern. Kelden scrambled to keep up.

The interior of the tavern was a study in rustic simplicity, its rough-hewn walls and sturdy wooden furniture bearing the marks of countless patrons who had sought respite within its confines. The air was heavy with the aroma of a hearty fish stew, its savory scent mingling with the earthy notes of freshly-baked bread and the sharp tang of small beer.

Finley and Kelden settled themselves at a table near the entrance, their eyes adjusting to the dim light that filtered through the single window that faced the street. The tavern keeper, a stout man with a ruddy complexion and a shock of graying hair, bustled over to take their order, his weathered hands wiping down the table with a well-worn cloth.

"The stew," Finley said. "And two small ales."

The man nodded and bustled off.

Kelden raised an eyebrow and Finley grinned. Likely the younger man's stomach was still rolling with them motion of the boat that had carried them here. "As the locals," he said softly, his grin widening as Kelden rolled their eyes and nodded assent.

The villagers went about their daily business, their faces etched with the lines of hard work and the weight of life's burdens. A group of children darted past the tavern, their laughter and shouts a bright counterpoint to the somber atmosphere within.

Their order arrived and they ate in silence, taking turns to glance out the door at the street. As they spooned up the last of the excellent stew, Kelden raised an eyebrow.

Finley nodded. "Looks fine." He left a few human coins on the table as they rose and stepped back onto the street.

As they blinked in the bright midday light, the human church loomed before them, its simple yet imposing structure a stark contrast to the bustling village life surrounding it. The white-washed walls gleamed in the midday sun, the light reflecting off the tall, narrow windows that punctuated the facade. The steeple rose from the center of the roof, a slender spire reaching towards the heavens, a weathered copper icon glinting at the apex.

The roads on either side of the church were well-trodden, the packed earth bearing the imprints of countless feet and hooves. Villagers hurried past, their arms laden with baskets of produce and freshly-caught fish, their faces lined with the cares of daily life. The air was filled with the mingled scents of baking bread, smoked meats, and the ever-present tang of the lake, a heady bouquet that spoke of the simple yet fulfilling existence of Little Bay's inhabitants.

Finley's sharp eyes scanned the surroundings, his gaze alighting on a weathered wooden sign that hung from a wrought-iron bracket beside a modest, two-story building adjacent to the church. "There."

Kelden looked and nodded as they spotted it: a carved wooden sign depicting a serpent coiled around a staff. Then he frowned. "You didn't mention a knife." A simple depiction of a blade had been carved at the top of the sign, lying horizontally across the top of the staff.

"Chirurgeon," Finley said. "The ones who heal people by cutting into them. That's actually a strong candidate for us."

"Wouldn't there be more than one?"

"In a village this small? Doubtful. There'll be other healers, ones who deal mainly in herbs and poultices. There wouldn't be enough work for two chirurgeons, I wouldn't think."

"Do we go in?"

"Let's walk."

They joined the busy stream of humans and walked past the healer's, not sparing it even a glance as they did. Kelden seemed confused, but then their eyes started darting back and forth and Finley knew they'd realized the tactic. He led them down the street, turned up another, and down yet another, until they were passing the church on its opposite side. They cut in front of it to return to the healer's.

"Now we go in," Finley said quietly. "With discretion.

Ready?" Finley felt familiar warmth within him as he unconsciously reached for his reserves of Earth and Flame magic.

"Always," Kelden replied, and together they stepped into the shop.

The wooden door swung quietly shut behind them. Fortunately, the healer's shop appeared unoccupied, save for a young girl minding a small desk just inside the door. "May I help you?" she chirped, giving them both a bright smile.

"We were told to seek out Master Johan," Finley said hesitantly.

"For an injury or a sickness?" the girl asked.

"An injury," Kelden said, holding out his arm.

Finley's eyes widened and he almost gasped as he caught sight of the angry, inflamed gash that marred Kelden's forearm. The wound was several inches long, its edges ragged and puckered, as if torn by some vicious creature. The skin surrounding the laceration was an alarming shade of red, contrasting starkly with Kelden's medium-brown complexion. Tendrils of infection snaked outward from the wound, tracing ominous paths beneath the surface of the skin.

Though the injury appeared to be a few days old, it showed no signs of proper healing. Instead, a thin, sickly discharge seeped from the depths of the cut, glistening in the muted light of the healer's shop. The pungent odor of infection hung in the air, mingling with the earthy scent of dried herbs that lined the shelves.

Finley suppressed a smile as he studied the wound more closely, and a telltale itching sensation began to prickle behind his eyes—a subtle yet unmistakable indication that the injury was not entirely as it seemed. *Fast reaction,* he thought approvingly. *And his Sky magic would create a better illusion—obviously—than my own.*

"Goodness," the girl said, peering over the desk. She didn't sound alarmed or look the least bit discomfited. "This looks to be a few days old."

"Seemed to be healing fine," Kelden said with a shrug. "Kept it clean and covered."

"Infection can be difficult to prevent, especially in something so deep," she mused. "Let me get Father. Why don't you step into the back? He can see you there."

Finley and Kelden followed the girl through the doorway into the back room, their footsteps echoing softly against the aged wooden floorboards.

The room was spacious, its walls lined with shelves that reached towards the ceiling. Upon these shelves rested an array of jars and bottles, each containing herbs, tinctures, and salves in various hues. Labels, meticulously handwritten in a neat script, adorned each container, hinting at the potent remedies within. The air was heavy with the mingled scents of medicinal plants—the sharp tang of peppermint, the earthy aroma of valerian root, and the sweet fragrance of lavender.

In the center of the room stood a sturdy wooden table, its surface worn smooth by countless years of use. Atop the table lay an assortment of surgical instruments, their polished metal gleaming in the soft light that filtered through the room's small windows. Scalpels, forceps, and needles were arranged with meticulous precision, a testament to the chirurgeon's skill and attention to detail.

Adjacent to the table, a small brazier smoldered, its glowing embers casting a warm, flickering light across the room. From the brazier's depths, tendrils of fragrant smoke curled upwards, carrying with it the subtle scent of burning herbs—a blend designed to purify the air and soothe the senses.

As Finley and Kelden took in their surroundings, the door at the far end of the room opened, and a man stepped through. He was of an age that was difficult to determine, his features both youthful and wise, as if he had witnessed the passing of many seasons yet retained the vigor of a man in his prime. His hair, a rich chestnut hue, was neatly combed and pulled back, revealing a high forehead and a pair of piercing blue eyes that seemed to hold a depth of knowledge and understanding.

The man's attire was simple yet elegant, consisting of a well-tailored tunic in a deep shade of green, paired with trousers of a darker hue.

"I am Master Johan," he introduced himself with a gentle smile. "Who's got this gash that sent my daughter running?"

"She didn't look the slightest bit alarmed," Kelden chuckled, holding out his arm. "I'm Kelden."

Master Johan took Kelden's arm in one hand and studied it closely. "Animal?"

"Hunting accident. My own fault."

"Those claws contain more maladies than you can imagine. Almost impossible to clean out, truth be told. Infection set in a couple of days ago?"

"The redness and swelling?" Kelden asked. "Yeah. Seemed fine until then. Hurts the blazes now, I don't mind telling you."

"Well, I've just the thing." The healer turned to a shelf behind him, pulling down a glass jar filled with a blue-green powder. "I'll need to pack this into the wound. I'll be honest with you—it'll hurt a bit. And I'll give you some to take with you. You'll need to wash it out with clear water every day, and re-pack it. That'll need to go on for around seven days at least— no less, even if the infection seems to clear. Is that acceptable?"

Finley and Kelden exchanged glances. The visually compelling wound wouldn't hold up to much manual inspection, especially not packing it with a blue-green powder. Finley gave Kelden a slight nod and started pulling together an Earth magic construct that would lend some tactile veracity to the "wound."

"What is that stuff?" Kelden asked uncertainly, playing for time.

Master Johan chuckled. "Bread mold."

"I'm sorry," Kelden said after a moment. "Did you say 'bread mold?'"

"My daughter says I'm foolish for not keeping it a secret, but I don't believe in secrets when it comes to healing. Yes, bread mold. From clean wheat bread, in fact. Grows in a few days if you leave it in the open, with a bit of indirect light and a comfortable temperature. Scrape it off, grind it up, and you've got this powder. It'll grow back on the same piece of bread in a couple more days, and you just repeat." He shrugged. "There's doubtless some bread in here as well, but it won't do any more harm than you've already experienced."

"Bread mold," Kelden repeated, genuinely amazed.

"Bread mold," Master Johan nodded with a grin. "Seems to kill whatever causes the infection. I can't explain it, but it's worked for over a month now."

"Well, might as well get on with it," Finley suggested. He'd had a moment to do some gentle sculpting of Kelden's forearm skin, so that it would feel a bit more like the open wound it appeared to be.

Master Johan got to work, moving quickly and skillfully as he packed a small amount of powder into the wound. Kelden winced and grunted appropriately at the "discomfort," and then stepped back and inspected the result. "That's it?" he asked dubiously.

"That's it." The healer turned back to his shelves, replacing the glass container and turning back with seven small paper packets. "And this is for the next seven days. Remember: clean the wound as thoroughly as possible, preferably before bed. Use clean water—boiled for quite some time, if you can, although absolutely let it cool before using it. Clean your hands as well as you can, and then pack in a full packet of powder. Cover the wound—a wrap of linen will do well. And *keep* it clean, understand? All day. If it's dirtied, wash it again, repack it, and use a clean wrap. You can come back for more powder, if you need."

"Or leave some bread to go moldy," Finley joked.

Master Johan shrugged. "If you like. That's two pieces for everything."

Finley frowned. "Only two?"

"You've been in here for a short period of time and I've given you bread mold," the old man smiled. "Only two."

They paid three, insisting the extra piece was for his honesty and ingenuity, and made their way back into the must market square.

"So do we let this one go?" Kelden asked, wiping the powder off his uninjured arm.

"Absolutely. In fact, I'm going to put it out that Master Johan's invention is something we should be spreading around. No reason everyone can't benefit for this knowledge, especially as he's been so free with it."

"So what next?"

"A meal, I think," Finley said after a moment's thought. "We can touch base with some of our kitchenware dealers here, and keep our ears to the ground for any... opportunities." *Rumors of inventions and off-the-map villages,* was the unspoken translation.

"Anything," Kelden said firmly, "but more fish. That stew was fine, but I find myself quite uninterested in more of the stuff. And I'd like to insist on a land journey home."

"Agreed," Finley laughed.

CHAPTER 6

Any Pier in a Storm

Finley stood by the small hearth in the little room he'd adopted as an office, while Kelden leaned uneasily against the adjacent wall. A crackling fire cast flickering shadows on his dark skin. His green eyes, usually bright with purpose, now reflected frustration and wariness.

"I dislike giving the humans any advantage," Ram growled as he sunk into the chair behind Finley's desk.

Dmitry bustled over, setting a steaming mug of *kava* in front of Ram.

"It's hardly an advantage," Finley said mildly, holding his frustration in check. "It's not like we've ever used magic to heal humans."

"Maybe we should," Ram grumbled, staring at the fireplace and ignoring the mug.

"You know it wouldn't work. We can't use magic on them directly."

The Order's Head simply grunted.

Finley and Kelden waited.

"Perhaps—" Dmitry started.

"Agreed, then," Ram interrupted, his voice gruff as he conceded. "There was no other choice—no action to be taken."

Finley nodded slowly, his thoughts already shifting. The debriefing had been terse, the mission closed with a sense of unease that clung like morning fog over the fields.

Ram's eyes snapped to Finley's. "You will not be not idle for long. A new assignment has arrived."

"We can be ready to leave in the morning, I think," Finley agreed as, from the corner of his eye, he saw Kelden stiffen. Sending them back out so quickly, even after such an uneventful mission, was unusual, if not exactly against protocol.

Dmitry watched them both carefully, but said nothing.

"The humans' ingenuity has again led them astray," Ram began, his eyes flashing. "A fishing pier, built by their hands, is our target."

Finley frowned. "Why does it concern us?"

"Because it was damaged in a storm, and they've used recycled iron as reinforcement as they rebuilt," Ram replied sharply.

"Wouldn't the Fisherwitches—" Kelden began.

"None left," Dmitry said softly. "Haven't been witchkind in this little place for years."

"The runes on the pier would have faded, then," Finley said slowly. "Is that how it was damaged?"

"Probably."

"And so we're to fix it?" Kelden asked uncertainly.

"Destroy it entirely," Ram said, his voice growing even harder. "We've put the word out to see if a Fisherwitch family is interested in moving, but until then... no magic, no piers. No docks. Let them wonder why their structures fail and fall."

"But destroy it?" Kelden's brow furrowed. "Why not just remove the iron? Seems a waste of a perfectly good—"

"Because," Dmitry interjected, his voice steady, "we

cannot reveal ourselves. And we want it to appear as if the strapping failed naturally. Reduce their confidence in the metal."

"Exactly," Ram agreed.

"Where's the village?" Finley asked.

Ram snorted. "Less than a village. There'll be a map in your kit."

Finley's breath caught in his chest. "How much less than a village?"

Ram nodded slowly and rose from the chair. "No church. An older settlement than we've seen before, but..."

"Be careful," Finley finished.

"Very."

"We'll leave at first light."

Dmitry's eyes tracked them as they left the office.

***

"Look at it, Kelden," Finley said, his voice barely audible over the crash of waves against the damaged pier. The structure stretched along the shoreline before them, a testament to human ingenuity and ignorance—a once-sturdy platform now crippled by their unwitting use of iron. "See there? The runes themselves are damaged. Half are missing. They must have faded completely. Without a Fisherwitch's care, the rest are as good as dust. And now with the iron..."

Rough iron bars had been attached to the pier's remaining structure, attached by iron nails thicker than Finley's thumb. It was an inexpert job, and even with the heavy sturdy iron, the pier creaked ominously.

"Looks like parts from the iron roadway," Kelden noted.

"Old parts," Finley agreed. "And heavily rusted. The sea water will make short work of them."

"How short?"

Finley considered. "A few months, perhaps, before those spikes begin to give way."

"Can we just let that happen?"

Finley sighed and shook his head. "Ram's in a mood. He's sent us here to make it happen *much* faster."

Kelden nodded, their violet eyes scanning the horizon where dark clouds began to gather. "Storm's brewing. Give it a few days, and this pier will be nothing but memories and driftwood."

"A few days..." Finley murmured.

"Help you?" a wizened voice asked from behind them.

Finley and Kelden turned to see a hunched old man squinting at them, his weathered face etched with deep lines. His clothes, showing signs of numerous repairs, hung loosely on his frail frame, and his gnarled hands gripped a twisted wooden cane.

"Ah, no, we're just passing through," Finley replied smoothly, forcing a pleasant smile. "Admiring your pier here. Looks like it's seen better days though, hasn't it?"

The old man hobbled closer, his rheumy eyes studying the battered structure. "Aye, that she has. Was a mighty storm that did her in, it was. Waves higher than the rooftops, crashing and smashing all night long. Thought the whole village might get swept away."

He paused, his gaze distant as if reliving the harrowing memory. "But she held, at least some of her. Enough for the young lads to patch her up best they could. Used bits of that fancy metal roadway they're rebuilding inland. Strong stuff, that is. Figured it might keep her standing a while longer."

The old man shook his head slowly. "But between you and

me," his voice dropping to a conspiratorial whisper, "I don't think she'll last more than a few days once this next storm hits. The sea, she's a fickle mistress. Takes what she wants, and no bit of metal will stop her when she's in a temper."

Finley exchanged a glance with Kelden, a silent understanding passing between them. The storm would provide the perfect cover for their task.

"You may be right," Finley said, turning back to the old man. "Best to stay clear of her when the winds start to howl, I'd wager."

The old man chuckled, a dry rasping sound. "Oh, I learned that lesson long ago, lad. These old bones know when to seek shelter." He squinted at the darkening sky. "And it seems that time is coming sooner than later."

With a nod of farewell, the old man shuffled away toward the settlement, leaving Finley and Kelden alone on the windswept shore.

"An opportunity, then," Kelden said quietly.

"Agreed. But..." Finley paused as he cast his eyes out over the gray sea.

"What is it?"

Finley's affinity with Sea magic didn't extend so far as to let him read the weather, but he could certainly get a sense of the ocean's mood. "It doesn't feel like that strong a storm, to be honest."

Kelden slowly nodded agreement. "Feels like a lot of blow and bluster. A Fisherwitch would know for sure." Those of witchkind who made their lives on and next to the sea were renowned for their ability to read the weather days into the future.

"If we had a Fisherwitch," Finley said wryly, "the pier probably wouldn't have been damaged."

"True."

"Think we can whip it up a bit?"

Kelden chewed their lip for a moment and then nodded. "I think so. It'll take me some time."

"I had intended to spend the evening. The map indicated there's a small inn."

Kelden sighed. "More fish stew?"

"Very likely."

The apprentice looked up. "I'll handle the storm. By the time I'm done, they'll think nature's fury claimed the pier, not us." They spoke with methodical certainty, each word underscored by the stiff, salty breeze.

"Good. I should be able to coax the sea into lending some added corrosion. The iron will rust faster than time alone would allow."

"Does it bother you?" Kelden asked suddenly, watching Finley's concentration. "To destroy what they've built without them knowing why?"

"Every time," Finley admitted, opening his green eyes to behold the pier's imminent demise. "But our purpose is greater than our comfort. We preserve the balance, even if it means unmaking what should never have been made." He considered the pier. "I'll need some time as well. Let's head into the village."

"'Village,'" Kelden snorted. "Ram wasn't kidding."

Finley and Kelden turned away from the battered pier, their footsteps crunching on the rocky shore as they made their way toward the cluster of weathered buildings huddled against the slate-gray sky. The settlement, if one could call it even that, consisted of a handful of structures that seemed to lean on each other for support, their rough-hewn walls and sagging roofs a testament to the hardscrabble existence eked out by the hardy souls who called this place home.

As they drew closer, the scent of woodsmoke and brine

mingled in the air, carried on the relentless wind that whipped at their cloaks and tugged at their hair. The buildings, constructed from a patchwork of driftwood, salvaged timber, and stone, appeared to have been built and rebuilt countless times over the years, each repair a defiant act of stubborn independence in the face of an unforgiving environment.

The narrow, winding paths between the structures were little more than well-worn tracks in the hard-packed earth, lined with bits of broken shells and the occasional tuft of wiry grass that had managed to take root in the unyielding soil.

A few scrawny chickens pecked and scratched in the dirt, their feathers ruffled by the cold, persistent breeze. An old, half-blind dog lifted its head as Finley and Kelden passed by, its tail thumping once against the ground in a halfhearted greeting before it settled back into its spot.

The local inn, if one could grace such a structure with the name, was little more than a slightly larger version of the other buildings, distinguished only by a weathered sign hanging crookedly above the door. The faded lettering, barely legible, proclaimed it to be "The Salty Dog."

Finley pushed open the heavy wooden door, its hinges protesting with a rusty creak. The interior was dimly lit, the air thick with the scent of smoke, ale, and the unmistakable aroma of fish stew simmering over the hearth. A few rough-hewn tables and benches were scattered about the room, their surfaces worn smooth by countless elbows and tankards.

The innkeeper, a stout, middle-aged woman with a no-nonsense air about her, looked up from the hearth as they entered.

Her sharp eyes appraised them quickly, taking in their travel-worn cloaks and the subtle air of otherness that clung to them like a second skin.

"Strangers, eh?" she said, her voice rough as the sea wind.

"Don't get many of those 'round here. What brings you to our little corner of the world?"

Finley stepped forward, a disarming smile on his face. "Just passing through, ma'am. We were hoping you might have a room available for the night, and perhaps a bit of that stew we smell simmering."

The innkeeper's gaze lingered on them a moment longer before she nodded, wiping her hands on her apron. "Aye, I've got a room. It ain't much, but it's clean and dry. As for the stew, you're in luck. Just pulled a fresh pot off the fire. This morning's catch, too." She offered a firm smile. "We may be small, but we ain't savage." She gestured to one of the tables. "Have a seat, and I'll bring you a bowl. Ale to wash it down?

"Please," Finley said as he and Kelden settled onto the benches, the rough wood creaking beneath their weight.

"Fish," Kelden sighed quietly.

"Be alert," Finley warned, his voice barely audible. "If there's going to be a trap, it'll be here."

The innkeeper returned a few moments later, setting down two steaming bowls of stew and two tankards of ale before them. The rich aroma of the stew filled their nostrils, and despite Kelden's earlier reservations, their stomach rumbled in anticipation.

Finley and Kelden ate in silence, their senses on high alert for any signs of danger. Other patrons wandered in, ordering stew and perhaps an ale before wandering out. They paid the two strangers little mind, too engrossed in their own conversations and meals to spare more than a cursory glance at the newcomers.

As they finished their stew, the innkeeper approached their table once more, a curious glint in her eye. "So, where you headed?" she asked, her tone casual but her gaze sharp.

Finley met her eyes steadily. "Just passing through, as I said.

We've been on the road a long while and thought to rest here a night before moving on."

The innkeeper nodded slowly, seeming to weigh his words. "Funny thing, that pier out there," she said, jerking her chin toward the door. "Been standing longer than anyone can remember, through storms that would tear the roof off this very inn. But lately..." She trailed off.

"Time and nature will break anything," Finley said sagely. It was a phrase he'd heard more than a few times back home.

"Aye," the innkeeper said heavily, turning to greet another pair of customers.

"I could use with some time," Kelden said softly. "If you think it's safe."

Finley's eyes darted around the room. "It should be. Let's see this room of ours."

***

The room was small, barely large enough to accommodate the two narrow beds that stood on either side, their rough-spun blankets and lumpy mattresses a testament to the inn's rustic simplicity. A single, flickering candle illuminated the space, casting dancing shadows on the whitewashed walls and the low, raftered ceiling.

The floorboards creaked underfoot as Finley and Kelden entered, the worn wood polished smooth by countless footsteps over the years. A small, shuttered window looked out over the windswept shore, the sound of the waves crashing against the rocks a constant, muted roar in the background.

A battered wooden table stood between the beds, its surface marked with countless rings from tankards and bowls, each stain a silent story of the many travelers who had sought shelter within these walls. A chipped ceramic basin and pitcher rested on a shelf above the table, the water within cold and fresh, drawn from the inn's well.

Finley set his pack down on one of the beds, the frame groaning slightly under the weight. He ran a hand over his face, feeling the weariness of the road settling deep into his bones. Kelden moved to the other bed and sat on the edge, closing their eyes and beginning a breathing exercise.

"Have you ever worked tandem?" Finley asked quietly.

Kelden opened their eyes. "No. It isn't exactly... I mean, Thornwaithe's..."

"Right. Of course," Finley said quickly, flushing with embarrassment. "We didn't either, at school. It's not... taught."

"I've heard of it," Kelden allowed.

"My parents learned it from my mother's parents," Finley explained. "It's kind of a family tradition."

"And they showed you?"

Finley's flush intensified. "They explained. But you... I mean..."

"You have to have someone you're close to."

"Normally, yes." Finley spoke faster now. "But I have dual gender affinity. You do as well. That kind of changes it."

Kelden's eyebrows rose. "How so?"

"It's the flow of the magic." Finley sat on the edge of his own bed. "I don't know if it'll work, but given that we have to move both Sea and Sky..."

Kelden nodded slowly. "It might pay to work together. You have a rune construct in mind?"

So to speak, Finley thought anxiously. His Rune Smith talent had been poking at him ever since he laid eyes on the damaged pier. "Sort of."

Kelden's eyebrows rose again. "Your..."

"Talent, yes," Finley nodded. "It's... unusual."

"I can't wait."

"No, really. It's nothing like any rune you've ever seen."

"At Thornwaithe's—"

"It's not Old Runic. Or Middle Runic."

"I feel like you should just show me."

Finley nodded and held his index finger in the air. *"Transkribuoti."* The tip of his finger began to glow a gentle orange, and the glow lingered as he started tracing the rune.

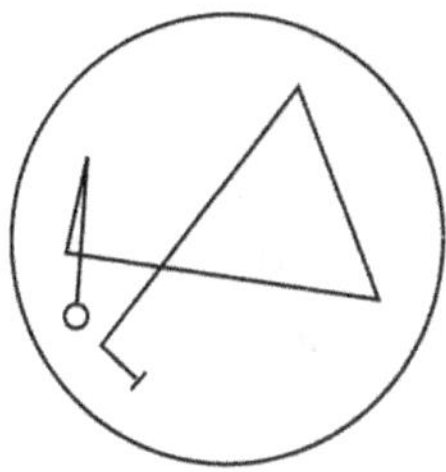

Finley wasn't even halfway through when Kelden's eyebrows reached maximum height, but the apprentice stayed silent until Finley finished. The glow faded from his fingertip, but the completed rune remained hanging in the air, a dull orange shot through with yellow.

"Well, you weren't wrong," Kelden chuckled. "You're sure this'll work?"

It'll work, something whispered in Finley's mind. "If we do it together, yes," Finley said, forcing into his voice a confidence he didn't quite share.

"A rune for a storm," Kelden said appreciatively. "Well. Let's get started."

. . .

***

The wind howled like a pack of wolves and the sea churned wildly, as Finley and Kelden watched from their concealed vantage point. The pier, once a proud structure jutting into the ocean, now bore the scars of nature's ferocity and the hidden hand of witchkind. Iron strappings, meant to be a quick human fix, screamed against the relentless push and pull of the elements.

"Look at it buckle," Finley said, his voice steady despite the turmoil before them. "They didn't mean any harm—just humans with their iron and ignorance."

They'd lay in their shared room for the entire afternoon, holding the strange new runes in their minds as they fed it with magic. They'd fallen into the ancient, half-forgotten rhythm of tandem magic without even trying, Sea and Sky magic complementing each other. The rune led their thoughts, conscious and unconscious, into the proper pattern, and their magic filled the construct with power.

"Intentions don't change the outcome," Kelden shouted over the roar, violet eyes fixed on the pier. "Better a lost dock than a war between worlds."

The water in the settlement's shallow little bay had grown warm, while the air above had grown cold. Before long, moist, warm air was rushing up, pushing the colder, drier air aside. But the updraft's energy didn't last long, and it quickly collapsed, falling to the side as fresh air shot up from beneath.

"True." Finley nodded, focusing back on the task. With each wave, he sent a subtle pulse of Sea magic, encouraging the rust that crept over metal like a deadly vine. It was painstaking work, forcing decay without a trace of witchkind influence.

Before long, the storm had become a self-sustaining monster, the air whirling in a tight vortex. Moisture from the ocean lost its warmth and began falling as a fierce, pounding rain. Finley and Kelden's eyes had flown open in the same moment, and they'd rushed outside to fine-tune their work and observe its results.

"Safer night to stay abed!" the innkeeper had called after them.

"More?" Kelden asked, hands outstretched to maintain the tempest they had summoned.

"Nearly done," Finley assured them, drawing upon his Flame affinity to quicken the oxidation process. Steam rose as heat met cold saltwater, the stench of corroding metal filling the air.

"Make sure the strapping is what gives way first," Kelden reminded him, eyes narrowed in concentration. "It needs to look like a structural failure, nothing more."

Finley poured more Flame magic into a simple heat spell, keeping his focus well away from the actual iron and instead feeding energy into the seawater he'd churned up. "Right." His gaze didn't waver from the task. He pictured the structure's integrity hanging by a thread, the iron yielding under the onslaught of nature and his hidden craft, wishing he could just focus his power directly on the offending metal. "Almost there," he murmured, feeling the magic respond, a symphony of destruction played on an invisible stage. He looked away from the pier for a moment, catching Kelden's eye. "That feel good?"

"More than," Kelden affirmed, the storm above echoing their resolve.

With one final nudge of power, Finley released his hold on the elements. A crescendo of cracking timber filled the air as the central section of the pier gave way, the iron strapping snapping loudly as if to punctuate the end of their task. The remaining structure swayed perilously before succumbing to the ocean's embrace, leaving behind a jagged silhouette against the stormy backdrop.

"Let's go," Finley said, clapping a hand on Kelden's shoulder. "Our work here is done." Together, they turned their backs on the wreckage, retreating into the shadows as the storm began to abate, leaving only the sound of waves devouring what remained of human endeavor.

"Back to the inn?" Kelden called through the howling wind.

Finley shook his head, cold water splashing down his face. "I've no appetite for it. Let them think we fell in."

Kelden grinned as rain streamed down his head, plastering his hair to his face. "I know a great travel spell."

"Do you have enough magic?" Finley asked warily. "I'm all but tapped out."

"If the choices are to head home or eat more fish stew," Kelden sighed, gathering more Sky magic to himself, "I've more than enough magic to head home."

CHAPTER 7

Construction Technique

"And no sign of the human cabal?" Ram asked suspiciously.

"Not that we saw," Finley replied wearily. He and Kelden had scarcely set foot into the Farm's main building before Ram had cornered them. "To be fair, we didn't stay long."

"They'll know it was magic," Ram muttered.

Once again, Dmitry leaned against the far wall, saying nothing.

"They might not," Kelden offered, earning a foul glare from the Head. "There was a storm already brewing. We just encouraged it—and we did that from within the inn. We didn't go out until it was already in full blow, and nobody else was crazy enough to join us."

"That you know of."

"The mist was so thick we could barely see each other," Finley assured the older man. "They may suspect, but we weren't observed."

"And that storm will take days to blow out completely,"

Kelden added, a tinge of regret in his voice. "And it'll drift, just like any storm. It *is* just like any storm—we just used magic to make it more powerful."

"And the pier is gone?" Ram asked for the third time.

"Gone, and the iron strapping corroded and snapped in the doing," Finley said. "If there thought was that iron could beat a storm, we've disabused them of the notion."

"Humph," Ram muttered. Then he shrugged. "Mission's done, then. Rest up. New one for you tomorrow."

"New—" Kelden began, heat in his voice.

"We could use some rest to Gather," Finley said more gently. "We expended a lot of magic."

Ram stared at him for a moment and then nodded. Even the too-tense Head of the Order couldn't change how magic worked. "Sleep, then. Gather. See me in the morning, but this one can wait a day. Perhaps two." He gave them a cold smile. "It's a sheet of music you've seen before. Dmitry will have a pack ready for you."

And with that bare clue, he stalked off toward his rooms, leaving Finley and Kelden to dry themselves off and find a dinner than wasn't fish.

Dmitry's expression was unreadable as he followed Ram.

***

"I wouldn't have expected Pease to be the innovator in construction," Kelden said quietly as the village came into sight.

"This... is a recurring issue, actually. Like printing presses were. But consider it: Pease sits on the edge of one of the largest forests on the continent." Finley shrugged. "Plenty of wood. So people tend to experiment."

"You've seen this before?"

"Sadly, yes."

"Care to explain it to me?"

Finley sighed. "Human buildings, at least as they're usually built, are really just solid boxes. They raise four walls, lay a few beams across them for a roof, and thatch the roof. Usually thatch. Some places use slate, when they have it. But the technique is the same. It's why none of their buildings can be that big—the walls can't be furthest apart than a beam can support, and even with a village full of people, you can only hoist so large a beam. And I mean, trees only grow so big. So they hit the upper limit pretty quickly. Went past it, really."

"Which is where we come in."

"Exactly. The right runes carved into a beam can let it support a good bit more weight. That's how they got to two-story structures. Runes carved into the walls keep them from bowing—that's how the few three-story structures stay upright. Humans put the buildings up, witchkind creates some of our hidden spaces in them, and the witchkind residents or business-people or whatever, they're responsible for keeping the build-ing's runes charged."

"And this new technique disrupts that balance?"

Finley sighed again. "It threatens to."

"How so?"

"Stronger buildings. With less material, even. And entirely from wood—far easier to build than with stone. Bigger build-ings, potentially taller buildings. But certainly sturdier."

Kelden chuckled as they walked. "I guess my imagination doesn't extend to anything more than boxes with roofs."

Finley grinned. "It's straightforward once you see it, I guess. Come on, it's supposed to be on the outskirts. Experimental buildings almost always are. We should see it soon." Then he grew more somber. "And stay alert. *Very* alert. This kind of repeated 'innovation' is exactly where I'd expect a trap. Or at least to be observed."

"Got it."

Finley led Kelden to the edge of the village, where a large structure was taking shape. It looked like any other building at first glance, with walls and a roof, but as they drew closer, the differences became apparent.

"See how the walls are thinner?" Finley said, pointing. "And there are fewer of them. That's because the weight of the roof isn't resting on the walls anymore. It's resting on those big vertical timbers."

Kelden peered at the massive wooden posts rising from the ground at regular intervals. They were easily as thick as a man's torso and twice as tall as Kelden himself. Stout horizontal beams connected the posts at their tops.

"The posts are sunk deep into the ground for stability," Finley explained. "And those beams tying them together at the top create a sturdy frame. From there, they lay more beams across to form the roof. The walls become just a way to enclose the space, not support anything."

Kelden whistled appreciatively. "That's brilliant. You could make a much bigger building this way."

"Exactly. If you can get big enough trees, obviously. See how far apart those posts are spaced compared to the traditional beam spans in the other buildings? This design lets them create a significantly larger interior space."

Kelden nodded thoughtfully as he examined the framework. "I can see why this would be concerning. It could disrupt our hidden spaces if it catches on. Undermine our quiet influence."

"Not to mention make it easier for them to expand and progress even further without our magic to assist," Finley added grimly.

"So you've seen this before?"

"Once. And the Order has records of far more attempts than that. It's the kind of thing that's just... obvious. To humans, I mean. They seem to keep reinventing it."

"So what's the plan? Sabotage the building somehow?"

Finley shook his head. "Maybe. That's what we usually do. We might need to be more subtle." He scanned the area, noting the workers milling about, the tools and materials strewn across the site. "We have two problems. One is these humans. This experiment. Which is going well, by the way—they've moved quickly. And that brings us to the second, more worrying problem."

"This cabal you've mentioned."

"Exactly. They're documenting these innovations. I'm sure of it. We can sabotage them, but they catch us at it. Or now, they probably just assume it's witchkind. And our sabotage does no good, because they've documented what works."

"Have we tried altering the documentation?"

"We have. We do, when we find it. I invented a rune construct that makes it easier."

"Truly?"

"It's carved into the foundations of their churches, every-where on the continent. Which is why they've moved to the edge of town, or why they're working in smaller settlements with no churches at all. Worse, we know they've etched some of their documentation into iron plates."

"Dust and winter," Kelden swore softly. "It's that bad?"

"It's likely worse," Finley said grimly. "And Ram keeps it from most of the Order. He thinks everyone would panic and abandon him."

"But you're telling me."

Finley hesitated. "I don't entirely agree with Ram's approach. I don't... fully understand it."

"But you follow his orders?"

"I do trust him. He's led the Order for decades." Finley paused. "I *think* I trust him."

Kelden was quiet for a moment as they watched the workers hoist another beam into place. "So what do we do?"

"Ideally, something more permanent, this time. We plant doubt. Make them question the stability and longevity of this new method. A few well-placed magical 'accidents' to make the timbers warp or crack over time should sow enough uncertainty to stall the adoption of the technique."

"Won't they just think it's a flaw with this particular building though? Or blame the quality of wood?"

Finley's jaw tightened. "They probably will."

"So that won't work?"

"It probably won't."

"Then why—"

"Because I dislike the alternative."

"Then what—"

"Let's go talk to them."

***

"So you heard about us all the way from Nworlins?" The human who'd been introduced to them as the lead designer on the project gave them a suspicious look.

But Finley was quite practiced in spinning stories on the fly. "A colleague, actually. I work for a kitchenwares firm, and one of our salespeople comes through here pretty regularly. I guess you were just started out then, although it was only a fortnight ago. You've made remarkable progress."

The man's expression eased a bit. "No secrets, really. It's

just a better construction technique." The corners of his eyes wrinkled in mild amusement. "It's astounded me that the traditional buildings manage to stay intact, really."

If only you knew, Finley thought. "We actually had a couple of pretty bad failures in my hometown. That's why I decided to come see what you were doing."

"It's a solid design," the man said slowly, "but I'll be honest. We've had some problems. Sabotage, mainly. It's why we're a little careful with who we let into the site." Indeed, the man's crew had held them back a few dozen paces while one of them ran to fetch him. "But if we can prove it out, it'll be a revolution."

Finley nodded slowly. "I can appreciate the ambition, and I understand the desire to keep your methods secret while you're still perfecting them." He looked up at the building. "But I'm afraid I've got some concerns."

The man's brow furrowed. "Concerns?"

"Yes," Finley said. "I'm just an amateur, of course, but I've worked with wood all my life. And I can't help but notice that your beams are all resting on top of each other, rather than being mortised and tenoned together. Wouldn't that make them more susceptible to shearing forces?"

The man scoffed. "Shearing forces? This building is designed to withstand the worst storms nature can throw at it."

"I'm sure it is," Finley said soothingly. "But storms are one thing. What about earthquakes? Or even just the settling of the ground over time? Wouldn't it be safer to have the beams locked together?"

The man hesitated. "I suppose it wouldn't hurt."

Finley pressed his advantage. "And what about the roof? It seems to be relying on a lot of small, individual pieces. Wouldn't it be stronger if you used larger, more substantial timbers?"

The man's jaw tightened. "Look, I appreciate your concerns, but I'm confident in my design."

"I'm sure you are," Finley said with a conciliatory smile. "But wouldn't it be better to be safe than sorry? Just think of it as a way to buy yourself some peace of mind."

The man sighed. "I suppose you have a point." He looked up at the building again.

"There's more," Finley suggested. The man raised an eyebrow. "I mean, have you really thought hard about the wood species you're using? Softer woods might be more malleable, able to flex more in a storm or even a quake. And what about the moisture content? That will surely change over time and affect the stability. And the walls themselves—without the weight of the roof bearing down on them, aren't they going to be more susceptible to damage in a storm? I could think they'd even blow inwards."

The man's eyes narrowed and Finley cringed inside. He knew his arguments were specious, but he'd been hoping the man was more of a try-and-see experimenter, not someone actually experienced with the issues he'd raised.

"Who did you say you were, again?" the man asked, his voice hardening.

Finley held up his hands as if to forestall the builder's growing suspicions. "My name's Almet. And I'm sorry, I didn't mean to imply you weren't being thorough." Quickly, he called up a rune in his mind, and cringed again when his Rune Smith talent peremptorily discarded it and substituted one of its newer ideas.

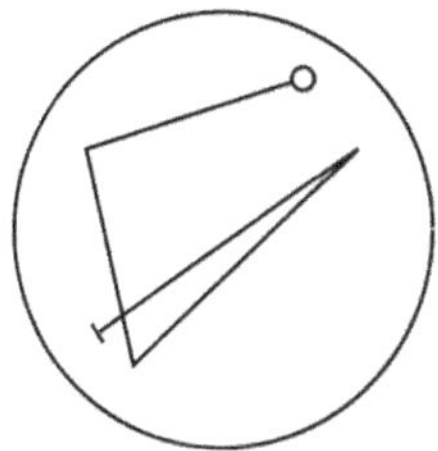

He trickled magic into it, and although his particular affinities weren't well-suited to this kind of work, he couldn't see a way to get Kelden to do this instead. The rune he'd called to mind was designed to sooth emotions, but this new one seemed more purpose-built to allay suspicion. But even as the magic took hold, he could feel it wasn't sufficient. His magic just didn't have the right nuance to it.

The builder took a step backwards. "I need to get back to work."

"Of course," Finley said, stepping back himself.

The man nodded curtly and turned to go. The members of his crew who'd remained followed him slowly, casting sharp glances back over their shoulders as they went.

"That went well," Kelden said quietly as the humans walked out of earshot. "I felt you doing something—didn't work?"

"It did not," Finley sighed.

"So now what?"

"We find an inn for the night. I have another idea, but I'll need your help."

***

. . .

The village of Pease had a couple of inns, and they were both nicer and less rustic than what Finley and Kelden had become used to. The first, the Sun and Moon, was small and cozy, with a warm fire in the hearth and a friendly innkeeper who served them a hearty meal of roasted chicken, mashed potatoes, and gravy. The second, the Blue Boar, was larger and more boisterous, with a lively taproom and a menu featuring a variety of exotic dishes. They opted for the Blue Boar, drawn in by the promise of a bustling clientele that would make it easier for them to blend in.

The inn was indeed lively, filled with the sounds of laughter and conversation. The air was thick with the smell of roasted meat and ale, and the walls were adorned with tapestries depicting scenes of hunting and battle. Finley and Kelden found a table in a corner and settled down to order their food.

"I'll have the wild boar stew," Finley said to the barmaid, a buxom woman with a warm smile.

"And I'll have the dragon steak," Kelden added. "What is it, exactly?"

The barmaid chuckled. "A bold choice, sir. It's just venison, but our cook has a way with spices that livens it up quite a bit. I assure you, it's the best dragon steak you'll ever taste!"

The food arrived promptly, and Finley and Kelden tucked in with gusto. The boar stew was rich and flavorful, the meat tender and falling off the bone. The "dragon steak" was surprisingly tender, with a highly spiced and smoky flavor.

"This is delicious," Finley said, licking his lips.

"I've never had anything like it," Kelden agreed.

They finished their meal and then retired to their room, which was small but comfortable. There was a bed for each of them, a chest of drawers, and a small table with two chairs.

"I'm going to go for a walk," Finley said. "Want to come?"

"Sure," Kelden said.

They stepped out into the cool night air. The moon was full, casting a silvery light over the village. They walked along the cobblestone streets, admiring the quaint houses and shops. The buildings here were sturdy, neatly decorated, and far less ramshackle than the last place they'd stopped.

"What's your plan?" Kelden asked.

"I'm wondering if we can have one of those timber beams split open. Maybe more than one," Finley said. "And have some kind of insects come pouring out."

Kelden tilted their head. "Insects?"

"There's no way they could have cut the trees to this point and not noticed an infestation, right?"

"Sure."

"So if the inside of those beams turns out to be mostly hollow and filled with insects—that's going to throw them off."

"Wouldn't they just... I don't know. Try new trees?"

Finley's lips thinned. "We have to try something short of... what Ram would actually want us to do."

Kelden stopped, and turned to face Finley. "He'll want them all killed, won't he?"

Finley nodded silently.

They stared at each other for several long moments until Kelden spoke. "In the past... I mean, I've read about some of the past missions. The human religion..."

Finley looked away as he considered it. "You're not wrong. We'll often try to find a way to make whatever they're doing objectionable to the religion."

"Isn't that something we could do now?"

"I don't... hmm."

"You have an idea?" Kelden asked after a few minutes.

"Did you ever," Finley said slowly, a grin spreading across

his face, "read about the time the Veil almost failed? A few hundred years ago? It was the beginning of the end of the Age of the Adherents."

"In school, we—wait. The dragon thing?"

Finley's grin widened. "The dragon thing. C'mon, we're going to need to find someone with Earth alignment, and I bet the inn has a hidden space where we can start looking."

***

Dawn broke over Pease, bathing the village in an eerie, misty light. The usual morning sounds of roosters crowing and villagers beginning their daily routines were shattered by an unholy creaking and groaning, like the tortured moans of a dying giant.

Three colossal trees, easily a hundred feet tall, were lumbering into the village center on gnarled, twisted roots that served as makeshift legs. Their branches, once lush with leaves, were now bare and razor-sharp, slashing through the air like the claws of a ravenous beast.

The trees' bark was blackened and cracked, oozing a foul, oily sap that sizzled and smoked where it dripped onto the cobblestones. Their trunks were riddled with knotholes that glowed with an infernal red light, like the eyes of a demon.

Leading the charge was an ancient oak, its trunk as wide as a house. With a bone-shaking roar, it reared back and brought its massive branches crashing down onto the roof of the village church. Timbers splintered and stone crumbled under the assault, the once-sturdy walls collapsing inward like a house of cards.

Villagers poured out of their homes, some still in their

nightclothes, their eyes wide with terror. Screams filled the air as they fled in all directions, desperate to escape the rampaging trees.

One tree lashed out with a branch, impaling a fleeing man and lifting him high into the air. His agonized shrieks were cut short as the tree shook him violently, then flung his broken body aside like a rag doll.

Finley watched in grim silence from the roof of the inn as the trees continued their rampage, smashing through buildings and crushing anything in their path. The experimental construction site was reduced to a pile of splinters in seconds, the sturdy posts and beams snapping like twigs under the onslaught. "That's enough," he called, a wisp of magic carrying his words into his room at the inn.

"I don't think Marta could keep this up anyway," came the reply, a whisper carried on the back of a breeze.

A sprinkle of dust held a curmudgeonly retort: "Marta can out-magic you all day long, boy."

"Do you need to march them out?" Finley asked.

Marta replied, "It'll be more impressive to just let them drop where they stand." Already, Finley could see the ambulatory trees flagging as Kelden and Marta's magic dwindled.

"You just don't want to march them back," Kelden teased.

"Quiet, boy," Marta snapped, although Finley could hear the good-natured fatigue in her tone.

As one, the trees toppled.

And that's when Finley saw her.

***

"You're sure it was one of their agents?" Kelden asked.

Finley cinched his travel sack tightly shut and nodded. "She was the only one not running around in terror. Certainly nobody else was staring at me, standing on the roof."

"So they'll know."

Finley laughed—a dry, hollow sound that lacked any mirth. "We marched a bunch of trees into town to attack their church. If you know that magic exists, and this cabal certainly does, we couldn't have left a better calling card."

"If we go back to the roof, I know a travel magic that—"

"We're going to go by the building site," Finley said firmly, looping his bag's strap over one shoulder. "You ready?"

"Yes, but—"

"We'll be careful. Keep a defensive rune on the edge of your mind, along with the iron-defense one I showed you."

The sun was well above the horizon by the time Finley and Kelden emerged from the Blue Boar. The once-lively village of Pease was now a scene of devastation, the streets strewn with debris and the air thick with the whimpers of the wounded.

Villagers picked their way through the wreckage, their faces ashen with shock and grief. Some were helping to carry the injured to the local healer, which had miraculously survived the attack unscathed. Others were sifting through the rubble of the damaged buildings, salvaging what little they could.

The church was a complete ruin, its once-sturdy walls reduced to a heap of shattered stone and splintered wood. The great oak tree that had dealt the final blow lay across the ruins like a fallen giant, its branches still twitching feebly as the last of Marta's magic drained away.

On the edge of the village, a group of men were struggling to lift a heavy beam off the crushed remains of the experimental construction site. The massive timbers that had once seemed so promising now lay in a tangled heap, their ends jagged and splintered where they had snapped like twigs under the onslaught of the rampaging trees.

The builder saw them walking past and trudged over to them. "I suppose you've lost interest in our project."

Finley feigned shock and amazement. "It seems clear that you're not meant to proceed! The trees themselves... if ever there was a clear message of the god's will, that was it. We were terrified for our lives this morning! Our inn would have been the next to go!" He glanced at Kelden, who'd managed a drawn, ashen expression and was nodding in silent agreement.

The builder opened his mouth to protest, but then closed it and shook his head. "I'm not normally a religious man..."

"The forest stirring itself to protest has given me a renewed commitment," Finley said firmly. "I assume you'll abandon these efforts?"

Again, the man opened his mouth and then snapped it shut. "Nobody will support us, now. And word will spread." He turned back to his ruined project. "I'm finished." He glanced at Finley and Kelden. "I hope your travels are safer than they've been."

Finley nodded silently, and he and Kelden began picking their way around the construction site, heading out of town on the main trade road.

"Do you know how many were killed?" Kelden asked quietly as the town slowly fell away behind them.

"Four," Finley said tensely. "And at least thirty injured."

They walked silently for a ways before Kelden asked, "Do you think he'll try again?"

"I hope not," Finley said, shaking his head. "Did you count his crew?"

"The builder's? I saw around three dozen."

"As did I. And we'd have had to kill them all. Anyone who knew what they were doing."

"But you said the cabal probably had the technique documented."

"Exactly. Their deaths would have been pointless, because the cabal would have just found someone else to try. Somewhere we might not notice. This way... the humans themselves might put a stop to it."

"Marta felt pretty confident of it."

"She's reason to. That kind of thing has worked well in the past, so long as there's no reason to suspect magic."

Kelden snorted. "Walking trees aren't magic?"

"Not if they're summoned by their god."

They trudged along the road for another ten minutes. "That's probably far enough," Finley said, stopping and scanning the road behind them. "I can handle the travel magic, this time. You must be spent."

"Mostly," Kelden admitted. "Finley..." he added, hesitation in his tone.

"Yeah?"

"Do you ever wonder?"

"Wonder what?"

Kelden hesitated again. "Wonder if it's really necessary? If the humans having better buildings, stronger homes... if it's so dangerous?"

Finley's jaw clenched as he began weaving magic into a traveling rune in his mind. "I do wonder. More and more, actually."

CHAPTER 8

More Bricks for the Wall

Ram was unexpectedly out when they returned to the Farm, giving them an equally unexpected reprieve. "Something urgent with the Taryba," Delcie, one of the Order's mission administrators, told them. "Dmitry's in charge until Ram's back."

Finley frowned. He'd been told that only one member of witchkind's Great Council even knew about the Order, and even that councilor was given only limited information about their operations and missions. What could have been so urgent that the Head of the Order needed to attend in person? Then he shook his head and let it go. Perhaps their reprieve would include a couple of nights in a comfortable bed around their own kind, before they were sent out again.

He was surprised to find a number of other field agents at the Farm for at least a few nights—more than he'd seen in the past year or so. Aistė, who specialized in long-term assignments where she strove to become part of small human communities; Dovilas, who'd made a career out of hindering expansions to the Iron Roadway; Genovaitė, one of the Order's oldest field agents, with a keen mind for forestalling technological advances; and Raimondas, who normally kept himself to the bitter-cold towns and villages of the northeast. Finley felt a pang of regret that Arcadia wasn't there as well—it had been months since he'd seen her, and they'd always been close.

As the sun dipped below the horizon, painting the sky in hues of orange and pink, the gathered field agents settled around the crackling campfire. The flames danced and swayed, casting a warm glow on their faces and creating flickering shadows that mingled with the lengthening shadows of the surrounding trees. The air was filled with the gentle chirping of crickets and the distant hooting of an owl, a soothing symphony of nature that helped to ease the tension from their weary bodies and minds.

Dovilas leaned forward, his elbows resting on his knees as he stared into the mesmerizing flames. "I've been trying a new approach lately," he began, his voice low and thoughtful. "Instead of just creating sinkholes to disrupt the Iron Roadway, I've been focusing on transforming the land into marshes."

The others looked at him with curiosity, their eyes glinting in the firelight. Aistė, her long blonde hair plaited into a neat braid, tilted her head. "Marshes? How does that help?"

Dovilas smiled, a hint of mischief in his expression. "Well, you see, the Iron Roadway requires firm, level ground to function properly. By turning the land into a boggy, waterlogged mess, it becomes nearly impossible for them to lay down the tracks and maintain the stability they need."

Genovaitė nodded slowly, her weathered face creased with understanding. "Clever. But don't they notice when land they'd previously surveyed is suddenly a bog?"

"Ah," Dovilas said, his smile widening. "I'm even more clever than you think. I've been timing the storms, you see. A little push at the right time and I can get a nearby stream to overflow its banks. Makes it look seasonal, which is even harder to deal with than just filling in a marsh." Then he frowned. "Although they're starting to experiment with raising stream banks." He nodded to Finley. "Your work ruining their Benoto blocks has set them back, though. They were relying on that material to build—well, sea walls, basically. 'Stream walls' sounds strange to my ears." His grin returned.

Aistė leaned back, a wistful expression on her face as she gazed up at the star-studded sky. "Speaking of sea walls," she began, her voice soft and melodic, "my last assignment was in a small coastal community called Svyturys. It was a picturesque little village, nestled between rolling hills and the vast expanse of the ocean. The people there were hardworking and determined, their lives intertwined with the rhythms of the sea. No Fisher-witches, though."

She paused, her eyes shimmering with memories. "Without magic, they had been struggling for years to build a sea wall that could withstand the relentless pounding of the waves and the fury of the storms that battered their shores. Their homes and livelihoods were constantly under threat, and they knew that they needed a solution that would stand the test of time."

Aistė shifted, drawing her knees up to her chest and wrapping her arms around them. "That's where the Benoto material came in, although they weren't calling it that. They named it *cementis*. It was a revolutionary new material, designed to be stronger and more durable than anything they had ever seen before. I never did learn where they got it from, but the villagers were thrilled when they learned that they would be among the first to use it in their sea wall construction. They imported wagonloads of the raw materials, built this incredible tube-shaped over out of solid rock—just an enormous amount of work."

Finley's stomach tightened.

She smiled, a hint of pride in her voice. "I worked alongside them, day after day, as they poured their hearts and souls into building that wall. I did every little thing I could to undermine the work, as ordered. The stuff was notoriously susceptible to an improper ingredient mix—really, really picky. But in the end, all I was doing was slowing them down. They'd managed to pour a length of wall taller than myself, and... well, Ram was getting irritable."

Why didn't he ever mention this to me? Finley thought, getting irritated himself.

Aistė shrugged. "But then it all stopped working. Even perfectly measured, they couldn't get it to work anymore. One of the key ingredients stopped arriving entirely. What they'd constructed already is still there, and I tell you—it's amazing. Half the Fisherwitches on the continent would probably use the stuff, and save their magic for other tasks."

"Which is, of course, the problem," Genovaitė said in her gravelly voice. "A slow progression to where magic itself is no longer needed. And then, once we're discovered... nothing stopping them from Hunting us to extinction."

"Oh, surely it's not so bad as that," Dovilas scoffed. Finley raised an eyebrow—Genovaitė was simply repeating the Order's well-established dogma. "Magic keeps everything together in a thousand little ways. Sure, the Iron Roadway has been a disaster, but sea walls? Or street lamps that don't blow out in the slightest breeze? Or glass windows you can actually see through?"

"They've been improving windows?" Kelden asked, speaking up for the first time that evening.

Genovaitė leaned forward, her eyes gleaming with a mixture of fascination and concern. "Indeed, they have been making remarkable strides in glassmaking. It's quite astonishing, really." She reached into her satchel and pulled out a small, perfectly square pane of glass, holding it up for the others to see. The fire-light danced across its surface, revealing a clarity and smooth-ness that was unlike anything they had ever seen before—without the use of magic in the process.

"This," she said, her voice barely above a whisper, "is what they're calling 'crown glass.' The process is quite ingenious, actually. They take a glob of molten glass on the end of a blow-pipe and spin it rapidly, using centrifugal force to flatten it into a large, circular disk. As it spins, the glass becomes thinner and more uniform, with any bubbles or imperfections being pushed toward the edges."

The others leaned in closer, their eyes wide with wonder as they examined the glass. It was so clear, so flawless, that it almost seemed to disappear in Genovaitė's hand. Finley reached out tentatively, his fingertips brushing against the cool, smooth surface. "Incredible," he murmured, shaking his head in disbelief.

Genovaitė nodded, a hint of a smile playing at the corners of her mouth. "But that's not all. Once the disk is formed, they allow it to cool slightly before cutting it into smaller panes like this one."

"How did you stop them?" Kelden asked.

Genovaitė's smile widened, a glint of mischief in her eyes. "Oh, I had a few tricks up my sleeve," she said, leaning back and crossing her arms over her chest. "You see, the key to the crown glass process is maintaining a precise temperature throughout the spinning and cooling stages. Too hot, and the glass becomes too fluid, losing its shape and clarity. Too cold, and it becomes brittle, prone to cracking and shattering."

She reached into her satchel again, this time pulling out a small, intricately carved wooden box. Opening the lid, she revealed a fine, silvery powder that sparkled in the firelight. "This," she said, "is a special blend of minerals I created. When added to the molten glass, it alters the thermal properties ever so slightly, making it nearly impossible to maintain the perfect temperature range."

Dovilas let out a low whistle, his eyebrows raised in appreciation. "Clever. But how did you manage to get it into their supply without being noticed?"

Genovaitė chuckled, a mischievous glint in her eye. "Well, that's where a bit of glamour magic came in handy. I disguised myself as one of the glassmakers' apprentices and slipped the powder into their batch during the night shift. By the time they realized something was amiss, it was too late. The entire batch was ruined, and they had no idea what had caused it." She shrugged. "Lost interest in the project entirely."

Finley and Kelden exchanged a glance. The majority of the Order's operatives were unaware of the human cabal that opposed them, and Finley was all but certain that the 'crown glass' technique was well-documented somewhere. It would come up again, likely in some smaller settlement where the Order had fewer eyes.

Raimondas spoke next. "It seems like their pace of experimentation has increased," he said in his deep, rumbling tone. "I've been chasing down rumors of some miracle building material myself. *Sustiprintas molis*, it's called."

"The *humans* call it that?" Genovaitė frowned. "It sounds like something from the True Language."

It is, Finley thought. Yet another example of humans using the old tongue—a language they'd left behind centuries ago.

"They do," Raimondas nodded. "Although I've traveled to every town and village in the northeast and found no evidence of it. Apparently some miracle building block."

"The Benot—" Finley started.

Raimondas shook his head. "No, not those. Something made with the local clay, and reinforced, somehow."

Finley and Kelden exchanged another wary glance. "When you say every town and village," Finley asked slowly, "do you mean the smaller settlements that crop up between them? The ones mainly populated by malcontents? The ones not even big enough for a small church?"

Raimondas frowned. "Why would I bother with those?"

Finley groaned inside and gave a slight nod to Kelden. They'd look into this in the morning. *There goes a few days of home comfort,* he sighed to himself.

The conversation continued well into the deep of the night, but Finley's mind was now awhirl with planning.

And, strangely, his Rune Smith talent was murmuring softly in the back of his mind.

***

"This seems like it was a little too easy," Kelden remarked. He and Finley had visited just two small villages before finding their target on the outskirts of Landshire.

Finley shrugged. "Honestly, Raimondas isn't that creative. Like I told you, we just needed to find one village with new brick buildings going up, wait for a supply wagon to come in, and then figure out where it came from."

"By bribing the driver," Kelden grinned.

Finley smiled back. "Surely buying a man an ale or two isn't a bribe." Then he nodded to the brickyard they'd found. "And it isn't like this is being kept a secret. I mean, it's right here." Finding the brickyard hadn't even been difficult, as it seemed like a tenth of the town's population was employed there. They'd found a small inn that made its business housing the brick-wagon drivers in between runs, and settled onto a sturdy old table on the inn's front patio, directly overlooking the broad yard where piles of bricks were being loaded onto empty wagons. The brickworks building itself was set further off, but they could still see the neat piles being wheeled out.

"So what do you think the secret is?"

Finley considered. "I don't know, honestly. We have reinforced bricks already—the ones my parents used in sea walls had horse hair pressed into the wet clay to add strength and help prevent cracks. But they still broke fairly easily, which is why their runes were in such demand. But—look, did you see that?"

A pile of dark-red bricks had tumbled off their wheeled cart, scattering in the dry dirt.

Kelden let out a low whistle. "Not a single one broke."

"So they're doing something pretty different." Finley's eyes narrowed. "Hmm."

"What are you thinking?"

Finley didn't respond, but instead summoned his magic. There was a simple rune for cracking bricks, often employed in demolishing old structures to make way for new ones. He held the rune in his mind, ignoring his talent's sudden urge to rewrite it in the half-random, angular style it had invented.

In the brickyard, a half-dozen bricks cracked with a dull sound, even as the man who'd been pushing the cart tried to restack them.

"What's that prove?" Kelden asked.

"That they haven't stuck iron into them as reinforcement," Finley said, relief coloring his tone. "So it's something else, but at least something a little less immediately threatening to us."

"So we sneak in tonight?"

"That's my preference. Come on, let's see if this inn has an empty room to let."

As the two men stood, a young girl inside the inn's common room whirled and hurried out a back door.

. . .

***

"Do you have a light spell you prefer?" Kelden asked softly as they crept through the brick yard, threading their way through precise stacks of bricks.

Finley shook his head, his eyes already adjusting to the deep shadows that blanketed the brickyard. "Not in the open," he whispered back. "We don't want to risk alerting anyone to our presence."

The night was thick and heavy, the air redolent with the earthy scent of clay and the sharp tang of smoke from the brickworks' chimneys. A sliver of moon hung low in the sky, its feeble light barely penetrating the inky darkness that pooled between the towering stacks of bricks. The two men moved with practiced stealth, their footsteps nearly silent on the hard-packed dirt.

As they drew closer to the brickworks building, Finley could make out more details in the wan moonlight. The structure was long and low, constructed of the same dark-red bricks that surrounded them. Smoke curled lazily from a trio of tall, narrow chimneys, hinting at the furnaces that burned within. The windows were shuttered tight, not a glimmer of light escaping to betray the secrets that lay inside.

"I have a rune I'll teach you," Kelden whispered. "Better than a light spell. Something Thornwaithe's has used for years. *Aštrus įbrėžimas.*"

Finley's eyes felt like they'd received a sharp scratch of some kind, and then he blinked, marveling at the transformation before his eyes. The once impenetrable darkness had given way to a world awash in a soft, ethereal glow. It was as if the very fabric of the night had been peeled back, revealing a hidden realm.

The stacks of bricks, previously mere shadows in the gloom, now stood out in stark relief. Each brick was a tiny masterpiece, its surface etched with intricate patterns and subtle variations in color. The dark-red hues seemed to pulse with a life of their own, as if the clay itself held secrets waiting to be unlocked. The precise lines and angles of the stacks created a mesmerizing geometry, a labyrinth of form and function that drew the eye and captured the imagination.

The brickworks building, once a featureless silhouette against the night sky, now revealed itself in stunning detail. The weathered wood of the shutters and doors was a tapestry of texture, each grain and knot telling a story of the hands that had shaped them. The bricks themselves were a symphony of shades, from the deepest crimson to the palest rose, each one a testament to the skill and dedication of the craftsmen who had laid them.

Even the smoke that drifted from the chimneys took on a new life under the influence of Kelden's rune. The tendrils of vapor were no longer mere wisps, but rather sinuous dancers, weaving and twirling in an intricate, glowing dance.

"What does that even do?" Finley whispered in amazement. But his Rune Smith talent was already analyzing the magic. "Somehow amplify the moonlight?"

"Any light," Kelden whispered back, clearly satisfied with themselves. "Even on a moonless night, it'll pick up starlight. You do need to be a bit careful of any actually bright lights—they'll blind you until you dismiss the magic." They gestured to a small side door on the brickworks building, barely visible in the shadows. "There."

Finley nodded, his senses on high alert as they crept towards the entrance. The scent of clay grew stronger here, mingling with the acrid bite of chemicals that Finley couldn't quite place. The door was secured with a simple latch, easily overcome with a whispered incantation from Kelden. It swung open on well-oiled hinges, revealing a narrow passageway that led deeper into the heart of the brickworks.

The two slipped inside, closing the door softly behind them. The passageway was lined with shelves laden with an array of tools and supplies - trowels, molds, buckets, and strange metal implements that Finley had never seen before. The air was thick and heavy, the heat from the banked furnaces still seeping through the walls like a living thing.

As they ventured further, the passageway opened up into a vast, cavernous space. It was the sight at the center of the room that drew Finley's attention like a lodestone. There, arranged in neat rows, were the molds for the bricks themselves. They were, in and of themselves, unremarkable—simple rectangular blocks into which clay could be packed. But it's what they contained.

"Is that... iron?" Kelden asked, freezing in their tracks.

Each mold contained a simple cage, made out of thin rods of metal.

"It's metal," Finley said hesitantly. His talent's awareness drifted outward, tentatively brushing near the heavy wooden molds, but he didn't feel any draw on his magic. "But it isn't iron."

"It isn't copper, brass, or bronze, either," Kelden said, their brow wrinkling. "It's silvery."

"They're what's reinforcing the bricks," Finley said. "Silver would be too soft."

"Silvery, I said."

"True."

The interior of the brickworks must have been nearly pitch-black, with the single moon's thin light barely filtering through grimy windows high overhead. But Kelden's magic still showed the little metal cages sparkling silver-white.

"They must have more of it in here somewhere," Finley said, looking around. "There." He led Kelden to a large wooden drum, which had been tightly wound with the thin, silvery metal. "Thicker than horse hair, but not by much," Finley observed, gently running a finger over the densely wrapped metal. "My magic isn't responding at all. It's not iron."

"We call it *plienas,*" a voice said behind them.

Alarmed, the two men whirled just as a nondescript, middle-aged man carefully withdrew the shield that had hidden the light from the candle he was carrying.

"It starts as iron, but things are added to it. No," he said as Kelden opened their mouth to speak, "I don't know. But it is documented. In iron. You cannot take it from us. Any more than you can stop this innovation."

"Who are you?" Finley asked. His magic pooled into his mind, where a half-formed defensive rune was already taking place. Annoyingly, his talent was more focused on *that,* trying to twist it into a new shape.

"My name is unimportant. You know who I represent."

"We do."

"We knew one of you would come here, in time."

"Or one of the other places you're doing the same thing, I presume," Finley said.

The man shrugged.

"So what now?"

"I was sent to ask you a question."

Finley and Kelden waited silence.

"Why?" the man eventually asked.

"Why what?"

"You know what. Why must this be taken from us?"

Finley's shoulders dropped slightly. "I've had this conversation before."

"Before, it was things that you thought threatened you. How do stronger buildings threaten you? We presume you live in them as well."

He's not wrong, the whisper in Finley's mind pointed out.

"You let some things go. The curative mold."

"You know about that?" Kelden asked.

"We watch everything."

"I... don't have an answer for you," Finley admitted.

The man nodded slowly. "So what will you do here? Tonight?"

Finley hesitated. "I... nothing." From the corner of his eye, he saw Kelden's eyebrows rise.

The man's head tilted slightly. "Because it doesn't threaten your... magic." It was a statement, not a question.

Finley hesitated again. "I think so."

"This is a decision *you* are making. Not your superiors."

Finley nodded silently.

"We wondered. This *plieninė viela*—that is what it is called, this *wire*—we tested it. We suspect it would not affect your... powers."

"Why does it not?" Kelden asked.

The man shrugged. "We do not know. It also does not attract lodestone. We—some of us—have a theory they are related."

They're not, Finley's talent whispered dismissively. *But it's an interesting theory.*

So why doesn't it? Finley asked it.

He received a feeling of mild frustration. *It's complicated. The substance is... adulterated. Too far removed from what it once was. The roots... it is complicated,* it repeated before falling silent.

"What will you tell your superiors, then?" the man asked, unaware of Finley's inner conversation.

"I don't know."

"Well then. I will leave you to it."

With that, the man turned, not bothering to shield his candle, and walked calmly out of the brickworks.

When he was gone, Kelden spoke first. "We're doing nothing at all?"

Finley didn't trust the cabal to not still be listening, so he simply shook his head and gave his apprentice a searching stare. "We should go."

"To the inn?"

"What would be the point?" he snorted. And with that, he gathered the Earth magic that fueled his most powerful travel magic, whisking the two of them away.

***

"This isn't the Farm," Kelden said with some surprise as they materialized.

They found themselves standing in a vast, open meadow, the lush green grass swaying gently in the cool breeze. The air was crisp and invigorating, carrying with it the unmistakable scent of the nearby sea. In the distance, they could hear the soft, rhythmic babbling of a river, its waters rushing over smooth stones and cascading down small, natural falls. The meadow stretched out before them, a seemingly endless expanse of verdant beauty, even under the dim light of the single moon.

"No," Finley agreed. "I wanted to speak with you."

"About the man?"

"What did you think of him?"

"He sounded genuinely curious."

"And the bricks. If you were in charge, what would you have done?"

"I... honestly don't know," Kelden said, their brow wrinkling. "Metal reinforcement... it would make their buildings useless to us, on top of reducing their reliance on magic."

"But that metal doesn't affect our magic."

"Exactly. So... what's the harm? Shouldn't our magic be for more than just holding buildings together?"

"You could make the same argument for the timber construction we destroyed."

Kelden nodded. "I would, I think."

Finley fell silent for several moments, listening to the sound of water and the smooth breeze rustling the grass. "I think I'm getting tired. And... I think we work against ourselves."

Kelden frowned. "How so?"

"Consider: we stop the humans from advancing, yes?"

"Of course."

"And this cabal is aware of us. But every time we stop them, they simply become more determined to advance in spite of us."

"Sure."

"So when we stop them on these things—things that shouldn't truly be a threat to witchkind—does that not mean they'll simply try harder, and be more secretive, about everything? Even the things that do threaten us?"

Kelden considered. "I see your point. You're saying we should be more choosy."

"We used to be," Finley sighed. "I think the message we're sending is that we'll give them no quarter. And yet, with this brick issue, they come to us with a compromise."

Kelden's forehead wrinkled further. "I didn't hear a compromise."

"No? Kelden, they've invented a metal that they obviously think is as strong as iron, but it doesn't interfere with our magic. You heard the man—they even attempted to test it. Wasn't that an attempt at compromise? 'We've found a metal you can tolerate, now let us be?'"

Now the apprentice's eyes widened. "I see what you mean."

Finley tilted his head back a bit, looking at the moon's pale, blue-white light. "I think we need to learn a little more."

"About that man?"

Now Finley's eyes fell to his apprentice's. "About that wire. And I think I want someone to help us."

"Who?"

"An old friend."

CHAPTER 9

Reunion

"Dmitry is *not* happy about this," Arcadia said, her mischievous grin countering the seriousness of her words. "I'm supposed to be on the other side of the continent right now."

Finley couldn't help but smile back at her, despite the gravity of the situation. It had been far too long since he'd last seen Arcadia. Her porcelain skin seemed even paler than he remembered, almost translucent in the dim light. But her hair, once a shimmering platinum blonde, now held a dull, ashen hue—as if life had been especially wearing for her over these long months apart.

It was her eyes that captivated him, just as they always had. Those deep, obsidian pools seemed to hold secrets and mysteries. They sparkled with keen intelligence and a hint of mirth, even as dark shadows lurked beneath them, hinting at the trials and hardships she'd clearly faced in their time apart.

Despite the weariness etched into her delicate features, Arcadia's presence filled the room with an electric energy. Her sharp wit and brilliant mind were as intoxicating as ever, drawing Finley in like a moth to a flame.

"Well, when has Dmitry ever happy about anything, lately?" Finley quipped, falling easily back into their old rhythm of playful banter. "But exactly why? What's on the other side of the world for you?"

She shrugged and took a long swallow from her mug of ale. "The usual. Mission, mission, mission." She set the mug gently on the table and gave him a tired look. "Does it ever feel like the list of things humans can threaten us with has gotten impossibly long?"

Finley leaned back in his chair, surveying the inn's interior. The River's Respite was one of Carvendam's finest establishments, a perfect blend of rustic charm and modern comforts. Rough-hewn wooden beams crisscrossed the ceiling, while polished oak tables gleamed in the warm light cast by wrought-iron chandeliers. The floors were a patchwork of well-worn flagstones, smoothed by countless footsteps over the years.

At this time of day, the inn was quiet, with only a handful of patrons scattered about the spacious common room. A fire crackled merrily in the massive stone hearth, casting dancing shadows on the walls. The air was filled with the mouthwatering aroma of roasting meat and freshly baked bread, mingling with the subtler scents of ale and whiskey.

Finley couldn't help but feel a sense of comfort and familiarity wash over him. He had spent so much of his adult life in places like this, moving from one town to another, always on missions, never settling down. It was a strange realization, that he felt more at home in an inn than anywhere else. What did that say about his life, about the choices he had made? He pushed the thought aside and focused on Arcadia, who was studying him with those piercing eyes. "It does."

She nodded slowly before taking a quick glance around the

inn—an ingrained habit Finley had to actively suppress himself from mirroring. "So what's this about?"

"You're sure you're not going to get in trouble?" he asked.

She looked down at the trestle table for a moment, and then raised her eyes to meet his. "Trouble? No. You want to know something? I haven't actually done half the missions I've said I have."

Finley blinked in confusion.

"What's that mean?" Kelden asked.

Arcadia turned to him. "I'll assume Finley will stop me if you're not trustworthy." She waited a beat before continuing. "Some of these missions are *stupid,* and others are downright *evil.* You know what they asked me to do a moon ago? Wipe out all the willowbark within a two-day ride of Baythwaite."

Finley drew back in surprise. "What? Why?"

"Because they brew it into a tea to ease their hangovers."

Kelden's brow wrinkled. "I don't get it."

"They drink a lot there, but they also invent some of the most amazing things. The theory, as I was told, was that if they all had more hangovers, they'd invent less. Less willowbark, harder hangovers."

Kelden almost choked on a mouthful of ale. "That's ridiculous!" they sputtered.

Arcadia shrugged. "I don't know what missions you've been on, but that's what most of us are dealing with. Ridiculous."

"So you're just... not doing it," Kelden said, almost in awe.

"No."

"And nobody cares?"

Arcadia looked away. "I hate saying this, but the Order *trusts* us. Nobody's following up. I'm abusing that, I know. But I'm just... I'm sick of it. It doesn't make sense."

Finley nodded slowly. "So you're..." He paused. "You never cared much for humans, before."

Arcadia sighed. "They've both done bad things to people we know. And love. But... I'm not cruel. I joined to stop them from being a danger to themselves and to witchkind. But not to... not to stop them from preventing hangovers."

"Yeah," Finley said. "Us too."

"What do you mean?"

He relayed the story of the brickworks in Landshire.

"Exactly that," Arcadia said with conviction when he finished. "Why are better bricks a problem? Especially if they don't threaten our magic?" Her voice lowered on that last word, and she did another automatic scan of the common room. "Why," she continued in a low, dangerous voice, "does witchkind need to use *our* magic just to keep *their* buildings upright? Why are we *slaves* to the humans' ineptitude? An ineptitude *we* perpetuate!" She exhaled sharply and leaned back. "I can't even tell you how many smithies I've had to... you know. Because they were trying something new with iron." Then one of her eyebrows quirked upward. "Isn't that what you told me, when you said to meet here?"

Finley nodded. "New alloys."

"When you say 'new—'"

"Finley thinks," Kelden interrupted carefully before Finley could speak for himself, "they're trying to offer a compromise."

Arcadia's brow furrowed. "Compromise?"

"They know iron hurts us," Kelden continued.

"Of course they do," Arcadia snorted. "So what kind of—wait. New alloys." Finley could see it working through her brain. "You're talking about a metal that doesn't affect our... us."

Finley gave a shallow nod.

"But brass. Bronze. Copper. They've had—"

"They're all soft," he pointed out. "You couldn't make rails for their iron roadway from bronze or brass."

She paused, and then slowly nodded.

"And you couldn't reinforce brick with copper. It's too soft. It wouldn't make a difference."

"No," she agreed quietly. "But they've found something that works."

Finley nodded.

"And doesn't affect us."

Another nod.

"And you're letting it go."

"I have to, don't I?"

"Runes and ruin, Finley, what if that's what they're really doing? What if they're *trying* to work with us? And we're just coming in harder, taking them down at every possible turn?"

"And some of us have no... discretion," Finley said softly, thinking of Genovaitė's hardline devotion to the Order. "The smallest thing, the tiniest advancement, is met with..."

"Death and destruction," Arcadia muttered, emptying her stein. She looked up and waved to a server for another round. "This isn't what I signed up for. It isn't what the Order *used* to be."

"That's why I want to look into this 'wire,'" Finley said. "It's why I need your help."

"Why, exactly?"

He sighed. "Because I'm pretty sure it's true, but I need to test it more thoroughly. I mean, I was there, but..."

"You need to see it again."

He nodded.

She tilted her head and accepted another stein from the server. "That isn't the only reason you wanted me here. You've more than enough affinities to test it yourself."

"True," he allowed. "It's also because I'm pretty sure it's a trap."

"Ah," Arcadia grinned as she sipped her ale. "Now we're in territory I know."

***

Well past midnight, Finley led them back to the brickworks and watched with satisfaction as Kelden's magic unlocked the doors and let them in.

They crept through the darkened brickworks, their footsteps echoing softly on the stone floor. The cavernous space was filled with hulking shapes, casting eerie shadows in the faint moonlight filtering through the high windows. The air hung heavy with the scent of clay and coal dust, tinged with an undercurrent of something metallic that set Finley's nerves on edge.

They moved cautiously, senses heightened, alert for any sign of danger. Arcadia took the lead, her lithe form gliding silently through the gloom. Finley followed close behind, his magic pooled and ready in his mind. Kelden brought up the rear, their eyes darting nervously about, fingers twitching with barely restrained power.

Despite their thorough scan for iron before entering, Finley couldn't shake the feeling that they were walking into a trap. The brickworks felt too still, too quiet. The hair on the back of his neck prickled with unease, and he found himself straining to hear the slightest sound that might signal an ambush.

As they ventured deeper into the building, the shadows seemed to press in around them, thick and oppressive. The towering brick kilns loomed like silent sentinels, their gaping maws yawning open like portals to some dark, forgotten realm. Finley formed Kelden's *Aštrus įbrėžimas* rune in his mind, but his talent immediately seized upon it, disassembling its broad strokes and gentle curves. *Inefficient,* it muttered. In less than a heartbeat, it re-formed the rune in a dozen different ways, finally settling on an entirely new configuration.

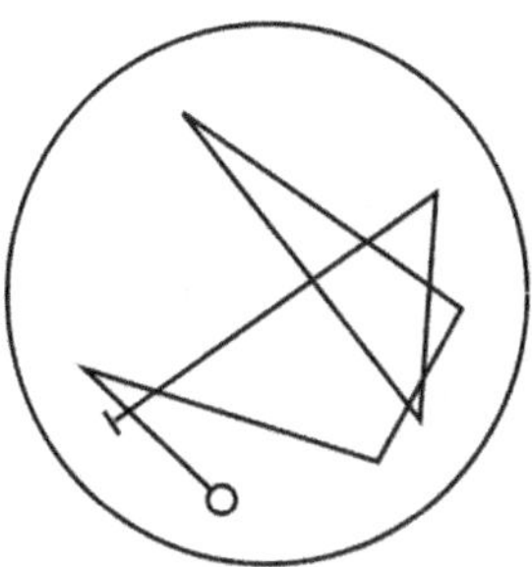

Far better, it said with satisfaction. Finley noted that the voice continued to seem more... *sentient.* More human, as if it wasn't him speaking to himself, but rather someone, or some*thing* else, speaking to him.

What's the difference? it mused in response.

Finley trickled a bit of magic into the new rune and the interior of the brickworks flared to life as the rune captured the dim, blue-white moonlight and amplified it for their eyes.

Arcadia gasped. "What did you do?"

"It's... the same *Aštrus įbrėžimas,* isn't it? You're using more power?" Kelden asked uncertainly.

"Later," Finley said softly. "Focus on the mission."

The interior of the brickworks was a marvel of engineering. Rough stone walls rose two stories high, enclosing a cavernous space filled with ingenious devices and contraptions. Massive wooden beams supported the vaulted ceiling, while narrow clerestory windows admitted shafts of silvery moonlight.

Finley's gaze was immediately drawn to the rows of wooden molds lining the far wall. Each one was a perfect rectangular void, precisely crafted to shape the clay into uniform bricks. Some of the molds still held their precious cargo—bricks in various stages of drying, waiting to be fired in the enormous kiln that dominated the center of the room.

But it was the contents of other molds that made Finley catch his breath. Nestled within the unfilled voids were more delicate cages of silvery wire, glinting in the enhanced light. The wire was impossibly thin and fragile-looking, yet it seemed to possess a strength and resilience that defied its brittle appearance. Each cage was a masterpiece of metalworking, its graceful curves and precise angles forming a lattice that would reinforce the brick from within.

Along the adjacent wall, neatly stacked wooden spools held coils of the same remarkable wire. It shimmered softly, almost as if imbued with an inner luminescence. Finley longed to reach out and touch it, to feel its cool smoothness against his fingertips and test its strength for himself.

"We're being watched," Arcadia muttered.

"How can you tell?" Kelden asked.

"*Akys pakaušyje,*" she replied tersely.

Finley's talent seized the phrase and constructed variations of the corresponding rune. One was in in the abbreviated, simplistic style of Middle Runic, while the next was a more complex and angular New Runic version. Both vanished from Finley's mind almost immediately as his talent seemed to scuttle off into one corner of his mind to consider them. *Fascinating,* it said as its presence faded. *I never worried about being watched.*

"That's the wire?" Arcadia asked, pointing to the molds.

"Like they've left them on display for us," Finley said, nodding.

"They did," Arcadia said, sounding absolutely certain. She turned and examined the spooled wire before stepping closer to it. She moved slowly, hesitantly, waiting for the iron in it to grab her magic and try to pull it from her, but even as she crept closer and closer, nothing happened.

It won't, Finley's talent muttered, preoccupied with its new puzzle. *Too far off from the roots.*

What does that mean? he asked, but it had already retreated further.

Arcadia reached out tentatively, her slender fingers hovering just above the nearest spool of wire. It was roughly the size of her head, and if the material was as heavy as iron, would weight quite a bit. She took a deep breath and gently brushed the gleaming metal, marveling at its smooth, cool surface. A shiver ran through her as she realized that she felt no ill effects, no draining of her magic. It was as if this strange new alloy was completely inert to her powers.

She picked up the spool with care, exhaling sharply at its weight and cradling it in one arm like a precious artifact. The wire was wound tightly around a wooden core, each loop perfectly aligned with the next. The wood of the spool itself was cheap and roughly cut, its grain highlighted by the glowing light from Finley's spell. Arcadia ran her fingertips over the surface, feeling the tiny ridges and whorls.

As she turned the spool over, she noticed a series of intricate markings burned into the other end of the wooden core. She traced them with a delicate touch. "Look at this," she breathed, holding the spool out for Finley and Kelden to examine. The markings, seared into the cheap wood with a careful hand, formed an intricate pattern of lines, dots, and symbols. To the untrained eye, they might have appeared as mere decorative flourishes or random scribblings. "These are carters' marks," she explained, tracing the symbols with a slender finger. "Shippers use them to track their goods—where they come from, where they're headed, and all the stops in between. I learned about them on a previous mission involving rope shipped on spools just like this one."

Finley leaned in closer, his brow furrowed in concentration as he studied the markings. The symbols were unlike any writing system he had encountered before. Some resembled stylized arrows or compasses, while others looked like miniature depictions of landmarks or geographical features. Tiny dots and dashes connected the larger symbols, forming a complex web of meaning.

"Can you read them?" Kelden asked, their voice tinged with awe and curiosity. "What do they say about where this wire came from?"

Arcadia nodded, her eyes still fixed on the spool as she deciphered the code. "This batch originated in Ironhold, up in the northern mountains. There's a huge mine up there, one of the few we haven't been able to keep shut down."

"It's pretty hostile territory," Finley agreed. One of their first missions for the Order had taken them into those mountains. They were isolated, desolate, wind-blown, and deadly cold even in the summer. Humans willing to work in those conditions would find few of witchkind willing to object, iron or no.

"But that was just the raw ore," Arcadia continued. "Here, this indicates where the wire itself was made. Spurham. They probably floated the ore across the lake and down the river."

Finley frowned. "Spurham doesn't have any large smithies or forges."

"Maybe somewhere nearby? One of the small settlements that doesn't appear on the map?" Kelden suggested.

"Likely," Finley acknowledged. "That will make it difficult to find."

"It shouldn't be that hard," Arcadia countered, setting the spool back in its place and pointing to additional markings. "That was lighter than I thought, but still heavy. Look, this is the carter that carried it. All we need to do is find the group that uses this symbol. And we can probably start in Spurham."

Finley nodded slowly, then came to a decision. "Then that's what we'll do." He raised his voice for the benefit of those watching. "If you can have the benefit of iron without its... effects... then I believe you should keep it." Kelden inhaled sharply but remained silent. "Arcadia, your... ability—"

"Intact," she assured him. "And look." She reached to the side of the spool, pulling the free end of wire back, bending a short length off the spool. "It's pretty strong, even for how thin it is."

Finley sent a lance of Flame magic into the wire, gradually increasing the flow until Arcadia snatched her hand back with a yelp. He kept adding more and more magic until the wire began glowing a cherry-red.

"You might have warned me," Arcadia said crossly. "How much are you using?"

"Enough to melt any of the copper alloys," he admitted, letting the magic fade. The wire quickly cooled to a dull red glow and then back to its silvery gray. "It doesn't look damaged at all."

Arcadia tugged gently at it. "Seems just as stiff as before."

Quite far from the roots, Finley's talent mumbled distantly.

"A possible compromise," Finley said, raising his voice again. "We'll look into it." He paused and considered before adding, "It would be helpful if nothing else... happened. While we're looking."

If anyone was still watching them, they didn't reply.

"Let's go," Finley said at last, dropping his light augmentation and heading for the still-open door.

***

The small, nameless settlement nestled in the foothills near Spurham was an unassuming cluster of rough-hewn buildings, easily overlooked by the casual observer. But to Finley, Arcadia, and Kelden's trained eyes, it was a hub of activity, a place where raw iron ore was transformed into the miraculous steel wire they had encountered at the brickworks.

As they approached the settlement, the first thing that struck them was the sheer scale of the operation. Towering piles of iron ore, each easily the height of a two-story building, dominated the grassy landscape. The dark, jagged chunks of rock glinted in the sunlight, their surfaces flecked with rust-red streaks. Massive wooden carts, their wheels creaking under the weight of their cargo, trundled back and forth between the piles and the nearby structures, ferrying the ore to its next destination.

All three of them shielded themselves from the iron's greedy draw on their magic, using the rune construct Finley had developed—now well-known throughout the Order—to contain their magic within themselves. They'd be unable to use it while it was bottled up, but they'd be protected from the iron draining it completely.

The settlement's buildings were an eclectic mix of styles and materials. Some were simple wooden shacks, their boards still fresh and new. Others were more substantial, with stone foundations and sturdy timber frames. The largest of these, a cavernous structure with a steeply pitched roof, emitted a constant plume of smoke and steam from its numerous chimneys, hinting at the intense heat and energy within.

As they drew closer, the trio could make out more details. Alongside the piles of iron ore, they saw neatly stacked cords of wood, each log carefully cut and seasoned to fuel the roaring furnaces. Teams of workers, their faces streaked with soot and sweat, moved with practiced efficiency as they loaded the wood and ore into the gaping maws of the furnaces.

The air was filled with the clamor of industry—the ringing of hammers on anvils, the hiss of steam, and the shouts of the workers as they coordinated their efforts. The acrid scent of burning coal and molten metal hung heavy in the air, stinging their nostrils and making their eyes water.

Finley led them towards the heart of the settlement, where the largest building stood. As they approached, they could feel the intense heat radiating from the structure, even from a distance. The ground beneath their feet was warm to the touch, and the air shimmered with the rising heat.

A burly man with a thick beard and a soot-stained leather apron emerged from the building, wiping his brow with the back of his hand. He eyed the trio with a mix of curiosity and suspicion as they drew near.

"What brings you folks to these parts?" he asked gruffly, his deep voice barely audible over the din of the forge.

Finley stepped forward, his demeanor calm and confident. "We've come to learn about the wire you produce here," he said, meeting the man's gaze steadily. "We're interested in it for reinforcing our own bricks."

"Not for sale," the man said flatly. "Proprietary material." He turned and stomped back to the nearest building, glancing over his shoulder to ensure they didn't follow.

"Look," Finley said quietly, nodding.

Finley directed their attention to the piles of materials scattered around the settlement, each one obviously playing a crucial role in the creation of the remarkable steel wire. Alongside the towering mounds of iron ore, they saw heaps of coal, the shiny black lumps glinting in the sunlight. The coal was clearly for fueling the furnaces, providing the intense heat needed to melt the iron and transform it into steel.

Next to the coal, they spotted piles of limestone, the pale, chalky rocks contrasting sharply with the dark hues of the other materials. "Limestone," Kelden said. "They already use that to remove impurities from molten iron."

"That one," Finley said, jerking his chin. It was a mound of shimmering, silvery-gray powder that seemed to dance and swirl in the breeze. Finley broke away from the other two and approached it cautiously, scooping up a handful of the fine, almost ethereal substance. It felt cool and silky against his skin, its texture reminiscent of Finley ground mica. "Manganese," he breathed, his eyes widening with recognition. "They're using manganese to create the alloy."

"I've never even heard of it," Arcadia said, walking over to join him.

"It's used to make certain pigments," Kelden said, following her. "I've never seen so much of it in one place."

"Glassmakers use it to *remove* color," Finley added. "It's how they get it to be so clear."

"And so this is the trick? This is what they're using? This is what... *changes* it?"

"I don't see anything else unusual," Finley said, casting his eyes around the site. "This must be it." He turned and realized that the settlement's activity had come to a near-halt, with three dozen or more humans simply standing and staring at them. Waiting. "We should go."

"But—" Kelden protested.

"Follow me," Finley ordered. He began walking briskly out

of the settlement, retracing the path they'd followed to get here, along the well-worn road to Spurham.

Do you want to know if they're following us? his talent asked suddenly, its presence growing in his awareness. *Try this.*

A new rune, in the angular, asymmetric style his talent seemed to have created, appeared in his mind.

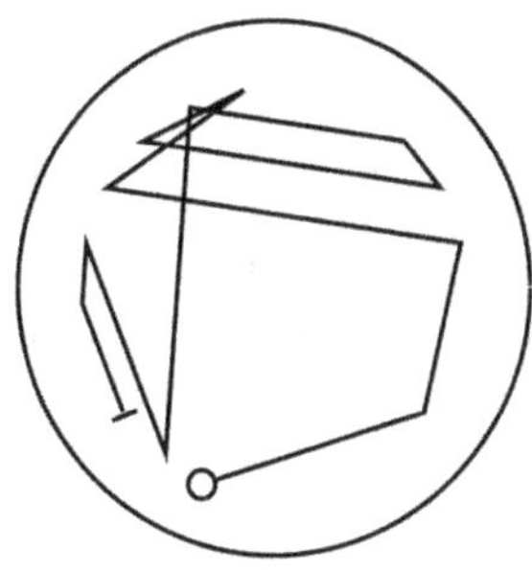

Finley immediately fed it magic, noting that it drew heavily on his affinity for Sky. He refocused, feeding it more of that gentle, subtle power. He felt it bloom around him, *felt* the humans' eyes on their backs, with a firm sense that nobody was setting out to chase them. "They're not following." He considered the signals the rune seemed to be sending him. "Nobody else is watching. Just stick with me."

"How can you tell?" Kelden asked.

Finley conjured another rune, using it to draw the new one in bright lines of light in front of him as he walked. "Arcadia's *Akys pakaušyje,*" he said.

"That isn't my rune," Arcadia objected. "That isn't *any* rune. None I've ever seen." She hesitated. "This is your..."

"Kelden knows I'm a Rune Smith," Finley said, letting the

glowing lines of the rune fade. "And yes. My talent... it's been going off in a new direction."

"Is that how you made *Aštrus įbrėžimas* better?" Kelden asked.

Finley nodded and quickly drew his talent's revised version in the air before him, letting it hang there for a moment before willing it to fade. "It's taking everything and... improving it. In this new style."

It's more direct, his talent said confidently. *Less ideographic. Less waste. I'm surprised I never considered it before. You're more... flexible.*

"You speak of it as if it's alive. Independent," Arcadia said.

He hesitated. "I'm not sure it isn't."

Independent, yes, it murmured with amusement. *Alive is complicated.*

They walked several more paces as Finley maintained the magic. The humans seemed to have returned to their duties.

"You've never been big on the Origin," Arcadia said slowly. "As a theory, I mean."

"I've been thinking of it a lot more."

"How can you not believe in the Origin?" Kelden asked incredulously. "It's not a 'theory.'"

"A single source where all magic comes from?" Finley asked, realizing that his usual skepticism was absent. "Always seemed too... neat for me. I guess."

Kelden chuckled. "When you can have your mind and body possessed by a force of pure magic, it's not that difficult to imagine. For Thornwaithe's alum, the Origin isn't a subject of debate. It's a fact."

"I... I'd never considered it that way," Finley admitted.

You can't seriously doubt it now, his talent insisted.

"Believe it or not," Finley said aloud, "I think my talent is telling me it's real, too."

"It probably *is* the Origin," Kelden said easily. Finley was struck but how matter-of-fact Kelden sounded." "It actually speaks to you? In words?"

Finley hesitated again. "Yes," he said at last. "It didn't, at first, but lately it—"

Arcadia stopped in her tracks. Finley turned quickly, scanning behind them, and realized they'd marched out of sight of the settlement. "What is it?" he asked.

"Sending," she said tersely. "From the Farm. From Ram. I'll be right back." And in a cool swirl of magic, she vanished.

"At Thornwaithe's, we've always wished the magic would *tell* us what it wants, rather than just taking control."

"You've felt it?"

"We all do. At the end of every school year, and it gets stronger year by year." His voice had gone low and quiet. Respectful. "It grows the bond we all share with it."

"I never knew."

"We *really* don't talk about it outside of school. Even with other alum. I mean... it's crazy, right?"

"Not if it's real." *And you* are *real, aren't you?* he asked his talent.

Probably more than I ever was, it replied.

Arcadia swirled back into existence between them. "New mission. Highly urgent. I'm to go alone." Her lips thinned. "Want to come with me?"

CHAPTER 10

A Meeting

"What do you think, sir?"

The room was dimly lit by a handful of flickering candles, their wavering light casting long shadows on the rough stone walls. The air was heavy with the scent of damp earth and the musty odor of ancient books and parchment—books that were no longer read, as they could not be trusted. Around the table sat a group of elderly men, their faces lined and weathered, their eyes sharp and calculating. They were dressed in dark, nondescript clothing, as if they wished to blend into the shadows.

The table before them was massive, hewn from thick, age-darkened wood. Its surface was covered with a scattering of thin iron sheets, each one etched with dense lines of tiny, precise text. The men ignored them for the moment.

The room itself was sparse, with no adornments or comforts. The only furniture was the table and a handful of simple wooden chairs. The walls were bare stone, damp with condensation, and the floor was packed earth. There were no windows, no hint of the world outside this secret, subterranean chamber.

The men spoke softly, their voices low and muted. They moved with a quiet deliberation, every gesture and glance laden with unspoken meaning. These were men accustomed to secrecy, to the weight of hidden knowledge and the burden of unspoken truths. They were the guardians of new mysteries, the keepers of yet-to-be-forgotten lore.

"Him bringing the woman was a good sign," one of them murmured. "She's left our work alone in the past."

"They took no action in the foundry settlement," another pointed out.

At the head of the table sat a man who seemed to embody the very essence of the room—ancient, inscrutable, and steeped in shadows. He was tall and gaunt, with a face that was more skull than flesh. His skin was pale and translucent, stretched taut over the sharp angles of his cheekbones and the jutting prominence of his chin. His eyes were deep-set and hooded, glinting with a cold, piercing intelligence that seemed to penetrate the very souls of those who met his gaze.

He was dressed in simple clothes of the deepest black, the fabric so dark that it seemed to absorb the light from the flickering candles. The clothes hung loosely from his narrow frame, the folds and drapes concealing the contours of his body and giving him an otherworldly, almost spectral appearance.

The man's hands rested on the table before him, long and slender fingers steepled in a gesture of contemplation. His nails were long and sharp, like the talons of a bird of prey. When he spoke, his voice was low and gravelly, with a sibilant edge that sent shivers down the spines of those who heard it. "Promising," he rasped, nodding slowly. "The process is documented?"

"In iron, so their magic can't change it," the man who had

first spoken assured them. "Copies in all of our major repositories."

"So we have a rift," the man at the head of the table mused. "A wedge. Three, at least, who are less blindly fanatical than the others. Could there be more?"

"These three will likely seek out others amongst their kind," someone asserted.

"Perhaps," the leader allowed. "Perhaps. Although perhaps not. There was a time not long ago when we could be assured of... *clemency,* for many innovations. Now..." he trailed off, his jaw clenching and unclenching in the flickering light. "We have paused other initiatives?"

"For the moment," someone said.

"And of the churches?" the leader asked.

"We've confirmed the carvings are identical. Many fresh." This voice was the youngest amongst them, and belonged to the only man at the table dressed in priestly vestments. "But they match the symbols in some of our oldest holy texts."

"They would," the leader muttered with a cough. "A clever way to use our beliefs against us."

"I am... hesitant to destroy some of those texts," the younger man cautioned.

The leader shrugged. "Little matter. We've lost the movable type project entirely, then. Hand-etching iron sheets will have to do, for now. We've preserved the basic process."

The priest hesitated before offering, "I have considered a mitigation."

"Oh?" The leader's eyebrows rose slightly.

"Many of the churches are old. Crumbling, in some cases, especially along the coasts. The weather can be—"

"And?"

The priest swallowed heavily. "We've had a success convincing one village to tear theirs down and start over."

"Theirs—the church, you mean?" The old man's tone was disbelief mingled with intrigue.

"Yes. So obviously, when the new one—"

"When the new one is built," the leader mused, "we work to prevent the carvings. See if that changes anything."

"That was my thought."

"Proceed. It surely cannot hurt. When will this occur?"

"Well, the first one has already been demolished and rebuilt. As yet, there have been no efforts to carve the symbols into the exterior."

The man at the head of the table nodded. "Keep us informed. But... be cautious."

"Your predecessor," someone muttered.

"Yes," the leader acknowledged. "He was... incautious, at the end."

"I'll be very careful," the priest assured them.

"Good."

"Sir, the post-and-beam experiment..." someone ventured.

"Was exactly that," the leader snapped. "An experiment. We have pressed, my friends. Pressed, and what have we found?

"Improvements to building design, no. Improvements to lighting, no. Medicine, sometimes. It appears to depend upon the operative. The general *idea* of innovation, no. Shipbuilding, no. Sea walls, no. Weapons, no. What are we left with? Some few medicinal projects. Agriculture. Anything else is apparently held together with their magic, and they will not let us shake their yoke. If we attack them as one, they can withdraw their power and everything we have will simply collapse. But the... what was the wire named?"

"*Plienas,* sir," someone said.

The leader scowled. "An uncomfortable word in the mouth."

"From the First Language, sir."

"Notwithstanding."

"Someone had suggested *cruach,*" someone offered.

The leader's scowl deepened. "Even worse."

"Hardfire," said a firm voice from the far end of the table.

The leader's eyebrows rose. "Hardfire," he murmured, tasting the word for the first time. "Hardfire," he repeated more firmly. "Yes. Let us use that, henceforth." A few mutters of agreement circled the table. "The next projects are prepared?"

"Ready at your word, sir," someone assured.

"Then let us nurture our new compromise," he said heavily, leaning back in his creaking chair. "And let us hope it does not come to the war we all desperately seek to avoid."

"And if these three are not enough to turn the tide?" someone asked as others began pushing back their chairs.

"Then," the leader said, his voice thick with conviction, "there will be no avoiding it."

CHAPTER 11

Woodcarver

"They want you to *what?*" Finley asked, aghast.

They stood in the center of Nek, one of the smaller villages along the continent's western coast, just north of the peninsula that contained Farreach in the South. It was a fishing village, prospering from the plentiful seafood catch its fishermen—and fisherwitches—brought in every morning. The village square had once held a sturdy but incredibly weatherworn human church, built in one of the most traditional styles Finley has seen.

But that church was now gone.

It had been fully rebuilt on the footprint of its predecessor in a newer and simpler style, but using no less sturdy, traditional construction of stone and hefty timbers. Only the boards of its eaves looked unfinished to Finley's eyes, lacking the intricate fretwork that usually adorned these buildings.

Fretwork where the Order was accustomed to hiding the various runes Finley had developed to stifle specific types of innovation.

Finley felt his heart began to beat faster.

The village square now bustled with activity as the morning's catch was brought in and sorted. Fishermen hauled baskets brimming with silvery fish, crabs, and shellfish, their weathered hands deftly handling the squirming creatures.

Around the square, quaint wooden buildings with colorful shutters and flower boxes lined the cobblestone streets. The salty sea breeze carried the aroma of baking bread from the village bakery, mingling with the pungent scent of drying seaweed and fish. Seagulls wheeled overhead, their raucous cries echoing off the stone walls.

In the center of the square stood a magnificent fountain, carved from the same sturdy stone as the church. Water cascaded from the open mouths of intricately sculpted sea creatures—whales, dolphins, and mythical beasts of the deep. Children darted between the adults, laughing and splashing in the cool, clear water.

A vibrant open-air market occupied one side of the square, its stalls overflowing with fresh produce, handcrafted goods, and sparkling trinkets made from sea glass and shells. Villagers haggled good-naturedly with the merchants, their voices rising and falling like the tides.

At the far end of the square, an ancient, gnarled tree stood sentinel, its twisted branches reached out like the tentacles of a kraken, casting dappled shadows across the cobblestones.

"Collapse it," Arcadia said, her voice tense.

"Why?" Kelden asked, although Finley suspected he already knew the answer.

"They finished it a week ago, but nobody from the Order has been able to get near it to add our runes. Even to the donation box on the door." The boxes whose runes carried the Order's message tokens back to the Farm.

"Why not? We've never had a problem—" Finley started.

"The priest. They've brought in someone new, and he says he's not having it. Won't allow anyone with a chisel nearby."

"We could certainly do it at night, from a distance," Kelden pointed out. "There's Sky magic that could—"

"There's none of the usual fretwork," Finley pointed out. "Anything we add would stand out pretty sharply."

He felt his talent sniff toward the new structure with interest.

"The full mission," Arcadia said grimly, "is to execute another change in their holy books, to—"

"Not again," Finley moaned quietly.

"—to forbid worship in an undecorated house," Arcadia finished. "And to then collapse it in the middle of services the next holy day. Tomorrow." Finley could hear the tension in her voice.

"This is because they're on to us," Finley murmured.

"Obviously," Arcadia agreed.

"Are you any good at the book modifications?" Finley asked slowly.

"I'm okay," Arcadia admitted.

"I'm excellent," Kelden offered.

"Truly?"

"Extremely," they confirmed. "It was a special focus for my class, actually. Never knew why."

"Well," Finley said, sighing heavily, "you're about to find out."

***

As dawn broke over the village of Nek, Finley stepped into the bustling square, his humble woodcarver's garb allowing him to blend seamlessly into the crowd. The early morning light cast a golden glow across the cobblestones, illuminating the faces of the villagers as they went about their daily tasks.

The scent of freshly baked bread wafted from the village bakery, mingling with the salty sea breeze that carried the distant cries of seagulls. Finley watched as the fishermen hauled their morning catch into the square, their weathered hands deftly sorting through the glistening piles of fish, crabs, and shellfish. The baskets overflowed with the bounty of the sea, a testament to the skill and perseverance of the fisherwitches who had braved the early morning tides and kept their ships intact.

Finley made his way through the throng of villagers, his eyes scanning the square for any signs of the previous day's events. The magnificent fountain still stood at the center, its intricately carved sea creatures spouting crystal-clear water that sparkled in the sunlight.

The priest stood in front of his church, on the elevated platform that helped keep dirt and mud from the front doors. He was watching the crowd, an expression of mild suspicion on his face as his eyes darted nervously to and fro. As Finley maneuvered through the crowd, making as direct a line as possible for the church, the priest finally spotted him.

As Finley approached, he could see the priest more clearly. He was a middle-aged man, with salt-and-pepper hair cropped close to his head and a neatly trimmed beard that framed his angular face. His piercing blue eyes were set deep under bushy eyebrows, giving him an intense, almost hawk-like gaze that seemed to bore into Finley's very soul.

The priest wore simple robes of deep blue, cinched at the waist with a woven belt adorned with intricate silver embroidery that glinted in the morning light. Around his neck hung a heavy silver pendant in the shape of a cresting wave, the symbol of the human god and its dominion over the sea. His hands, clasped in front of him, were strong and calloused, a testament to a life spent in service and labor.

As Finley drew nearer, the priest's eyes narrowed, his deepening suspicion evident in the tightening of his jaw and the slight forward tilt of his head. He stood tall and proud, his shoulders squared and his feet planted firmly on the stone steps of the church, a bastion of faith and tradition amidst the bustling chaos of the village square.

"Good morning, Father," Finley called out as he neared, his voice carrying easily over the din of the crowd. He raised a hand in greeting, a disarming smile playing across his lips. "I hope this day finds you well."

The priest's gaze remained fixed on Finley, his expression guarded and unreadable. "Good morning, stranger," he replied, his voice deep and resonant, carrying a hint of wariness. "What brings you to our humble village on this fine day?"

Finley maintained his friendly smile, stopping a respectful distance from the church steps. "Father, I am but a humble woodcarver, seeking to offer my services to your magnificent church. I couldn't help but notice the lack of adornment upon its eaves, and I believe my skills could greatly enhance the beauty of this holy place."

The priest's eyebrows raised slightly, a flicker of interest sparking in his intense blue eyes. "Is that so?" he mused, his gaze sweeping over Finley's simple attire. "And why, pray tell, would we not leave this wood in the condition it creator has made it?"

"Does it not say in the Book of Worship that we are to 'adorn the house with our work, so that the god might know of our labor?'"

The priest shrugged and Finley's chest tightened a bit. "It might. Frankly, it says a lot of things. I suppose you're like the others, come to carve your lines and swirls and symbols?"

Ah, Finley's talent murmured gently in his mind. *We've been preceded.*

Arcadia said as much, he replied. Aloud, he said, "No, Father, not at all. May I show you?" From the battered leather satchel he'd acquired the evening prior, Finley withdrew an equally battered, leather-bound journal. He opened it, holding it out in both arms for the priest to see. "I have traveled far and wide, studying the intricate fretwork and carvings that grace the most revered churches and temples across the continent. I have come to believe, and I hope this is not presumptuous, that the carvings should not try to reflect the creator's work. No symbols for fire or water, no curves and and strokes. Merely symbols like these."

The priest's eyebrows rose slightly, and Finley thought the man's jaw unclenched slightly as he looked at the journal pages. "Oh?" he said with some small amount of interest.

Throughout the previous night, Finley's talent had guided him through a few simple runes in its new, "more direct" style.

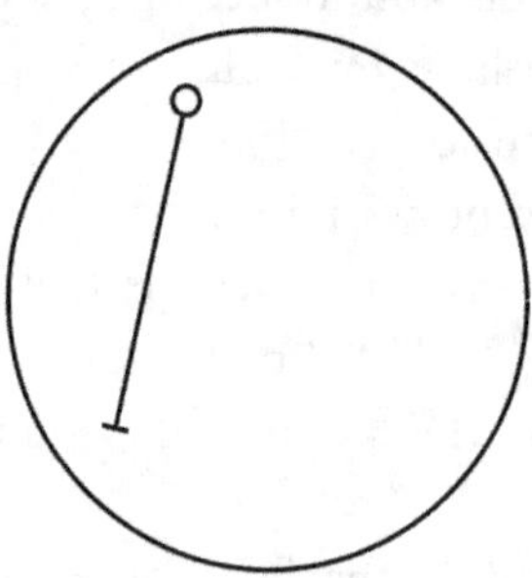

"It seems... simpler," the priest acknowledged, stepping closer.

It's literally nonsense, Finley's talent smirked.

"I have been thinking, Father, that—if we were to take the Book in its most literal sense—that the decorations which might please the god the most would be ones that purely show our labor. Our effort." He turned the page.

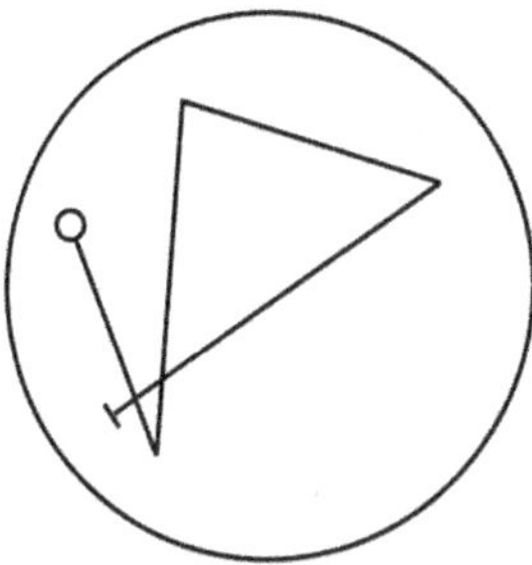

Runes which, when empowered, will keep this structure sturdy despite the unstable roof supports they've used, his talent noted. "Every one different, Father. None with any intrinsic meaning. All designed to take our time, the creator's gift to us, and gift some back." He turned the page again.

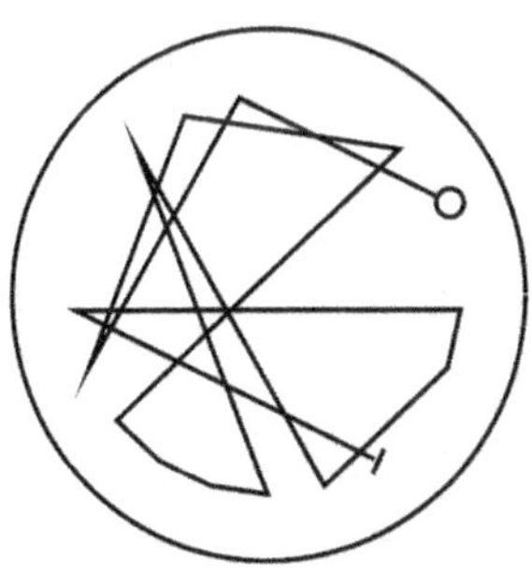

And that will create a deep uneasiness in anyone experimenting with movable type, his talent said. *Much more efficiently than the original one we created. Don't know why I didn't stumble on this sooner. Lack of perspective, I suppose.*

"I make each one as I go, sir," Finley continued as the priest leaned closer. "However the mood takes me. However the creator bids me."

"You carve these deeply?" the priest asked.

Finley blinked.

Tell him no.

"No, Father. Not too deeply. The, ah—creator is free to change them, of course. Especially here, where the wind and the rain are so dominant." *But won't they fade after a few years?*

They'll be fine.

"I... see." The priest looked up sharply, meeting Finley's eyes and once again seeming to bore into his soul.

Try this.

Another strange, angular rune-within-a-circle assembled itself in Finley's mind:

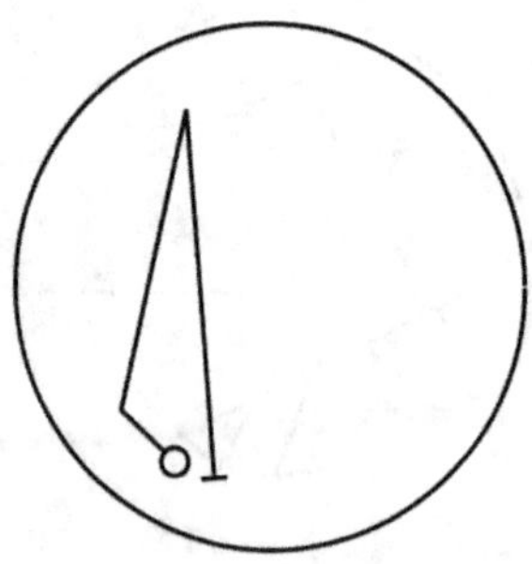

Finley didn't question it. He began feeding his magic to the rune, adjusting the flow when it seemed to gently seize magic of Sky and Flame. A combination that many thought to be unusual, but Finley knew the two fed each other quite well. He leaned into the Flame aspect, sensing the enchanted energies float outward from his mind in a diaphanous cloud. It drifted over the priest, whose eyes narrowed slightly. *But magic can't affect humans,* Finley thought.

It doesn't need to affect him, his talent whispered back.

The rune's pull on Finley's magic ebbed, even as the rune's effects were drawn fully into the priest, gathering momentum and grounding themselves into the earth.

"Agreed," the priest said in a low, softer voice. "But there will be no payment. You do this for the glory—"

"Of course, of course," Finley said quickly.

"You have an apprentice? Someone to help speed the work?"

"Of course," Finley said again, ducking his head. "I'll fetch him. We can begin—"

"Immediately."

"Yes, right away. Thank you, Father."

"*Nekęsk ragana gyventi,*" the priest said gravely, before turning, stepping into the church's and closing the doors firmly behind him.

Finley's eyes widened in alarm and he stumbled back into the throne of busy humans.

Suffer not a witch to live.

***

. . .

"We're being watched, aren't we?" Kelden asked softly from their perch on the rickety old ladder.

"Yes," Finley said tightly, his own ladder creaking in protest as he shifted his weight.

"Are we going to do anything about it?"

"No."

They'd managed to secure the two ramshackle ladders from a workshop nearby, paying far more than they were worth to close the deal quickly. Their purchase had also included two dull, chipped bronze chisels and two brass hammers so badly pitted that Finley expected them to fall apart at any moment. Fortunately, only the ladders needed to function: he and Kelden pretended to use the chisels, but in reality it was their magic carving the runes into the eaves of the church.

"Why not?"

"This mission is more important. And they're only *watching,* so far. And Arcadia's watching *them.*" Finley turned his attention back to the rune he was finishing.

This one next, Finley's talent mused.

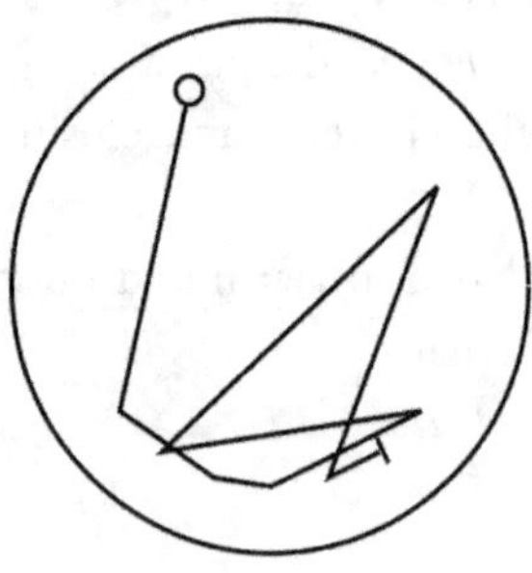

Finley's conscious mind was developing a knack for "reading" these new runes without fully empowering them. *Really? "Trust Magic?"*

His talent seemed to shrug. *Can't hurt. This one after that.*

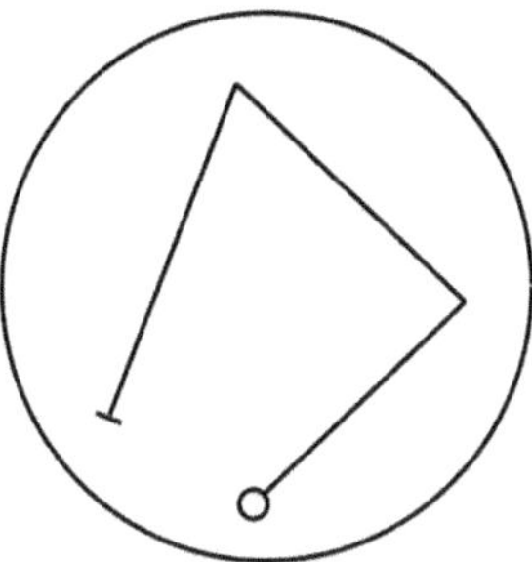

What exactly did that do to the priest? Finley asked. *Magic just grounds itself in humans.*

Mmm, not exactly, his talent said distractedly. *Humans are actually full of magic. Pure magic, so full that almost anything you throw at them just gets lost in the wash. But if it's simple enough, it can leave a... flavor. This one next.*

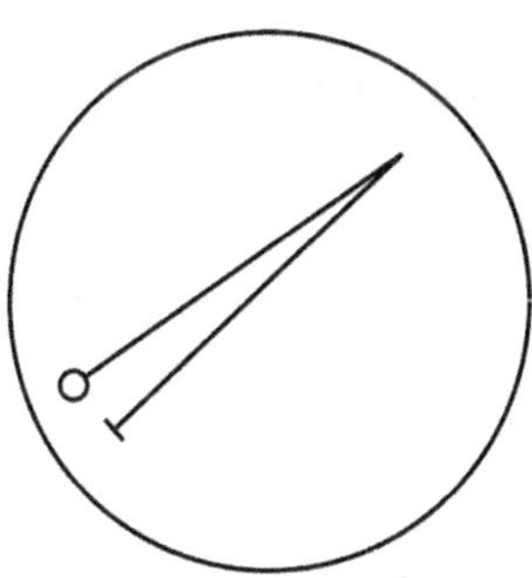

Finley was so taken aback he almost missed the new rune. *Endure.* At least that one would have a physical effect on the church's structure, helping it withstand the constant wind and rain from the nearby coast.

That's enough, his talent said sleepily, withdrawing into the recesses of his mind. *Just repeat them all.*

What do you mean, 'humans are full of magic?' Finley asked quickly.

But there was no reply.

"Should I keep copying the same ones?" Kelden asked.

"Um... yes," Finley said, his mind in a sudden whirl. *Humans are full of magic?* he repeated to himself. "Keep repeating these ones, and empower them as you go," he added in a low voice. The sensation of being watched, enhanced and made an almost physical feeling by his version of Arcadia's rune, bored into his back.

"Won't they wonder what we've done?" Kelden whispered, their voice barely audible over the noise of the crowd behind them.

"I imagine so," Finley said tightly. "I'm coming up with a story. I'm sure we'll be asked soon enough."

The two worked in companionable silence for several long minutes, the pointless *scritching* of their chisels against the wood, and the light ringing of the hammers against those chisels, acting as a soft counterpoint to the hubbub of the busy humans in the village square.

"These new runes," Kelden said after a while, "you're making them up as you go, aren't you?"

"Obviously," Finley chuckled.

"I can... feel it. I think."

Finley's eyebrows rose. "Oh?"

"Through magic," Kelden said softly. "There's a... current,

around you. When you're doing it. Making new ones, I mean. It *is* the Origin, you know. I'm convinced of it."

"I..." Finley paused, tapping his chisel a few times as his magic carved another rune into the flat wood of the eaves. "I guess. Maybe. Probably. It feels... strange."

"It still speaks to you?"

"Yeah. More now than ever."

"I'm jealous."

"I'm... not sure you should be," Finley said very quietly.

"What was that?"

"Nothing."

***

As the sun began its slow descent toward the horizon, painting the sky in a breathtaking array of oranges, pinks, and purples, Finley and Kelden stepped back to admire their handiwork. The intricate carvings they had etched into the eaves of the church seemed to glow softly in the fading light, the play of light and shadow making the runes dance and shimmer with a life of their own.

The village square was bathed in the warm, golden hues of the setting sun, the cobblestones reflecting the light like a mosaic of burnished copper and bronze. The once-bustling market stalls were now empty, the merchants having packed up their wares and headed home for the evening. The fountain at the center of the square continued to burble softly, the water gleaming like molten gold as it cascaded from the mouths of the stone sea creatures.

A gentle breeze wafted through the square, carrying with it the scent of the sea and the distant laughter of children playing on the beach. The ancient, gnarled tree that stood sentinel at the far end of the square cast long, twisting shadows across the ground, its leaves rustling softly in the wind like the whispers of ancient secrets.

As Finley and Kelden gathered their tools and prepared to depart, a familiar figure emerged from the lengthening shadows. Arcadia strode toward them, her dark hair billowing behind her like a banner in the breeze. "All done?"

"We are," Finley said, stretching his back. "I'm definitely done standing on ladders all day."

"Your watchers have left," she said as they walked slowly through the nearly empty square.

"A couple of hours ago, yeah," Finley agreed. "Did you spot them?"

"Two women and a man. All pretty young."

"Where'd they go?"

"An inn on the edge of the village."

"Well," Finley sighed, "let's ditch these tools and go have a meal."

"What, at the same inn?"

"Don't you think," he said in resignation, "it'll make their jobs easier?"

They deposited the tools in a narrow alley between two shops, and made their way to the inn. A village this size rarely had more than one or two inns, and this was clearly the more prosperous.

As they approached the inn, a weathered wooden sign swung gently in the evening breeze, bearing the name "The Mermaid's Tail" in faded gold lettering. The two-story structure was built of sturdy stone and timber, its walls adorned with climbing ivy and colorful wildflowers that spilled from window boxes. Warm, inviting light poured from the latticed windows, casting a golden glow onto the cobblestone path leading to the entrance.

Finley, Kelden, and Arcadia stepped through the heavy oak door, its iron hinges creaking softly as they entered the bustling common room. The interior was a cozy haven, with exposed wooden beams and a large, stone hearth that crackled with a welcoming fire. The air was filled with the mouthwatering aroma of roasting meats, herbs, and freshly baked bread, mingling with the rich scent of ale and the faint hint of pipe smoke.

Patrons of all sorts filled the room, their laughter and chatter rising and falling like the tides. Fishermen, their skin weathered by the sun and salt, sat at long tables, swapping tales of the day's catch and the mysteries of the deep. Merchants, their fine clothing a stark contrast to the humble attire of the locals, huddled in corners, negotiating deals and exchanging gossip. A group of musicians played a lively tune in the corner, their fiddles, flutes, and drums weaving a tapestry of sound that danced through the air, inviting patrons to tap their feet and clap along.

As Finley, Kelden and Arcadia wove their way through the crowded common room, they spotted an empty table tucked away in a quiet corner. They settled onto the rough-hewn benches, the worn wood smooth beneath their hands. A buxom serving girl with rosy cheeks and a mischievous glint in her eye approached their table, her skirts swishing as she walked.

"What'll it be, my lovelies?" she asked with a wink, her voice carrying over the din.

"Three ales and whatever's on the spit," Finley replied with a charming smile. The girl nodded and sashayed away, leaving them to their thoughts.

Arcadia leaned in, her voice low. "Did you see them when we came in? The watchers from earlier."

Finley nodded almost imperceptibly. "Yeah. Sitting by the hearth, trying to blend in. Not doing a very good job of it, are they?"

Kelden chuckled. "Amateurs. You'd think they'd know better than to stare so blatantly."

The serving girl returned with their drinks, the frothy ale sloshing over the rims of the tankards as she set them down. Finley took a long pull, savoring the rich, malty flavor. Then he set his tankard on the table, looked pointedly at their watchers, and gave them a single, deliberate nod.

The three exchanged glances, and one of the women—a short, sturdily built brunette with hazelnut skin and flashing brown eyes—rose from her seat, walked over to their table, and slid into the single empty chair.

"You've a message? Or questions?" Finley asked bluntly.

"You did something new," the woman said, her voice hard and flat.

Finley shrugged. "Our people have traditions as well. But this won't... hold you back."

"So the others did."

Finley shrugged again.

"We can have those boards replaced."

"You could," Arcadia spoke up. "But then our... *colleagues* will send another group. Probably take more drastic action. If you leave it, they'll leave it as well."

Suspicion was still carved deeply into the woman's expression, but after a few moments of silence, she gave them a curt nod and rose from her seat. She gestured to her companions, and the three of them filed quickly out of the inn.

"You really put nothing in to restrict innovations?" Arcadia whispered.

Finley quickly empowered a rune that guarded their words.

The noise of the pub became muffled. "I put a few. Things we've handled in the past. The printing press. A couple of others. Mainly to see if they work, and if the humans continue to try them. Nothing that is... well, harmless."

"Their printing machines aren't harmful," Arcadia pointed out.

"True, but they're the first thing the Order will notice. We've gone rogue here, you know that, right? We'll be called to account for it."

"I know," Arcadia sighed, sipping her ale. "Word that the church is still standing will get back quickly, and they'll send someone. They'll see your new runes. That's what Ram will want explained." Kelden nodded agreement.

"I... have some ideas in that direction," Finley said. "He knows I'm a Rune Smith. The truth might serve us best, in this instance. That this was the only way we could get anything carved into the church."

"He'll want to know more about your runes."

"Again, I'm... not even sure of them myself. Have either of you tried to use them?"

Kelden nodded. "They seemed to take up readily enough when I was empowering the carvings."

"Not much of a test," Finley mused. "Try one now."

"Like what?"

Finley extended a finger, and with the slightest lick of magic, carved a rune into the scarred tabletop.

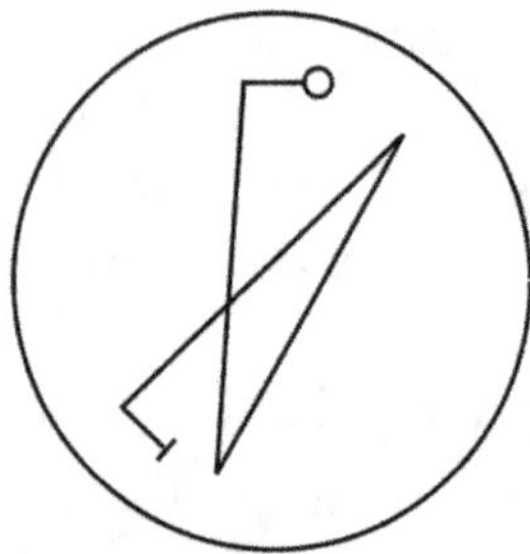

"Sky magic," Arcadia mused.

"You can tell?" Finley asked, surprised.

She nodded slowly. "It... there's kind of a pull. It knows what it needs." Her eyes narrowed and Finley could sense a gentle flow of magic trickling into the rune.

The rich smells of the inn was replaced by a fresh breeze. A few patrons turned to see if the main door had been opened, saw that it was still tightly closed, and shrugged before turning back to their meals and conversations.

The breeze lasted only a moment before Arcadia let it fade.

"Well, that answers that," Finley said quietly. "How did it feel?"

"Weird. I mean, it felt normal. Usual. But also... strange. The shape of it is different. It's the same as *gaivus vejelis?*"

Finley nodded. "Only more efficient."

"I think that's why it felt strange. It's very... to the point. Direct." She frowned. "It's efficient, but there's no beauty to it."

Finley nodded more slowly this time. "Yeah, I can see that."

"It speaks to me," Kelden said very softly.

"The magic?" Arcadia asked, her eyes widening.

"Yes."

"The Origin," Arcadia whispered.

"That's enough," Finley said, draining his tankard and pushing his chair back. "Let's go home."

CHAPTER 12

Flood Control

Ram was off in Evermore again, giving them a brief respite before the grilling they all fully expected to receive. That meant an unexpected three days on the Farm with nothing to do but *relax.* Dmitry gave them an uncharacteristically curt greeting as they handed over their report. "Stay ready," he added sharply.

Which was easy, given that both Arcadia and Finley had completely forgotten how to do anything as prosaic as *relaxing.*

The Farm sprawled across gently rolling hills, a patchwork of green fields and pastures stitched together by weathered wooden fences. The buildings were simple and functional—a sturdy barn with a battered wood-shingle roof, a cozy farmhouse with a wrap-around porch, a few outbuildings for storage and the small livestock that was kept more as a hobby than a profession. The air was crisp and clean, carrying the earthy scents of freshly turned soil, wildflowers, and distant chimney smoke.

Arcadia wandered restlessly through the orchard, the leaves above casting dappled shadows across her face. She plucked an apple from a low-hanging branch and turned it over in her hands, examining its shiny red skin as if it held the secrets of the universe. With a sigh, she took a distracted bite and continued pacing, her mind churning with thoughts that refused to settle.

Finley had claimed a spot on the porch swing, long legs stretched out before him as he rocked back and forth with a steady creak of old chains. A book lay open in his lap but his eyes kept flickering up to scan the horizon, searching for something he couldn't quite define. The peacefulness of the Farm seemed to mock him, a tranquility he couldn't match no matter how hard he tried to slow his racing thoughts.

Even Kelden, usually so unflappable, had an air of tension about him as he walked the perimeter of the Farm, checking the fences with a thoroughness that bordered on obsessive.

They came together for dinner that night, along with a half-dozen others who worked full-time at the Farm as schedulers, support staff, and so on. Dinner was an oddly subdued affair, as if the staff had picked up on their restlessness.

After the quiet meal, Arcadia found herself drawn back to the orchard, the gentle rustling of leaves a soothing whisper in the gathering dusk. She climbed the wooden rungs of the old ladder leaning against one of the larger trees, settling herself on a sturdy branch with her back against the trunk. From this vantage point, she could see the warm glow of lamplight spilling from the farmhouse windows, a beacon of comfort in the darkening landscape.

Finley appeared at the base of the tree, his face tilted up to meet her gaze. "Mind if I join you?"

Arcadia shrugged, scooting over to make room for him on the branch. They sat in silence for a while, listening to the chirping of crickets and the distant hooting of an owl.

"Do you ever wonder," Finley began, his voice barely above

a whisper, "what it would be like to just... stay here? To leave everything behind and just live a simple life?"

Arcadia turned to look at him, surprised by the wistfulness in his tone. "You mean give up on the Order? Give up everything we've worked for?"

"I don't know." Finley sighed, running a hand through his hair. "Sometimes I just feel like we're caught up in something bigger than ourselves, something we can't control."

Before Arcadia could respond, a twig snapped somewhere below them. They both tensed, peering into the shadows.

"Hey," Kelden said quietly.

Arcadia and Finley relaxed at the sight of their friend. "You startled us," Arcadia said, a slight admonishment in her tone.

Kelden's lips quirked into a brief, apologetic smile. "Sorry. I saw you two heading out here and thought I'd join you." He paused, his expression growing more serious. "I couldn't shake the feeling that something's off."

Finley nodded, his brow furrowing. "I know what you mean. It's like there's this... tension in the air. Like something's about to happen."

"But what?" Arcadia asked, frustration edging into her voice. "We're in the middle of nowhere, on a farm that's supposed to be a safe haven. What could possibly happen here?"

"It's this waiting for Ram," Finley sighed. "We're all on edge."

"It's what we'll be sent out to do next," Arcadia added.

"Even Dmitry seems wound tightly," Finley added. "I feel like..."

"Like there's something going on," Arcadia agreed. "Something someone's not telling us."

"Magic is... tense as well," Kelden murmured.

"Tense?" Finley asked.

They nodded. "It always felt like this before the end-of-year ceremonies at school. You knew nothing bad was happening, nothing was *going* to happen, but... magic isn't subtle. Not in that way. When we brought it out for the bonding..." They stopped and shook their head. "Sorry. We're really not supposed to talk about this outside of the school."

"You don't have—" Arcadia began.

"No, you should know. It's just that... for us, for Thornwaithe's, I mean, magic isn't... intelligent. It's this huge, slow-moving, blunt force. If it's threatened, it strikes, but it's a big, clumsy response. That's why so many alum work in areas to try and keep that from happening. Spot threats and deal with them quietly, in small ways."

"Like the Order," Finley said.

They shrugged. "I guess. A little. It's more just... watching. Making sure people don't threaten the Veil. But when we deliberately called on magic, for the bonding ceremonies... it felt like this. Tense."

"Anticipatory," Arcadia said.

Kelden chuckled. "Yeah, maybe that." They turned back toward the farmhouse. "We should go back."

"Face the music," Finley sighed.

"Ram's back, isn't he?" Arcadia asked quietly.

"Had to happen eventually," Finley said. He slid off the tree branch. "Come on."

***

Finley had been in Ram's office only a few times, as the elderly Head of the Order typically sought *him* out when a conversation was needed. But Ram had indeed returned to the Farm, and the moment they'd set foot in the farmhouse, they'd been sent directly to his office.

Arcadia and Kelden followed Finley into Ram's office, and a sense of unease settled in Finley's stomach as he took in the austere surroundings. The room was spartan, with little in the way of decoration or personal touches. The walls were painted a stark white, the only adornment being a single painting hung above the fireplace—a bleak landscape of barren trees and a leaden sky.

A large, heavy desk dominated the center of the room, its dark wood polished to a high shine. Behind it sat Ram, his lined face impassive as he watched Finley enter. Despite the mild weather outside, a fire burned low in the grate, its flames casting flickering shadows across the room. But even the fire seemed cold and uninviting, providing little in the way of warmth or comfort.

Finley's gaze was drawn to the mantelpiece, where a curious collection of objects was displayed. A tarnished brass compass, its needle spinning aimlessly. A small, intricately carved wooden box, its contents a mystery.

Dmitry was there as well, leaning against a wall, his arms crossed and a scowl on his face.

Ram cleared his throat, drawing Finley's attention back to the matter at hand. "Sit," he said, gesturing to the three straight-backed wooden chairs positioned in front of the desk. He grimaced sipped from a heavy mug, steam roiling around his face. "Dmitry, don't we have something less bitter?"

"Healer's orders," Dmitry murmured. "Just drink it." He pulled himself off the wall. "I'll fetch some *kava*. You can have it when you finish that." He stalked out of the office.

The others lowered themselves into the chairs with a shared sense of trepidation. The wood was hard and unyielding, and Finley shifted uncomfortably, trying to find a position that didn't make his spine ache. Arcadia and Kelden seemed equally ill at ease, their postures stiff and their faces carefully neutral.

Ram steepled his fingers, his elbows resting on the desk as he regarded them with inscrutable eyes. "I trust you've enjoyed your respite." The three said nothing. "So. Nek. The church stands."

"We were able to convince the priest to let us carve runes," Finley said.

"I'm told."

Ram stared at them until Kelden, no longer able to stand the silence, offered, "Finley came up with new runes. They look different enough that—"

"I've seen." The room fell into an uneasy silence for several more moments. Finally, Ram cleared his throat and continued in a gentler tone. "A new rune language?" Finley shrugged. "Your talent, then."

"Yes."

"Hmm. Well. Served us well enough, this time. Although I'm curious how you became involved when the assignment was for Arcadia alone."

"They've been thick as thieves again," Dmitry said, returning with a mug of *kava* in one hand. "Just like when they joined." He held the mug until Ram let out a resigned sigh and then downed whatever was in the first mug. Dmitry exchanged mugs, setting the empty one down on a small table to the side of the room before once again crossing his arms and leaning against the wall.

"I knew I needed help," she said firmly. "You know they're watching us. Testing us."

"*They.* You mean the human cabal." Ram's expression grew tight.

"Obviously."

"Mmm. Perhaps. You felt that modifying their holy book, giving reason—"

"They *know* we do that," she said, heat rising in her voice. "It's probably what they expected of us, in fact."

Ram stared at her for a long while and then nodded. "Perhaps. Our book of tricks is too thin, it seems."

I want to try something, Finley's talent said abruptly. Immediately, half-formed runes began flickering in the corner of Finley's mind. He released a thin stream of power into them, watching Ram carefully as the runes glimmered and shifted. A subtle magic began to whirl gently through the room, wafting around Ram, Kelden, and Arcadia. *No way to be more precise about it. Hmm.* His talent seemed mildly displeased with this, but the proto-runes, like nothing Finley had ever seen, continued dancing in his head.

"I've been to see the Taryba," Ram said suddenly. His eyes narrowed at once, as if he'd let something slip he hadn't intended. In the corner of his eye, Finley saw Arcadia's hands clench into fists on her lap. "Councilor Adomaitis." Again, Ram's eyes twitched as if he hadn't meant to offer a name.

"Ram—" Dmitry protested.

"It's fine," Ram snapped.

"And?" Finley prompted.

"The risk of human innovation continues to grow, despite our best efforts. Despite *your* best efforts."

"Some of that innovation—" Arcadia began, but Ram cut her off.

"Is unacceptable. We're to hold the line."

"Our instructions from the Taryba?" Arcadia asked coldly.

"You've grown some love for the humans?" Dmitry asked mockingly.

Finley's stomach clenched. Arcadia had a long dislike of

humans in general, and their shared experiences from school had done nothing but reinforce her distrust.

"Hardly. I simply thought we were an independent Order. If I'd wanted to be employed by the Taryba, I—"

"Witchkind stands as one!" Ram snapped, slapping an open palm on the desk. "We have our remit. Our mission. The Taryba watches over us all. And *humans* threaten us *all*."

Dmitry's nod was shallow, but Finley noticed it regardless.

"Sir," Finley said quickly, seeking to lower the tension in the room, even as whatever his talent was doing continued to eddy around the other three, "has something new happened?"

Ram's lips twitched and he reached into one of the desk's drawers, withdrawing a thick sheaf of papers. Finley recognized them as field dispatches as the old man let them *thump* to the desktop. "Something, yes. Some *things*. Some perhaps innocent. Most perhaps not." He flipped open the top paper. "A farm in Middlevale. River runs through it, floods annually, witchkind protects against the flooding. Now, the farmer is building some *structures* to contain the river."

"They can't build those blocks any—" Finley began.

"She's not using blocks, boy, she's using boulders."

Arcadia frowned. "Then what possible—"

"She won't need magic anymore!" Ram shouted. His eyes were flashing and his face flushed slightly.

Finley glanced at Dmitry, but the older man's expression was unreadable.

"But *she* doesn't know that," Arcadia objected. "So what are we to do? Just—"

"Observe," Ram hissed. "Discover if her actions are hers alone or if they're being *driven*. Directed from without."

"By the cabal," Finley said, realizing where Ram was going.

"Yes," the Head said, calming slightly. "All agents have been told to *observe and report*. No further actions. We go quiet. We see what the humans do, and we discover if they are acting alone or as one."

"This is purely for discovery," Dmitry added, his tone soothing. Ram glanced at him with a scowl.

Convenient timing, Finley thought with relief. If the human cabal held up their end of the nascent compromise, then the only "innovation" would in fact be from humans working alone. Not that that—

"The brickworks," Ram said, interrupting Finley's thoughts.

"It was nothing," he said quickly. "A new bronze alloy. Not especially innovative, even, but it let them spin very thin rods to reinforce the bricks. It won't work well. The metal is still too soft."

Ram gave him a hard stare, but then nodded. Slowly, the runes flickering in Finley's mind began to slow and fade, and the ambient effect in the air faded with them. *What was that?* he asked, but his talent didn't deign to reply.

Finley's eyes darted back to Dmitry, who was again staring back with an inscrutable expression.

"Go," Ram ordered, leaning heavily back in his chair. "All three of you. Middlevale. See to this river. Observe and report."

***

"Ram seems... more," Arcadia said quietly.

Her travel magic had taken them well outside of Middlevale itself, and about a half-mark walk from the edge of the farm. Another thread of her Sky magic had tugged a small cloud over them, cutting off the worst of the midday sun's bright heat.

"I've never seen him so tense," Finley agreed.

"Dmitry seemed worried about him," Kelden added.

"Dmitry's... *hovering*," Arcadia said. "He's never done that before."

"And this connection with the Taryba..." Finley said.

"It's what I said before," Arcadia muttered. "Something's happening, and nobody's telling us. More than just the human cabal and all the inventions. I *hate* not knowing what's going on."

"You don't like the Taryba, do you?" Kelden asked.

Arcadia grimaced. "It's not dislike. It's just that my parents have been on our *local* council for a long time, and the Taryba has been taking on more and more to itself. Stripping the local councils of authority. All in the name of 'protecting' everyone, but they're never clear on exactly what the threat is."

"Sounds like a familiar tune," Finley mused.

"Now that you mention it, it does," Arcadia agreed. "Ram's wound up about *anything* the humans do. You think the Taryba has gotten to him?"

"Or the other way around," Kelden said darkly.

"Save it," Finley sighed. "We're almost there."

As they approached the Middlevale farm, the lush, verdant landscape unfolded before them like a patchwork quilt of vibrant greens and earthy browns. The farm stretched as far as the eye could see, a vast expanse of carefully tended fields and orchards that spoke of generations of hard work and dedication.

The air was filled with the sweet scent of ripening fruits and the earthy aroma of freshly turned soil. Rows upon rows of fruit trees lined the edges of the fields, their branches heavy with plump, juicy apples, pears, and peaches. The leaves rustled gently in the warm breeze, creating a soothing symphony of nature's music.

In the fields, an array of vegetables flourished under the

nurturing sun. Leafy greens, plump tomatoes, and crisp cucumbers grew in neat rows, their colors a vibrant testament to the farm's fertility. The occasional scarecrow stood sentinel, its tattered clothing fluttering in the wind, a whimsical guardian of the crops.

The centerpiece of the farm was the wide, meandering river that cut through the land like a shimmering ribbon. Its crystal-clear waters sparkled in the sunlight, reflecting the azure sky above. The river's gentle current created a soothing sound, a constant murmur that seemed to whisper ancient secrets to those who listened closely.

Along the riverbanks, willow trees draped their long, slender branches into the water, creating secluded spots of dappled shade. Reeds and cattails swayed in the gentle breeze, providing sanctuary to a diverse array of wildlife. Dragonflies darted across the water's surface, their iridescent wings glinting in the sunlight, while frogs croaked their melodic songs from hidden perches.

As they drew closer to the heart of the farm, Finley, Arcadia, and Kelden could see the massive boulders that had been hauled into place along the riverbank. The stones were arranged with meticulous care, forming a sturdy barrier against the river's seasonal flooding. It was an impressive feat of engineering, a testament to human ingenuity and determination. As they watched, a horse-drawn cart was being maneuvered into place, its bed laden with another enormous boulder. Two men jumped out of the cart and began working with stout levers to roll the giant rock out onto the ground.

The cart's driver caught sight of them and frowned slightly. They realized, in the inexplicable way of witchkind, that the driver was one of them. She hopped down from the driver's box, said something they didn't catch to the two workers, and began walking toward them.

"Help you?" she asked as she neared, wiping dust from her hands.

She was tall and lean, with skin the rich, deep brown of freshly tilled earth. Her face was angular and striking, with high cheekbones and a proud, aquiline nose. Her eyes, a startling shade of amber, seemed to hold both the warmth of the sun and the sharpness of a hawk's gaze.

She wore simple, practical clothing that spoke of a life spent working the land. A loose-fitting shirt of cream-colored linen hung from her broad shoulders, the sleeves rolled up to reveal strong, sinewy forearms. Her trousers, made of a sturdy brown fabric, were tucked into well-worn leather boots that bore the scuffs and stains of countless hours in the fields.

Around her waist, she wore a wide belt of supple leather, its buckle a simple brass clasp that gleamed in the sunlight. From the belt hung an assortment of tools - a small, sharp knife for pruning, a coil of twine, and a pouch that likely held seeds or other small necessities.

Her hair, a mass of tight, springy curls, was pulled back from her face with a brightly colored scarf, its vibrant hues of red and orange standing out in stark contrast to her dusky skin. A few stubborn curls had escaped their confinement, framing her face with a halo of dark, kinky locks.

"I'm Finley," Finley said, nodding politely. "My friends, Arcadia and Kelden. We'd caught wind of this... project, and wanted to take a look. My parents have worked on sea walls for my whole life, but I'd never heard of a... what do you call it?"

"I'm Agne," the woman said, her face splitting in a wide grin. "And believe me, this was a new one on me as well. The owner of the farm's very own idea. She's calling it a riverwall."

"And you're not... you know. Helping?" Kelden asked.

Agne's grin grew even wider. "Nope. Not a trickle of magic. Which, I will tell you, I'm no little amount of grateful for."

"Oh?" Arcadia asked with surprise. "Why so?"

"Magic's thick enough out here," Agne said with a sigh.

You're welcome, Finley's talent said. Finley thought he detected a trace of irony in the statement.

"But we use an awful lot of it," Agne continued, "keeping the nutrients in the soil. There are five others of witchkind here, including my husband and son. Like most of the fields, the owner doesn't know much about soil health. We're all Earth-affinity, though, so we can *feel* it. I will tell you, it is no small task keeping these fields fertile. When the spring floods come, and sometimes in the fall, dealing with that river is the last thing any of us want. Not one of us has Sea affinity anyway."

"So how'd you tame it?" Finley asked.

"Carve a trough through the bottom where it's worst," Agne replied. "Doesn't hold more than a few months, although that's usually enough. Wasn't last year, which is what got Roze —she's the owner—thinking. We might still have to tough out the riverbed a bit when it's really bad, but she's planning to build it up to a full man's height where it tends to flood the worst, and that'll get us through most years."

Finley and Arcadia exchanged a quick glance. "Is she— Roze, that is—does she usually have ideas like this on her own?"

Agne tilted her head. "She does. She's quite clever for someone with as little formal education as she's had." Then her eyes narrowed. "But you're dancing around a question, young man. Ask plainly."

"It's just... well, there have been a lot of 'innovations' recently. Especially in the cities. Things that would reduce their reliance on... us. We've been looking into some of them, and sometimes they're coming to people who've never shown a creative or clever idea in their lives."

Agne nodded slowly. "That would be worrying. But not the case here. Roze doesn't take many guests. Her hands do all the carting and trading for her. And she's *damned* clever, if you ask me. If anything, we've had to hold her back a bit."

"Oh?" Arcadia asked, intrigued.

"Couple seasons back, she came up with this idea for a tiller that could be hitched to a team of horses. All bronze. Could till up a quarter of a field in one pass."

"And that's... bad?" Kelden asked, confused.

Agne laughed. "It is if you're the one moving soil around under the surface to even out the nutrients. She'd have outworked us by half. We started moving smaller rocks up closer to the surface—tore up the blades on the prototype she build. Eventually she gave up and we put everything back the way it was."

That's what the Order should *be doing,* Finley thought wearily. "Well. I suppose we'll leave you to it, then. Although... purely out of family interest, would you mind if we stayed and watched a while?"

"No problem. I'll let the boys know you're no problem. There's another couple of wagons coming in, so plenty to see." She smiled. "Good day, then."

"Good day," Arcadia said, matching the older woman's smile. "Thank you."

Agne bobbed a quick nod and hurried back to her cart, which was now empty. The two workers were wiping their brows and making plans to roll their boulder to an empty space in the growing wall, as Agne climbed aboard her cart and drove it off.

As Agne drove her empty cart back toward the distant barns, a second horse-drawn cart came trundling down the dirt path toward the riverbank. This cart was piled high with two boulders, each one slightly smaller than the massive stone the first two workers had just wrestled into place, but still impressively large. The cart's wooden wheels creaked and groaned under the weight of its heavy cargo as the sturdy draft horse plodded forward, its muscles rippling beneath its gleaming chestnut coat.

Two new workers walked alongside the cart, their faces glistening with sweat in the warm afternoon sun. They were both broad-shouldered men with sun-weathered skin and calloused hands that spoke of years of hard labor. One wore a faded blue shirt with the sleeves rolled up past his elbows, revealing arms corded with lean muscle. The other had a red bandana tied around his neck, the knot resting at the hollow of his throat.

As the cart drew closer to the growing wall, the workers guided the horse to a stop. One of them unhitched the animal from its traces and led it a short distance away, where it could rest in the shade of a towering oak tree. The other worker climbed up into the cart bed and began the arduous process of unloading the boulders.

These workers seemed to be better-equipped than the first pair.

He worked a thick leather strap around the first boulder, securing it tightly before attaching the other end to a sturdy metal hook. This hook was in turn connected to a series of pulleys and ropes that had been rigged up to a nearby tree. The worker gave a sharp whistle, and two more men emerged from the shade, each grabbing hold of a rope. Together, the three of them began to heave and strain, slowly lifting the boulder out of the cart.

Finley watched the process with rapt attention, marveling at the ingenuity and cooperation on display. The boulder swayed gently as it was hoisted into the air, the ropes creaking under the immense weight. Slowly, carefully, the workers guided the suspended stone over to the wall, lowering it into place with a dull thud that sent a small cloud of dust billowing into the air.

As the first boulder settled into position, the workers wasted no time in moving on to the second. They repeated the process with practiced efficiency, their movements synchronized and purposeful. Finley couldn't help but admire their skill and dedication. Building a wall of this magnitude was no small feat, and yet these men tackled the task with a resolute determination that bordered on the inspiring.

Arcadia, too, seemed impressed by the display. She watched the workers with a keen eye, her brow furrowed in concentration as she studied their techniques. "They make it look so easy," she murmured, almost to herself. "But the amount of strength and coordination required..."

Kelden nodded in agreement. "And to think they're doing it all without magic. It's remarkable, really."

"Are they?" Arcadia said, squinting at the activity.

Try this, Finley's talent suggested.

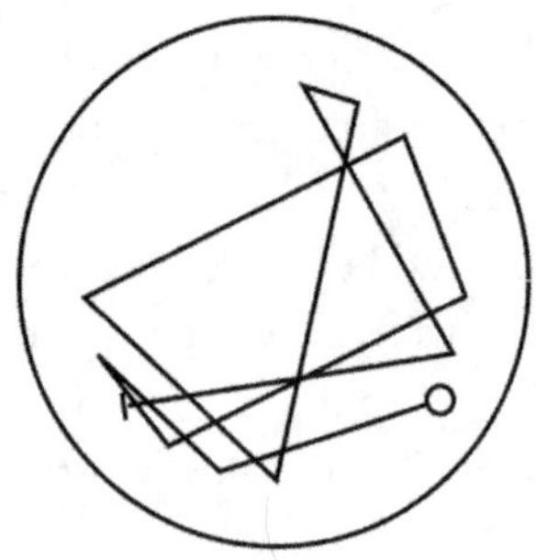

Finley fed the rune with magic, noting that it didn't seem picky about which affinity it received. The workers, the boulders, and the workers' equipment came into sharp focus as the magic went to work. He looked closely, but didn't see any signs of runes—traditional or otherwise. "They are," he said softly. "Not a rune in sight."

"So Ram's right," Arcadia said. "They don't need us."

"Weren't you the one talking about our magic being enslaved to humans' incompetence?" Finley asked wryly. "But we're the ones making it that way."

"I did," Arcadia admitted. "I mean for... everyday things. Ongoing things. But... they don't need us for *this*. I wouldn't have imagined it."

"It's not that strange," Kelden said. "I grew up in Carvendam. They use the same things, the ropes and pulleys, for moving lumber up the city's dam for repairs." He shrugged. "And that's *with* runes on the timber to resist wear. Even magic isn't permanent."

"Mmm," Arcadia murmured.

"We've seen enough, here?" Finley asked. "No sign of the cabal driving this, just a clever farmer and hard workers?"

"More the latter than the former," Arcadia sighed. "But yes."

One of the workers turned and gave them a curious look as they turned to go.

CHAPTER 13

Carronade

They returned to a Farm in chaos.

People were running everywhere, from the main farmhouse to the outbuildings used for storage and training. Travel magics were being used so frequently, and in such close proximity, that an acrid heaviness permeated the air.

Finley's heart began beating faster and his vision seemed to sharpen as even his talent became more alert.

"What's happening?" Arcadia asked, grabbing the arm of the first person who hurried past within her reach.

"Guys..." Kelden said, their voice low and urgent.

They ignored him as the woman began speaking. "There's an emergency. And Ram's fallen ill. We're to—"

Finley didn't hear the rest as he invoked his own travel magic, directing it to take him to wherever Ram was.

That turned out to be Ram's office, where the normally sturdy old man was being helped into his chair. Dmitry glanced up sharply as Finley arrived. The three people helping Ram—Finley recognized only Ella, the Order's young Healer—were focused entirely on getting him situated. Ram's skin was ashen, his eyes bleary, and his hands trembling.

"Finley," Dmitry snapped, stepping over to him. "This isn't a good—"

"What happened?" Finley asked.

"You know the pressure he's been under," Dmitry muttered, glancing back at Ram. Ella was holding her hands over the old man's forehead, doubtless invoking some rune or other. Finley's talent seemed to sniff at the air, trying to catch the scent of whatever magic was being used.

"Someone said something about an emergency."

"Yes. Lakewood. We got an urgent report of another carronade."

"Another—that's impossible! The church runes—"

"Seemed to have missed this one," Dmitry snapped.

"The Taryba," Ram said loudly. "I must—"

"Stay right where you are," Ella insisted. "Dmitry, I could use your help, here. Keep him calm."

"Go be useful," Dmitry said, turning from Finley.

More magic took Finley back to Arcadia and Kelden.

"How is he?" Arcadia asked.

"He doesn't look good. Stress. Ella is with him. Arcadia, Dmitry said there was a carronade. In Lakewood."

Her eyes widened. "They said they wouldn't—"

"Go find someone. Dmitry's busy with Ram. Tell them we're going, and to not send anyone else."

"Guys," Kelden repeated, their voice tense.

"What?" Finley asked as Arcadia's magic whisked her away.

"Something is happening."

"I know, it's—"

"No," Kelden insisted. "With magic."

Finley's eyes widened.

He's right, his talent said, its tone filled with alarm. You need to go.

<hr>

Finley's magic took them to the outskirts of Lakewood, where the dense construction began to thin. "It would have to be here," Finley said, pointing to the metalsmith's shop at the edge of town. An uncanny sense of déjà vu washed over Finley as he took in the scene before him. The shop appeared abandoned, its windows dark and door slightly ajar, swaying gently in the breeze. Rusted tools and scraps of twisted metal littered the ground around the building.

"This feels...familiar somehow," Arcadia murmured, her brow furrowed. She took a tentative step forward, leaves crunching beneath her boots. "Like we've been here before."

"The building looks the same, doesn't it?" Finley agreed.

"It's a smithy," Kelden said. "They all look the same."

"One of our first missions for the Order," Arcadia said quietly, "was in a shop very much like this one. It was also abandoned. Or looked like it. And it contained a carronade."

"It was a trap," Finley added.

"I don't know what a carronade is," Kelden said.

"A long, thick, heavy tube made of cast iron," Finley explained. "Closed at one end. Meant to be packed with black powder, and topped with an iron ball. Light the powder—"

"A weapon, then," Kelden said dourly.

"A weapon," Arcadia agreed. "Finley, this has to be a trap. We can't—"

"I'll go," Kelden said striding forward.

"You can't!" Arcadia said, grabbing for his arm and missing. "I can feel the iron from—"

"He's fine," Finley said, pulling her back. "He's immune."

"Imm—what does that even mean, 'he's immune?'"

"His magic isn't affected by iron. No, I don't know how," he added as Arcadia opened her mouth to speak. "But I tested it. He can still use his magic. He thinks it has something to do with Thornwaithe's, although I've never heard of anyone else being immune to iron."

They watched as Kelden approached the smithy's open door. He pulled it open wider and peered inside. "It's empty," he called back. "There are stacks of iron bars in here, but the forge is cold." He let the door swing partly shut. "Whatever was here is gone."

Interesting, Finley's talent mused.

Finley turned, gazing back toward the heart of Lakewood. The town was a charming picture of bustling activity, belying the grim purpose that had brought them here. Cobbled streets wound between busy shops and simple homes constructed of sturdy timber and fieldstone, their wood-shingled roofs glinting in the midday sun. Townsfolk in colorful garb strolled the avenues, pausing to peruse the wares displayed in shop windows or to exchange friendly greetings.

The air was filled with a symphony of sounds—the clopping of horse hooves on the cobbles, the creak of wagon wheels, the lilting melodies of songbirds in the trees lining the streets. Delectable aromas wafted from the open doors of bakeries and taverns, hinting at savory meat pies and hearty stews within.

At the center of town, an impressive fountain carved of rosy granite burbled merrily, the spray casting miniature rainbows in the air. Flower sellers hawked brilliant blooms from baskets and bouquets were thrust into the hands of sweethearts.

"I doubt they rolled it into town," Arcadia murmured.

"It's getting worse," Kelden said tensely, rejoining them.

"I want to see," Finley said, turning back to the smithy. He envisioned the rune that would bottle up his magic, protect it from being pulled away by the greedy iron.

We need to come up with something better than that, his talent grumbled, its voice muffled and distant in Finley's mind.

Finley stepped cautiously through the doorway into the smithy, his senses on high alert. The interior was dim, illuminated only by thin shafts of sunlight filtering through gaps in the weathered walls. Dust motes danced lazily in the beams, and the air hung heavy with the tang of iron and coal.

The main space at the center of the smithy was indeed empty, as Kelden had reported. An anvil stood solitary and silent, its surface marred by countless dings from hammering. Tongs, hammers, and other tools hung on racks along the walls, coated in a thin layer of rust. The forge sat cold and dark, ashes from its last firing scattered across the brick floor.

Yet as Finley's eyes adjusted to the gloom, he noticed signs that the smithy had been recently active. A few embers still glowed faintly in the depths of the forge. Water droplets glistened on the inside of a slack tub, as if something hot had been plunged into it not long ago. Scraps of metal lay strewn across a workbench, hastily abandoned.

In the far corner of the smithy, partially obscured by shadows, Finley spotted the remnants of what appeared to be a massive mold. He approached cautiously, his boots crunching on the scattered debris littering the floor.

The mold had clearly been used to cast something immense —a cylindrical object at least ten feet in length. He noted piles of sand, iron bands, and wooden staves.

The sand was the color of tarnished brass, flecked with glittering bits of mica that caught the dim light. It lay in haphazard heaps around the mold, as if hastily shoveled aside once the casting was complete. Finley knelt and scooped up a handful, letting the grains trickle through his fingers. It was cool to the touch.

Thick iron bands, their surfaces pitted with rust, lay discarded among the sand piles. They had served to reinforce the mold, ensuring it could withstand the immense pressure and heat of the molten iron. Some of the bands were bent and twisted, testament to the incredible forces at play during the casting process.

Shattered remnants of wooden staves were scattered throughout the debris. The staves had been used to create the initial shape of the mold, arranged in a cylindrical framework and then packed with sand.

"But what will they fire it with?" he murmured.

"Here," Arcadia said.

Finley turned quickly, surprised that she'd followed him in. Kelden was behind her, and they were peering at a small barrel that sat on a worktable, which ran the length of one wall.

Finley crossed to the worktable, leaning in to examine the small barrel. It was crafted of dark, oily wood, the staves bound together by iron rings that showed spots of rust. A crude plug of waxed cork sealed the bunghole at the top.

Arcadia gingerly pried the plug loose with her fingernail, and a sharp, acrid scent immediately assaulted Finley's nostrils. He recoiled slightly, blinking as the fumes stung his eyes. The odor was reminiscent of rotting fruit mixed with harsh chemicals, with an underlying tang of something almost metallic.

Peering into the opening, Finley saw that the barrel was filled nearly to the brim with a viscous, oily liquid. It had a sickly yellowish tinge, like spoiled milk, and seemed to emit an unsettling greenish sheen where the dim light struck its surface. Noxious-looking vapors curled lazily from the liquid, dissipating into the musty air of the smithy.

"What in the Origin is that?" Kelden asked, warily eyeing the barrel's contents.

"I'm not certain," Finley replied, "but I'd wager it's some sort of explosive concoction. Not black powder, but something more volatile and unstable."

He dipped a finger into the liquid and quickly withdrew it, rubbing the substance between his thumb and forefinger. It felt slick and greasy, with a consistency akin to thick syrup. As Finley rubbed it between his fingers, the liquid seemed to tingle and burn slightly against his skin, as if it contained some caustic agent.

"Don't touch it!" Arcadia exclaimed, grabbing Finley's wrist and pulling his hand away from the barrel. "We have no idea what that stuff could do. It smells awful."

Finley nodded, wiping his fingers clean on a scrap of dirty cloth lying on the worktable. "You're right. Whatever this is, it's clearly not meant for any good purpose."

Kelden leaned in closer, sniffing tentatively at the open bunghole. They immediately recoiled, coughing and sputtering as the acrid vapors assaulted their throat and lungs. "Gah, that's foul! It's like inhaling pure evil."

Can we stop it? Finley asked in his mind. Like we did with the black powder?

I don't know how this works, his talent said, its voice still muffled. I might need to see it in action.

Let's hope we don't, Finley said grimly. "We need to find out where they've taken the carronade," he said aloud, replacing the cork plug and sealing the barrel once more. "And what they intend to do with it."

"It must have been huge," Kelden observed, pointing to the piles of sand and broken staves. "How would they even move it?"

"On a cart," Finley said, pointing down. A set of wheel

tracks cut through the soot and grime on the floor, leading from the center of the space toward a large sliding door at the rear of the building. The heavy barn-style door was latched firmly shut.

"We can follow the tracks," Arcadia said, heading for the open door.

They emerged into the bright light, blinking as their eyes adjusted.

The road stretched out before them, a winding ribbon of hard-packed earth that disappeared into the distant horizon. The midday sun beat down mercilessly, casting shimmering heat waves that distorted the air and made the landscape seem to ripple and dance. Dust kicked up by passing carts and horses hung suspended in the still air, creating a hazy veil that softened the edges of everything.

Finley squinted against the glare, his eyes watering as he scanned the road for any sign of the carronade's passage. But the surface was a confusing jumble of tracks—deep ruts carved by the wheels of heavily laden wagons, the delicate imprints of horse hooves, the scuffed indentations of countless human feet. The intricate web of markings overlaid and crisscrossed each other, rendering any individual track indistinguishable from the rest.

A farmer's cart trundled past, pulled by a plodding mule. The weathered boards of the cart were heaped high with plump orange pumpkins, their thick stems curling like vines. A few stray wisps of straw poked out from between the pumpkins, and the earthy scent of fresh produce mingled with the dust in the air. The farmer tipped his broad-brimmed hat to Finley and his companions as he passed, his sun-browned face creasing into a friendly smile.

"So much for that," Arcadia groused. "How much of a head start do you think they have?"

"A day. Two at the most," Kelden said.

"How can you tell?" Arcadia asked.

"There's a rune that tells you when a place was last occupied."

"Oh. Handy. Do you think they kept to the road, then?" Arcadia asked.

"For at least a way," Kelden said, although they didn't sound certain. "I don't know why—"

Finley turned back to the smithy. "Oh, no."

"What?" Arcadia asked.

"What's due north of here?"

She frowned as she considered. The downside of using magic to take you everywhere is that the actual geography of the world becomes less relevant to you.

Her eyes widened as she realized the answer.

"Evermore," Kelden said grimly. "We need to hurry."

The difficulty with iron, Finley's talent groused, is that you can't track the stuff directly. Glowing lines and curves shimmered and snapped in his mind as his talent tried combination after combination.

"How could they have recreated a carronade?" Arcadia asked. She'd used her magic to jump them toward Evermore in small increments, hoping they could catch some sign of the humans and their weapon before the trade road turned east.

"Instructions on iron sheets," Finley said distractedly as his talent wrestled with the problem. "We didn't do anything to make them forget. We just made it bad enough we hoped they'd regret it."

"You left a crater, true," Arcadia said. "But you said black powder wouldn't be explosive anymore."

It can't be, his talent confirmed.

"Whatever was in that little barrel is obviously the replacement," Finley said. "How far do you think they stayed to the trade road?"

"Not far," Kelden said, their voice flat. "They're heading toward Evermore."

"You're certain?" Finley asked.

"It's... yes. We're being summoned. That's the only reason we would be."

"This is the cabal, then," Arcadia said.

"It has to be," Finley said.

"I—" Kelden started. They turned, and saw the life drain out of their expression, their face going flat and hard and their jaw clenching shut. With a snap, their magic carried them away.

This is a very strange sensation, Finley's talent said. Something is very angry.

If you're the Origin, can you stop this? Finley demanded.

I don't actually know what's happening, it replied. I can feel it, but this isn't... this is older. Something more basic. The image of an inhuman face flashed in Finley's mind for less than a heartbeat. He had a brief impression of deep blue skin, sharply angled ears, glossy black hair, and an expression of incalculable anger twisting its lips. It's calling them. It won't tolerate an attack on Evermore.

"We can't track iron, but we can track him," Arcadia said tightly. Before Finley could respond, Sky magic closed around them.

They arrived in a wide meadow bordered by dense forest. Finley didn't recognize it.

About halfway to Evermore, his talent supplied.

Finley and Arcadia stood at the edge of the meadow, taking in the alarming scene before them. The carronade was an imposing sight—a massive iron tube nearly ten feet long and two feet in diameter, its muzzle aimed ominously forward. The weapon sat heavily upon a sturdy wooden carriage with thick iron-banded wheels that had carved deep ruts into the soft earth during the arduous journey off the main road. Smaller crates and barrels lined the sides of the cart on either side of the enormous weapon.

A team of six powerful draft horses strained against their harnesses, their coats lathered with sweat from the exertion of hauling the tremendous weight. The animals rolled their eyes and tossed their heads, clearly agitated by the tension crackling in the air. Leather leads creaked as the horses stamped and snorted.

Tending to the horses and the carronade were a group of humans, their faces set with grim determination. They moved with practiced efficiency, checking the carronade's mounting, inspecting the carriage's axles and wheels. One man held a long rod, doubtless intended to be used as a rammer once the weapon was loaded. Another gripped a blazing torch in one white-knuckled fist, the orange flames dancing and sputtering in the breeze.

The men themselves were a ragtag bunch, dressed in an assortment of rough woolen trousers, sweat-stained linen shirts, and tattered coats that had seen better days. Despite their threadbare appearance, they carried themselves with an air of purpose, their eyes glinting with a fervor that sent a chill down Finley's spine. These were not mere peasants or laborers—they were true believers, zealots willing to risk everything for their cause.

Arrayed before them were a dozen of witchkind, their dull-colored clothes livened with colorful scarves, belts, hair ties, and more. Their postures were rigid, their faces masks of cold, hard fury. They seemed to vibrate with barely restrained energy, all of their hands clenched into fists at their sides. Kelden stood near the center of the line, which was clearly a message to the humans: Come no further. Turn back.

"Kelden!" Arcadia called out, her voice cracking with desperation. "What are you doing?"

"It's Thornwaithe's," Finley murmured. "It's magic. He's not himself."

A strange, undefinable, indescribable pressure began building around them.

CHAPTER 14

Attack on Evermore

Whether the humans felt it or not, Finley couldn't know, but they clearly recognized an attack, and wasted no time. Four of them reached under the huge carronade and pulled out... something. Finley didn't recognize the devices, but they had the unmistakable menace of weapons.

They were shaped like a capital T, with a thick stock and a short, stout bow mounted crosswise at the end. The bow was made of gleaming metal, tightly strung with what looked like thin wire. A groove ran along the top of the stock, and nestled in it was a short, stubby arrow, its tip wickedly barbed.

One of the humans hoisted the weapon to his shoulder, sighting along the groove. With a sharp twang, the bow released, and the arrow leapt forward, almost too fast for Finley to follow. It struck one of the Thornwaithe's alum square in the chest with a meaty thunk. The man crumpled soundlessly to the ground, blood gushing from the wound.

The other three humans let fly as well, and two more of the alum fell, pierced by the deadly bolts.

It happened faster than Finley could blink once.

Crossbows, his talent supplied. *I don't know why I know that. They're...* right *here, somehow. Notwithstanding,* it added, and a new rune flashed into Finley's mind.

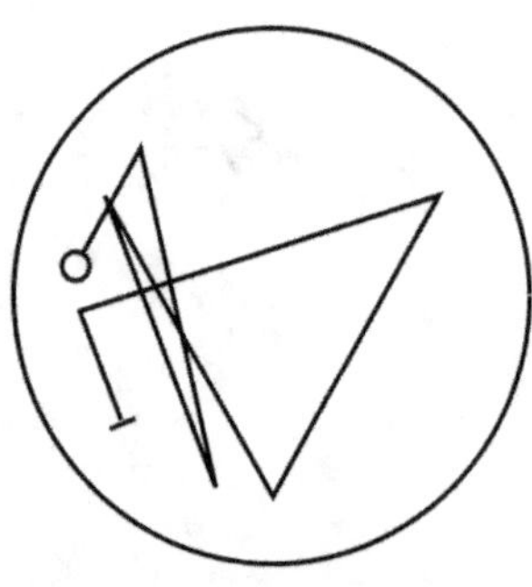

I'm liking this technique, it said abstractedly as Finley poured magic into the rune.

Purple fire sparked off the metal parts of the crossbows, but the wooden stocks and sharply curved bows instantly burst into flames. The humans shouted with alarm, dropping the weapons as the wood components crumbled into ash and sparks continued to cascade from the metal remains.

Arcadia was taking action as well: Sharp lances of Sky magic threshed through the ankle-high grass of the meadow, arrowing toward the horse's hooves. The horses panicked, rearing and screaming, letting the cart roll back a foot or so into the ruts it had created in the soft earth. "Kelden!" she shouted. "Look—"

***

. . .

"—out!"

Kelden heard the distant, fuzzy warning through the cold, pounding anger that filled his mind. It was unnecessary, irrelevant: all that mattered was the existential, intolerable threat before him. All that mattered was the insult of being attacked by iron bolts, sharp metal spears that drove through the wall of pure magic that should have protected them and their fellows. They felt their lips peel back from his teeth in a snarl, as if it was something happening to someone else.

A prickle of magic heralded the arrival of a half-dozen more Thornwaithe's alum. Replacements and reinforcements, although at a cost: Kelden could already feel magic's pressure lessening as it redistributed itself across them all. This, they knew, was the downside to how Thornwaithe's worked. More alum meant more magic could be channeled, but that magic's focus would be spread thinner, forcing its responses to less nuanced approaches.

Right now, the alum needed to spread out, encircle the threat and crush it back into the earth from whence it had come, but the sheer mass of iron before them was playing havoc with magic itself. Kelden could feel magic prodding them all to *move,* while at the same time it gnashed its teeth at the interference from the immense amount of iron before them.

Kelden's eyes gleamed with magical fury as they surveyed the scene before them. The huge iron carronade loomed like a malevolent presence, its bulk distorting the very fabric of magic. Sickly green and purple sparks sputtered and danced across its pitted surface, the semi-sentient magic of the Thornwaithe's alum now vainly trying to corrode and destroy the offensive metal. But the carronade resisted, an impenetrable bastion against the onslaught. Kelden could feel the magic moving through them, its direction and purpose set not by runes but by magic's own frustration and fear. But they could also feel the iron pushing back, sucking their power into itself and grounding it into the earth. Magic that could have destroyed an entire fishing fleet in a heartbeat was barely sufficient to create a light patina on the carronade's surface.

The humans had retreated to huddle in the shadow of their weapon, clearly realizing it afforded them some measure of protection against the alum's invisible attack. They crouched there like frightened rabbits, eyes wide and chests heaving. One clutched a blackened crossbow stock to his chest like a talisman.

Beyond them, magic swirled in iridescent eddies, pushed back by the carronade's presence. It pulsed angrily, a seething morass of barely restrained power seeking any outlet for its rage. Kelden could feel it beating against their skin like a living thing, demanding vengeance, demanding blood, demanding an end to this assault on witchkind.

They took a step forward, their boots crushing the scorched grass to ash. The magic rippled outward from their feet in visible waves, like the surface of a still pond disturbed by a cast stone. It lapped against the carronade and recoiled, repulsed.

***

"We need those humans alive," Finley said with a grimace. "We need to find out where this came from. Where it's going."

"Tell that to them," Arcadia said through gritted teeth. "Ah-ah," she added, sending a burst of air toward the human still holding the sputtering torch. The flame blew out just as the man managed to touch it to the back of the carronade.

"That thing's loaded," Finley realized with alarm. Then he remembered the small barrels of foul-smelling, oily liquid. "Arcadia, those little barrels—"

Her eyes widened in alarm. "Kelden!" she shouted again.

***

"Kelden!"

The cry was even more muffled as the magic in the meadow continued to build, as magic itself found more of its focus and energy. It vectored around the carronade, bright wisps darting around the iron, likely visible even to the humans who were conversing quickly, trying to device a response.

Kelden's jaw clenched tighter. More alum had been summoned, but the magic had reached a balancing point with the huge tube of iron, and travel magics sparked and failed as the additional alum tried to arrive. They'd be lying in pain wherever they'd originated—assuming they weren't injured or worse. Kelden pressed against the magic's dull intelligence. *Have them arrive further out,* they insisted. *They can run the rest of the way.* But they had no sense that the magic had heard them, let alone understood the tactic.

***

Finley set off at a run, heading for the carronade.

"Finley!" Arcadia shouted.

Magic here is getting very strange right now, Finley's talent warned him. It started forming a defensive rune in his mind, but the flickering lines couldn't seem to settle into a suitable pattern. Even Finley's personal magic roiled within him, upset by the magical storm happening around him and by the implacable magic-sink of the carronade he was sprinting toward.

He heard Arcadia sprinting behind him.

***

The magic tried a new attack, funneling immeasurable amounts of pure mystical energy through the alum. Kelden's head rocked back as every muscle in his body tried to contract at once in response to the rush of power. If it couldn't surround the threat and crush it as it usually did, then the magic would attempt to overwhelm it, blasting it to pieces in a single mighty blow.

It almost worked.

***

The horses were obliterated, situated as they were in front of the carronade. Finley and Arcadia threw themselves to the ground as a torrent of gore rushed past overhead. With a *crack*, the wooden cart shattered into a billion shards and splinters, shredding into the humans who'd taken refuge behind the carronade. The enormous metal tube itself crashed to the ground with a heavy *thump* that both Finley and Arcadia felt through the earth. Magic, visible as coruscating red and purple lighting, sparked from the carronade, the metal fittings of the cart, and the iron bands that had once wrapped around the rims of the cart's wheels.

The small barrels exploded.

The world erupted in a cataclysm of sound and fury.

Finley and Arcadia were flung backwards as if swatted by the hand of an angry giant, tumbling end over end through the air. The shockwave hit them like a physical blow, crushing the breath from their lungs. Finley's ears rang with a shrill, unending tone, all other noise drowned out by the deafening roar of the explosion.

The ground where the cart had stood was simply gone, replaced by a smoldering crater twenty feet across. Dirt and rocks rained down from the heavens, torn free and launched skyward by the titanic blast. Flaming chunks of wood pinwheeled through the air, the sad remnants of the sturdy cart transmuted in an instant to blazing projectiles.

Of the iron carronade, there was no sign. The immense tube must have been blown to atoms, vaporized by the unimaginable forces unleashed upon it. Only a twisted, molten stub of metal protruded from the center of the crater to mark its passing.

The humans had fared little better. Three charred corpses littered the edge of the crater, blasted beyond all recognition. Scraps of smoldering clothing and lumps of seared flesh were all that remained, still smoking in the aftermath of the explosion. Dark blood pooled beneath them, already attracting buzzing flies.

But against all odds, one man still lived. He lay on his back a dozen yards from the crater's edge, chest heaving as he gasped for air. His clothing was tattered and scorched, and blood seeped from a myriad of cuts and gashes. But his eyes were open, staring blankly at the smoke-filled sky.

Finley struggled to his feet, head still ringing from the blast. He stumbled towards the prone figure, Arcadia close behind. As they approached, the man's eyes flickered towards them, struggling to focus. His lips moved, forming words they couldn't hear over the persistent whine in their ears.

Finley knelt beside him, hands moving automatically to staunch the worst of the bleeding. The man weakly batted at his hands, still trying to speak. Finley leaned closer, straining to make out the words.

"...can't...stop..." the man wheezed, blood bubbling at the corner of his mouth. "More...coming...witches...will fall..."

A chill ran down Finley's spine at the ominous words. He exchanged a grim look with Arcadia. If this man spoke the truth...

"We need answers," Arcadia breathed.

"He's barely alive," Finley said. "I'm no good with the Healing runes—"

"Won't work on them anyway," she reminded him.

"Dust, I forgot. How can we—"

Clay is malleable, his talent mused.

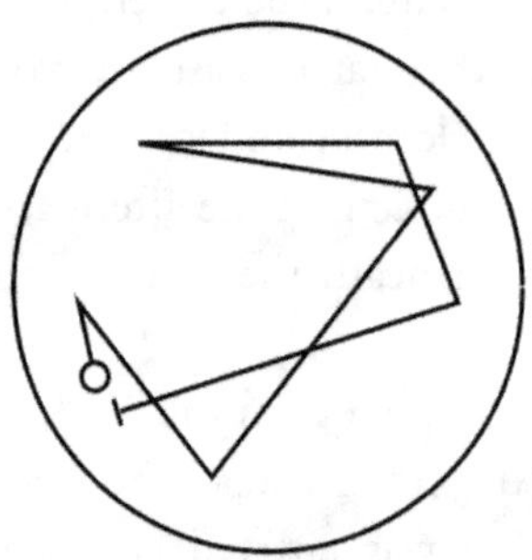

Finley didn't question it, and began pouring magic through the rune. It spread from his hands, settling over the injured human like a blanket. Instantly, a thousand thin cuts began to close.

"How—" Arcadia began.

Humans don't ground magic. I explained that. They're full of it. It actually comes from them, so strongly it drowns out almost anything you can do to them. It starts at the roots of the world, and fountains through the—well, we can discuss that later. But it's connected to their bones. If you're very careful, and if you use the right mix of Earth and Sky, you can heal the flesh. Not completely, but... enough.

The voice faded, as if that exposition had tired it. Finley relayed what it had told him to Arcadia.

"That's... incredible. As in I very literally don't know if I can believe it. And... it's talking to you that much now?"

"Entire sentences," Finley said wearily as the healing magic finished its work. "You," he said as the human opened his eyes. "Where were you going?"

The man shook his head slightly, his chest still heaving.

I can make him talk, Finley's talent offered.

I'm all but empty, he pointed out. The healing rune had taken more of his magic than he'd expected, and the local magic was still in disarray, unwilling to be Gathered.

"Are you both okay?" Kelden said, coming over and kneeling behind them.

"I should ask the same of you," Arcadia said.

"It's... gone. For now. I think... I didn't know it was possible, but I think it may have overexerted itself. But the carronade isn't going to move, so I guess the threat is over." You," they said, reaching past Finley to shake the man. "Where were you going?"

"I'd answer him," Finley suggested. "He's the one who did that to your weapon."

Kelden cocked an eyebrow but didn't offer a contradiction.

The man's eyes had widened. "We were told iron..."

"Some of us are immune," Kelden said, truthfully enough. "Where were you going? I won't ask again."

"Witch city," the man coughed, closing his eyes.

The three exchanged worried glances. "You know about that?" Arcadia asked.

"Scouted for weeks."

"And you were going to attack it?" Finley asked.

The man nodded silently, eyes still closed.

"How did you know how to build this?" Arcadia asked.

The man grinned weakly. "Can't steal our knowledge anymore," he whispered.

"Someone gave you the plans?"

No response.

"On iron sheets?"

His eyes flickered open and he looked at her. Then he attempted a shrug and let his eyes fall closed.

"You were supposed to stop," Finley said tightly, in as low a voice as possible, aware that the Thornwaithe's alum were closing in. "There was a compromise."

The man grinned again. "No compromise. Suffer not a witch to live."

The other alum had clustered closer, keeping a respectful distance between themselves and the remaining piece of iron. "If he knows, we can't let him go," one of them said coldly.

"We can't—" Finley began.

"When it recovers, the magic, it'll take us again and do it anyway," Kelden said quietly.

Finley looked at Arcadia, who simply shrugged. "No love lost. They killed three of us."

Finley rocked back on his heels and considered.

I could modify his memories, his talent offered.

"I could modify his memories," he repeated aloud. "Make him forget."

The man's eyes opened wide at that and he turned his head to stare at Finley.

The other alum looked at each other, and came to a silent conclusion. "If you can."

You're going to need magic, though. Sky would be best. A touch of Flame.

Can I show someone else?

His talent considered. *Probably. Show them this.*

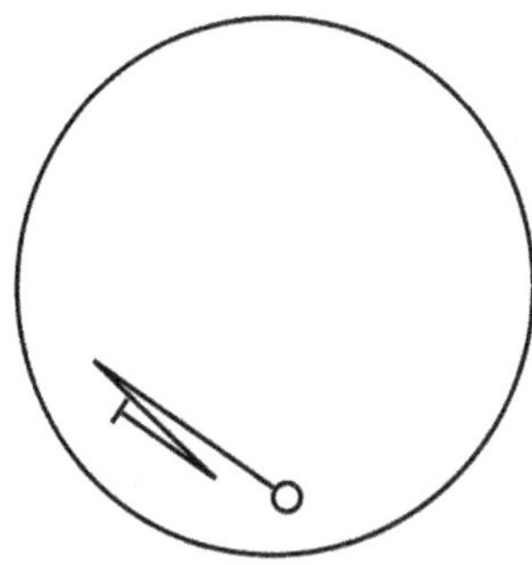

Finley used a finger to sketch the rune in a clear patch of earth. "It needs Sky magic. And a bit of Flame."

"I have both," one of the alum said, peering over Finley's shoulder. "What is it?"

"A rune," Finley said with a sigh. No sense keeping secrets at this point. "A new kind."

"Doesn't look like a rune," the woman said hesitantly.

"Just empower it," Finley instructed. "Mostly Sky, a bit of Flame. It'll... you'll probably feel it pull what it wants."

He turned to look at her and she frowned, but nodded. "What will he forget?"

Everything about magic and witchkind, his talent assured him. *It's... a bit of the Veil, in a way.*

Can we make them forget the carronade?

His talent hesitated. *No,* it decided. *There used to be a way, but... no.*

"Magic. Witchkind. Evermore. Everything we need him to. Cast it, and we'll leave him here."

"He'll die anyway," one of them observed.

"Not at our hand," Finley said firmly.

"What about this thing?" another alum asked, pointing at the crater and its lump of molten iron.

"If any of you are good with Sea and Earth," Finley said tiredly, rising to his feet, "we can probably get it to start corroding. If you can pull enough magic together it can be a rusted hulk before sundown. Then someone with Earth—and some magic left in them—can cover it up. Restore the meadow."

"I'm Sea," someone offered. More voices spoke up, volunteering for the effort.

"Okay," Finley said, crouching back to the ground. "Then you'll want to use this," as he sketched a new, angular rune into the soft earth. "But go slowly with it, and spread yourselves out."

Finley and Arcadia drew back as the alum went to work, several of them focusing their magic on the carronade, a pair pulling the human bodies out of the way, and the woman continuing to cast the slow, delicate magic that would modify the survivor's memories. Kelden was the only one who'd venture close to the carronade, and he began kicking at the earth, picking up pieces of wooden shrapnel. Most were dropped back to the ground, but he held onto a few. After some time, he walked over to Finley and Arcadia and showed him what he'd found.

Arcadia's eyes widened.

Well, that's unexpected, Finley's talent said softly.

"Those are runes," Finley breathed. "Middle Runic."

"Primitive," Kelden said, nodding agreement.

Hey, now, Finley's talent bristled.

"These were pieces of the cart," Arcadia said.

"Yes," Kelden agreed. "These are the biggest pieces left, I think. But it must have been carved all over." He looked to Finley. "You recognize them?"

Durability, strength, steadiness, his talent supplied.

"They would have made the cart stronger," Finley said aloud.

"It *was* a relatively light cart for such a heavy load," Arcadia said.

"So the question becomes," Finley said slowly, "whether this was a general use cart that someone routinely strengthened..."

"Or whether someone of witchkind was in league with these humans," Kelden finished bleakly.

"The iron would have interfered with the runes," Finley pointed out hopefully.

Not entirely, his talent said slowly. *My—these runes are less delicate. Around this much iron, they wouldn't have been fully functional, but... And look, that one. It would have reduced the overall mass, at least slightly. If there were more of those, it would have made the horses' work easier.*

"Maybe not," Finley amended, relaying the new information.

"I think," Arcadia said carefully, "we need to speak to someone about this."

"Dmitry," Finley agreed. "With any luck they've gotten Ram into a bed by now."

"I was thinking of someone else," Arcadia said quietly as she pulled a last bit of Sky magic around them and they vanished.

CHAPTER 15

Investigation

"Where are—" Finley began as Arcadia's magic deposited them on the edge of another small village. "Wait, is this Desivale?"

"It is," Arcadia said, leading them quickly into the village proper.

Desivale was a quaint hamlet nestled against the sprawling expanse of the Great Northern Wood. The village seemed to emerge from the very forest itself, with sturdy wooden homes and shops built from the towering oak, elm, and ash trees that populated the dense woodland. The main thoroughfare was a well-trodden dirt path that meandered through the heart of the village, flanked by cozy cottages with thatched roofs and small gardens bursting with herbs and vegetables.

As Finley and Arcadia walked deeper into Desivale, they couldn't help but feel a sense of warmth and welcome. The villagers, mostly humans with a smattering of witchkind, went about their daily tasks with a quiet determination. The blacksmith's forge glowed with the heat of molten metal as he crafted tools and horseshoes, his muscular arms glistening with sweat. The baker pulled fragrant loaves of bread from a stone oven, the aroma of fresh-baked goodness wafting through the crisp autumn air.

Children played in the small village green, their laughter and shouts of joy intermingling with the gentle clucking of chickens and the distant bleating of goats. An old woman sat on a bench near the well, her nimble fingers weaving a basket from supple willow branches as she hummed a haunting melody. A group of farmers loaded carts with the bounty of their harvest —plump pumpkins, crisp apples, and golden sheaves of wheat —preparing to take their goods to market.

Arcadia led Finley to a small, unassuming cottage on the outskirts of the village. The dwelling was surrounded by a well-tended garden, filled with fragrant herbs and late-blooming flowers. A simple wooden sign hung above the door, bearing the image of a mortar and pestle.

Finley's eyes scanned the structure automatically, quickly spotting the entry rune that'd been clever worked into a frieze along one corner. Arcadia made straight for it, and as she reached to touch it, both Finley and Kelden quickly laid a hand on her shoulders.

A quick, fresh swirl of magic took them, transporting them into the hidden space of the cottage's witchkind resident.

The small anteroom they found themselves in was a stark contrast to the simple, rustic charm of Desivale. The walls were draped in rich, vibrant tapestries depicting scenes of imaginary creatures and otherworldly landscapes. Plush, colorful cushions were scattered about the room, inviting visitors to sit and relax. The air was filled with the gentle tinkling of wind chimes and the soothing scent of lavender and chamomile.

A delicate crystal chandelier hung from the ceiling, casting a warm, ethereal glow throughout the space. The light danced off the surfaces of various trinkets and curiosities that lined the shelves—a shimmering geode, an ancient tome bound in deep blue leather, and a collection of intricately carved wooden figurines.

In one corner of the anteroom, a small fountain burbled softly, its water cascading over smooth river stones and filling the room with the gentle sound of flowing water. Floating candles bobbed on the surface of the fountain's basin, their flickering flames adding to the enchanting ambiance.

Arcadia approached a small, ornate bell hanging near the far wall and gave it a gentle ring. The clear, melodic chime seemed to hang in the air, reverberating through the room with a subtle magical energy. As the sound faded, a sense of anticipation filled the space, as if the very walls were holding their breath in expectation of the resident's arrival. She came quickly, bustling through an ornately carved wooden door, her eyes lighting when she saw Arcadia.

"Arcadia, my dear! Oh, and Finley! It's wonderful to see you!"

"Cat?" Finley asked, his eyes flying open in surprise.

Caitlin Novell, or Cat as she was affectionately known, beamed at her former apprentices with a warm, grandmotherly smile. Her face was a tapestry of laugh lines and wrinkles, each one a testament to a life filled with joy and wisdom. Her skin was a rich, warm brown, glowing with an inner radiance that seemed to defy her age. Her hair, a halo of silver curls, framed her face like a crown, catching the light from the chandelier and casting a soft, ethereal glow around her head.

Cat's eyes, a deep, soulful brown, sparkled with mischief and intelligence. They held a depth of knowledge and understanding that could only be earned through a lifetime of experience and learning. When she looked at Finley and Arcadia, those eyes were filled with a mixture of pride, affection, and a hint of playful mischief, as if she knew secrets that she couldn't wait to share.

She wore a flowing, deep purple robe that seemed to shimmer and shift with every movement, as if it were woven from the very fabric of magic itself. The robe was adorned with intricate embroidery in shades of gold and silver. Around her neck hung a delicate silver pendant in the shape of a crescent moon, inlaid with a single, shimmering amethyst.

"I had no idea you'd settled here," Finley admitted. "When you left, I—"

"I made it quick," she acknowledged with a smile. "I've never enjoyed goodbyes, especially in the Order. But I'd always wanted to live near the Wood, although not so much that I'd turn Woodwitch. This little village is the perfect compromise. But come, come! Let's get you comfortable. I'll make tea." She gestured them through the door, and Finley heard a gentle tinkling of dishwater from the next room as Cat's magic set a tea set into motion.

The sitting room was a haven of comfort and warmth, an inviting space that seemed to wrap its arms around Finley, Kelden, and Arcadia as they stepped inside. The walls were painted a soft, buttery yellow, like the first rays of sunrise filtering through a cozy bedroom window. The hardwood floors, worn smooth by countless footsteps and years of love, were covered in a patchwork of colorful, hand-woven rugs that seemed to tell stories of their own.

A large, overstuffed sofa dominated the center of the room, its plush cushions upholstered in a cheerful floral print of deep reds, vibrant oranges, and soft greens. Throw pillows in complementary patterns and colors were scattered across the sofa, inviting one to sink into their softness and let the cares of the world melt away. On either side of the sofa stood two well-worn, but undeniably comfortable, armchairs. Their faded blue fabric bore the marks of countless hours of contented reading and quiet contemplation.

A low, rustic coffee table sat in front of the sofa, its surface adorned with a vase of fresh wildflowers, their delicate petals dancing in the gentle breeze from the open windows. Stacks of well-loved books were piled haphazardly on the table, their spines creased and their pages dog-eared from frequent use. As they sat, a well-worn silver tray floated from the kitchen, bearing a mismatched tea set centered by a large, steaming, potbellied teapot.

The teacups filled and distributed themselves, and everyone took a moment to enjoy the light, herbaceous scent before Cat spoke. "So. Introductions, first. Who's this?"

"Kelden," Finley said. "Graduated, more or less, but working with me for a while."

"And I'm Cat, as you've gathered," she said with a smile. "I used to be in charge of wrangling you young ones for the Order, but I'd had my fill." Her expression grew more serious as she took a sip of tea. "Now, I can't imagine this is a mere social call, so why don't you get to it?"

Arcadia took over, explaining the attempted attack on Evermore and the carronade. She highlighted some of their recent missions, focusing on the Order's expanding desire to stop humans from having *anything*. She finished with Ram's collapse.

"He's also been conferring with the Taryba a lot more," Finley added. "Which I guess is fine, but—"

Cat frowned. "Not Adomaitis, I hope."

"That's the one," Arcadia muttered.

"Well," Cat said, leaning back with a sigh. "Unwelcome news."

"I will admit that I'm completely ignorant of the politics of this," Finley said quietly.

"Me too," Kelden said.

"There are more or less three factions at the present," Cat said. "Well, always have been, I suppose. The first, and traditionally largest, has been the maintain the status quo. Witchkind lives in secret alongside humans, as we have for centuries since shortly after the Forging of the Axes. We let the Veil cover our mistakes, and we use our magic to fill in where the humans can't."

"The second faction has always been smaller, but they've grown," Arcadia continued. "They're the ones who drove the creation of the Order in the first place. They hold that humans need to be actively held back. That some innovations are dangerous, and that their reliance on our magic is the lever we can use to protect ourselves if the Veil ever falls."

"And those two factions aren't entirely incompatible," Cat pointed out. "They've coexisted for... well, as long as anyone can remember. Certainly since the Thinning of the Veil, around the time that the Age of the Adherents ended."

Finley's talent muttered darkly in the corners of his mind.

"What's new is the third faction, which Adomaitis speaks for. They've grown substantially larger." Cat sighed and took another sip of tea. "They hold that witchkind should be the *masters* of humans. That we should not only reveal ourselves in time, but that we should *subjugate* the humans before doing so, and rule them afterwards."

That's not sane, Finley's talent said flatly.

"But that's who Ram's been speaking to," Finley protested.

"Which explains why the Order's priorities have broadened," Arcadia said grimly. "But this intersects with this cabal of humans I told you about, Cat."

"Yes, that's a disturbing new twist. Having a group of them actively working against you... is new."

"We thought there was a compromise," Finley said sadly.

"They've developed a metal, an alloy of iron, that doesn't affect our magic. It felt like... a peace offering."

Can nodded slowly. "That would certainly change the dynamic. If the humans were willing to abandon pure iron in favor of this alloy... many of witchkind could be persuaded to let them have their advancements. More of them, at least. But Adomaitis' faction?" She shook her head firmly. "Never." Then she sighed again. "But I honestly never thought Ram would go to their side. He was always so... *dedicated* to the Order's charter. He never *hated* humans."

"Did you know him well, then?" Kelden asked.

Cat snorted, almost spraying a mouthful of tea. "I should say so. We were married, for a time."

Arcadia and Finley were struck dumb, their jaws falling open as they stared at their former teacher.

"What?" she asked. "You didn't know?"

"Certainly not," Arcadia said.

Cat shrugged. "Well, there it is. We grew apart, though. Not in our dedication to the mission, or ever its direction. Just... the pressures of the job, I suppose. He was always so worried. There was just less and less room in him for *us.*"

"What do you think has changed him?" Kelden asked.

The germ of an idea sparkled in Finley's mind. "Did you know Dmitry well?"

Cat snorted. "Too well, if anything. Sneaky man. Never clear where his allegiances were. Ram took him on after he and I... separated. It was peaceable enough, but I know he felt badly about it. Us, I mean. Dmitry has been a field operative—one of our worst, I might add, clumsy and inefficient on his best days —and he wheedled his way into a permanent posting at the Farm."

"He's basically running things now," Arcadia said.

Cat nodded sadly. "Someone has to. It saddens me to hear

about Ram's health, but... honestly, this is why I had to break it off. This day was always going to come, and I think I needed to say my goodbyes on my own terms."

"Cat, what do you make of this?" Kelden asked, withdrawing the splintered remains of the carronade cart and sliding them to her across the low table.

She twisted the pieces this way and that. "Middle Runic? Don't see that much anymore. How old are these?"

"Not very," Finley said. "These are the remains of the cart that carried the carronade we told you about."

Cat shook her head. "Another of those in such a short time."

"They came up with a new explosive. That's what did most of the damage," Finley said.

Cat continued to stare at the shards. "My Middle Runic is rusty. I went to Duocastella's, you know. Very big on ancient history, but you forget when you don't use it all the time. Simpler runes, and they took a lot less magic. They'd have been partly functional even next to all that iron, you know." She frowned. "Was this cart repurposed for the carronade, or made special for it?"

"That's the question," Finley said. "Any of those runes would have been useful on any cart, making it stronger, lightening the load, and all that."

"And who would have helped do this explicitly for the carronade?" Kelden asked.

"And who would use Middle Runic, instead of New?" Arcadia added.

"Well," Cat said with another, heavier sigh, "in terms of 'who,' you'd be surprised. We don't talk about it much, but *išdavikų klanas* is a thing."

Finley's talent translated before he could do it himself. *Traitor clans. Don't get me started.*

"Traitor clans?" Arcadia said, her brow wrinkling. "Tell me I have that wrong."

"You do not," Cat said sadly. "They come up now and again, throughout history. We studied some of them at school, in fact—I was quite the student of history, back then. Fascinating stuff. There's even a theory that there has only ever been *one išdavikų klanas*, and that they've simply changed their clan name again and again to hide themselves."

Finley felt a sudden tension in his shoulders, and realized it was coming from his talent. "What," he asked carefully as a restless concern settled over his mind, "was the clan's name?"

"Well, as I said, it's only a *theory* that it's been one clan. Far more likely it's been multiple clans over the centuries. They all claim to be working for the betterment of witchkind, but most often it's for the betterment of themselves."

The name, Finley's talent insisted.

"What's *a* name, then?" Finley asked.

"The most famous was centuries ago," Cat said, frowning slightly as she tried to recall. "I believe it was Karal."

Finley's talent screamed with rage.

***

"Are you okay?" Arcadia asked Finley.

"Yeah, I'm better," he said quietly. His talent's rage had cooled into a simmering hatred, but at least he could think through it. "Thanks. What did you tell Cat?"

"That it was probably just fatigue."

"Thanks."

His talent's anger had come out in an involuntary and very audible cry, as Finley's face flushed so red it was almost purple.

Everyone had worked to calm him, and after he'd taken a few shuddering breaths and managed to speak in a normal voice, Arcadia had made excuses and they'd left Cat's comfortable home. They were now back on the edge of the village, its noises settling into a murmur as the sun neared the horizon.

"I don't want to go back to the Farm just now," Arcadia said, looking back toward the village. "Look, there's a perfectly good inn here. One of witchkind, so we can be ourselves. Can we stay the night? I have... something I want you both to see, but it'd be better in the daylight."

"Sure," Finley said tiredly. "I need to Gather anyway. I'm still near empty."

"Deal," Arcadia said. "Kelden, make sure he doesn't fall over on the way there. It's not far. I'll get us rooms, you get a hot meal into him, and we'll pass out until morning."

Finley gratefully gave himself over to Kelden, and combined with his talent's continued, fuming wrath, managed to ignore everything until his head sank into a soft, fresh-smelling pillow.

***

Arcadia awoke them before sunrise, her demeanor tense and drawn. "Change of plans. I've had a Sending."

"A mission?" Finley asked blearily as he used magic to clean himself and his clothes.

"No. A friend. Come on." She surrounded them with magic.

***

· · ·

"I always manage to forget that Chiton is never warm," Finley grumbled as they arrived. Chiton was a large enough town that witchkind had created several fully enclosed courtyards specifically for magical arrivals and departures, and Arcadia had taken them to one of these. They hurried to one side to clear the space as Finley empowered a rune that would blanket them with warmth. A rune carved into the stone wall of the courtyard whisked them into a narrow alley, which led to one of the town's main roads.

Chiton was a bustling, sprawling town that teetered on the edge of becoming a full-fledged city, rivaling even Evermore in size and population. The streets were a labyrinth of cobblestone paths, winding their way between towering buildings constructed from rough-hewn stone and polished granite slabs. The architecture was a testament to the ingenuity and resourcefulness of the town's inhabitants, with structures rising up to three stories high, their peaked roofs piercing the grey, overcast sky.

Despite the biting cold that permeated the air, the streets of Chiton were alive with activity. Throngs of humans, bundled in drab, heavy woolen cloaks and thick, fur-lined boots, hurried about their daily business, their breath forming ephemeral clouds in the frigid atmosphere. The cacophony of footsteps, creaking cart wheels, and the occasional whinny of a horse created a constant, pulsating rhythm that echoed through the narrow alleyways and broad avenues.

The town's main thoroughfare was a sight to behold. Tall, narrow buildings lined the street, their facades adorned with intricately carved wooden shutters and weathered, wrought-iron balconies. The ground floors of these buildings housed an array of shops and businesses, their wares displayed in frosty, fogged-up windows. The scent of freshly baked bread mingled with the pungent odor of tanning leather, creating a unique olfactory tapestry that hung in the chilled air.

As Finley, Arcadia, and Kelden navigated the bustling streets, they couldn't help but marvel at the resilience and determination of Chiton's inhabitants. Despite the harsh climate and the ever-present threat of winter's icy grip, the people here had built a thriving community, one that pulsed with life and vitality.

They passed by a blacksmith's forge, the heat from the glowing coals providing a momentary respite from the biting cold. The rhythmic clanging of hammer on anvil echoed through the street as the skilled artisan shaped a piece of red-hot metal into a horseshoe. Next door, a weaver sat at her loom, her nimble fingers guiding the shuttle back and forth, creating an intricate tapestry depicting a snow-capped mountain range.

Arcadia led them through a maze of side streets and alleyways, seeming to navigate the town's layout with an uncanny familiarity. They eventually emerged into a small, secluded square, its center dominated by a weathered stone fountain. The water in the basin had long since frozen over, creating a shimmering, icy surface that reflected the muted light filtering through the overcast sky.

A light dusting of snow began to fall from the sky.

"This way," Arcadia said, guiding them towards a nondescript wooden door set into the side of a squat, two-story building. She pushed through the door, gestured for Finley and Kelden to hurry in, and closed it firmly behind her. *"Liepsna,"* she whispered, and a series of oil lamps set into the stone walls flared to life, offering a dim, flickering view of granite steps leading down.

As they descended the granite steps, the air grew warmer and more humid with each step, a stark contrast to the biting cold outside. The flickering light from the oil lamps cast dancing shadows on the rough-hewn walls, creating an eerie, almost otherworldly atmosphere. The sound of their footsteps echoed through the narrow passageway, mingling with the distant, muffled sounds of activity from below.

At the bottom of the stairs, they emerged into a vast, high-ceilinged basement that buzzed with human activity. The space was dominated by a series of towering brass furnaces, their polished surfaces gleaming in the warm, amber light that suffused the room. The furnaces were fed by a constant stream of coal, shoveled into their gaping maws by a team of soot-stained workers, their faces glistening with sweat and their muscles straining with the effort.

From the top of each furnace, a profusion of brass pipes sprouted like the branches of a metallic tree, twisting and turning as they snaked their way across the ceiling and down the walls. The pipes were adorned with a myriad of valves, gauges, and dials, each one meticulously labeled with intricate, hand-painted signs. The air was filled with the hissing and clanking of the pipes as steam coursed through them, carrying heat and energy to unknown destinations.

The heat in the basement was oppressive, and the humidity clung to their skin like a damp, heavy blanket. Finley felt beads of sweat forming on his brow as he squinted through the hazy, steam-filled air, trying to make sense of the intricate network of pipes and machinery that surrounded them.

"What is this place?" Kelden asked, his voice barely audible over the constant hissing and clattering of the furnaces.

"Heat," Arcadia said, leaning close so they could hear her. "Those big boilers are full of water, and it's boiled into steam. The steam feeds out through those pipes, and into all the nearby buildings. It's *heat*. There are two of these in the town, and they're in the middle of building another one."

Finley's chest grew tight. "They sent you to destroy them, didn't they?"

Arcadia nodded, a defiant expression on her face. "Half the people here couldn't afford firewood. And there was a real treat of them cutting down every tree within a day's ride of the town. This is more efficient, and they all get to stay warm. But look."

She pointed, and they realized that one of the furnaces had been damaged. A gaping, ragged hole had been blown in its side, steam still floating lazily out. A group of people were gathered near that furnace, examining it and occasionally glancing with trepidation at the hole.

"Explosion?" Finley asked.

"Obviously," Arcadia said tightly. "But not a natural one. These don't produce much pressure."

"Wait," Kelden said. "Did... *we* do anything? For heat? Before these were built?"

Arcadia nodded again. "Nothing organized, but yes. Any building with a secret space in it was kept warm, but it took a constant stream of magic. Half the... of *us* in the town were near-exhausted, all the time. Shifts were organized, with people sitting up all night just to ensure the heat remained steady. But that still wasn't *every* building." She leaned even closer. "And the *idea for the invention was from one of us.*"

Finley's eyes widened.

She nodded at his expression. "I was surprised as well. But they'd seen the iron roadway's iron horses at a distance, and wondered if something similar couldn't be done here." She gestured to the giant boilers and their maze of piping. "No iron. Conserves magic. Makes life here better for *everyone.*" She pointed. "There, the woman with the blue headscarf. Vabaliene. This was all her idea."

"So you left it alone," Kelden said.

"Obviously."

"But this one still exploded," Finley said.

Arcadia shook her head. "Not on its own. Vabaliene sent for me. This happened late last night." The blue-scarfed woman had turned and noticed them, and was now walking quickly in their direction.

Finley slowly put it together. "You're saying the Order noticed. And sent someone else."

"I assume so."

"So what now?"

Vabaliene gave them a tight smile, and gave Arcadia a quick hug. "We must talk, but not here. Arcadia, do you remember Troi's?"

Arcadia nodded quickly and gestured for everyone to follow her. She led them back up the stairs and outside, and then to a tall, narrow building that hosted a pub on its ground floor. She walked directly to one side of the building and reached for an entry rune carved there.

They found themselves transported into a hidden haven within the walls of the human pub, another of the secret spaces known only to witchkind. The room they entered was a stark contrast to the rustic exterior of the building, exuding an air of refined elegance and sophistication that hinted at the early stirrings of a new era.

The walls were adorned with intricate tapestries, their vibrant threads depicting scenes of mythical creatures and enchanted landscapes. The rich hues of crimson, emerald, and gold seemed to dance in the warm, inviting light cast by the ornate brass chandeliers suspended from the vaulted ceiling. The chandeliers themselves were masterpieces of craftsmanship, their delicate curves and flourishes a testament to the skill of the artisans and magic that had forged them. The word *pub* was too crass, too coarse, for this space. *Dining establishment* was far more appropriate.

Beneath their feet, the polished hardwood floors gleamed with a warm, honeyed hue, reflecting the soft glow of the chandeliers above. The wood was inlaid with intricate patterns of lighter and darker shades, creating mesmerizing geometric designs that seemed to shift and change as they walked across the room.

The furnishings of the dining room were a harmonious blend of comfort and opulence. Plush, velvet-upholstered armchairs in deep shades of burgundy and forest green were scattered throughout the space, inviting patrons to sink into their luxurious depths. Arcadia nodded to a server, who directed them to an empty table and brought them menus printed in glowing letter on thick parchment.

"This is... *nice,*" Finley said in quiet awe.

"It's gotten to be a bit of a competition with the witchkind businesses here," Arcadia said. "Let's just have a round of small ale and something to nibble on," she directed the server, who smiled and hurried away. "And to answer your original question, no, nobody had noticed for *moons*. Ram gave me this assignment personally, and I never turned in a field report. I suspect... well, it's likely Dmitry didn't know I was sent here. He keeps Ram organized, and I figured if he didn't know, then nobody would follow up. Obviously someone did."

"Ram's been distracted," Finley admitted.

"And he never used to be," Arcadia said, lightly slapping the table with her hand. "He was always sharp. Always on it. This situation with the Taryba, and Dmitry is probably pushing him, it's all made him... distracted. Yes. Also..." she paused, and then shrugged. "I even took steps, in case anyone did follow up."

"Steps?" Kelden asked, his brow wrinkling.

"You can't see it unless you crawl under them, which I would *not* recommend doing when they're hot, but I added runes to the brass. On the bottoms."

A smile played across Vabaliene's lips.

"That do what?" Finley asked.

"Nothing. They're not empowered. But they *could* be, and they'd produce heat. So if someone really went looking, it'd—"

"—look like witchkind was really behind the whole thing," Finley finished, smiling. "Clever. Have you done that before?"

"In a few cases."

"So magic as a backup plan," Finley said.

"More or less. I guess. It just seemed... *wasteful.* And pointless."

"I wish I'd thought of that," Vabaliene sighed. "I was just trying to make things easier for everyone."

"Vabaliene, those things are staffed all night, aren't they?" Arcadia asked.

"They are."

"So nobody noticed anything?"

"Oh," she said flatly, "they definitely *noticed.*"

"What does that mean?" Finley asked.

"I was summoned as soon as it happened. I've grown used to working with the humans, and we try to have someone of witchkind in one of the boiler rooms at all times. Enrich wasn't in that one, but they knew to send for him to get me."

"And?"

Vabaliene's expression grew tighter. "The humans were muttering of *witchcraft.* They said a man appeared—he could have walked into the boiler room as you did, nobody pays much attention to people who come and go—and that his hands began glowing. He shouted some words, and the boiler exploded."

Everyone's eyebrows rose with alarm. "Just the one?"

Vabaliene gave them a menacing smile. "The people of Chiton are not easily cowed. They attacked, and they have a few iron tools on hand. The man vanished."

"I don't know what to say," Finley said quietly.

"I know there is a… group," Vabaliene said quietly, her expression now serious, "that tries to prevent dangerous human innovations. Arcadia, when we last met, you implied as much."

"There is, and we're part of it, but we're not happy with it, and regardless, our goal is *secrecy*. We don't blatantly show up wielding Flame magic and blow things up."

"Well, not usually," Finley amended, recalling the first carronade he'd encountered.

"So why would someone attack in this way?" Vabaliene asked.

"We *think*," Arcadia said slowly, "that there are a few—and they might not even be part of our Order—with a different agenda."

"Wait," Finley asked, confused. "What do you mean?"

"I mean, what better way to get the humans riled up than a stunt like this? And if they're riled up, they're dangerous. And if they're dangerous…"

"…then there's a reason to try and subjugate them," Finley finished, nodding. "Devious."

"And dangerous," Vabaliene said. "Threatening the Veil so… blatantly. I'm familiar with the political faction in favor of… subjugation. But they've always been a fringe element. Never a serious power."

"That seems to be changing."

"So we truly think one of them helped the humans with their carronade?" Kelden asked quietly.

Arcadia quickly summarized the abortive attack on Evermore.

"Unbelievable," Vabaliene sighed. "I wouldn't not have thought it possible. Is there truly a chance someone of witchkind assisted in such a… monstrous scheme?"

Arcadia sighed. "I don't know. I'd like to think not. Not with a weapon like that."

Show me the shards of wood again, Finley's talent insisted. Its anger had cooled further, but there was a hardness to its tone that chilled Finley to his core. He relayed the request, and Kelden spread the pieces in the middle of the table, runes facing upward. *This.*

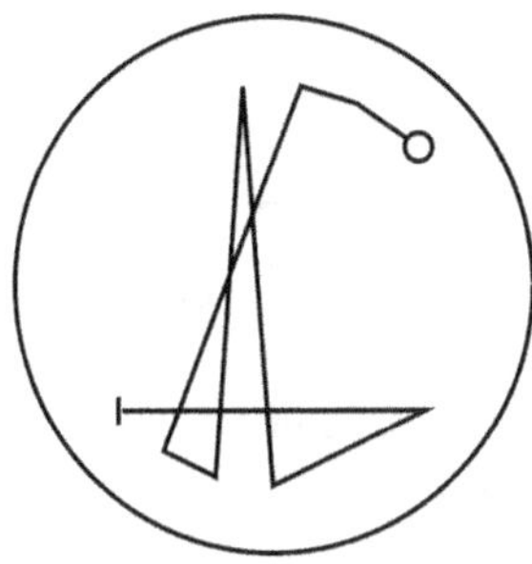

Finley empowered the rune—or tried to. His magic seemed to slip and slide around it, rather than sinking into it.

Irritating, this talent mused. *Your Earth affinity should be sufficient... ah. No, I see. You lack the necessary Control alignment as well. We will... adjust.*

Something inside Finley *twisted* and he gasped at the sensation. Arcadia and Kelden looked at him with concern. "I'm okay," he assured them. He refocused on the new rune and this time power flowed into it more easily. Glowing symbols, visible only to himself—and his talent—appeared above the pieces.

These runes are just days old, his talent informed him.

"The runes are new," he relayed to the others.

"Which is what we were afraid of. I don't know any other reason to use Middle Runic than its resistance to iron."

Less resistance to it, and more ignorance of it, his talent said. *But same outcome.*

"Doing a history project?"

All four of them started as their server set glass steins of ale on the table, followed by a large bowl of crisped potato slices.

"What do you mean?" Arcadia asked carefully.

"Those," the server said, pointing to the shards of wood. "My grandfather teaches at Duocastella's, and he's got a whole collection. Middle Runic, right?" She nodded appreciatively. "I doubt there are a half-dozen people in the world who could read those. He goes on and on about them, if you let him," she added with a chuckle. "How simple they were, how frugal they are with magic, all that." She shrugged. "I'll take the precision of New Runic nonetheless, thank you."

"May I ask your grandfather's name?" Arcadia asked.

"Jokubas Gelbėtojas," she said. "Look him up if you're studying the subject, but don't forget that I warned you! He won't stop, once he starts!" She chuckled again and walked away, leaving them to their light meal.

"Gelbėtojas," Arcadia mused. "You know, in the True Language, that means—"

Savior, Finley's talent said bleakly. *They're never subtle.*

"What if," Kelden said slowly, "and I'm only getting used to the levels of paranoia the Order appears to deal with, so bear with me, but what if..." He paused. "What if someone of witchkind helped with the carronade specifically to turn more people to Adomaitis' political faction?"

Arcadia and Finley's eyebrows rose to their hairlines.

"What," Finley said slowly, "is Dmitry's clan name?" Then he gasped as a jangling filled his head. "I've got a Sending," he said, mentally triggering the message to reveal itself.

He frowned as it played out in his mind, as Kelden and Arcadia waited expectantly.

"I have a mission," he said.

CHAPTER 16

An Urgent Call

"Who did the Sending come from?" Arcadia asked as her magic landed them in far-off Lastpointe. "Ram? Or Dmitry?"

"Neither," Finley said, tension in his voice. "Callum called me directly."

Arcadia's brow furrowed. "Callum? He's not in administration."

"No."

"Did he say—"

"No," Finley cut her off. "We're to meet him at the Inn of the Second Moon."

"I have family here," Kelden said quietly. "I know the place. It's on the other side of the village, away from the shore. This way."

As they made their way through the narrow streets, Arcadia couldn't help but marvel at the quaint charm of Lastpointe. The slabs of thick slate beneath their feet were worn smooth by centuries of foot traffic, and the buildings that lined the streets were a hodgepodge of styles and materials - some built of sturdy stone, others of weathered wood, and still others of a peculiar iridescent shell that seemed to shimmer in the moonlight.

Above them, the twin moons hung low in the sky, casting an ethereal glow over the sleeping village. The larger of the two moons was a brilliant silver-white, its cratered surface clearly visible even from this distance. The smaller moon was a shade of cream, its warmer tone diminishing the starkness of its silvery sister's glow.

The air was heavy with the scent of the sea, and in the distance, they could hear the gentle crashing of waves against the rocky shore. A cool breeze blew in from the water, carrying with it the faint aroma of salt and seaweed.

As they turned a corner, they caught a glimpse of the harbor, where a handful of fishing boats bobbed gently in the calm waters. The masts of the boats cast long shadows across the surface of the sea, like inky fingers reaching out toward the shore.

Despite it being early in the evening, there were only a few signs of life in the village. This was a working village, relying on its fishing fleets for its sustenance, and the villagers—human and witchkind alike—tended to rise and retire early.

As they approached the Inn of the Second Moon, Arcadia couldn't help but feel a sense of unease at the unusualness of Finley's summons. The inn was a tiny, two-story building, its timber frame covered in weathered slate that seemed to absorb the moonlight rather than reflect it. A single lantern hung above the door, its flickering flame casting a warm glow across the threshold.

Kelden pushed open the heavy wooden door, and they stepped inside. The ground floor of the inn was a small dining room and pub, with a handful of tables scattered throughout the space. The room was dimly lit by a few candles and a crackling fire in the hearth, which cast dancing shadows across the walls. The air was thick with the scent of roasted meat and ale, and the low murmur of conversation from two old men occupying a small table in one corner.

Callum was in another corner, nursing a pewter tankard of ale. His eyebrows rose as the three of them approached. "I wasn't expecting an army," he said mildly.

"We were on another mission," Finley said quickly. "And you seemed especially urgent."

"Does anyone at the Farm know about this, whatever it is?" Arcadia asked.

Callum shook his head. "I didn't want to disturb Ram if they'd managed to get him to rest."

"You could have told Dmitry," Kelden pointed out.

Callum gave him a long look. "I don't know you, boy."

"Kelden's doing a post-apprenticeship with me," Finley said quickly.

"Ah. Welcome, then." He looked away as he added, "I'm not sure telling Dmitry would have been for the best. He's... very busy, just now."

Interesting, Finley observed. "You didn't provide much in the way of details."

"I'm not even sure what I'm dealing with," Callum admitted. "I read about the carronade, a couple of years back, and you seem like the best one to deal with this."

Finley's heart started beating faster. "Another one? *Here?*"

"Not exactly."

"What, then?" Arcadia asked, her voice just as tense as Finley's.

"It's... smaller." From a pocket inside his vest, Callum withdrew a much-folded piece of parchment. He spread it out, showing them a sketch he'd made. "It's maybe as long as my arm. The tube part isn't much thicker than my thumb."

"A portable carronade," Arcadia breathed.

"Have you seen it used?" Finley asked.

Callum shook his head. "It was on the blacksmith's work-bench. I happened to be walking past and overheard him discussing it with another man. That one wanted to know how quickly more could be produced."

"And?" Finley prompted.

"I cast *tolimoji klausa* so I could keep listening without sticking around and looking obvious, but... I'm not very good at it, I admit. What I heard was garbled. I couldn't make much sense of it."

I have an idea, Finley's talent said suddenly. *Have him take you there.*

"Take me to the smithy," Finley said firmly, rising from his chair. "Kelden, Arcadia, you two wait here. Arcadia, you're better at *tolimoji klausa*. Cast it on me. You'll know if I need help."

Arcadia's fingers were already twitching through the somatic component of the magic. Her touch was so light that Finley didn't even feel it settle on him, but she nodded when she was done.

"Callum, let's go."

Finley and Callum made their way through the deserted streets of Lastpointe, their footsteps echoing hollowly off the slates. The village seemed to be holding its breath, as if aware of the impending danger that lurked in its midst. The twin moons cast an eerie glow over the slumbering buildings, their light painting the scene in shades of gray and black.

The air grew colder as they approached the smithy. A tension in his talent made it seem inappropriate to use magic to warm himself, and so Finley pulled his cloak tighter around his shoulders.

Their destination was set back from the street, surrounded by a low stone wall that was covered in a thick layer of moss.

The smithy itself was a squat, unassuming structure, its walls made of the same weathered slate as the rest of the village. The only indication of its purpose was the massive chimney that rose from its roof, its blackened bricks a testament to the countless hours of work that had taken place within.

As they drew closer, Finley noticed that the smithy was closed up tightly, its heavy wooden door secured with a thick iron padlock and sturdy wooden shutters were bolted tightly over the windows.

"We could try a window," Callum said, glancing uneasy at the iron lock.

"I—" Finley started.

We don't need to go in. Empower this, his talent said.

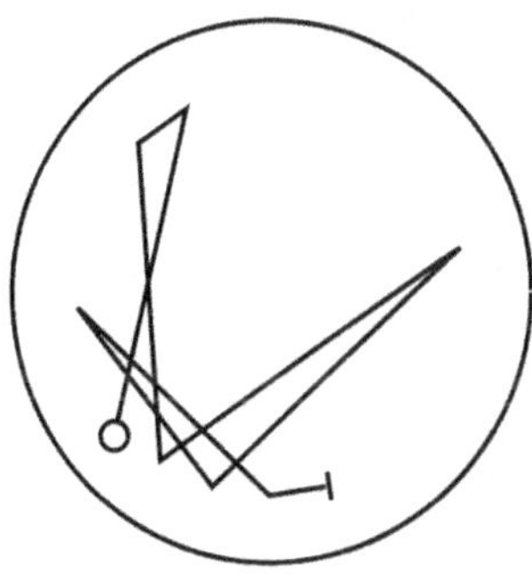

Finley did as he instructed, and jumped slightly when he heard a voice in one ear.

"You've tested it?"

"Aye, and the most terrifying thing it was, too. Even two drops of that concoction of yours is too much, I think. It'll blow out the breech, over time."

"I'll pass that along. How many more can you make? How quickly?"

"As many as you like, but not quickly. I'd thought to make them in flat sheets and roll them, but you were right—the seam never holds long. Casting tubes is difficult enough, especially when they're this small. And then the boring took nigh most of a day."

"So how long?"

"It's the precision that makes it difficult. I had to keep re-checking those figures you gave me, and—"

"Again, how long?"

"Mmm. I think I can manage four at once. Figure a day for the casting, a day for the boring if I get my boy to help. You know, my brother owns a smithy across the channel in Westhead. You could—"

"No. You're more isolated here. We don't want... people copying this design. Not until we're ready."

"Aye, well, four of them every two to three days is the best I can offer."

"It will have to do."

Finley shook his head as the words faded. Callum's eyes were wide and his jaw was slack, answering Finley's question about whether the other man had heard the words as well. "What was that?" he asked incredulously.

I used to think everything had an Ending, his talent said distractedly. *Turns out nothing Ends. Not really.*

"Just... something I've been experimenting with," Finley said. "I'll show you sometime."

"So now what?"

Finley started at the closed-up smithy, chewing his lower lip. "Arcadia," he said softly.

An instant later, she and Kelden arrived in a gust of breeze. "We heard. Well, I did, and I relayed to Kelden. What's the plan?"

"Kelden, do something to hide us," Finley said, his thoughts still running in circles.

Kelden nodded, and whispered *"Neregėtas vaizdas."* The moonlight seemed to dim around them, and the shadows grew taller and darker. The small sounds of the village faded as well.

"We have to take it," Arcadia insisted.

"It wouldn't do any good," Finley said, shaking his head. "The smith already knows how to make more."

"We could—"

"They'll have the designs on iron sheets. We can't touch them."

"Well..." Kelden offered.

Finley raised an eyebrow. "Good point. If they're here."

"They're either here, in the smith's home, or with the other man," Arcadia pointed out. "The smith said he had to keep re-checking figures, which—"

"Suggests he has the design, yes," Finley said, nodding. "But those won't be the only copies."

"The other man seemed in a hurry. If we can slow them down, it would give us time to... do something more."

"You both know this is probably a trap, right?" Kelden said urgently.

"Oh, probably," Finley sighed. "Arcadia, did you happen to check for watchers? I'm so frazzled I didn't even—"

"I did in the pub, and I am right now, and... no."

Finley frowned. "You don't sound certain."

"I'm not. Can't you feel it?"

"Feel—" he started, but then he stopped and waited a moment. "Iron," he spat. "It's everywhere."

Callum nodded. "My magic's been slightly off-kilter ever since I got here. I just figured I was tired."

"What brought you here in the first place?" Arcadia asked.

"Routine checkup. Nothing specific."

"You do that on a schedule?"

"Once every other moon. Pretty regular."

"It's definitely a setup," Kelden said.

"We should assume it is," Finley agreed. He looked again at the smithy, this time casting his senses about and feeding a thin tendril of Earth magic toward the innocuous-looking building. *You look as well,* he instructed his talent.

I'm still pretty stuck in your head, it muttered, but he could sense it riding on Finley's own perceptions, hopefully analyzing them with its greater experience and unique perspective.

"Well?" Arcadia asked after a few moments.

Finley sighed. "It's almost certainly a trap. There's a basement. I can feel the void in the earth. And the whole thing is subtly twisting my magic—there's iron. Probably bars in the walls, but spaced pretty wide. The roof has a lot more, but—"

"That's not uncommon here," Callum said slowly. "There's an iron mine in the middle of the island, and they use a lot of it to reinforce their buildings. Except where witchkind lives, of course."

"I can't believe anyone lives with all this iron around," Arcadia groused.

Callum shrugged. "You get used to it a bit, and almost everyone here is a fisherwitch anyway. They're always out to sea, and everyone knows it's bad luck to have iron on a boat."

Finley snorted. "We started that superstition. Centuries ago, my parents told me."

"Okay, so what are we doing?" Arcadia asked.

Finley considered, and then shrugged. "We have a bit of a secret weapon. So let's fall into their trap." Arcadia's eyes widened further than Finley would have thought possible, and he gave her a tired smile. "You and Callum go back. Far back, actually. Go to Westhead, even. Kelden and I—"

"Finley, that hearing spell won't work over that kind of distance," Arcadia protested.

"It wouldn't work reliably through all the iron anyway," he countered. "And it's fine. We won't need it."

"But how—"

"Just go," Finley said wearily. "Trust me. If you're not looking me in the eyes by this time tomorrow, get help. Get the entire Order, if you have to. But I don't think it will come to that."

She frowned uneasily at him, and then reluctantly nodded. "Callum, do you need to get anything?"

"I've a few things at the inn I should grab," he said softly. "Finley, are you certain—"

"Yes."

He sighed. "Fine. Let's go, then."

As Arcadia's magic took the two of them away, Kelden spoke quietly. "You seem certain about this."

"Good. She needed me to be. But I'm not. If you don't want to do this—"

"No, I trust you. I assume you need my... immunity."

"Yeah."

"I'm in. What's the plan?"

Finley shrugged and walked toward the smithy's door. "Basically just this." He held a hand out, and before his talent could start tweaking it, summoned the rune for *mušamas avinas* in his mind. He fed it a stab of Earth magic laced with Sea, and the door blew inward, in a miniature recreation of what had happened to the carronade's wooden cart.

"Oh," Kelden said mildly, dropping their concealment spell as they followed Finley into the smithy.

"*Dienos šviesa,*" Finley murmured, and the inside of the smithy flooded with bright, even light. "No sense being subtle," he added as Kelden blinked furiously.

As their eyes adjusted to the sudden brightness, Finley and Kelden took in the interior of the smithy. The space was dominated by a large forge set against the far wall, its coals still glowing with a dull red heat. The air was thick with the scent of smoke and hot metal, and the stone walls radiated a palpable warmth.

Scattered about the room were various tools of the blacksmith's trade - hammers, tongs, and anvils of varying sizes, their surfaces worn smooth by countless hours of use. Barrels of water and oil stood in one corner, ready to quench the heat of newly forged metal. Racks along the walls held an assortment of finished and half-finished projects - horseshoes, hinges, nails, and other everyday items essential to village life.

But it was the object sitting on the workbench that immediately drew their attention. The miniature carronade gleamed in the magical light, its metal surface polished to a high sheen. It was a strange and alien thing, unlike anything either of them had seen before.

The device consisted of a long, slender tube, roughly the length of a man's arm from elbow to fingertip. The tube was made of some dark, dense metal—*Iron*, Finley thought. Its exterior was smooth and unblemished, save for a few small protrusions and fittings whose purpose was not immediately clear.

One end of the tube was open, its circular maw an inky black void that seemed to swallow the light. The other end was sealed, with a small, circular piece of metal protruding from its center. This protrusion was threaded, as if meant to screw into something else.

Finley approached the workbench cautiously, his senses on high alert for any sign of danger. He could feel the subtle twisting of his magic as he drew closer to the iron device, a faint but persistent discomfort that set his teeth on edge.

Kelden moved to stand beside him, his eyes fixed on the miniature carronade. "It's so small," he murmured, reaching out a hand as if to touch it before thinking better of it and pulling back. "Hard to believe something like this could be dangerous."

"Size doesn't matter," Finley said grimly. "It's what's inside that counts." He leaned closer, squinting at the device. "There's some kind of mechanism here, at the sealed end. Probably for igniting the explosive."

Kelden nodded. "And the open end is where the projectile comes out, I assume."

"Most likely." Finley straightened up, his gaze sweeping the room. "We need to find those design sheets. They have to be here somewhere. Look for thin sheets of iron."

They began to search the smithy, rifling through drawers and shelves, looking for anything that might resemble a schematic or blueprint. The iron in the walls and roof made it difficult for Finley to use his magic, and even his talent was grumbling in the back of his mind.

As they searched, Finley couldn't shake the feeling that they were running out of time. When would the trap close on them?

After several tense minutes, Kelden called out softly. "Finley, over here."

Finley hurried over to where Kelden was crouched by a heavy iron chest tucked into a corner. Kelden had already pushed the lid open, and a small corner of Finley's mind gibbered with panic at the thought of even touching the deadly metal. But Kelden seemed unfazed by it.

Something started clacking, the low, sharp sound of two pieces of metal gently tapping against each other. Finley looked around for the source of the noise, but didn't see anything. He returned his attention to the chest.

Inside, stacked neatly, were several thin sheets of iron. Kelden carefully lifted one out, angling it to catch the light. Etched into the metal in fine, precise lines was a detailed diagram of the miniature carronade. Measurements and notes crowded the margins, the handwriting small and cramped.

"That's it," Finley breathed. "The design for the portable carronade."

Kelden quickly flipped through the other sheets, confirming they held similar schematics and notes. They frowned. "Should we take them? Destroy them?"

The floor fell out from beneath them.

***

"Ow," Finley said, rubbing his head gingerly.

You have good reflexes, his talent murmured. *You bottled up your magic as you fell.*

"We're surrounded by iron bars," Kelden said quietly.

"Yeah, I'm familiar with the tactic," Finley said ruefully. "How long was I out?"

"A moment or two. So what now?"

Finley pulled himself upright and looked up. His magical light had extinguished itself when they fell, but a beam of moonlight stabbed in through the open doorway of the smithy above, providing a slight bit of illumination. They'd been standing on a trap door, Finley saw, which had swung down and dropped them here. A new barrier, this one composed of more iron bars, had slid into place to cover the opening. "You think you could open that?"

Kelden peered up. "Possibly. It seems to just be resting there against that latch. Want me to?"

"Not just yet. Let's meet our captors, first. I have some questions for them."

They didn't have to wait long before two sets of boots

thudded their way into the smithy and over to the barred opening in the floor. Finley couldn't make out much more than their shapes, backlit as they were by the moonlight.

"Fell right in, then?" one of them asked. His voice was deep and coarse.

"That was your plan, wasn't it?"

"Aye."

"I thought we'd arrived at a compromise?"

The man snorted, and the other figure spoke. "You were meant to think that." A woman's voice, deep and smooth.

"Marching a carronade to our city didn't maintain the illusion, much."

"Those idiots moved ahead of schedule," the woman admitted.

"I'm guessing you meant to have a collection of those hand-held ones ready first?"

"It's called a *šautuvas,*" she said. "And yes, that was the plan. We'll make it work anyway."

Odd that they use the True Language for so many terms, Finley thought. Aloud, he said, "So you mean to attack our city?"

"We do," she confirmed. "But there's no reason for you and your friends to get caught up in it."

"No need—what are you talking about?" Kelden asked, sounding genuinely confused.

"We know you've passed on opportunities to hold us back. To slow us down. Not every time, but you've left us some things. Things less dangerous to you. The wire. So we're making you a simple offer: stay out of it, and you won't get hurt."

"I'm not sure you understand the nature of the resistance you'll face," Finley said carefully. "Have you actually seen what's left of your carronade?" The two were silent for a moment. "Our city... it defends itself, in a way. Firing iron balls, or those—what were they called, cross bows? Those iron shafts won't do it either. This isn't like attacking a human village."

"We've done our research," the man said, but he didn't sound certain.

"We have to do something," the woman said more firmly. "We can't stand by and let you oppress us. Subjugate us. Make us your slaves."

"Most of us—and I do mean *most*—don't want that either," Finley said flatly. "You're seeing a very small faction that's been growing through lies. You know about the heating boilers in Chiton?"

"What about them?" the woman said uneasily.

"One of them was damaged. A great hole tore through the side of it. But one of *us* did that. And was *seen* doing it. They're doing it to inflame you, rile you up. So the rest of my people *do* see you as a threat. You can stop all this. Don't start up the Hunts. We can... we'll make changes. We'll leave you your innovations. There can be a peace between us. A secret peace, but a peace."

The two shadows turned to each other for a long moment, saying nothing. Then one shook its head. "It's gone too far for that," the woman said, and Finley thought he could detect a hint of regret in her voice. "You've found what you were meant to find. We'll leave, and in the morning the smith will let you out. He doesn't know anything about... about you. Tell him you're petty thieves, and he caught you. Worst case, you'll deal with the local lawkeeper."

"But stay out of it," the man warned.

"If we tell our people what you're doing," Kelden said, "they'll just make a case for moving faster."

The woman shrugged. "Then don't tell them. Or do. It's going to turn out the same either way."

"You don't *know*, do you?" Finley said, suddenly overcome with weariness. "You don't truly know what's arrayed against you?" The two said nothing, but continued staring down into the iron-lined pit. "For *centuries*, for *millennia*, we've kept your buildings sturdy. We've kept your boats afloat. Your street lamps, the crops on the farms, *everything* you have is held together by our magic. That's our lever. We take that away, and everything you have... collapses."

The two shadows were quiet for a long, long moment. Then, the woman spoke in a soft, resigned voice: "Maybe that's what needs to happen."

The two turned and left, their footsteps thudding away into the distance.

"This is bad," Kelden said.

"I know. Get us out."

"I'll need a boost."

Finley held his hands out and boosted Kelden up. They grabbed onto the iron bars covering the opening, steadying themselves while they worked the simple iron latch. It released with a click, and Kelden kicked their feet, swinging to one side and pulling the cover to one side. They dropped back to the dirt floor, crouched, and leapt up again. This time their fingers found purchase on the edge of the opening and they quickly pulled themselves up. A moment later, a coil of heavy rope thudded next to Finley, and Kelden helped him climb out.

They walked out of the smithy, brushing dust from their clothes. "Well," Kelden began, "I guess—"

Finley's mind was filled with the jangling noises of an urgent Summons. "It's Arcadia," he said quickly, pulling his magic around them. "Something's happening."

CHAPTER 17

Bad Actor

"It's my cousin, Calliope," Arcadia said breathlessly when Finley and Kelden materialized. "She did a Sending when I was in Westhead. I left Callum there. The trap! You got out okay—"

"Arcadia, slow down," Finley said. "What's going on? Your Sending only said—"

"It's Landon!"

Finley froze in mid-sentence.

"Who's Landon?" Kelden asked.

"He joined the Order at the same time we did," Arcadia explained quickly. "Didn't do well. It went bad. He wound up fighting us. Calliope met him, before then, on one of our school breaks."

"Why would your cousin call you about—"

Arcadia blushed and looked away for a moment. "We're like sisters. I told her—nothing, really, just that Landon—"

"Fine, fine," Finley said, forcing himself to calm down. "Runes and ruin, Arcadia, I thought you'd been attacked or something."

"But Landon shouldn't—"

"Yes, yes, I know." Finley ran a hand through his hair, a sure sign of his frustration. "We'll track him down. Where did your cousin see him?"

"She was in the commercial district. I'll show you."

Arcadia led them through the winding streets of Twynsits, the cobblestones uneven beneath their feet. The residential quarter was a labyrinth of narrow alleys and leaning houses, their upper stories jutting out precariously over the street. Laundry fluttered from lines strung between windows, and the air was thick with the smells of cooking and the chatter of families settling down for the evening.

As they hurried on, the streets began to widen, and the houses gave way to shops and taverns. The commercial district was still bustling, even at this late hour. Merchants called out their wares, and the clatter of hooves and wagon wheels filled the air. The mighty river that split the town in two was visible now, its dark waters glinting in the moonlight.

Arcadia paused at a crossroads, peering down each of the four streets in turn. "This way," she said at last, turning left toward the river. The buildings here were larger, the shops more prosperous.

Arcadia led them onward, past the grand facades of the merchant's guildhalls and the ornate storefronts of the jewelers and silk merchants. The streets narrowed again as they approached the river, the buildings growing more utilitarian. Small warehouses and artisans' workshops lined the way now, their shuttered windows dark and silent.

The scent of the river grew stronger, a mix of damp stone and the pungent odor of fish. Somewhere nearby, a night bird called, its eerie cry echoing off the close-set buildings. Arcadia shivered and pulled her cloak tighter around her shoulders.

As they rounded a corner, they found themselves in a small

square. A fountain stood at its center, the water still and mirror-like in the moonlight. And there, milling about in the shadows of the surrounding buildings, was a crowd of people.

Finley frowned, his hand going instinctively to the hilt of his sword. "What's this? It's far too late for a market or a festival."

Arcadia shook her head, just as perplexed. She scanned the faces in the crowd, looking for her cousin's familiar features, but saw only strangers. They were an odd assortment, she realized. Men and women, old and young, some in the fine clothes of the wealthy, others in the plain garb of laborers. What could have brought such a disparate group together at this hour? "Excuse me," she asked a woman. "What's happening?"

The woman's face was lit with excitement. "It's Master Jacoby! He's promised to demonstrate his new miracle again tonight! I missed it last night, but my neighbor Etta says her husband saw it and—I just have to see it for myself! She said it's like *magic!*"

Finley, Arcadia, and Kelden exchanged worried glances. "Follow me," Finley said in a low tone, beginning to push his way through the crowd. Behind him, he heard Arcadia whispering under her breath, and the people in front of them began turning to either side, opening a path between them. Despite the situation, Finley grinned. He couldn't see her magic, but she was using an old Sky trick: creating whispers in the air, causing people to turn to one side or another and ask 'what?'

They finally came to the front of the crowd. A sturdy wooden fence stood between the street and a small open courtyard, which was backed by a single-story workshop made from simple framing and enclosed with battered wooden planks. A table had been set up in the middle of the yard, and a... contraption of some kind was sitting on it.

The device on the table was unlike anything Finley, Arcadia, or Kelden had ever seen. It consisted of a large glass sphere, nearly three feet in diameter, mounted on a wooden stand. Inside the sphere, two discs of some strange, glossy material were suspended, one above the other, with only a hand's breadth of space between them. The discs were connected by a rod that passed through the center of the sphere and emerged from the top and bottom, where it was attached to a crank handle.

As they watched, a man stepped forward from the shadows at the edge of the courtyard. He was tall and thin, with a shock of wild gray hair and a neatly trimmed beard. He wore a long coat of deep purple velvet, embroidered with intricate silver designs that caught the moonlight as he moved.

"Good evening, my friends!" the man called out, his voice rich and resonant. "I am Master Jacoby, and I have come to share with you a wonder the likes of which you have never seen!" Then he chuckled. "Unless, of course, you were here last night, when we made our first trial run. But fear not! We've repaired the damage and should suffer no such problems tonight!"

The crowd murmured in anticipation as Jacoby stepped up to the table and laid a hand on the crank handle of the strange device.

"This, my friends, is machine capable of producing pure energy," Jacoby declared. "It harnesses a force that can move objects without being touched!" He gave the crowd a wan smile. "Now, we're still not sure what good it all is, and we have many more experiments in front of us, but we think this is an exciting start." He looked around, took a deep breath, and cried out, "Are you ready?"

The crowd cheered.

Master Jacoby began to turn the machine's crank, slowly at first, then faster and faster. As the discs inside the sphere began to spin, a strange hum filled the air, rising in pitch and intensity as the speed increased. The crowd fell silent, watching in rapt attention.

Suddenly, a brilliant arc of light leaped from the top of the sphere, sizzling through the air like a miniature bolt of lightning before grounding itself on the metal rod at the bottom. The crowd gasped in unison, some stepping back in fear while others leaned forward for a better look.

Jacoby laughed with delight, his eyes shining with reflected light as he continued to crank the machine. The arcs of energy came faster now, crackling and snapping, the air filling with the sharp scent of ozone.

Finley, Arcadia, and Kelden stood transfixed, their eyes wide with shock. This was no magic they had ever seen or heard of. It couldn't be magic at all. Magic was the domain of witchkind, not humans. And yet, here was this man, this Master Jacoby, wielding a power that seemed to defy the very laws of nature.

"How is he doing that?" Arcadia whispered, her voice trembling slightly. "It's not possible..."

Finley shook his head, at a loss for words. His mind raced, trying to make sense of what he was seeing. Could it be some trick, some sleight of hand? But no, the energy was real, he could feel it prickling his skin even from this distance.

Then whatever strange energy Jacoby was creating *surged*.

The sparks from the machine grew in intensity, their *snapping* becoming louder, as the air filled with a sharp, acrid smell. Jacoby's eyes widened, and he began slowing the machine's crank—but it didn't seem to matter. More and more bolts of blue-white energy flew from the machine, now reaching out into the empty yard, leaving scorch marks on the hard-packed earth as they grounded themselves.

"Finley—" Arcadia said nervously, taking a step back.

"What's happening?" Kelden asked.

Finley's hands clenched into fists as he watched the machine spin seemingly out of control. "I don't know, but it can't be good. We need to get these people out of here."

Jacoby was frantically working the crank backwards now, trying to slow the furiously spinning discs, but to no avail. The air crackled with energy, the bolts of lightning growing larger and more erratic by the second. The crowd, which had been murmuring in excitement just moments before, now broke into shouts of alarm as they began to back away.

"Everyone, please, remain calm!" Jacoby called out, his voice strained. "I have it under control, just give me a moment to—"

But his words were drowned out by a deafening crack as a particularly large bolt leaped from the machine, striking the wooden fence and setting it ablaze. Panic erupted as people screamed and surged backward, trying to escape the flames.

"Arcadia!" Finley shouted over the chaos. "Can you douse the fire?"

Arcadia nodded, her face pale but determined. She raised her hands, whispering the vocal companion to a firefighting rune, and a gust of wind swirled around her, gathering moisture from the air. With a flick of her wrists, she sent the miniature storm toward the burning fence, the water dousing the flames with a hiss of steam.

Meanwhile, Kelden had pushed his way through the crowd to the table where the contraption was still spinning out of control. Jacoby finally stepped back. "Be careful, young man!" he warned as another bolt of power sparked out of the machine, grounding itself next to Finley's feet.

Then he spotted it.

A rune, carved in the tiny, precise lines of curves of New Runic, set into the wooden base of the machine.

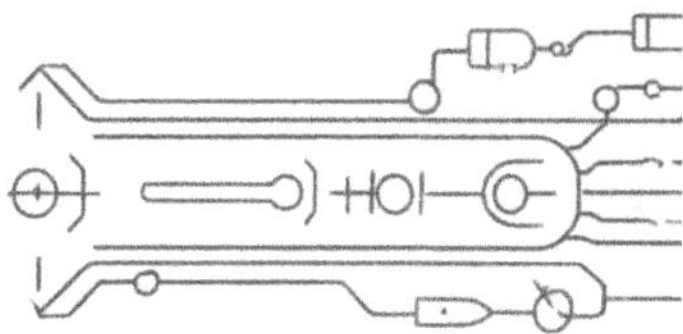

The rune glowed softly, which meant—"Kelden, someone's empowering this!" Finley took a step back and began scanning the crowd. "There!" he shouted, pointing. "It's Landon!"

Arcadia whirled, spotting Landon, who was grinning madly even as his fingers danced through the renewing motions that were keeping his rune empowered. She immediately summoned a blunt column of air, aiming for Landon's stomach, but he dodged it adroitly.

Kelden attacked next, attempting to sweep Landon from his feet, but the other man leapt to one side, aided by Flame magic.

Destroy the rune, Finley's talent suggested.

Finley turned to comply, drawing on his Earth magic to change the structure of the wood itself. He knew the active rune would fight this change, and he'd need to pour—

Allow me.

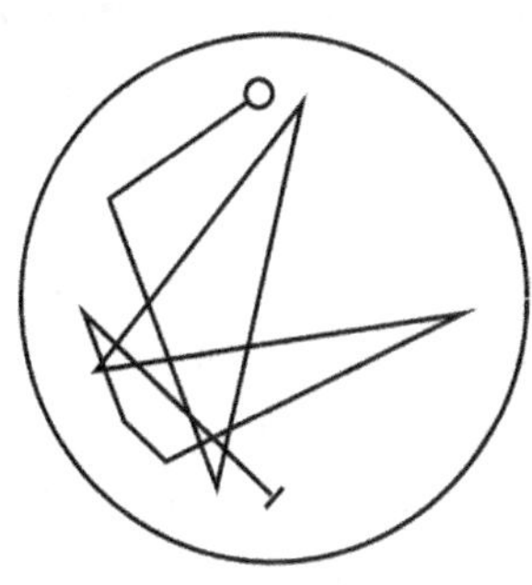

Finley empowered the new rune and watched as the device's wooden base flowed and twisted. Landon's rune was pulled apart, and its energies—

—backlashed.

The rush of magic was a sight to behold. As Finley's rune tore apart Landon's, the conflicting energies collided in a dazzling display of raw power.

A blinding flash of pure white light erupted from the ruined machine, illuminating the night sky like a second sun. The light pulsed and swirled, tendrils of energy dancing and intertwining in a mesmerizing ballet. Shimmering sparks of every color imaginable burst forth, cascading through the air like a rain of gleaming jewels.

The very air seemed to come alive, crackling and humming with barely contained power. Waves of shimmering, iridescent force rippled outward, distorting the world around them like heat haze on a summer day. The ground trembled beneath their feet, and a deep, resonant thrumming filled their ears, as if the earth itself was groaning under the strain of the clashing magics.

Collision of Axes, Finley's talent whispered, sounding awed.

Finley's rune, focused on creation and change, collided with Landon's, which had been powered with his Flame magic— magic of change, true, but more often of destruction and empowerment. Landon's well-known lack of Control alignment meant his magic was free to act on its own, and the resulting combination was... otherworldly.

Amidst this maelstrom of light and sound, strange, ethereal shapes began to coalesce. Ghostly figures of animals, plants, and things that had no name swirled into being, only to dissipate moments later, like wisps of cloud scattered by the wind. Eerie, haunting melodies seemed to emanate from the very fabric of reality, the notes alien and discordant, yet strangely beautiful.

Memories of a distant past, Finley's talent mused.

The crowd, already on the verge of panic, could take no more. Their screams of terror pierced the night as they fled in all directions, trampling each other in their desperate bid to escape the unnatural spectacle. Some fell to their knees, hands clasped in prayer, while others simply stood transfixed, their eyes wide with a mix of awe and horror.

Finley, Arcadia, and Kelden, their own magic swirling invisibly around them in a protective cocoon, stood at the heart of the maelstrom. They could feel the raw, primal power of the colliding magics tugging at their very souls, threatening to tear them apart and scatter their essence to the winds.

Finally, the conflicting magics began to run out of power. The unreal visions faded, the eerie sounds died. What few humans still remained in the street struggled to their feet and began hurrying away.

The only sound was Landon, laughing with delight. "That couldn't have gone better if I'd planned it that way!" he crowed. "Stories of magic and witchcraft will be all over the town by morning!"

He's not wrong. Do you feel that? Finley's talent whispered with sudden alarm.

Finley focused his senses, reaching out with his magical awareness. At first, he felt nothing out of the ordinary, just the usual gentle hum of the world's magic. But as he concentrated, he began to perceive a subtle change in the fabric of the world.

It was the Veil. The thin, gossamer magic that protected witchkind. That made humans explain away any odd traces of magic they happened to catch from the corner of their eye—a person appearing out of thin air, or a lance of fire lighting a lamp.

But now, it was as if the Veil was *vibrating,* a barely perceptible tremor that sent ripples through the magical ether. The sensation was so faint that he might have dismissed it as a figment of his imagination, but his talent's warning urged him to press on.

He closed his eyes, blocking out the chaos of the world around him, and delved deeper into the mystical realm. As he did so, the vibrations grew stronger, more insistent. It was like standing on the edge of a great chasm, feeling the ground tremble beneath your feet as some ancient, slumbering beast begins to stir.

The Veil was not just vibrating, Finley realized with a start. It was resonating, like a lute string plucked by an invisible hand. The magical barrier that separated the world of humans from the realm of the supernatural was singing a haunting, discordant melody that set his teeth on edge and made his skin crawl.

He could see it now, in his mind's eye. The Veil was like a vast, shimmering curtain, woven from strands of pure magic. It stretched across the sky, an infinite expanse of faint light that shifted and danced.

It's too thin, his talent said. *It can't handle this.*

Finley forced his awareness back to the present, where Landon was continuing to gloat. "Get him," he ordered.

Kelden had obviously prepared something already, because his magic flew outward before Finley's words had even settled into the air. A textbook *dvasios narvas*, bindings of thickened air, lashed out, surrounding Landon, who simply grinned.

And then, in a flash of light and heat, Landon was gone.

Kelden's construct collapsed in on itself, deprived of its target, and they snarled in frustration.

"What the—he *never* mastered Flame's travel magics," Arcadia protested.

That was a Forged item, Finley's talent said.

"He had a token of some kind," Finley relayed.

"Well, I know him well enough to trace him," Arcadia growled, her fingers already flicking through the motions of a tracing rune. Sky magic was superior to any other for this task, but after a moment, Arcadia let out an incoherent cry of frustration. "It's blocked! He's done something to *block* it!"

"He anticipated this," Finley said, frustration rising in his chest.

Be calm. We just need a different approach.

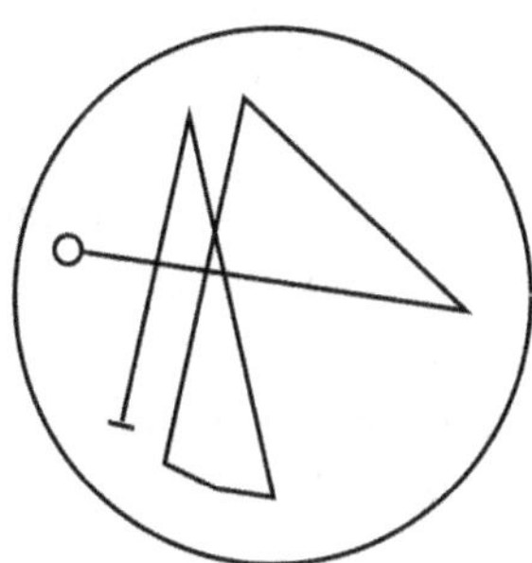

Have her do it, his talent instructed.

"Arcadia, use this," Finley said, quickly sketching the new rune in glowing lines in the air between them. Arcadia studied it for a moment, nodded, and began feeding Sky magic.

"That's got it," she said a moment later, a tight grin of satisfaction on her face. "Grab my arm."

Finley and Kelden moved to comply, and a moment later a dervish of cold wind surrounded them and they were gone.

***

"What—this is the Farm," Kelden asked, confused. "Did you get it wrong?"

"I did not," Arcadia said firmly. "This is where he came."

"That's—" Kelden began.

"Don't say 'impossible,'" Finley warned. "This is starting to come together now, isn't it?"

Kelden's mouth snapped shut and they nodded. "Where do we go?"

"The trace puts him in the farmhouse," Arcadia said, her tone low and dangerous. "In Ram's office."

"Yeah," Finley said bleakly. "Let's go. Be ready for... anything." He pooled magic from his own reserves into his mind, preparing for whatever action he might have to take.

As they approached the farmhouse, a sense of unease settled over Finley, Arcadia, and Kelden. This place had always been a sanctuary, a refuge from the chaos and danger of the outside world. The sprawling, rustic building held countless memories of laughter, camaraderie, and the warmth of belonging. It was a place where they had honed their skills, formed unbreakable bonds, and found a purpose greater than themselves.

But now, an unfamiliar dread seemed to permeate the very walls of the farmhouse. The once welcoming facade now loomed before them, the weathered wood and stone taking on an ominous air in the moonlight. The windows, usually aglow with the soft light of lanterns and the flicker of hearth fires, were dark and lifeless, like the hollow eyes of a skull.

As they stepped over the threshold, the familiar scent of herbs, old books, and the faint tang of magic greeted them, but it was now tinged with something else—a subtle, unsettling odor that set their nerves on edge. The air felt thick and heavy, as if the house itself was holding its breath in anticipation of some impending doom.

Their footsteps echoed unnaturally loud on the worn floorboards as they made their way through the entry hall. The usual clutter of boots, cloaks, and staves that lined the walls was absent, lending the space an eerie, abandoned feel. The silence was oppressive.

As they cautiously approached Ram's office at the end of the hall, they could hear muffled voices engaged in a heated discussion. Finley held up a hand, signaling Arcadia and Kelden to pause. They strained their ears, trying to make out the words.

"—went exactly as planned," came Landon's voice, tinged with smug satisfaction. "With a few more demonstrations like that, the humans will be whipped into a frenzy. They'll start seeing magic everywhere, and then they'll all see. I wouldn't be surprised," he bragged, "if they call a Hunt based solely on tonight."

"Good," replied a second voice, deep and authoritative. Finley's blood ran cold. It was Dmitry. "The time has come for witchkind to take our rightful place. For too long we have hidden in the shadows, constrained by our fear and the humans' numbers. But no more."

Arcadia shot Finley a look of disbelief and horror. Kelden's hands clenched into fists, their knuckles white.

Dmitry continued, "We will no longer need to hide—or to fear them. They will see us for what we truly are - their superiors in every way. And they will have no choice but to bow before us."

"What of the rest of the Order?" Landon asked. "Surely they will oppose this."

A cold chuckle emanated from the office. "Adomaitis has convinced the rest of the Taryba to expand the Order. Take it public. Let all of witchkind see us hold the humans in their place."

Finley marched forward, pushing open the office door. Landon turned at the intrusion, but Dmitry's smile widened a bit. "Some of us *do* oppose this."

Dmitry nodded. "We expected as much. But you'll find—"

A moment, please, Finley's talent said, the rage from earlier now boiling to the top. *This, please. Sea magic would be best.*

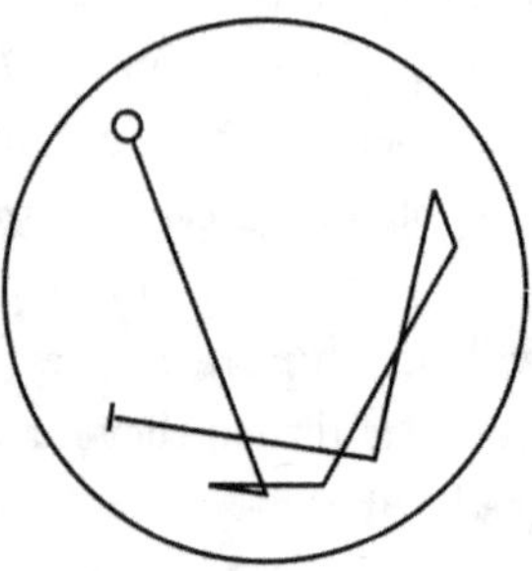

The magic darted forward, spun once around Dmitry, and then surfaced a glowing rune.

In the True Language of witchkind, it read *Gelbėtojas.*

I knew it, Finley's talent seethed.

"You're the *išdavikų klanas,*" he blurted out.

Dmitry's demeanor changed in an instant, the look of calm bemusement replaced by scarcely controlled fury. His face flushed dark red as he snapped, "*Never* use that phrase with me!"

"But you are, aren't you?" Finley insisted. "You helped the humans with their carronade. You've sent *him* to openly display magic! You *want* them riled up, you *want* them attacking us!"

Dmitry's expression was stony now. He flicked an index finger, and the office door slammed shut behind them. In the same instant, a sheet of glowing energy flickered and glowed along the walls, ceiling, and floor of the office.

What's that? Finley's talent asked, startled.

Finley's heart began beating faster and faster. A *šeimininko narvas,* he replied. *Energy cage. Extremely powerful, extremely complicated. I had no idea Ram had placed one here.*

Hmm.

"You listen to me, *boy,*" Dmitry was saying, his tone nearly a snarl. "Witchkind have lived in fear long enough. The carronade? It was no threat to Evermore. Its defenses were well-prepared. Landon's... missions? Nothing more than to highlight how dangerous humans have become. Our people have become *sheep!* Livestock! We lend the humans our magic in exchange for *nothing!* Nothing save fear. An entire people in *hiding* for *millennia!* It ends *now!*"

He's mad, Finley thought in panic.

You'll find it runs in the family, his talent said wryly.

"But the Veil!" Arcadia joined in. "It can't hold against that kind of—"

"The Veil is a *myth,* girl!" Dmitry barked. "Our own cowardice is all it takes to keep magic a secret!"

If only he knew, Finley's talent said sadly.

"You will all remain here, at the Farm," Dmitry said coldly. "Clearly, you have been infected with something that is driving you to ignore your vows to this Order. Ram would be... saddened, at the least. You—"

"Ram would never have approved this," Arcadia shouted. "Where is he, anyway? What—oh, no," she moaned as she caught sight of the glee on Landon's face. "You've done something to him, haven't you?"

Dmitry's eyes narrowed. "Ram is *resting* comfortably after the... stress placed on him by the humans. I'm quite certain he will revive once all of... *this* is over."

They've poisoned him with something, Finley's talent said. *You've been saying he wasn't himself.*

Later, Finley replied. "So what—"

Once again, Finley's head filled with the urgent jangling of an emergency Sending.

From his family.

"Finley?" Arcadia asked, putting a hand on his forearm. "You've gone ashen."

"It's my family," he whispered.

"They'll be fine," Landon sneered. "Probably. If they're smart."

The seething rage of his talent combined with Finley's own sudden, dire fury. Power pooled inside him—Sea and Earth, his longtime companions, but equal measures of Flame and Sky, each coupled with a new, strange *something* that whirled gray and white in his soul.

Every Ending is a Beginning, his talent whispered through the raw emotion and growing power. *And it's time you Begin to be free of this cage.*

More lines and curves began flickering madly in Finley's mind as his talent sought to assemble something new. *Earth, for preservation,* it said, its bodiless voice both cold and searingly hot at once. *Hmm. Perhaps a different approach.*

Be free.

The rune exploded out of Finley in a dazzling display of raw power, a blinding white light tinged with shimmering hues of blue, green, red and gray. The energy surged outward in a pulsing, expanding sphere, slamming into the glowing walls of the *šeimininko narvas* with a deafening crack like thunder.

For a moment, the energy cage held, its shimmering surface rippling and flexing like a soap bubble straining against a gale. But Finley's magic, fueled by his righteous fury and the arcane knowledge flowing from his talent, was relentless. The rune of freedom battered against the cage's glowing barrier, seeking out the minuscule flaws and imperfections in its structure.

Then, with a sound like a thousand panes of glass shattering at once, the *šeimininko narvas* burst apart. A million fragments of glowing energy flew in all directions, ricocheting off the walls, floor and ceiling of the office. They sparkled and flashed as they whirled through the air, like a blizzard of luminous snowflakes caught in a cyclone.

The occupants of the room were momentarily stunned by the explosion of light and sound. Dmitry and Landon threw up their arms to shield their faces, while Arcadia and Kelden staggered back, their eyes wide with awe at the display of Finley's newfound power.

The outrush of energy left Finley suddenly empty, and Kelden caught him as he sagged. "Home," he croaked, and a tempest of Arcadia's Sky magic whisked them away.

CHAPTER 18

Crossing the Line

Exhausted and frantic, Finley gratefully accepted Kelden's offer to take them to the tiny village west of Sowsee. The village nestled in the cove like a hidden gem, its thatched roofs and rough-hewn stone walls illuminated by the eerie glow of the false dawn. Normally, the scent of salt air and the gentle lapping of waves against the shore would lend the scene a peaceful ambiance, but this morning, an unsettling energy crackled through the narrow, winding streets.

As Finley, Arcadia, and Kelden approached, the clamor of urgent voices grew louder. Men and women, some still in their nightclothes, rushed about with torches held high, casting long, flickering shadows that danced across the faces of the weathered cottages. The orange light glinted off the scales of the day's catch, strewn haphazardly across the cobblestones as if abandoned in haste.

The air hung heavy with the acrid scent of smoke and the metallic tang of fear. Children clung to their mothers' skirts, wide-eyed and trembling, while the village elders conferred urgently, their lined faces grave in the wavering light.

"Mom!" Finley shouted, spotting his parents. They were holding each other tightly, standing across the street from the small, humble building that played host to the vast, cavernous secret space that held their home.

"Finley!" his mother called back, breaking off from her husband to wrap her son in a tight hug. "We don't know what's happening!"

Finley turned and looked at the building, his jaw dropping with amazement. What had once been a simple building of native stone and hand-cut timbers was now... changed.

The once-ordinary tailor's shop had transformed into a fantastical sight. Lush, verdant vines burst forth from the cracks in the stone walls, their tendrils curling and twisting as they reached for the sky. The leaves, a vibrant green that seemed to pulse with an otherworldly energy, were adorned with the most peculiar of decorations.

Nestled among the foliage were tiny, intricately crafted pieces of furniture, as if a skilled artisan had created a miniature world within the plants. Delicate, ornate chairs no larger than a thimble perched precariously on the edges of leaves, their velvet cushions still plump and inviting despite their diminutive size. Miniature mahogany tables, their surfaces polished to a high sheen, balanced on the slender stems, laden with silver platters bearing minuscule feasts fit for a fairy court.

As Finley's gaze traveled higher, he noticed the glimmering of crystal caught in the vines. Miniature chandeliers, their delicate arms draped with strings of tiny, twinkling lights, hung suspended from the tendrils, casting a soft, enchanting glow upon the scene. The crystals refracted the light, sending shimmering rainbows dancing across the stone façade, as if the building itself had been touched by magic.

The upper floor, once the tailor's humble abode, had undergone an equally astonishing transformation. The windows, once simple panes of glass, now resembled the stained-glass masterpieces found in grand cathedrals. Vibrant hues of ruby, sapphire, and emerald danced across the surface, depicting scenes of mythical creatures and fantastical land-scapes. The intricate designs seemed to move and shift with a life of their own, as if the figures within the glass were engaged in a silent, eternal dance.

The roof, once a simple thatch of straw and reeds, had been replaced by a canopy of shimmering, iridescent leaves. Each leaf was as large as a shield, their edges gilded with threads of gold and silver that caught the light and sent it cascading down the walls in a mesmerizing display. The leaves rustled softly in the breeze, their gentle whispers carrying the promise of secrets waiting to be unveiled.

Clever, Finley's talent allowed.

"Mom, what—"

"There was no warning," Finley's father said, his voice heavy with sorrow. "One minute we were sleeping, and the next minute the magic was faltering."

"Falt—oh, no," Finley moaned, finally seeing it. A group of humans had clustered near one side of the tailor's shop, where it abutted the adjacent bookseller. With a *clang*, they began hammering an iron spike into the wall, wedging it into the tight mortar lines. Leaves and tiny pieces of furniture fell to the cobbled walk. More tellingly, every blow sent sparks of blue-white energy rippling up the building, as the magic holding his parents' home was disrupted by the iron. Each cascade of sparks brought more cheers, rumblings, and shouts from the humans scattered up and down the street.

"Is everyone out?" Finley asked quietly.

His mother nodded. "It was just us."

Listen to them, his talent prompted.

Finley turned his attention to the crowd. Murmurs of

witchcraft and *Hunt* were rippling between the small knots of humans who'd gathered. Two women detached themselves and ran toward the village's church, doubtless to fetch the local priest—although Finley couldn't imagine why the man wasn't already here.

With a resounding clang that echoed through the narrow streets, another iron spike was driven deep into the mortar of the tailor's shop. The moment the metal pierced the stone, a blinding flash of blue-white light erupted from the point of impact, illuminating the faces of the gathered villagers with an eerie, otherworldly glow. The air crackled with energy, the hairs on the back of Finley's neck standing on end as the magic that had once sustained his parents' home began to unravel.

As the iron spike sank deeper into the wall, the acrid scent of burning leaves and scorched wood filled the air, mingling with the tang of salt and the metallic odor of the iron itself. The verdant vines that had once adorned the building began to wither and blacken, their leaves curling and crumbling to ash as the magic that had given them life drained away. The miniature furniture that had nestled so charmingly among the foliage burst into flames, the delicate chairs and tables reduced to smoldering embers in mere seconds.

The stained-glass windows shattered in a cascade of glittering shards, the intricate designs and vibrant colors lost forever as the glass rained down upon the cobblestones below. The iridescent canopy of leaves that had once crowned the roof dissolved in a shower of sparks, each golden and silver thread winking out of existence like the dying embers of a once-glorious fire.

With the runes on the building broken, it too began to show signs of weakness. Mortar flaked from between the stones of its walls, and its timbers—carefully and lovingly carved, but inexpertly set and joined—began to tremble. The building wouldn't collapse immediately, Finley knew, but the next strong storm that blew in would likely damage it beyond repair. This was the symbiosis between humans and witchkind, but with the runes destroyed and the magic ended, the humans' works would begin to crumble.

One starts to think we shouldn't have held them back, his talent said sadly. *If it hadn't been for the damned iron, your Order would never have even begun.*

Finley's misery kept him from replying.

His mother was sobbing, and his father held her tight. "Years of hoarding our magic," he whispered, a single tear trickling down his cheek, "and it's all gone."

Two more of witchkind approached, their expressions full of sadness. "You can stay with us," they offered quietly. "As long as you need."

The humans' fervor grew with each passing moment, their voices rising in a cacophony of fear and anger. They surged forward, emboldened by the destruction of the magical building, their faces contorted with a mixture of righteous indignation and primal terror. Torches held high, they cast long, flickering shadows across the narrow streets, the dancing flames reflecting the chaos that had taken hold of their hearts.

The village priest, his robes billowing in the early morning breeze, finally arrived, his face a mask of grim determination. He held a heavy, iron-bound tome in his hands, the ancient pages crackling as he opened it to a well-worn passage. His voice boomed above the clamor, reciting words in a long-forgotten tongue, each syllable imbued with the weight of centuries of suspicion and mistrust.

As the priest's chanting grew louder, the villagers began to take up the cry, their voices blending in a discordant chorus of accusation and condemnation. "Witchcraft!" they shouted, their eyes wide with a feverish intensity. "Hunt them down! Purge the evil from our midst!"

The air grew thick with the scent of smoke and sweat, the palpable fear and anger of the crowd mingling with the acrid tang of the iron spikes driven into the stone.

The once-peaceful village had transformed into a seething cauldron of hostility, the gentle lapping of waves against the shore drowned out by the roar of the frenzied mob. Finley's heart raced as he watched the scene unfold, his mind reeling with the sudden, devastating loss of their magical home and the looming threat of the villagers' wrath.

"I don't know that you'll be safe," Kelden cautioned. "This isn't over yet." Already the villagers had begun hammering a stake into a nearby building, waiting for some reaction. When nothing happened, they moved on to another. "They may do this to every building in the village before they're satisfied."

Finley's parents and their friends exchanged glances. "The inn," the one man suggested. "The hidden space isn't in the main building, it's in the stables. They won't think of that."

"Possibly," Finley allowed. "Go. We'll—"

"Go with them," Kelden insisted. "Arcadia and I will stay out. We'll keep an eye on things. We can wake everyone if the mob gets close. And... I have some ideas on how we can protect everyone. Go. Rest."

Finley started to protest, but then nodded. With one last glance at his ruined family home, he pulled his parents away and led them to the village inn.

***

. . .

As Finley stepped out into the morning light, he could see that the village was a changed place. The once-bustling streets were now eerily quiet, the only sounds the distant cry of seagulls and the soft whisper of the sea breeze. The cobblestones were littered with the detritus of the night's chaos—broken glass, scorched wood, and the occasional glint of a discarded iron spike.

The buildings that bore the brunt of the mob's fury stood like wounded sentinels, their facades marred by gaping holes where the spikes were driven in. Some of the structures seem to sag, as if the very life had been drained from them, their timbers creaking and groaning in the salt-laden air. The once-vibrant paint on the shutters and doors is now faded and peeling, as if the color itself had been leached away by the iron's touch.

"Were any more homes—"

"None," Kelden said, proud through evident fatigue. "Arcadia and I cast some illusions—nothing big. Lights playing up one side of a building, shadows scampering down another. But only on buildings we knew didn't contain any secret spaces. So the spikes only got hammered into plain buildings."

"They still managed to take out a rune here and there," Arcadia added, nodding to one sagging structure, "and they're going to lose those come the next storm. But nobody else is displaced."

"Where are they all?" Finley asked. At this hour, the little village should have been bustling, preparing for the return of the fishing fleet—which Finley could see was still bobbing at their berths.

"Some of them are sleeping it off," Kelden said with a wry grin. "The liquor came out a few hours ago. Some are in the church, doing some kind of ceremony." Then he frowned. "This isn't going to be the last of it."

"Mom and Dad are already spreading the word. There's to be a meeting tonight."

People without physical homes are going to be noticed, his talent warned. *The Veil is... thinner. More than I've seen, especially here and now.*

Finley relayed that.

"It never occurred to me," Arcadia mused, rubbing her eyes.

"What?" Kelden asked.

"You have all these people, our people, working shoulder-to-shoulder with the humans every day," she said with a shrug. "It never occurs to anyone that some of those people go to a home, and others just... vanish? Nobody ever wonders where they *live?*"

"The Veil," Finley confirmed. "It's more than just making people explain away something odd they've seen. It keeps them from thinking about all the things they *don't* see."

"And it's failing," Kelden said.

"It's getting—" he began.

"Finley," Arcadia warned, her tone suddenly alert and low. "It's Landon."

Finley spun to see their former classmate and colleague sauntering down the deserted street, a smug grin plastered across his face.

Finley, don't— his talent warned.

Finley's world exploded in a red haze.

Distantly, he realized that he retained access to all four elements of magic, as if his affinities had doubled. But at the front of his mind was nothing more complex than *revenge.*

He lashed out with a battering ram of Earth magic, rocks and soil gathering themselves from the road and into a solid form. It punched Landon in the stomach, sending the larger boy flying backwards, gasping for breath. But he quickly rose to one knee, an expression of *hunger* hardening his features. His grin was now feral and cold, and he brushed aside Finley's follow-up attack.

Landon's eyes glinted with a cruel, predatory light as he rose to his feet, his movements fluid and assured despite the force of Finley's attack. He brushed dirt from his clothes with a nonchalant air, as if the assault had been nothing more than a minor inconvenience.

"Well, well, Finley," he drawled, his voice dripping with condescension. "I see you've learned a few new tricks. But do you really think you can match me?"

Finley gritted his teeth, his hands clenching into fists at his sides. The rage that had consumed him moments before still simmered beneath the surface, but it was now tempered by a cold, calculating fury. He knew he couldn't allow his emotions to control him, not if he hoped to stand a chance against Landon's formidable power.

"What have you done, Landon?" he demanded, his voice tight with barely contained anger. "Why are you doing this?"

Landon threw back his head and laughed, the sound harsh and grating in the stillness of the morning air. "Why? Because I can, Finley. Because I'm tired of hiding in the shadows, pretending to be something I'm not. Tired of skulking in the shadows. Dmitry's bringing us into the light. It's time for witchkind to take our rightful place in this world, and I intend to lead the charge."

He spread his arms wide, and Finley felt the crackle of magic in the air, the hairs on the back of his neck standing on end as Landon gathered his power. The ground beneath their feet began to tremble, small pebbles and bits of debris rising into the air as if suspended by invisible strings.

"You're mad," Finley breathed, his eyes wide with horror. "You can't possibly think that revealing ourselves to the humans will end well. They'll hunt us down, just as they did in the past."

Landon's grin only grew broader, his eyes glinting with a manic light. "Oh, they'll try," he purred, his voice silken and dangerous. "But they'll soon learn the folly of their ways. With the power we possess, we can crush them like the insects they are."

He thrust his hand forward, and a bolt of searing white energy shot from his palm, hurtling toward Finley with terrifying speed. Finley barely had time to throw up a hasty shield of Sky magic, the bolt shattering against the barrier in a shower of sparks. He was dimly aware of Arcadia and Kelden moving to support him, vaguely aware of his talent trying to cut through his anger.

Landon slammed Finley with a rapid-fire series of assaults. But Finley realized that his opponent's attacks were one-dimensional: with his affinity limited to a single element, his options for offensive maneuvers were limited. And, he'd never been a particularly apt student. Finley began adjusting his approach, letting Kelden and Arcadia defend—something their Sky magic was well-suited for—and shifting his own efforts toward Sea and Flame. The only two elements that truly opposed each other, he managed to quickly weave them into a succession of quick jabs, forcing Landon to give ground and defend himself.

Rune after rune flashed through Finley's mind, distracting even his talent. This is where Finley had excelled in school, and even after that in the Order: his mind was fast, and he had an encyclopedic memory for runes, even the most complex constructs. And now, with all for magical affinities open to him, his options were all but endless.

But it was Kelden who managed the decisive blow, likely thanks to the greater emphasis on combative magics taught at Thornwaithe's. They stepped forward, their eyes narrowed in concentration as they drew upon the power of Sky magic. The air around them began to swirl, gentle at first, like a soft breeze playing through the leaves of a tree. But as they focused their will, the wind grew in intensity, whipping about them in a frenzy of motion. Finley had mistaken it for a defensive construct at first, but Kelden quickly dispelled that notion.

Dust and debris were caught up in the maelstrom, forming a vortex that spun faster and faster, its edges shimmering with an otherworldly light. Kelden's hair and clothing whipped about them as they stood at the center of the storm, their hands outstretched, fingers splayed as they shaped the currents to their bidding.

With a sudden, sharp gesture, Kelden sent the whirlwind hurtling toward Landon. It moved with the speed of a lightning bolt, faster than should have been possible, the air screaming as it was rent asunder by the force of Kelden's magic. The vortex engulfed Landon, lifting him off his feet and sending him tumbling head over heels, his limbs flailing helplessly as he was tossed about like a rag doll.

But Kelden wasn't finished. Even as Landon struggled to right himself within the swirling winds, Kelden began to weave another spell. Their hands danced in intricate patterns, his fingers tracing arcane sigils in the air. The wind around Landon began to change, the howling gale giving way to an eerie, unnatural silence. The dust and debris that had been caught up in the vortex suddenly stopped moving, hanging suspended in midair as if frozen in time.

Landon's eyes widened in shock as he realized he was trapped, his body held immobile by the strange, oppressive stillness that now surrounded him. He struggled to move, to break free of the invisible bonds that held him, but it was as if he were encased in solid stone.

But Landon couldn't just surrender.

With a *crack*, the earth around him split, a jagged breach in the ground opening. From it, a profusion of rocks began rising.

Earth magic can be so literal, Finley's talent said, finally managing to break through. *Try th—*

There was no time. Kelden had seen the attack building as well, and acted decisively. A solid column of air crashed down into Landon from above, a miniature of the kind of battle-ending tactic so commonly associated with Thornwaithe's alum under the control of magic itself. The pillar of air—visible only by the distortion it caused around itself—hammered Landon into the ground. This time, the audible *crack* came from Landon's bones as his arms and legs slammed into the earth by his side. He screamed.

"I—" Finley started, intending to thank Kelden for his quick action.

"Stop him!" Arcadia shouted. A gush of air rushed from her and toward Landon, who was managing to rummage for something inside his shirt.

In a burst of Flame magic, he vanished.

A silence descended on the street, one so absolute it was almost tangible. Dust settled slowly as a few small rocks rolled this way and that.

"Finley," Arcadia said, her voice now low and urgent.

Finley refocused and saw the half-dozen humans who'd ventured from their shops and homes, each taking in the scene with eyes like saucers.

Witchcraft, someone whispered.

Finley felt a strange sensation, like the time he'd once bent over and felt the seam in his trousers give way.

The Veil, his talent said, its voice filled with resignation.

Arcadia's magic, weaker and more jittery than Finley had ever experienced, carried them away.

CHAPTER 19

A Dream

"Everyone's preparing to leave the village," Kelden said, slumping into a chair.

Arcadia had taken them to her own home town, to an inn run by witchkind. She'd leased rooms for them all, insisting she couldn't deal with her family until she'd had a full sleep. They'd managed a quiet, filling lunch before Finley's eyelids, struggling to remain open, threatened immediate unconsciousness.

"Off to bed, then," Arcadia insisted. "At least six marks. We need to be rested for... whatever comes next."

"We have to find Landon," Finley insisted, forcing his eyes open.

"He's doubtless at the Farm being Healed," Arcadia said, failing to suppress a yawn. "We're all wiped out. I need to sleep and I need to Gather. Go."

Finley considered protesting until his talent nudged him. *She's right.*

Fine.

He rose silently, made his way to his assigned room, and collapsed into the bed.

***

Finley's mind, exhausted as it was, couldn't completely give over to a restful, blissful sleep. Instead, it seemed to toss and turn like a fishing boat on a stormy sea, casting up a vague sense of threat and a desperate longing for slumber.

But then, with an almost perceptible *snap,* his mind went blank. The half-formed visions of danger faded, the nearly unconscious pressure to *do something,* the nebulous sense of dread... they all slipped away.

The darkness in Finley's mind slowly came to life. At first, it was just a faint glimmer, a barely perceptible shift in the endless void. But then, as if drawn by an invisible hand, gentle swirls of color began to emerge from the depths. They were soft and ethereal, like wisps of smoke dancing in the breeze. The colors were muted at first, pale shades of blue and green, but as they twirled and intertwined, they grew more vibrant, more alive.

In the distance, two moons hung in the sky, their pale light casting a ghostly glow over the dreamscape. They were dim and far away, like distant beacons in the night. And even further still, a sparkling blue-green mote of light twinkled, a tiny pinprick of brilliance amidst the vast expanse of darkness.

But it was the swirls of color that truly captured Finley's attention. They moved with a mesmerizing grace, weaving intricate patterns in the air. As they drifted closer, Finley realized that he could taste them on his tongue, each one a unique flavor that seemed to embody the very essence of the elements.

The first swirl, a deep blue-green, tasted of the Sea, a briny tang that brought to mind crashing waves and salt-kissed breezes. It was cool and refreshing, like a gulp of icy water on a hot summer day. The second swirl, a light and airy blue, tasted of the Sky, a crisp, airy flavor that filled Finley's lungs with the essence of freedom and flight. It was like inhaling the very breath of the heavens, a rush of exhilaration that made his heart soar. The third, brown and green, was the taste of the Earth, loamy and rich, with hints of moss and wildflowers. It was the flavor of life itself, of growth and renewal, of the deep, abiding strength that flowed through the roots of ancient trees. And the fourth whirl, all oranges and reds, tasted of Flame. Hot and smoky, but bright and demanding, it reminded him of the spicy foods of the south.

As Finley drank in these flavors, these elemental essences, he felt a strange sensation wash over him. It was as if he were being filled with a new kind of energy, a force that flowed through his veins like liquid fire. He could feel it pulsing in his fingertips, crackling in his mind, a wild, untamed power that begged to be unleashed.

And then, as suddenly as it had begun, the dream shifted. The swirls of color faded away, and Finley found himself standing in a vast, empty space. Before him, hovering in the midst of the darkness, was a very young man, with the same rare, pale white skin as Arcadia, neatly combed black hair, and flinty gray eyes. His lips slowly bent upward in the barest introduction of a smile, and he said, "Well. This is new."

Finley recognized the voice immediately as that of his invisible talent. "You're... in my head."

Now the man chuckled. "I've been in your head your entire life."

"Who are you?"

One aquiline eyebrow rose. "Now *that* is a very good question."

"You're the Origin, aren't you?"

"No. Not... no, I'm not. I thought I might be, but I'm distinct. Separate. But I'm *in* the Origin." The stone-gray eyes took on a faraway look. "The place where the four intersect. Earth, Sea, Sky, and Flame. All surrounded by the circle of Ending and Beginning."

As he spoke, the swirls of color returned, drifting lazily around the enigmatic figure like ethereal ribbons. They were more muted now, their vibrant hues softened to gentle whispers, but they still carried the essence of the elements—the smoky heat of Flame, the rich loam of Earth, the briny coolness of Sea, and the crisp freshness of Sky.

Finley watched, transfixed, as the wisps of color wove intricate patterns in the air, their movements almost hypnotic. They seemed to respond to the man's words, pulsing and swirling in time with his speech, as if they were an extension of his very being.

The swirls of color began to change, their hues shifting and blending in a mesmerizing dance. The deep green of Earth gave way to the shimmering blue of Sea, which in turn melted into the pale azure of Sky. And then, in a burst of brilliant orange and red, Flame emerged, its fiery tendrils licking at the edges of the other elements.

"Where magic comes from," Finley whispered.

The figure shrugged. "Sort of. Not really. It's as I told you —magic comes into the world through humans. They draw it up from the roots of the world, the bones of the continent. More comes from... there's a font, or sorts, but... for our purposes, it's from the humans. It spills from them, pure as can be. The Origin... *colors* the magic. Lends it the flavor of the elements. Makes it so that we—so that you—can manipulate it."

"Oh."

And now Finley could see it: the distant blue-green mote is the world, and it is filled with millions of points of pure light. Humans, pouring magic into the world. As it does so, the magic flows into the Origin, gaining tints of color before spreading across the land like a thick, multicolored blanket.

"I was asleep a long time, in the Origin. Floating there. Not really aware of anything."

"How long?"

"I'm guessing a couple of centuries."

"What woke you up?"

"I think *you* did. When you were born. I... it's still indistinct. But I remember a light, just a tiny pinpoint, but incredibly bright. Something I could latch on to. Something I can relate to. There's something about *you* that's... special, somehow. And slowly, as you grew up, I became more and more aware. It's been a slow process." He frowned. "And now Karal's return... I suspect my anger is bringing me out of it faster, now."

"You said that name before," Finley remembered.

His talent nodded. "I've had dealings with them. Always selfish, always putting both humans and witchkind at risk. Always justifying it, somehow. They always burn out their identity runes, change *who* they are. It's not just their name, you know. They cut much deeper when they change."

"You're sure it's the same?"

He nodded. "It's the same. It's their pattern. They've been doing it... well, forever. That clan goes back a long ways, if you trace it far enough. Through a hundred different names, a hundred different identities, back to the founding of the world. Then the Forging of the Axes. They meant to capture the Fifth Axis for themselves, but it... well, they couldn't do it. So they wound up with nothing. And oh, they *hated* having nothing. They *long* for power. Crave it. I think it's the only thing they care about. The one constant in their history."

"Can we stop them?"

His talent sighed. "I don't know. You felt the Veil, didn't you?"

Finley nodded. He could feel it even now, as if once he'd noticed it he couldn't *not* be aware of it. It was stretched taut, and he thought he could sense the tiniest of tears beginning to form.

Finley focused his mind's eye on the Veil, and as he did, it came into sharper focus. It was a gossamer layer, so thin and delicate that it seemed almost insubstantial, like a wisp of smoke or a breath of mist. And yet, there was a strength to it, a resilience that belied its fragile appearance.

The Veil was woven from countless strands of ancient magic, each one as fine as a spider's silk and as luminous as starlight. They crisscrossed and intertwined, forming an intricate tapestry that stretched as far as Finley's imagination could reach. The strands glimmered with a soft, ethereal light, pulsing gently like the beating of a distant heart.

As Finley watched, mesmerized, he began to discern patterns in the weave of the Veil. There were swirls and eddies, whirlpools of energy that seemed to draw the eye and the mind into their depths. There were also vast, sweeping currents, rivers of power that flowed majestically through the fabric of the Veil, carrying with them the very essence of magic itself.

And yet, for all its beauty and intricacy, Finley could see that the Veil was under immense strain. It was stretched taut, like a rubber band pulled to the very limit of its elasticity. In some places, it seemed to vibrate and hum with barely contained tension, as if it were on the verge of snapping at any moment. And there, just as Finley had sensed, were the beginnings of tears - tiny, almost imperceptible rips in the fabric of the Veil, like frayed threads in a well-worn garment.

As Finley peered closer, he could see the edges of the tears glowing with a sickly, greenish light, as if infected by some malevolent force. The strands around these rips seemed to writhe and recoil, as if trying to pull away from the spreading corruption.

"Can it be... fixed?"

His talent hesitated, and then shook its head. "It might be impossible. It's old magic, incredibly ancient. Older than our entire world. It was... repurposed, in a way, to form the Veil. If it tears... the only way to fix it isn't available anymore. There's a source, an anchor, so to speak, and it's out of reach. Of you, of me, of any of witchkind."

"And then we're exposed."

His talent nodded slowly, its demeanor somber. "Yes. It's not as simple as making humans explain away the odd gaffe, you know. It's not just making them ignore us when we appear out of nowhere. It's more subtle. It makes them ignore our runes. Makes them... not think about things. Why the street lamps can stay lit in the strongest wind, even with cracks in their glass. Why the fishing boats steer themselves away from storm fronts. Why the fishing nets never seem to twist themselves into knots. It's a hundred tiny things, a thousand, that just never occur to them. But if the Veil tears, they'll start thinking about it. All of witchkind could completely forswear any more magic, and the humans would still suspect. We make everything too *neat*. Too automatic. We contradict what *should* be." It shook its head again. "And if it tears, there's no going back."

"Could we really... I mean, could *they* really subjugate the humans?"

He snorted. "No. It's not just how they outnumber us. They're *immune* to magic, right? We can't affect them directly.

I've... what I've done is probably the limit. I don't think anyone other than you and I, working together, could nudge their minds, convince their flesh to heal. Certainly not across the entire world." He leaned toward Finley, his eyes piercing. "They would *know* they were being oppressed. And they would fight it, with every fiber of their being. Just as we would." He stood straighter, and glanced away for a moment. "But I'm starting to think the Veil wasn't the right way, any more than the Axes were."

"How so?"

"What do they teach you now, about the Forging?"

This was some of the earliest lore they'd been taught at Disemstoke's. "Humans had grown greedy for magic, and sought to control it. To control witchkind. They visited unspeakable horrors on us, took families hostage, all to bend us to their will. The Axes were formed to consolidate power in a few protectors, the Adherents, who could fight back against the humans."

His talent actually rolled its eyes. "Still the same story, then. And it's wrong. The Axes were Forged to consolidate power in a *few greedy men and women.* Nothing more, nothing less. They sought to raise themselves above the rest of witchkind, and above humans. Our—the runes used then, they *had* to be simpler—"

"Because magic itself was thinner, then. Less of it."

"No. Less of it *for everyone else,* yes, but there was *ample* power for the adherents."

"You were one of them, weren't you?"

A simple nod.

"You... were the last one, weren't you?"

Another nod, slower and deeper this time as understanding bloomed in Finley's mind.

"That means you're—"

"Don't," his talent cautioned. "I was. But I'm not. And naming me won't help. It might... constrain me, as I am now."

"So if the Veil was a mistake..." Finley said, picking up the earlier comment.

"I don't think we should have Sundered the relationship between humans and witchkind," his talent said, seeming grateful for the conversational turn. "That was before... my time, of course. The Sundering happened sometime after the Forging, once everyone realized the humans weren't going to give in. They started fighting back. And even the Adherents weren't immune to iron."

"So if the Veil falls now..."

"It will be horrific," his talent said firmly. "The relationship is broken, and has been for millennia. The only way to go back would have been to rebuild that. To create trust. To openly be the partners that humans and witchkind secretly are, now. But... it may be too late. If the Veil tears before that trust is built, it will be... chaos."

"Landon and Dmitry—they haven't been building trust."

"No. They've been sowing fear. Fear to make the humans dangerous to us. To restart the Hunts *again*. Because *that* will make witchkind fearful. Make them willing to take steps they wouldn't have, without that fear."

"It's working," Finley said sadly.

His talent nodded. "I know." Then it winked at him. "I'm more awake now, more aware now, than I have been since... well, since I went into the Origin. I'll help. I don't know if it will be enough, but I'll help."

"Can I ask you a question?"

"An easy one. You need to get some sleep."

"Am I really a Rune Smith? Or was it just you all along?"

His talent quirked its lips into a grin. "Can't both be true?"

CHAPTER 20

Confrontation

"Son, is this something *you* have to do?" Finley's father asked.

His son nodded. "It is, Dad. I'm probably... I might be the only one who can. And Arcadia's going to go regardless, and I owe it to her." Finley had managed to fall into a deep and uninterrupted sleep after his talent spoke to him, and he felt at least moderately refreshed. If nothing else, he'd Gathered sufficient magic during those few hours of sleep to fully replenish his reserves.

Arcadia and Kelden were speaking in hushed tones, across the inn's spacious common room from Finley and his parents.

Finley's father nodded slow acceptance. "I understand, then. Be... careful. If you can."

"I will. Where will you go?"

"With your aunt and uncle in Harbsmouth. We did a Sending last night, and they've told us there haven't been any riots or anything."

"Be careful. Please."

"We will. The plan is to look for someplace in Evermore, at least for the time being. If we're not safe there…"

"Yeah. I'll come find you when… we're done." Father and son embraced, and Finley joined Arcadia and Kelden. "I assume we're going to the Farm?"

Arcadia frowned. "Why would we do that?"

Finley's brow wrinkled. "I mean… Dmitry?"

She gave him a tight grin. "Why not go straight to the top?"

"Straight to—wait, do you mean Evermore?"

Her grin grew, and a wicked gleam lit her eyes. "I believe that's where we keep the Taryba, yes."

Kelden rolled his eyes. "I've been trying to talk her out of it."

"It hasn't worked," she countered.

Finley shrugged. "I guess I'm in. What's the goal?"

"Simple. We confront Adomaitis. We make sure *everyone* on the Taryba—Councilors, staff, everyone—knows what he's done. That he and Dmitry have been stacking the deck. That everything was *fine* before they started pushing the humans. That they've been the ones stretching the Veil."

Finley considered, and then nodded slowly. "Yeah, I guess that's it."

"Then off we go."

Fresh-smelling Sky magic surrounded them and spirited them away.

***

They arrived in one of Evermore's many bustling squares. By common agreement, witchkind never arrived directly inside one of Evermore's buildings unless it was a private residence and they'd received consent from those living there. With no concern about displays of magic, any other approach would have resulted in chaos, with people popping in and out of existence at all times. As it was, they still had to clear the square quickly to make room for new arrivals.

Evermore stretched out before them, a dazzling city of magic and wonder. The buildings were crafted from smooth white stone that seemed to glow softly in the mild morning sunlight. Graceful towers soared into the sky, their spires twisting and curving in whimsical shapes that defied gravity. Large windows of stained glass or crystal clear panes sparkled in every edifice, inviting in light and air.

The streets were paved with gently rounded cobblestones that chimed softly and melodically underfoot, the notes changing subtly as one strolled through different quarters of the city. Greenery and flowering vines cascaded from balconies, rooftop gardens, and window boxes, splashing the ivory cityscape with vibrant color. Gentle breezes carried the mingled scents of a thousand blooming flowers.

In the squares and plazas, fountains danced with enchanted waters that leapt and spun in mesmerizing patterns. The air thrummed with a palpable aura of magic that permeated every molecule. It was the very lifeblood of the city, as much a part of Evermore as the ancient stones from which it was built.

Witchkind strolled the avenues garbed in robes of every hue, some walking with purpose towards unknown destinations, others meandering languidly as if they had all the time in the world. Which, Finley mused, they very well might. Here there was no need to rush. While many of witchkind preferred the simpler existence of the human villages and towns, those who lived in Evermore lived a life full of magic and few burdens. Especially since the Fall of the Adherents and the return of abundant magic to the world, Evermore was the closest thing to a paradise anywhere on the continent.

Finley, Arcadia and Kelden strode purposefully down the cobbled streets towards the grand hall where the Taryba convened. Myriad thoughts swirled through Finley's mind as he mentally prepared himself for the confrontation to come. He knew Adomaitis would not yield easily, that he would fight tooth and nail to maintain his newfound grip on power. But they had to try. For the sake of witchkind, for the very survival of their world, they had to succeed.

As they approached the imposing marble edifice housing the Taryba chambers, Arcadia turned to her companions, eyes flashing with determination. "Remember, we stand united. No matter what tricks Adomaitis tries to pull, we do not waver. We get him to admit it, and we expose him."

Kelden and Finley nodded their assent. Taking a collective breath, the trio ascended the sweeping stairs and pushed open the heavy oaken doors.

The interior of the Taryba chambers was a breathtaking spectacle that dazzled the senses. The grand foyer soared several stories high, its vaulted ceiling adorned with an intricate mosaic crafted from thousands of precious gemstones. Rubies, sapphires, emeralds and diamonds glittered in elaborate patterns that depicted key moments from witchkind's storied history—the mythical Founding of the World, the Forging of the Axes, the Sacrifice of the Last Adherent, and more. The effect was mesmerizing, the way the light danced and refracted off the polished facets.

The walls were paneled in richly grained wood imbued with preservation magic to maintain their luster for centuries. Opulent tapestries hung at intervals, their threads woven into runs that made the scenes of witchkind's greatest triumphs and achievements seem to move and shimmer as if alive.

Underfoot, the floor was an expansive marble mosaic that formed a grand map of the lands witchkind called home. Each tile was inlaid with chips of colored stone and mother-of-pearl to denote some of the key landmarks in the world, like a giant map. As one walked across it, faint chiming notes would sound, indicating the region being traversed.

Throughout the space, pedestals and alcoves displayed ancient magical artifacts and relics, each with a fascinating story. Some were said to still hold residual power from the great magic-workers who created and wielded them ages ago.

Hallways branched off in every direction, hinting at immense volumes of space that the building itself couldn't possibly contain. Witchkind's signature space-expanding magic on its greatest display, used here not to hide homes and shops, but to provide all the space needed for the government of witchkind, its record keeping, its tribunals, and more.

Arcadia stepped up to a small podium that glowed with a scintillating blue-green-purple light. "Councilor Adomaitis," she said clearly.

A glowing point of pink light detached itself and rose in front of them before drifting quickly and with purpose through the foyer.

The pink light led them down a hallway that exuded an air of stately formality, a marked contrast to the grand foyer's opulence. The walls were paneled in rich, dark wood polished to a mirror sheen, reflecting the soft glow of the floating witch-lights that hovered at intervals near the ceiling. Intricate brass sconces held flickering flames that cast dancing shadows, creating an interplay of light and dark that seemed to imbue the space with a sense of gravitas.

Underfoot, the floor here was crafted from alternating planks of honey-hued oak and deep mahogany, arranged in a herringbone pattern that drew the eye forward with its precise geometry. The wood had been worn smooth by centuries of footsteps, yet it retained its luster, a testament to the preservation runes carved like a decorative frieze along the floor's edges.

At evenly spaced intervals, alcoves housed life-sized bronze statues of witchkind's most revered leaders from ages past. Each figure was rendered with astonishing detail, from the drape of their robes to the wise, knowing expressions on their faces. Small plaques beneath each statue bore their names and a brief synopsis of their greatest achievements. Finley recognized a few from History classes in school—Valerius the Wise, who brokered the first peace accords with the humans; Isadora Stormweaver, who harnessed the power of the tempests to turn back the Blight; and even one of the Last Adherent himself, Daniel Scratch.

Good likeness, his talent murmured.

Finley's heart began to beat faster.

The pink light finally stopped before a set of double doors carved with an intricate tree motif, its branches spreading wide to encompass the entire portal. With a soft chime, the doors swung open of their own accord, revealing Adomaitis personal offices.

The offices' foyer was a large, circular room with a soaring, domed ceiling overhead. It was conservatively decorated in panels of honey-colored wood, and a small desk made from darker wood occupied the center of the room. Behind the desk was a young, friendly-looking man who smiled as they entered. "Welcome to Councilor Adomaitis' offices. How may I help you?"

"We're here to see him," Arcadia said firmly.

The receptionist pulled a well-practiced sigh of regret. "Alas, I'm afraid the Councilor is not available to take—"

Finley waved his hand, and the foyer's doors slammed shut. A rune carved itself into the wood, glowing with Earth magic as it knitted the two doors into a single slab of wood. "It's not a request," he said mildly. "I'm Finley Coughlan. This is Arcadia, and Kelden. We represent the Order of Some. The Councilor will see us. Tell him we're here."

The young man blinked as he processed what had just happened. "He, ah—" he stammered, clearly unprepared to deal with something this far off-script.

"Is he here?" Arcadia demanded.

"Not at—that is to say, I couldn't—"

"Sure you can," Finley offered.

"You know, you can't just fling magic—"

"That's not all we're going to be flinging," Arcadia said sweetly. "Where's he at?"

The receptionist's eyes flicked back and forth between them.

Try this, Finley's talent offered. *Old, but good. I'm curious to see if it still works.*

Middle Runic? Okay, Finley responded, trickling a healthy flow of magic. It seemed to accept a combination of everything he'd absorbed, drawing an equal share of Sky, Sea, Flame, and Earth, along with something... else.

Beginning and Ending, his talent supplied. *Focus it on him.*

Finley did so, and was surprised to see a gentle blue haze settle over the receptionist, who immediately looked tense and wary. "Where's Councilor Adomaitis?"

The man's mouth opened, and judging from the expression on the rest of his face, it was doing so of its own accord. "He's not here. He's almost never here. Only for full sessions of the Taryba, in fact."

Arcadia frowned. "Wait, that can't be right. Ram has been seeing him all the time, lately."

"Ram who?" the receptionist asked.

"Don't pretend—" Arcadia started with some heat.

"I don't think he can, right now," Finley said quickly, holding up a hand to calm her. "Do you know who Ram is? The Head of the Order?"

"No."

"But you know about the Order?"

"Yes."

"Would it be possible for Ram to have met with Adomaitis without you knowing?"

"Of course. Anywhere but in the office, really."

"And Adomaitis isn't here."

"No."

Arcadia asked, "Then where is he?"

"I don't know."

She frowned. "Who would know, then?"

The man's expression twisted a bit before he replied, "That's the thing. I *should* know. But he only ever shows up for council sessions, now. He comes here to retrieve his agenda, and then he goes into the main chamber, and that's the last I see of him until next time." He snapped his mouth close as if trying to hold back any further information.

"Okay," Finley said, dismissing the magic. *That's impressive,* he told his talent. *I've never heard of anything like that.*

And that's only the Third Form of the Axis, it replied cheerfully. *You should see the Fifth.*

"So what now?" Kelden asked.

"You could start by putting the door back," the receptionist said nastily.

Finley projected another rune, and the doors quickly resumed their original form and swung open. As they walked out, he said, "Do you think a trace would work?"

Arcadia nodded. "It's worth a try." She stopped as Finley pulled the doors shut behind them and they moved to one side of the hallway. A passing staffer gave them a curious look, but continued on her way. After a moment of concentration, Arcadia shook her head. "No good. Something in here's blocking it."

"Let's try mine," Finley said, recalling the rune in his mind.

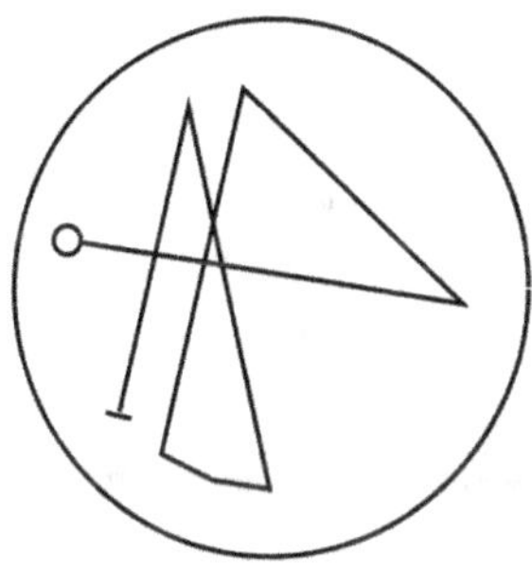

He focused his will, channeling magic into the rune. It drew both Sky and Flame, the two most ephemeral and flexible magics, well-suited to this task. He immediately felt his consciousness expand, reaching out like ethereal tendrils to find any trace of Adomaitis' magical signature.

At first, there was only a vast blankness, an empty void that seemed to swallow his probing magic. He pushed harder, pouring more power into the spell, determined to break through whatever was blocking him. The rune pulsed brighter in his mind, glowing with an intense blue-white light.

This is odd, his talent said.

Suddenly, he sensed something—the barest whisper of Adomaitis' presence. It was faint and fleeting, like a half-remembered dream upon waking. Finley latched onto it, trying to follow the faded trail, but it seemed to splinter and fragment, pulling his mind in a dozen different directions at once.

It was like grasping at wisps of smoke with his bare hands. Every time he thought he had a hold of it, the trace would dissolve, leaving him clutching at emptiness. A dull throbbing started behind his eyes as he strained to maintain his focus.

The magic twisted and writhed, as if actively fighting against his attempts to track the Councilor. Finley gritted his teeth, a bead of sweat tracing down his temple as he redoubled his efforts. But it was like trying to catch the wind—the more he struggled, the more elusive the trace became.

"It's not working," he said with a frown. "It's not even being blocked, just... misdirected. I think."

Give me a moment, his talent said, clearly intrigued. Flickering lines of white and blue arranged and rearranged themselves, seemingly trying hundreds of new configurations with every beat of Finley's heart. *How odd. And I'd grown so attached to those. Oh well.* Now the possibilities seemed to expand a thousandfold, glimmering through Finley's mind so quickly they blurred into a bright, twinkling light. *Oh, I see,* his talent said after a few more heartbeats. *They've done something to discourage order. So we embrace chaos. Try this.*

Finley focused his mind on the new rune, feeling its power coalesce in his thoughts. As he channeled magic into it, the rune ignited with a flickering orange glow shot through with erratic streaks of indigo—Flame magic intertwined with something more abstract and mercurial.

The sensation was wholly unlike his previous attempts at tracing. Instead of the focused, probing tendrils of before, this magic seemed to expand in all directions at once, like a swarm of fireflies dispersing into the night. It was chaotic, unpredictable, yet oddly freeing.

Finley let his mind drift, not trying to direct the magic but simply allowing it to flow where it willed. It was like trying to glimpse something in his peripheral vision—the harder he looked, the more it eluded him. So he relaxed, letting his thoughts unspool into randomness.

Suddenly, he caught a flicker of Adomaitis' presence, dancing at the edges of his perception. It was there and gone again in an instant, a mote of light flickering in and out of existence. Finley resisted the urge to pounce on it, instead letting his unfocused mind simply observe.

The trace reappeared, slightly stronger now, like a skittish creature slowly gaining confidence. It darted and weaved in erratic patterns, never quite where Finley expected it to be. But by not looking directly at it, by embracing the chaos, Finley was able to grasp snatches of the elusive trace, his mind dancing along its convoluted path. It led him in dizzying spirals and sudden sharp turns, defying any sense of linear direction. He let himself be pulled along, a leaf caught in the eddies of a whimsical breeze.

The trace grew stronger, coalescing into a shimmering thread that pulsed with an otherworldly light. It was a strange, almost unsettling hue that seemed to shift and change even as Finley tried to perceive it—now a sickly green, now a bruised purple, now a color that had no name.

The thread wove a meandering path through the hallways of the Taryba chambers, passing through walls and doors as if they were no more than mist. Finley's consciousness followed, unbound by the constraints of physical space.

He caught glimpses of rooms and chambers he had never seen—a vaulted library with towering shelves that stretched into infinity, a shimmering pool that reflected a night sky filled with unfamiliar constellations, a hall of mirrors that fractured his sense of self into a thousand shards.

On and on the trace led him, deeper into the labyrinthine heart of the building. The air seemed to thicken, taking on a cloying, almost oily quality. Finley's thoughts felt sluggish, as if he were trying to swim through honey. But still he followed, driven by a growing sense of urgency. He knew, with a certainty that defied logic, that he was getting close.

So interesting, his talent murmured, as if peering over his shoulder.

The thread pulsed brighter now, its uncanny hue searing itself into Finley's mind. It was leading him downward, spiraling ever deeper into the bowels of the earth. The air grew colder, damper, and a sense of ancient, brooding malevolence seemed to press in on him from all sides.

Suddenly, the thread went taut, quivering like a plucked bowstring. Finley's consciousness hurtled forward, pulled inexorably towards its destination. He braced himself, unsure of what he would find...

And then he was there. A cavernous chamber, hewn from living rock and suffused with an eerie, pulsating light that seemed to emanate from the very walls. The air was thick with the tang of ozone and something else, something dark and acrid that caught at the back of Finley's throat.

"I've got him," Finley said hoarsely. He began pulling magic to himself and pictured a travel rune in his mind, but Arcadia laid a hand on his arm.

"No magic," she warned. "Not here. You won't believe the alarms, and it might not even work, depending on what rune you have in mind. Can you see the way there?" Finley nodded, reaching for more magic to reinforce the glowing thread in his mind. "Lead the way."

Finley led the way, his eyes half-closed as he followed the shimmering, erratically pulsing thread that only he could perceive. It wove a dizzying path through the hallways, penetrating barriers as if they were mere dreams. Arcadia and Kelden followed close behind, exchanging glances of mingled anticipation and trepidation as they walked in Finley's wake. They had to dodge hurrying staffers, and double back more than a few times as the thread wound back on itself.

The hallways grew increasingly maze-like as they progressed, the opulent wood paneling giving way to rougher, older stone. The air took on a musty quality, redolent with the scent of ages past. Witchlights flickered fitfully in sconces that looked as if they hadn't been tended to in decades, casting an uncertain, wavering light.

Finley made an abrupt turn, veering towards what appeared to be a solid expanse of wall. As they drew closer, however, the stones seemed to shimmer and dance, revealing the ghostly outline of a door that had been cleverly concealed, the seams blending almost perfectly with the surrounding masonry. Finley reached out, his hand passing through the seemingly solid stone as if it were no more than an illusion. With a soft grinding sound, the hidden door swung inward, revealing a narrow staircase that spiraled down into darkness.

The hidden staircase wound down into the earth, the rough stone steps worn smooth by centuries of treading feet. The air grew colder and damper as they descended, their breath misting before their faces in the chill. The only light came from the flickering witchlights that cast eerie, dancing shadows on the close walls.

Down and down they spiraled, the passageway growing narrower with each turn until they had to hunch their shoulders and walk in single file. Finley kept his eyes half-closed, his attention focused inward on the chaotic, pulsing thread of Adomaitis' magical signature. It was stronger now, throbbing with an almost manic intensity that set his teeth on edge.

"We must be getting close," Arcadia murmured from behind him, her voice oddly muffled in the oppressive closeness of the stairwell.

Kelden grunted in agreement. "Can't imagine this goes on much deeper. We've got to be well below the foundations by now."

As if in response to his words, the staircase terminated abruptly in a small, circular antechamber. The walls were rough-hewn bedrock, glistening with moisture and shot through with veins of some dark, crystalline substance that caught the witchlights and fractured it into strange, unsettling colors.

And there, in the middle of the small room, was a solid, translucent crystal pillar.

"Adomaitis," Arcadia whispered.

In the center of the antechamber, the crystal pillar glowed with an inner light, pulsing softly like the beat of a distant heart. It stood taller than a man, its facets perfectly smooth and symmetrical. And there, suspended within its translucent depths, was the unmistakable figure of Councilor Adomaitis.

He hung motionless, his robes drifting about him as if he were submerged in some invisible, viscous fluid. His eyes were closed, his face slack in an expression of profound repose. His skin had taken on a pale, almost luminous quality, as if he had been carved from the same crystal that imprisoned him.

Finley stepped closer, marveling at the intricacy of the magic at work. Through his talent, he could sense the complex web of enchantments woven through the crystal, a tapestry of spells so dense and interwoven that it was almost a physical presence in the room. Sky magic to suspend, Earth to preserve, Flame to energize, and Sea to stabilize—all bound together in a configuration of staggering power and precision.

As he studied the suspended figure, Finley noticed details he had missed at first glance. Adomaitis' hands were folded across his chest, his fingers interlaced in a gesture that seemed almost ritualistic. And around his neck hung a heavy gold medallion, inscribed with runes that pulsed with the same unsettling light as the crystal itself.

Arcadia circled the pillar slowly, her brow furrowed in thought. "This is advanced magic. Beyond anything I've ever seen or even heard of. What could possibly be the purpose of keeping him like this?"

Such things were possible, once, Finley's talent murmured. *I wouldn't have thought they still were.*

Kelden shook his head, his expression grim. "Nothing good,

that's for sure. It's like he's in some kind of stasis or suspended animation."

"It's nothing more than a piece of artwork," came a sharp voice from behind them.

They whirled to see...

"Councilor Adomaitis?" Kelden asked, their brow wrinkling in confusion.

Adomaitis stood in the entryway to the antechamber, his hands clasped behind his back and a thin smile playing across his lips. He was a tall, imposing figure, with broad shoulders and a regal bearing that seemed to fill the small space. His robes were of the finest silk, a rich burgundy hue that shimmered softly in the witchlight, adorned with intricate golden embroidery along the hems and sleeves.

His face was angular and aquiline, with high, prominent cheekbones and a sharp, pointed chin. His skin was pale and smooth, almost unnaturally so, as if carved from alabaster. Jet-black hair, shot through with streaks of silver at the temples, was combed back from his high forehead in smooth, precise waves.

But it was his eyes that commanded attention—a piercing, icy blue that seemed to bore into the very soul. They glittered with a keen intelligence and an undercurrent of something darker, more calculating. When those eyes fixed upon you, it felt as if he could see through all pretense and deception, straight to the core of your being.

He stepped further into the chamber, his movements fluid and graceful, almost predatory. The air seemed to chill and crackle with his presence, a palpable aura of power that set the hairs on the back of Finley's neck standing on end. "Obviously," he said imperiously. "And you're trespassing. Quite significantly." Two men stepped out from behind the second

Adomaitis, their hands poised to cast something that Finley had no doubt would be combative.

This isn't right, Finley's talent warned.

With no further prompt, Finley cast the rune they'd used on the receptionist.

As Finley channeled magic into the Middle Runic figure, the air in the chamber seemed to vibrate and hum with building power. The rune ignited in his mind, glowing with a brilliant blue-white light that pulsed in time with his heartbeat. He focused his will on the figure of Adomaitis standing before them, pouring all his intent and desire for truth into the spell.

For a moment, nothing seemed to happen. Adomaitis stood there, a smug smile playing across his lips, his icy blue eyes glittering with disdain. But then, something shifted. It started as a barely perceptible flicker, a ripple across the surface of his form, like the disturbance on a pond from a thrown pebble.

The ripple grew, spreading outward from Adomaitis' core, gaining speed and intensity with each passing second. His form began to waver and distort, as if he were a reflection in a funhouse mirror. The colors of his robes bled and ran together, the rich burgundy and gold melting into a sickly, iridescent swirl.

Adomaitis' face contorted, his features stretching and warping in grotesque ways. His eyes bulged, the icy blue darkening to a stormy, turbulent gray. His mouth opened in what might have been a scream or a snarl, but no sound emerged. Instead, fracture lines appeared, spreading across his skin like a cracked porcelain mask. With a sickening crunch, Adomaitis' form shattered into a thousand glittering shards that hung suspended in the air for a heartbeat before dissolving into motes of sickly, greenish light that winked out like dying fireflies.

In his place stood a figure that they knew well.

"Dmitry," Arcadia said with disgust.

Finley felt her pulling power from her reserves.

"Kill them," Dmitry sneered.

Dmitry's henchmen moved with blinding speed, their hands weaving intricate patterns in the air as they summoned their magic. The first, a burly man with a shaved head and a scar running down his cheek, slammed his palms against the stone floor. Instantly, the bedrock buckled and heaved, jagged spikes of rock erupting from the ground like the teeth of some monstrous beast. They shot towards Finley and his companions, the air shimmering with the heat of the Earth magic that propelled them.

Arcadia reacted with lightning reflexes, her own hands moving in a blur of motion. A shimmering shield of Sky magic sprang into existence before them, a wall of cerulean energy that pulsed and undulated like the waves of a storm-tossed ocean. The stone spikes slammed into the barrier with a resounding boom, shattering into a thousand razor-sharp fragments that ricocheted off the magical shield in a dazzling display of sparks and shards.

But even as Arcadia deflected the first attack, the second henchman was already in motion. He was tall and lean, with long, stringy hair and eyes that glowed with an almost feverish intensity. He thrust his hands forward, and twin jets of searing Flame magic erupted from his fingertips, twisting and coiling like serpents of living fire. They struck Arcadia's shield with a roar, the force of the impact sending her stumbling back, her face contorted with effort as she struggled to maintain the shield against the onslaught of Flame magic. The air crackled and sizzled, the acrid stench of ozone mingling with the coppery tang of blood magic that flowed from the two henchmen like a noxious tide.

Finley leapt into action, his hands moving in a complex pattern as he channeled a torrent of Earth magic. The floor beneath the lean henchman's feet suddenly turned to quicksand, the solid rock liquefying and sucking him down like a malevolent quagmire. The man let out a yelp of surprise, his concentration broken as he struggled to free himself from the grasping morass.

Kelden seized the opportunity, their hands weaving a net of shimmering Sky magic that engulfed the burly henchman. The man roared in fury, his muscles straining against the ethereal bonds, but the more he struggled, the tighter the net constricted, until he could barely draw breath.

Dmitry snarled, his eyes flashing with a malevolent light. "Fools!" He raised his hands, and the air around him began to warp and distort, as if reality itself was bending to his will.

For Finley, time froze.

You're not going to win this, his talent warned him.

His talent expanded his perception. Suddenly Finley could see magic itself, laid bare before his eyes in all its intricate, awe-inspiring complexity.

It was like stepping into a whole new plane of existence. The air around them was alive with shimmering strands of power, weaving and dancing in mesmerizing patterns. Each type of magic had its own distinct hue and texture. Sky magic manifested as translucent ribbons of cerulean and aquamarine that rippled and flowed like wind-tossed currents. Earth magic was a tapestry of rich greens and browns, the strands as strong and sturdy as ancient tree roots delving deep into the soil. Flame magic coruscated in vivid reds, oranges, and golds, the threads crackling and sparking with barely contained energy. And Sea magic undulated in shades of blue-green and turquoise, its strings eddying and swirling like the ever-shifting tides.

But it was more than just seeing the individual types of magic. Finley could perceive how they interacted, the way they wove together in endlessly intricate configurations to create spells of staggering power and complexity. Runes, he realized, were merely the physical anchors, the way a caster's mind could interpret and shape the raw stuff of magic. But this... this was magic in its purest, most primal form.

And at the center of it all was Dmitry, a maelstrom of dark, pulsating energy that seemed to draw in the very fabric of magic around him. Tendrils of oily black and sickly green snaked out from his form, ensnaring and tainting the strands of purer magic, bending them to his twisted will.

Stolen power, his talent realized. *An old family trick.*

Finley and his talent were momentarily frozen as they took in the spectacle before them. Dmitry was a master of magic, his control and power far surpassing anything they had ever seen. It was clear that he had perfected a feel for the raw energy that surrounded them, far beyond simply memorizing runes.

And what he was constructing here would end them.

Then what do we do? Finley asked desperately, his mind racing.

I'll show you, his talent said, and here Finley sensed a tinge of reluctance and regret, *but you can never use it again. And you must* focus. *You must direct it* only *at this man and these fighters. No-one else. Do you agree?*

I do, Finley said.

You will regret this, his talent warned. *Do you still agree?*

Finley hesitated less than an eye blink before deciding. Arcadia's life, and Kelden's, were at stake. *I do.*

Then empower this, his talent said, seeming to shake its head in resignation. *And* focus.

Finley fed the rune all the power it could handle... and it demanded *more.* He emptied himself, grasping to Gather more power as the rune sucked him dry.

I didn't— his talent started.

The rune reached out to Finley's allies, and Arcadia screamed as her magic was pulled from her. Kelden grunted and fell to one knee, breathing heavily as his own magic was smoothly ripped from him.

Focus, his talent reminded him.

Through blurred, red-tinged eyes, Finley *focused.* He stared at Dmitry, held the man's image firmly in his mind. *Dmitry of Clan Gelbėtojas,* he roared in his mind.

NO! his talent screamed.

Time returned to its usual pace.

An unholy shriek rent the air as a seething mass of dark wraiths exploded into existence, bursting forth from the very fabric of reality. They were living shadows, writhing and twisting in a grotesque parody of life. Their forms were vaguely humanoid, but stretched and distorted in impossible ways, with elongated limbs that ended in razor-sharp claws and gaping maws filled with rows of needle-like teeth.

The wraiths moved with a terrifying swiftness, their shadowy forms blurring and phasing through the air like a nightmarish swarm. One of them lunged at Dmitry, its inky black form engulfing him in an instant. Dmitry's scream was abruptly cut off as the wraith consumed him whole, his body and magic alike devoured by the insatiable darkness.

Two more wraiths descended upon the henchmen, their claws rending flesh and their maws devouring souls. The men's agonized wails echoed through the chamber for a brief, horrifying moment before they too were silenced forever, their essences absorbed into the ever-growing horde.

Thousands more wraiths poured forth, a tidal wave of living shadow that surged through the walls and out into the world beyond. They passed through solid stone as if it were nothing more than mist, leaving behind only a bone-chilling cold and a lingering sense of dread in their wake.

Finley fell to his knees. To one side, Arcadia was sobbing uncontrollably, blood dripping from her nose. To the other, Kelden had fallen forward, supporting himself on his elbows as blood seemed to ooze from the very pores of his skin.

We've one more task, his talent said. Its tone was cold and distant, full of disappointment and... regret. *Adomaitis.*

Right, Finley thought wearily, wiping his forehead and

gasping at the slick of blood that came away on the back of his hand. *What do I do?*

You already know the rune.

Finley started to protest, and then realized that he did.

Finley focused his mind on the rune for Freedom, feeling its gentle power coalesce in his thoughts. He channeled the last dregs of his magic into it, the rune glowing with a soft, pulsing blue light as it drew upon the soothing, restorative essence of Sea magic.

The rune's energy reached out, tendrils of cerulean light extending towards the crystal pillar that held Councilor Adomaitis suspended. As the magic touched the crystal's surface, it began to change, its hard edges softening and its facets turning cloudy. Tiny fissures appeared, spreading across the crystal like a delicate web of frost on a winter window pane.

Then, with a gentle sigh, the crystal began to dissolve. It didn't shatter or break, but rather seemed to sublimate, trans-forming directly from solid to a cool, swirling mist. The fog curled and eddied around Adomaitis' suspended form, caressing his skin and playing through his hair like an ethereal breeze.

As the crystal fell away, Adomaitis slowly descended, the invisible forces that had held him aloft releasing their grasp. His feet touched the ground with the lightness of a feather, and he drew in a deep, shuddering breath, as if his lungs were relearning the feel of air.

The mist swirled around him for a moment longer, a final cool caress, before dissipating.

"Councilor," Finley croaked. Beside him, Arcadia and Kelden had managed to pull themselves upright, although both were still bloody and shaken.

"What's—" the councilor began.

"You were... frozen. In crystal," Finley answered roughly.

Adomaitis frowned. "Dmitry."

"Yes. He's taken your... *movement* and... witchkind is in danger, now. He's put on displays of dangerous magic." Finley took a deep, heaving breath to try and control the shudders that were taking over his own body. "The Veil is stretched, if not pierced. This idea of subjugating the humans... let it go."

Adomaitis flushed. "Who are you, to tell me—"

"We're the people who will put you back in a crystal," Arcadia snapped. "And hash out the details later. Dmitry was impersonating you, with as solid an illusion as I've ever seen. And he wasn't doing *nice* things. You've a lot to answer for."

"I?" Adomaitis blustered. "I've done nothing! *You* on the other—"

"Enough!" Kelden roared. He stepped toward Adomaitis, leaning in so the two were almost nose-to-nose. "I am of Thornwaithe's. You understand?"

Adomaitis' flush of anger instantly faded, his dark skin going gray.

"I see you do. I will Testify."

Finley could *hear* the capital letter, and made a note to ask Kelden what that meant.

Adomaitis went even paler.

"We're leaving now."

Kelden's Sky magic was the bitter cold of the mountains, and it shocked Finley back to full awareness as it took them away. A small, absurd part of his mind wondered if the Taryba's alarms worked in the basement.

***

"It's been a reckoning," Finley's father said, shaking his head. "Adomaitis is not only off the Taryba, he's been imprisoned. All of Evermore is in chaos. That's why we decided to stay here."

Finley nodded silently. Arcadia and Kelden had joined him at his aunt and uncle's home, given that Harbsmouth had remained fairly quiet.

"There have been Hunts, in other villages," his mother added softly.

"They may die down," Kelden said. "If everyone can just stay low for a moon or so."

Next to him on the comfortable, worn couch, Finley felt Arcadia stiffen.

"A Sending," she said, her voice tense as she received the message. Then her brow wrinkled. "We're to go to the Farm."

"I don't know if—" Finley began.

"I think you will," Arcadia said with a heavy sigh, rising.

And sometime soon, his talent said just as heavily, *we will need to talk about what you've done.*

CHAPTER 21

Order Restored

"Well," Finley observed, a grin on his face, "being in charge certainly suits you."

Arcadia rolled her eyes. She sat in Ram's old office, behind his old desk, a stack of field dispatches neatly arranged before her. "It's not like I asked for it."

"Ram was too sick to continue," Finley pointed out.

"And once Father found out about the Order, he started pushing every lever he could reach," Arcadia sighed. "And Ram earned his retirement. Besides, the mission now is... different."

Finley snorted. "That's an understatement. And you've certainly not held back in changing."

Arcadia stood up from the desk and walked to the large window that overlooked the Farm. The sight before her was a far cry from the secretive, understated compound it had been mere months ago.

Everywhere she looked, the Farm was alive with activity. The main farmhouse, once a quaint, if sprawling, structure, was now enveloped in scaffolding as teams of witchkind workers used their magic to expand and reshape it. The weathered white siding was being replaced. New wings were being added, the framework already in place and imbued with strengthening charms. A new second story was being added over the majority of the structure as well.

Out on the grounds, the old barn and stables were barely recognizable. Their rustic wooden exteriors had been stripped away, revealing the magically reinforced stone and timber skeletons beneath. Carefully carved runes adorned the structures, each pulsing with power. Teams of witchkind swarmed over the buildings like industrious ants, carving new runes to add durability, and in some cases, protective wards around the areas where new apprentices would practice.

Even the fields and gardens were undergoing a metamorphosis. Earth-affinity workers tilled the soil with gestures, enriching it with nutrients and charms for abundance. Other with Flame affinity reworked the many fireplaces, upgrading their runes to provide more warmth while protecting against escaped embers.

"The mission isn't just different," Arcadia mused. "It's so much bigger."

"You're keeping Kelden on scouting?"

She nodded, turning back to him. "He's good at it, and anyone with Sky affinity is joining him. We're reworking all the runes on the churches, making them all listening posts, but someone has to sit and actually *listen* to everything that comes back. Thanks for those runes, by the way."

You're welcome, Finley's talent said.

"So how goes it?"

Arcadia sighed and walked back to her desk, flipping through the top few dispatches. "Two Hunts put down so far. We've managed to create the idea of a rogue group of priests trying to overturn the church hierarchy. That's been pretty effective."

"The cabal?"

"No sign of them. But we've stopped pushing back against… well, everything. They're working on an extension to the damned iron roadway, pushing south toward Baythwaite. Perilously close to Disemstoke's, in fact. That's the one place we're still active, just keeping them away. We've filled in more marshland than we've created, ironically. But so far, manipulating information is proving more effective." She paused, and gave him a close look. "How's the Veil?"

Finley closed his eyes and focused on the dim, vague sense of the Veil that always seemed with him. He took a deep breath, his brow furrowing as he concentrated on the ethereal sensation that had become a constant presence in his mind. The Veil felt distant, far more removed than it had in the past. It was as if he were reaching out to touch a gossamer curtain that hung just beyond his fingertips, tantalizingly close yet frustratingly out of reach.

The fabric of the Veil itself felt foreign, its once familiar threads now imbued with an alien, unsettling quality that sent a shiver down Finley's spine. It was as if the very essence of the barrier between the ordinary and magical had been altered, its fundamental nature transformed by the events that had transpired.

By the stress it had experienced.

As he probed deeper, Finley became acutely aware of the Veil's precarious state. It was stretched taut, like a rubber band pulled to its limits, ready to snap at the slightest provocation. The tension was palpable, a thrumming energy that set his nerves on edge.

Scattered across the expanse of the Veil, Finley sensed tiny rips, minuscule tears in its fabric. They were like loose threads in a tapestry, seemingly insignificant on their own, but harboring the potential to unravel the entire structure. Each rip was a vulnerability, a weak point that could be exploited by those with malicious intent.

"Not great," he said aloud.

"And there's no fixing it?"

His talent said nothing, but Finley had a clear impression of regret and resignation.

"I don't think so. No, there's not. It's unbelievably old. Older than our entire world he... it... says."

"Your talent."

"Yeah. It says the Veil originated in an entirely different world, and we repurposed it here. But the anchor for that is out of reach, and that would be the only way to try and repair it."

Arcadia slumped into her chair. "So we're going to lose."

Finley's heart broke for her. She's always been such a perfectionist, even back in school. Always top of the class, always first to finish. "We can probably prevent further damage. But... eventually. Probably. Yeah."

She shook her head. "We're going to push some innovations of our own. Try to sneak them into human awareness without them knowing. The boilers in Chiton are a good example. There are a few others. There's a team building more riverwalls along farms—runes to make boulders lighter, aid in the construction, that kind of thing."

"Maybe that'll be enough to keep the cabal happy."

She shrugged. "Maybe. Maybe not. It all went too far. What if... Finley, what if what happened in your village just gives them confidence?"

He hesitated. "Yeah. I've thought about that."

"I've... had a couple of crazy ideas. I haven't told anyone about them."

Finley arched an eyebrow.

"What if... this is going to sound crazy."

"Just say it."

"What if we... *told* them? Some of it, at least?"

"Told... the humans? What?"

She leaned forward, resting her elbows on the desk. Her eyes were bright now. "What if we just *came out* and *told them* about witchkind? About magic? They've been benefitting from it for millennia, now. They just haven't known. Yes, we've held them back, especially recently, but a lot of what we've done is still beneficial. We still make the boats better, the buildings stronger. Our work with weather, the work on the farms—they can't duplicate that. Not yet."

I don't think we should have Sundered the relationship between humans and witchkind, his talent had said.

"You mean, live alongside them. Openly."

She nodded. "It seems like the only option, apart from..."

"War."

"Yeah."

Finley took a deep breath. "You're going to face a lot of opposition."

Arcadia leaned back. "I know. It's why I haven't told anyone else. I keep hoping we can just get things back to the way they were."

"And the Taryba?"

"Doing what they can. Telling people to keep their magic out of sight. Assume the Veil won't protect them. One Councilor—there's something of a movement, especially in the smaller villages, for witchkind to move into ordinary homes. Physical ones, I mean. Abandon the secret spaces. Be seen *as people*, all the time."

"I guess that could help," Finley said doubtfully. "There've always been some who do that anyway."

"But it won't matter in the bigger villages and towns," she said. "None of them can just suddenly add a quarter to their population. There's nowhere to *put* everyone."

"So we... just keep doing what we're doing."

She nodded glumly. "For now. I guess we wait for an opportunity."

Wait, but prepare, Finley's talent whispered.

"Yeah."

"More and more people are noticing," one man said.

The old men had once again seated themselves around the sturdy, battered table in their cold, moist subterranean retreat. The sheets of inscribed iron had been carefully stacked this time, and they all turned toward their leader.

"Noticing," he acknowledged. "Wondering."

"Their group," someone said. "It seems to have pulled back. Perhaps—"

"Too late," the leader said, shaking his head slowly. "We might have wished. But all they'll do is focus on our most... hmm. *Egregious* innovations. But focus they will. Yet at the same time... people are *noticing*."

"Waking up," someone said.

"Opening their eyes," said another.

"It's in the oldest of the holiest books," a third offered. "*Nekęsk ragana gyventi.*"

"Suffer not a witch to live," the man at the head of the table translated. "Yes." He paused, and seemed to come to a decision. "The mines at Ironfast remain productive?"

"As much as they can," someone grumbled. "We still lose a third of the shipments to... mishaps."

"We will take a more active stance," the leader said heavily. "It has come too far." He tapped one small stack of iron sheets. "Begin executing the plans, Reinforce the carts with iron. Clad the wheels. Drape the horses."

"Northsea, then?" someone asked.

"And Soloton," the leader confirmed. "North of the Great Northern Range. Chiton next, although it's so large we may be forced to abandon it."

"The Iron Roadway—" someone began.

"Will wait," the leader insisted. "We must end this threat before we can move forward as a... people."

"They'll resist," someone pointed out.

"They'll lose," the old man at the head of the table sighed.

***

The leader emerged from the dank underground chamber into a small, narrow alley, his breath misting in the frigid night air. He pulled his worn cloak tighter around his shoulders as he began to walk, his footsteps echoing off the cobblestones. The others would take their own paths home, as they always did, to avoid drawing attention.

The village was quiet at this late hour, the windows of the ramshackle wooden houses shuttered tight against the biting cold. A few feeble oil lamps sputtered on the corners, casting flickering shadows. The leader passed the old stone well in the center of town, its bucket rimmed with ice.

He paused for a moment, closing his eyes and inhaling deeply through his nose. There was a sharpness to the air, a crisp tang that made the hairs on the back of his neck stand up. The scent of impending conflict, of a great change stirring. It had been absent for too long, the people lulled into complacency. The old ways, the *oldest* ways, had been fading.

But there was something else on the wind tonight too. Faint and elusive, threading through the smell of woodsmoke and frozen earth. The enticing aroma of freedom, of shackles cast off. Of ancient strength awakening once more.

A dog barked somewhere in the distance and the old man started slightly, then smiled. Even the animals could sense it. The wheel of fate was beginning to turn.

He continued on.

***

The consciousness, now old beyond reckoning, was blinking itself back into existence. It had slept for so long, waiting for someone who could hear it. Now, it had been heard, and its awareness of the broader world was slowly returning.

Perhaps I could have prevented this, it thought for a moment. Then, *No. This probably always had to happen.*

It cast its sleep-blurred gaze across the continent, noting the bright fountain of power that still rose upward in the great, empty northwest. It sent its sight downward, deep into the continent, examining the roots of the world and the thick tendrils of magic wrapped around them.

I've always wondered what would happen, it thought.

Award-Winning Fiction

Daniel Scratch: a story of witchkind

- Kirkus Starred Review
- Winner, American Fiction Awards—Best Fantasy (2023)
- Finalist, American legacy Book Awards—Best Fantasy (2024)

Clara Thorn, the witch that was found

- Winner, American Fiction Awards—Best Young Adult (2023)
- Runner-Up, American Fiction Awards—Best Fantasy (2023)
- Finalist, American Legacy Book Awards—Best Fantasy (2024)

- Finalist, American Legacy Book Awards—Best Young Adult (2024)

Find these books and more at DonJones.com

About the Author

Don Jones spent two decades writing tech books before he finally penned his first sci-fi novella, *A History of the Galactic War*. His well-reviewed and award-winning novels span fantasy and science fiction, with a focus on world building and relatable characters.

Connect, get free novels and short stories, and learn about upcoming releases by visiting Don's author website at DonJones.com.

Magical Worlds.
Incredible Adventures.

stories of witchkind consist of two trilogies of light fantasy, suitable for ages sixteen and up:

Daniel Scratch

Master of the Tower

The Fifth Axis

The Order of Some

The Conspiracy of One

The Truth of All

———

the *Clara Thorn* trilogy is suitable for younger readers aged 13 and up.

Clara Thorn, the witch that was found

Clara Thorn, the witch that fought

Clara Thorn, the witch that won

———

The Endless Sky series is sci-fi themed GameLit, following the adventures of characters who are playing a fully immersive game.

Truthsayer

New Worlds

tales from the broken claw are shorter "cozy fantasy" novels, featuring deep character building, low stakes, and fantastic baking.

Pubs & Pegasi

The Never: A Tale of Peter and the Fae is a retelling of the classic *Peter Pan* story, told from the fairies' point of view. The story begins long before that boy comes to Neverland, and its epic conclusion comes long after he's gone.

Stay in touch!

I love to hear from readers—hop on DonJones.com and hit the "HMU" (hit me up) link to drop me a note. And, if you've enjoyed this novel, know that an honest review on your favorite book-related website means more than you can probably imagine to an independent author. Thank you for reading!

www.ingramcontent.com/pod-product-compliance
Lightning Source LLC
Chambersburg PA
CBHW072010190726
48293CB00001B/222